I0526302

UNEXPECTED FRIENDS

BOOK THREE

SAHAR ABDULAZIZ

SHAGGY DOG PRODUCTIONS, LLC

To all the women who were not believed.
I believe you.
I stand with you.
Behind you.
Next to you.
With you.
I stand for you.
I am you.
We are not victims, but survivors.
And our truth, like our minds and bodies,
have the unmitigated human right to exist and thrive
without the fear of retaliation,
humiliation,
or the expectation
of further victimization.
No More.

"Our job is not to deny the story, but to defy the ending—to rise strong, recognize our story, and rumble with the truth until we get to a place where we think, Yes. This is what happened. And I will choose how the story ends."

– Brené Brown

CHAPTER 1

HIS HEAVY-SHOED FOOTSTEPS echoed against the nearly emptied bedroom's wood floors. By the still-curtained window stood a single dresser. One of the last items left undisturbed. Until today.

Here goes nothing.

Irwin slid the old top drawer out as far as it would go, stretching his arm toward the far backside until his overextended fingertips brushed against a familiar felt-covered small box. The one with a tiny white bow fastened to the top. He took it out and held it close against his chest, hesitant to lift the lid. Inside, lay a white gold heart necklace, inlaid with diamond chips, sparkling ever so slightly whenever a glint of light hit upon it just right.

"Irwin!" Harper called up from the bottom step. "We need to get going."

"I'm coming," he muttered softly to himself.

"—*Irwin*." The impatience in Harper's voice rose.

"I'm coming, I'm coming," Irwin replied louder, his mouth set in a taut, brittle line. Irwin hung his head, smacking his palms noiselessly against the top of the dresser as if bracing for the next round of anguish, all the while overcome with the enormity of what had yet to happen.

Why—

Irwin sighed, slamming the drawer shut behind him, his choppy breaths discharging in angry, anxious bursts. In frustration, he clenched his fist and pounded the side of his thigh, over and over, and over again, powerless to make this achingly sad reality disappear, yet wise enough not to barter with the heavens for one last-minute reprieve or miracle.

Irwin kissed the gold heart, placed it in the box and snapped it closed, knowing today would forever mark the end of what had been a long and painful journey; shadowed all the while by a foreboding so ominous, that even at his foulest, he would never have wished it upon his worst enemy.

"We have to go," whispered the soft, choked-up voice waiting for him at the door.

"Are your parents downstairs?" Irwin kept his back purposely faced forward, needing a moment to pull himself together.

"Yes," Harper murmured. "They sent me up here to get you. They're waiting in the car." She sniffled.

"Christopher?"

"He's here," murmured Harper.

Irwin placed the box on top of the dresser and turned. He scrutinized Harper's face, sadden by the blotchy-red eyes from crying, engulfed in a perpetual stream of salty tears. So reminiscent of the troubled, frightened young girl he had met years earlier.

"Are you ready to go?" she repeated.

Unlike Harper, who wore her heart on her sleeve, Irwin kept his emotions bottled up tight inside, disinclined to let even those closest to him know how genuinely terrified he felt.

Standing rigid-still, Irwin tucked his arms by his sides, squaring his bony shoulders as if preparing to walk the plank. His heart sank to see the next round of pooling despair fill Harper's eyes. It hurt to see how her antsy gaze bounced from surface to surface, or the way her arm muscles seemed to jolt beneath her skin.

Then, much to Irwin's dismay, he watched her flex her fingers in and out, expanding all ten digits as if preparing to vault.

Uh-oh.

Suddenly, Harper, sobbing hysterically, tore across the bedroom lunging full speed into Irwin's stiff body.

No, no, no—

Like a cornered animal with no place to run, Irwin curled his shoulders like an accordion, his arms locked against his sides.

Harper flung both trembling arms around Irwin's much too-thin waist, burying her wet cheek against his gaunt chest.

Arms still clamped down at his sides, Irwin strained to break free, flapping his hands like a trapped guppy.

—I. Can't. Do. This.

Irwin couldn't bear to be touched, no less squeezed. At the same time, he felt miserable, frustrated by his pitiful inability to provide even a modicum of comfort to the closest thing he'd ever have to a granddaughter. So instead, he gritted his teeth, wincing—stretching his neck as far as possible until the point of his chin jutted up and forward.

Mustn't. Give. In.

Overcome with the desire to get away, Irwin tried backing up, only to be rewarded with a sharp jab from the dresser's corner for his effort.

He next tried upraising his pinched narrow shoulders, lifting them almost clear up to his ears under the false expectation of masking the dread creeping across his concaved cheeks.

"*Ahem*," he fake-coughed. "You shouldn't hug me. I might be coming down with something," he sputtered, which only served to make Harper grip him tighter and sob louder.

Helpless, Irwin glanced away. "*Please*," he pleaded from bloodless pinched lips. "You don't want to do that."

Wracked with tears, Harper discharged a gut-wrenching sob so loud, so painfilled, that it shredded whatever reserve Irwin's guilt-ridden damaged soul had left. His throat tightened like a vice as he inhaled a strained, stuttered breath of courage.

"There, there," he sputtered, managing to tug one arm free to *pat-pat-pat* Harper on the back.

Harper peered up to stare at him through puffy, red eyes, her mouth fastened into an offended scowl.

"Seriously, Irwin? 'There, there?' Is that all you can say to me?"

Irwin tried swallowing, but the lump lodged in the back of his throat refused to budge.

Harper retracted her arms, "You're such a pedantic dork, you know that?"

"So, I've been told," he exhaled, relieved when she released him from the agonizing embrace.

Annoyed, Harper took a half-step backward, her arms folded across her stomach. "*Oh, wow*, I'm so sorry," she apologized after spotting the splotched wet spots she'd left all over Irwin's previously pressed, crisp white shirt. She dug into her pocket for a tissue, but came up empty-handed.

"There's nothing to be sorry about." Irwin, scarcely able to see clearly through his own welled tears, handed Harper his backup hanky. "Well, there is, but this certainly isn't it."

Harper sniffled a few more times, dabbing at her eyes. She slipped her hanky-less hand into Irwin's to gently tug him along. "We have to hurry *before*—"

Irwin understood and followed Harper out. As he stepped over the threshold, he placed his trembling palm flat against Cornelia's doorframe, summoning the strength to endure from its strong-willed former inhabitant.

Midway to the stairs, Harper stopped and turned. "Irwin—" she whispered.

Irwin cleared his throat. "I'm right behind you."

They descended the steps, cutting through the kitchen and out the side door to join the others already waiting in the car. Without a word, Harper slipped into the backseat next to her parents, while Irwin slid into the front passenger seat. No one spoke. No one needed to.

Christopher shifted into reverse and slowly backed out of the short, graveled driveway, righting the vehicle onto the lovely tree-lined block imbued by the Pocono's summer sun.

Rich, deep green foliage complemented by splashes of vibrant blushes were scattered everywhere. Stunning flower baskets and potted plants adorned many a porch as the air erupted with the sounds of lawnmowers, giggling youngsters sprinting through sprinklers, and the protests emanating from heat-exhausted shoppers, perched under shaded, full-leafed trees in search of relief.

However, Irwin, consumed by anguish, could not appreciate any of this neighboring beauty. Neither the scent of fresh-cut grass nor the enchanted sounds of children celebrating summer's treasures. Not even the warmth and light from the sun's rays possessed the power to grant Irwin's chiseled-out, troubled soul any consolation on this terrible day.

HARPER PRESSED her forehead against the car window, ignoring her mother's fidgeting. Olivia, sitting in the middle seat, used her fingers to twist the corner of her peasant blouse into a dull point as she stared, glassy-eyed ahead at nothing. Meanwhile, Darren, Harper's dad, held Olivia's other hand to lend his wife much-needed support.

Irwin held the jewelry box clasped tight in his fist, glaring face-forward, his gaze locked and unwavering.

Harper slumped against the back of her seat, thinking about how a relatively short car ride across town, one they had taken hundreds of times before, would suddenly feel monumentally longer.

They sat in silence. Each lost in thought, until out of nowhere, just when the air in the car turned inconsolably heavy and unbreathable, the silence burst apart. Irwin, of all people—was humming! Something no one present had ever heard him do before.

"*Duh, duh, du-du, duh, duh, du-du, duh, duh, du-du, duh, duh, du-du. Doodledoo, doodledoo, doodle doo, doo-doo...*"

Darren's head perked up. "Isn't that the theme for *Mission Impossible?*" he whispered into Olivia's ear.

Cornelia would often hum random refrains and show tunes in an attempt to quiet her nerves whenever she felt either overwhelmed or afraid.

Olivia nodded, "It sure is." The corner of her mouth lifted into a half-taut smile.

"*Doodledoo, doodledoo, doodle doo, doo-doo...*" continued Irwin.

Without standing on ceremony, Harper joined in. Olivia soon followed, then Christopher. Eventually, Darren did as well—humming way off-key, but nobody either noticed or cared. The solemn bunch hummed for the entire car ride, a melodic tribute to their fallen friend, and they didn't stop belting out their last *doodle do* until reaching their final destination.

Christopher cut the engine. "I hate this," he said aloud to no one in particular, before stepping out and slamming the car door shut.

Harper sniffled and hugged herself. *You and me both, luv.*

THE GROUP FILED out of the car one by one like an army of ants, making their way single file into the portentous brick building, with Irwin leading the pack.

"Can I help you?" asked the cheerful young receptionist seated behind a large desk, her perky face half-hidden behind a computer screen. Her name tag read, '*Hi! My name is Amy.*'

"We're here to see Cornelia Parish," announced Irwin brusquely.

"Are you family?" cheerful Amy inquired, sizing up the group.

"Yes," blurted Harper, confrontationally. "We are."

Olivia darted forward to take over. "Dr. Newport contacted us a short while ago, Amy," she clarified, sounding absurdly pleasant. Olivia pushed forward, wedging herself in front of her surly daughter and the all-too-acerbic Irwin. "He told us to come immediately."

The receptionist smiled at Olivia, then glanced over the counter to count heads.

"Five," snapped Irwin, losing his patience, only to get a sharp elbow to the ribs by Olivia.

After clicking away at her keyboard for what seemed like an eternity, Amy produced five visitor passes which she slipped into individual plastic badge holders, each connected to long blue lanyards. "You're all set," the young woman said, all smiles. "Have a pleasant visit."

Irwin's jaw dropped.

Have a pleasant visit?

Irwin's lips opened, then closed. He was ready to give ole Amy a piece of his mind when from the corner of his eye, he caught Olivia's threatening glare.

You don't scare me.

Irwin tugged at his earlobe and contemplated his next move, finally settling on glowering right back at her.

Undaunted, Olivia leaned in closer, her hands resting on her hips, and a scowl on her face that said, *try me.*

Irwin's right eye twitched, but he refused to surrender. Instead, he squared his shoulders, furrowed his bushy brows, and prepared to show Olivia he meant business.

Olivia, eyes open wide and nostrils flaring, didn't even break a sweat as she continued to stare Irwin down, seething.

From where they stood, Darren, Harper, and Christopher could watch the two exchange an entire heated conversation, skillfully deploying nothing more than eye twitches, inaudible snorts and death glares. The battle of the wits continued until Irwin, no longer able to maintain his snarl, slumped his shoulders in reluctant defeat.

"Go down the hall, and you'll find an elevator on your far right," said chirpy Amy, the mind-blowingly, perpetually smiling receptionist who apparently remained completely oblivious to the less than subtle, quite intense exchange happening right before her.

Amy handed the stack of prepared passes to Olivia. "Take the elevator to the fourth floor, room 412 - B."

"Thank you," mumbled the group before traipsing across the tiled lobby heading to the elevator. While waiting, Darren held Olivia's hand. Behind them, Christopher kept a protective arm firmly around Harper's waist. Irwin, his angular head held high, chose to stand stoically in the back with his sharp chin jutted forward.

"Did you remember to bring it?" Olivia asked, turning around. Her irritation from moments earlier, forgotten.

Irwin patted his shirt pocket.

Two people were already inside Cornelia's hospital room by the time they arrived. One, clearly a nurse, and the other, a familiar face—Joanne Burberry, Cornelia's professional health coordinator. Through the partially curtained window, Joanne noticed the group huddled outside the door and gave them a brusque nod. She held a finger in the air to indicate she needed them to give her another minute.

Sensing the nurse close to done, Joanne mouthed to Irwin through the glass, *I'm going to need to talk to you.*

Irwin nodded showing he understood.

"Blaire, Cornelia's family is here," Joanne said to the nurse. "I'll be right outside."

Blaire offered Joanne a slight, indifferent nod as her full attention remained transfixed on adjusting Cornelia's medications.

Joanne quietly cracked open the door. "I'm glad you're all here," she said, speaking to them in trained hospital whispers. She counted heads. "We've set up a few extra chairs inside the room, but we can always bring in more."

"Thank you," murmured Irwin.

"Joanne? Can you tell us how Cornelia's...? I mean, if she's, you know, in any pain?" Harper's choppy question came out in a throaty whisper.

"No pain. Dr. Latimer has Cornelia on the highest dosage to keep her comfortable." Joanne gazed into each of their sullen faces. "Listen, I'm not comfortable making predictions, but Cornelia's body is sending us a clear signal that she's almost ready to go. She's struggling and putting up one hell of a good fight but barely holding on. And to be quite frank, I think she's been fighting this hard to give you all time to get here." Joanne turned to Irwin. "Mr. Abernathy, I'm sorry to have to do this, but Cornelia relies on you. She's going to need to hear you tell her that it's okay for her to let go, and that you will all be okay when she does."

Irwin bowed his head. "Understood."

Joanne squeezed Irwin's arm in a sympathetic show of support. "I'll let you get to it, then. If you need anything, please don't hesitate to let Blaire know. I'll be back in a little while to check on things." She gave each a slight nod and left, her heels clacking down the hall.

Irwin drew in a deep breath, working up the courage to proceed inside while Harper, Christopher, Olivia, and Darren took up the rear.

"Come in," smiled Blaire now that her tasks were completed. "Cornelia," Blaire turned to her unconscious patient and in a loud but pleasant voice said, "Your beautiful family is here." One of the machines sounded. "Excuse me." Blaire scooted past Darren to get to the monitor on Cornelia's far side. "I'll be out of your way in a sec."

Christopher moved to wait by the windowsill, while Darren, his tatted muscular arms crossed, leaned against the wall next to him. Irwin and Olivia chose to stand on one side of the bed with Harper on the other. The room felt unusually still, except for the constant soft swishes, clicks, and beeps resonating from Cornelia's intravenous infusion and telemetry monitors.

"Hey, Cornelia," mumbled Harper, holding Cornelia's veined, thin hand in hers.

Olivia bent over and placed a soft kiss on Cornelia's forehead, whispering something only Cornelia's subconscious could have heard.

Irwin, stiff and rigid, puffed out his chest to clear his

throat, and in doing so, produced the loudest and most appalling grousing sound—a sound that one could imagine a flock of horny birds making during the peak of mating season.

He did it once, twice, then a third time.

"Stop already!" Harper wrinkled her nose in distaste. "Are you trying to spew?"

"Spew? I don't spew. Don't be absurd. I was trying to clear my throat."

"—to spew."

"Not to spew," Irwin contested, growing annoyed. "Why am I even discussing this with you?"

"Do you need a tissue?" Olivia already had her hand digging deep into her purse.

"—*to spew!*" Harper repeated, her mouth forming into a tiny grin.

Irwin, ready to scoff and protest, stopped when he realized Harper was only playing with him. "To spew, or not to spew," he said, "—that is the question."

Harper smiled. "'Whether 'tis nobler in the mind to suffer the slings and arrows of outrageous fortune—or to take arms against a sea of troubles...and by opposing end them. To die—to sleep, no more—and by a sleep, to say we end the heart-ache, and the thousand natural shocks that flesh is heir to—'tis a consummation." Harper tilted her face playfully at Irwin.

"'Devoutly to be wish'd. To die, to sleep," recited Irwin, taking over. "To sleep, perchance to dream—*aye*, there's the rub. For in that sleep of death what dreams may come when we have shuffled off this mortal coil...'"

In her heyday, Cornelia had enjoyed reciting Shakespeare aloud. She'd often swap-out the author's original words with colorfully concocted proses, all to better torture her friends with.

The heart monitor bleeped, and although not loud, its din caused everyone in the room to panic. Harper dashed out into the hall, yelling for the nurse to come back. Within in seconds, Blaire reappeared, pushing past Irwin to Cornelia's side. In a ballet of fluid well-practiced motions, she checked the machines, Cornelia's pulse, her eyes, then pushed the intercom to call for Dr. Latimer and Joanne.

Out of nowhere, Cornelia started making a wet crackling sound, akin to choking or drowning.

The time had come.

"She can't breathe," cried Harper, her legs visibly quaking against each beep. "Somebody do something," she sobbed, her knee's buckling. "Help her."

Christopher rushed to grab hold of Harper, locking his hands around her waist, while doing his best to shield her face with his neck.

Irwin moved in closer. He had witnessed enough people dying in his life to recognize a death rattle when he heard one. With no time to waste, he grasped Cornelia's hand gently in his, bending down so his lips almost touched her ear. "I promise, old gal. You don't have to worry about me anymore," he said in barely a whisper. Tears escaped from his distraught, ravished eyes, landing on Cornelia's cheek. "It's my turn to take care of everyone. You have done all you can." Irwin's voice broke. "Let go, my friend, and rest," he sobbed, choking up. "I will ... always ... love ... you ..."

Right on cue, the machine's blipping sound flatlined. Blaire rushed to switch it off.

Overwrought with grief, Olivia spun away sobbing, hiding her head in Darren's chest.

Harper, still being supported upright by Christopher's embrace, flailed her arms, moaning, "No, no...don't go, Cornelia...please don't go..."

"I'm so sorry," said Blaire, her eyes welled with tears like the rest of them. "We adored Cornelia, and we're going to miss her greatly." She turned off the rest of the machines and rolled them out of the family's way, removing any tubes and conduits from Cornelia's lifeless body. Before making herself scarce, she slipped Cornelia's wedding band off and pressed it in Irwin's hand. "You should have this," she whispered.

"Thank you."

Blaire left the family alone to mourn, almost colliding with the doctor and healthcare coordinator on their way into the room. She waved them out into the hall where she filled them in on what had transpired inside.

"Mr. Abernathy?" asked Joanne softly, peeking her head into the room. "I'm sorry to disturb you, but when you have a minute, I'd like to have a word with you out in the hall. Alone."

"Yes." Irwin nodded, wiping his eyes, still in disbelief his best friend was gone. "Of course."

"This is for you," Joanne said, pulling a manila envelope from a folder to hand to Irwin. "Cornelia asked me to give this letter to you immediately upon her passing. She also insisted I tell you not to wait to read it."

The envelope had Irwin's name scripted across the front in Cornelia's recognizable flowery handwriting.

"Thank you." Irwin pressed the letter to his heart. "I need to go now." Without uttering another word, Irwin turned and walked back inside to join the others.

Irwin took a seat. He wanted to read Cornelia's letter first to himself while the rest of the group spent their last few minutes saying their private goodbyes. Once everyone had finished, they followed Irwin out to the empty visitor's lounge to talk and pass out tissues.

"I-I-can't believe she's gone," whimpered Harper, leaning her head on her mother's shoulder.

Olivia clutched her daughter's arm in support and kissed her forehead. "I honestly can't either," she said.

"I don't think any of us can," Darren added sadly.

"That's because none of us want to," Christopher corrected in a strained, croaky whisper.

"Well, none of us are going to have to," Irwin blurted out, waving the letter indignantly in the air.

Olivia frowned at him. "What are you talking about now?"

"This," he nodded, signaling the paper clutched in his hand. "Cornelia's written a letter to all of us. Joanne Burberry just handed it to me a few minutes ago."

"A letter?" asked Darren. "What kind of letter? About what?"

Irwin sighed. "It seems our beloved Cornelia left us detailed instructions as to what she'd like done with her remains."

"You mean a will?" inquired Christopher.

"No." Irwin shook his head. "Not exactly. However, she has written down her explicit wishes, namely to have her ashes spread in the Pacific Ocean. Specifically, off a beach in La Jolla, a small city north of San Diego."

"In California?" Darren whistled softly through his teeth. "But why California?"

Irwin shrugged. "She doesn't say."

"What's the big deal?" Harper bristled. "If that's what Cornelia wants, then that's what Cornelia will have. I'll do it."

"We both will," Christopher chimed in, massaging Harper's lower back.

Harper's mouth curved into a forced smile, grateful for her partner's support.

Irwin shook his head. "Thank you both, but Cornelia indicated that she wants all of us to go."

"All of us?" Harper's tight smile faded. "Well, all right.

Still, not the biggest deal. We can fly out to La Jolla and do-the-do."

"Not so fast," said Olivia, dabbing her eyes. "I mean, I'm not saying I won't go, but I need to know a whole lot more before I agree to go off traipsing halfway across the country."

"Not half, Ma," corrected Harper. "The entire country— all the way across."

"Yes, well, let's not get ahead of ourselves," muttered Irwin.

"Meaning?" asked Christopher, always the calm, sensible one in the bunch.

"Meaning that not only does Cornelia want us—*all* of us— to make this trip," Irwin said, emphasizing *all*, "but she's gone ahead and laid out an entire itinerary, including various pitstops we're to make along the way."

"That knocks out flying," said Harper.

"Pitstops?" Darren rubbed his forehead. "To do what? Pour a cup of her ashes in each different place?" Darren shrugged. "Come to think of it, that's kind of a cool idea. I can remember a guy from a band back in the seventies who did that with his mom's ashes. He'd sprinkle some on the stage of every place he performed as a tribute to her."

Irwin arched an eyebrow, amused to see Darren's face pale under his wife's glowering glare.

"Then again," Darren backpedaled. "I hope Cornelia doesn't expect us to stop in all fifty states. That would take longer than a—"

"Dad! —Gosh. Not now." Harper shot her father a sharp, impatient glare. "You better read the entire letter to us, Irwin. I get the feeling this is about to get a whole lot more complicated."

"Oh." Irwin's face contorted into a strange grin. "You have no idea." He cleared his throat, "*Ahem*," and began to read.

. . .

DEAR FAMILY,

If you're reading this, it means I finally kicked the bucket. But hey, C'est la vie. And don't get all doom and gloom about it. I mean, be a little sad. That's only natural, but if you feel the need to cry, rip your hair out by its roots, or drown yourself in vats of alcohol, do so while packing because you, my anything but adventurous friends, are going on a trip. A trip? Did I say a trip? Yes, I sure did. In fact, think of this as our last hurrah together. Because surprise—I'm coming with you.

Well, not my body...at least not my body in one piece. That would be too weird. Plus, I'm assuming carting a dead body across the country on a road trip is uncivilized, not to mention possibly illegal.

Can you imagine having to figure out a way to prop my body up in the backseat? Which, depending on when we leave, could be in rigor mortis. Or better yet, sticking me in a pine box in the trunk and risking hearing me slide around. Ha! —not even I could do that to Irwin.

IRWIN SNORTED.

THEREFORE, to make life easier—yours—not mine, because ding, ding, ding, I'm already dead, I want you to just stuff my ashes in a jar. Easy-peasy.

OLIVIA CLAMPED one hand across her mouth and moaned while the fingers of her other hand disformed the hem of her shirt, twisting and twisting.

Irwin continued to read.

So, a big heads up, buttercups. You'll need to find something sturdy to carry me around in, and I strongly suggest that whatever you decide on, it has a secure top. Don't stand on ceremony. Feel free to dump my ashes in any bargain basement, run of the mill, everyday urn. Nothing fancy. It's an urn, for goodness sake. Not some swanky designer handbag.

IF IRWIN GAMBLED, he would have bet the entire bookshop and his less than impressive pension that Cornelia had cracked herself up laughing when she wrote this.

Now, I'm sure whatever you decide on will be fine. Just don't let any of those sly, conniving undertakers guilt you into buying something ridiculously expensive or ornate. Trust me, any old mayonnaise jar or coffee can will work — it'll just need a tight-fitting lid. Lord knows I would die a second death knowing the darn thing popped open on you.

Can you imagine? There I am, spilling out all over the place, my ashy remains getting stuck on some dirty pavement and mixing in with old melting chewing gum or worse, pigeon droppings.

HARPER'S NECK disappeared as her shoulders rose and pulled forward. "*Ewww—*" she moaned, scrunching her nose, dry gagging.

Irwin looked up from reading. He wanted to gauge how the rest were handling what they'd heard. Thus far, Olivia, her skin as pale as a ghost, seemed the most mortified, while Darren and Christopher, both with their arms crossed over their chests, appeared marginally amused.

Irwin glanced over at Harper, her nose still discolored from crying. There was no mistaking the profound sadness clouding over her entire being. The grief—palpable. Nevertheless, Irwin had to hand it to Cornelia and her ill-timed and shockingly morose gallows humor that she had at the least, and for the time being, worn-out Harper's exhaustive flow of tears.

"Should I continue?" Irwin asked, voice flat.

"Yes," resounded the group, noticeably less enthused.

"But not here." Olivia started to walk away. "Let's go home."

CHAPTER 2

HARPER HEARD the phone ringing through Irwin's back door as soon as she stepped out of the car. Shattered, she had to drag herself up the steps to stand behind Irwin. She peered over his shoulder, watching his shaky fingers fumble with the keys.

"Here." Harper held out her palm, antsy to get inside. "Let me do it," she offered, hoping she didn't sound as impatient as she felt. Irwin ignored her, so she nudged his shoulder, jutting out her arm farther, but Irwin wasn't having it and blocked her hand with his body.

"I got it," he told her gruffly, just before dropping the keys to the ground, causing him to have to start all over again. "If you wouldn't mind?" He shooed her back. "I need room to work here."

"Pardon me, Houdini." Harper raised her hands in mock surrender, then took less than a half step back, leaning her frame against the metal railing. She couldn't help but notice Irwin's hands continue to shake. "Any day now," she teased, hoping to get him to relax.

Irwin, an expert at ignoring taunts, stuck the key into the lock and jiggled it.

"Come on already," he muttered under his breath, listening for the familiar click to catch and *clack*. "Bingo." Irwin twisted the doorknob to the far left, while at the same time shoving his shoulder against it just so.

Whoa. Harper made a mental note to ask her dad to take a look at the door before Irwin wound up cracking a shoulder blade.

The ringing continued, but Irwin, in his usual fashion, did not rush. Instead, he held the door open for Harper, and then trudged his way to the counter to answer the phone.

"Hello?" Irwin practically shouted into the receiver. "Yes. This is Irwin Abernathy speaking."

Harper noticed his face tensed.

"And you are? ... Oh. Yes. I see ... No. It's all right, I understand." *Pause.* "Could you hold on for a quick minute? I'd like to switch phones ... Yes, thank you. One moment." Irwin hooked the receiver onto the side of the telephone. "Harper, when I yell, please hang up."

"No problemo, *Cap-i-tan*," she answered, already busy sifting through Irwin's paltry pantry, grabbing first for the saltines. Harper shook the box to make sure something was actually inside before flipping it over to check the expiration date—two safety precautions everyone had begun to adopt as a matter of course at Irwin's house.

Next, Harper stuck her nose in the box and sniffed, mistakenly inhaling a larger lungful than planned, causing her to violently cough. "Oh, man," she hacked, "He got me again."

"I already put the water up," announced Olivia, looking unfazed by Irwin's latest pantry poison. "No special requests this time, folks. It's tea for all," she said, facing the stove and waiting for the kettle's whistle to blow. "I'm exhausted."

"Better make mine a double, Liv." Darren slid an extra chair over to the kitchen table and plopped down. "Man." He propped both elbows onto the table to knead the aching crick in his neck. "What a day."

"Stiff?" asked Christopher, pointing to the back of his neck, grabbing the seat next to Darren.

"I think I slept wrong."

"Hang up, Harper," Irwin shouted from his study.

"Yup," she confirmed, tossing the box in the trash before taking her usual seat at the table, her mouth stuffed with the only salvageable saltine cracker.

"Who do you suppose Irwin's talking to?" asked Olivia in a conspiratorial whisper, walking the kettle over to the table.

"No idea." Darren lifted his cup, giving Harper a quizzical look.

"Don't look at me." Harper shrugged and grabbed for a teaspoon. "Are you using this?" she asked Christopher.

"Nope. It's all yours, my lady."

"Cool." Harper slid the sugar bowl closer and dug in, lifting out a sizeable mound. "I couldn't hear who, but he sounded upset." She dumped the spoonful into her mug, stirred briskly, took a reserved sip, and cringed.

Blech.

Harper watched as her mother's one discerning brow arched, just as her spoon got ready to dig in for the second shovel of sugar. When the glower didn't work, Olivia shot her never-paying-attention husband a series of overly exaggerated glares, but when subtly failed to do the job, Olivia resorted to pinching Darren on the side of his neck.

"*What?*" he balked, shoulders scrunched to his ears.

Irritated, Olivia lifted both brows pointedly in their daughter's direction.

Darren glanced at Harper, his focus eventually landing on the spoon in question. He squinted back at Olivia, raising his palms in the air with the— *I'm not doing it, you deal with her*—gesture.

Olivia, lips pouting, bypassed Darren's cup and poured Christopher's water first.

"Well, Irwin certainly doesn't need any more bad news right now," she said, somewhat brittle. Then, just as she turned to walk away, something caught her eye. Unable to stop herself, Olivia froze, watching in horror as her daughter's spoon once again targeted the sugar bowl for round three.

"Oh, heck, no." Olivia scurried over to the table like there was a fire and plucked Harper square in the shoulder. "Are you insane?"

"*Ouch!*" Harper flinched, holding a hand in front of her for protection. "I'm not a kid anymore. You need to stop doing that."

"You got no argument from me," groaned her dad, continuing to knead the side of his plucked neck.

Without looking, Harper could sense her mother hovering. "I'm in shock, okay!"

Olivia didn't answer; her deadpan stare never once wavering from Harper's glutinous hand.

For a split second, Harper weighed the risk of sugar consumption against her mother's likely retaliation.

Plunk.

"That's the last one, I promise," she said, tossing trepidation bravely to the wind.

Meanwhile, in the next room...

Irwin slid down into the chair behind his finely crafted wooden desk, bracing himself for the probable onslaught of more bad news.

"Thank you for waiting, Mr. Davenport. Please continue with what you were saying."

"Thank you, Mr. Abernathy, and again, please accept my deepest condolences on the loss of Ms. Parish."

"Thank you."

"I'm not sure if you are aware, but Cornelia and I also go way back. She had been one of my first clients when I put my shingle up in town. I often liked to tease her, telling her how she alone kept me gainfully employed." Davenport paused. "Cornelia will be sorely missed."

Irwin thought Davenport's jest probably held more truth to it than Irwin cared to admit or explore.

Thinking about that reminded Irwin of Cornelia's many entertaining anecdotes about 'my friend the attorney.' Although, surprisingly, she never felt obligated to provide anyone listening an actual name. Merely a title. Nonetheless, the stories were shared with good-humor and respect. Out of curiosity, a part of Irwin wanted to confirm if Davenport had, in fact, been Cornelia's 'friend the attorney,' but under the circumstances, he chose not to ask.

"As Cornelia's probate lawyer, I am calling to inform you that you have been appointed executor of her will."

Irwin's eye twitched. "Me?" he grizzled. "But I don't know the first thing about probate issues."

"Which is why I will make myself available to advise and assist you on how to settle best the remainder of Cornelia's final affairs, including that of her beneficiaries." Mr. Davenport paused. "Of course, you are certainly under no obligation to serve, Mr. Abernathy. You are perfectly within your rights to decline."

Irwin's mouth clamped shut while his mind wrestled against the deluge of conflicting thoughts racing through his head. Although Irwin's hand had mercifully stopped trembling moments earlier, his knees apparently didn't get the message. They continued to bob under his desk, making thud-like drumming sounds muffled only by a thick area rug. "What happens if I decline?"

"Then, the court will appoint someone else. They usually select next of kin—either a surviving spouse or an adult child."

"Cornelia had neither," said Irwin, thinking aloud.

Mr. Davenport cleared his throat but stayed mum.

Irwin crouched over his desk, propping his chin on his palm, trying to think. "This seems complicated."

"It can be. But if it's any consolation, Cornelia anticipated your trepidation. In fact, I feel comfortable telling you she made these plans prior to her diagnosis being confirmed. With sound mind and body Cornelia went above and beyond to make sure this process, however unpleasant, would, at the least, be as simple and as straightforward as possible for you. I hope knowing this provides you some small consolation as to her intentions and clarity of thought." The attorney waited for an answer. "Mr. Abernathy?" Davenport waited. "Mr. Abernathy, are you still there?"

"I'm here."

Irwin heard Davenport titter. "I thought I lost you for a minute."

"No. I'm listening." Irwin drew in a deep, exhausted breath. He leaned back in his chair. "I'm finding it difficult to process everything, Mr. Davenport. It's been a long day."

"I can well imagine."

Irwin sat up straighter. "Will it be necessary to go to court?"

"Not necessarily. Probate is essentially the assembling of a deceased person's assets, paying any taxes or debts from that, and then distributing whatever is left to the inheritors. Mostly paperwork, and again, pretty straightforward, unless family members or creditors are fighting."

Assets, estates, inheritance, court—and now ashes.

Irwin sighed again, wiping away a tear ready to spring out from the corner of his eye.

"Mr. Abernathy?"

"Yes, Mr. Davenport."

"Is that an affirmation?"

"Yes."

"So—to be clear, that's a 'yes'—as in you agree to be Cornelia's executor?"

"Yes. That is correct. I agree," Irwin confirmed. "I will see this duty through, but before doing so, I need to do something first. It should only take a few weeks. May I give you a ring when I return? Then we can do whatever's necessary to sort out whatever legalese."

"That would be more than fine, Mr. Abernathy. There's some paperwork I can finish up on my end until I hear back from you. Perchance, do you have something to write on? I'd like to give you my contact information."

AFTER FINISHING the phone call with Mr. Davenport, Irwin returned to the kitchen feeling a bit flustered but determined. He tugged out the deepest bottom drawer at the farthest end of the kitchen counter. Huffing as if out of breath, he bent over and started his search, aware of how everyone had stopped to watch him toss and flick stuff around. Harper and Olivia exchanged quizzical looks, but Irwin didn't care.

"*Ah-ha!* I found you," Irwin proclaimed, victorious after his many under-the-breath comical complaints and assorted colorful grumblings. "I knew I had one."

"Had one, what?" asked Harper, her attention focused on scraping a dried blob of jam stuck on her shirt with her thumbnail.

"A large map," he exclaimed as if that should explain everything.

Irwin made everyone remove their cups and saucers from the table's surface to make space. He then pressed down on the map's well-worn creases for easier reading. "And there you have it, my friends. A map of The United States."

Everyone, excluding Harper, appeared genuinely interested.

"Of course, we will still need to get a road map," explained Irwin, pleased with himself, "but this will do for now."

Harper reached for her cell phone. Without skipping a beat, she swiped and tapped away, her fingers sprinting over the small keyboard.

Irwin, the only one standing, stared down at her. "*Ahem.*"
Nothing.

Irwin cleared his throat again. "*Ahem,*" but much louder this time. "Are you texting?"

"No," answered Harper, never glancing up.

Irwin frowned but waited. "Perhaps you would prefer pen and paper?" he said, his tone shifting between utter annoyance and caustic sarcasm.

"Nope. I'm good, but thanks."

Harper, seemingly unperturbed, kept her eyes downcast and her fingers busy pattering away.

Irwin frowned, exasperated by Harper's unhinged adoration for anything technological, a reoccurring thorn in his rump for years. For Harper's part, she never missed an opportunity to show him up. Today, Irwin would come to find out shortly, would be no different.

Although not appreciating the distraction, Irwin decided to wait for Harper to finish anyway. However, it didn't take Irwin long to realize she had no intention of stopping. Irritated, he tapped her on the shoulder.

"What exactly are you doing, then?"

"Who?" Harper glanced up. "Me?"

Irwin snorted, his eyes doing a hard flick in the direction of her phone.

"*Umm*, well, so far, I've looked up the cost of van rentals. I went ahead and also roughly calculated our gas mileage from here to California—incorporating, of course, making several pitstops." Harper paused. "Understandably, I'll be better able to calculate these numbers once I know exact addresses. Then I'll figure out approximately what we will be paying for gas, factoring in what different states along with our route charge per gallon, so we know what to budget for." Harper's mouth twisted into a sardonic smile. "Next on my list— hotels, pet-friendly—if we decide to take Bones, and possible restaurants."

Harper toyed with a lock of her hair. "Oh! —and I almost forgot," she blurted out. "I also googled the most efficient routes to take while avoiding unnecessary tolls as opposed to the ones I assume you're about to plot with your antiquated map."

Christopher turned his head to hide a grin.

Darren, his stubby finger tapping on the table's edge, leaned back in his chair, his mouth clamped shut, careful not to make eye contact with anybody—especially Olivia.

However, Olivia, the group's unanointed gatekeeper, perched herself at the edge of her chair and leaned in, pointing to Irwin's map. "Is this our first stop, Irwin?" she asked, sounding genuinely interested. "Wait." Olivia twisted her neck to get a better read. "I still can't see it clearly. What does it say? ... Columbus, Ohio?"

"Yes. That's our first stop," nodded Irwin. "We'll need to make a pitstop probably in Missouri to rest, and then on to Amarillo, Texas. After a brief stopover, we head to someplace called Las Cruces in New Mexico. Afterwards, we'll drive through Arizona to our final and last stop, La Jolla, San Diego. There are four scheduled stops in total, not including necessary fill-ups, bathroom breaks, hotels, and food." Irwin lifted a single challenging brow toward Harper, who, much to his amusement, had already slumped back in her chair, evidently unamused.

"We should probably contact these people before we show up at their doorstep," grumbled Olivia, fanning her damp neck with a useless paper napkin.

"Excellent point," agreed Christopher. "I mean, it's got to be weird for them to have a load of strangers pull into their driveway claiming to bring them letters from the dead."

"—with ashes stuffed in a mayonnaise jar," said Darren.

"—or coffee can," Harper added.

"Which isn't a problem as long as the lid is tight," Darren kidded. "But joking aside, I'd sure hate to get shot for trespassing."

"Or arrested," said Olivia.

Darren's smile fell. "Please don't remind me."

Nobody, especially Darren, ever wished to revisit last year's fiasco when the police arrested Darren of killing Alastair Brooke, the troublesome, blackmailing antique dealer neighbor, next door to the bookshop. Although Darren had been eventually cleared of all charges with the help of his family and friends, it wasn't before spending a couple of terrifying, lonely nights behind bars. Although those awful memories had dulled over time, they still lingered—and not just for Darren, either.

Irwin slid out four hand-filled, stamped postcards from the larger packet and plopped them on the table. "Cornelia's already thought of that."

"Of course, she did." Harper's snicker, somewhat restrained, soon morphed into fits of laughter.

Irwin scowled. "What's so funny?"

Irwin's indignation alone caused the group to join Harper in her hysterical meltdown.

"Would somebody care to share the joke with me?" Irwin complained.

More laughter.

Fits of laughter.

Laughter with tears, and laughter with snorts.

Irwin took a seat, determined to wait them out.

"I really don't think this is a laughing matter," Irwin managed to eke out, baffled as to what had prompted such a strange and inappropriate outburst. At one point, he noticed Harper, visibly still deep under the spell of joviality, turn her face fully away from him, since any glance in his direction would start her hooting all over again, which of course, caused the rest of the group to fall back apart.

Irwin stroked his throat, grimacing, waving a hand in the air as if ready to throw in the towel.

Harper, trying to steady her breaths, wiped her face with her sleeve.

Christopher flat out gave up and buried his entire face under folded arms.

Red-faced, Darren hid his laughter behind his wife's quaking shoulder, while she pinched her nose, trying to make herself stop. All with little success.

"Not you too, Olivia?" Irwin sulked, sounding somewhat disappointed.

"I'm sorry," —*giggle*—"but Irwin," —laughter—"can't you see," —*more giggles*—"the ridiculousness in all of this?" Olivia panted through her mouth, trying to calm down. "I mean, look at us!"

Irwin glanced around and shrugged. "What am I supposed to be looking at?"

"Okay...let me explain it this way." Olivia dabbed at her eyes. "Here we are, at your kitchen table, only a few hours after watching our mutual friend take her last breath. Correct?"

Irwin nodded.

"And presumably, we are here to plot out a cross-country excursion to the other side of the country, all along debating on whether to put Cornelia's ashes into a mayonnaise jar or a coffee can. And, we are doing this so we can then spread them in the Pacific Ocean—which, fine, okay, I get, except we don't know why we're doing it because Cornelia never bothered to say."

"It's her last request," said Irwin, defensively.

"But that's the thing," countered Harper. "It's not really a last request, though, is it? I mean, let's remember, shall we, that Cornelia also wants us to stop at four strangers' homes to deliver whatever she's got for them. Letters, mementos, or whatnot. I can't remember which now—"

"She didn't say," said Irwin.

"Correct, because she didn't say," repeated Harper.

"Exactly my point," said Olivia.

"Okay," nodded Irwin, still not grasping the entire picture, but getting closer. "And this is funny because?"

Olivia blew out a long breath. "Let me try to put it another way for you. Are we expected to do all this stuff, everything Cornelia wants—with *you*?"

The table exploded again with another round of hilarity.

Irwin lifted an eyebrow, dismayed. "Again, I'm failing to

find the humor in any of this," he grumbled, wishing they would stop fooling around.

"Oh, you will," Harper managed to cackle out between laughing spasms and snorts.

Darren, the only one close to being under control, cleared his throat. "Listen, Irwin—no offense, but the thought of all of us traveling together for what? Two weeks? Going across the whole country just to dump Cornelia's ashes in an ocean when we have a perfectly fine one less than two hours away, is sort of crazy."

The group murmured in agreement.

"On top of that," continued Darren, "this is Cornelia we're talking about. Who in the heck knows what else she's got in store for us? I mean, Irwin, old buddy— you gotta see how insane this is, right?"

Irwin sat up a bit straighter. His right eye twitched as he ran the presented scenarios through his head. Everyone stared, waiting...looking like they were teetering on the precipice of renewed hysterics.

After a good half-minute, Irwin only managed to mumble a limp, "I see," and that was all it took for giggle-fest, round three to commence.

"Oh, for Pete's sake." Irwin glared around the table at his friends. "Fine! Maybe you're right, and this is crazy. Quite possibly certifiably insane, but certainly not the least bit amusing," he huffed. "This is a serious undertaking we're about to embark on and one we are tasked to complete by our dearly departed friend, Cornelia Parish. How can you all sit here goofing around at a time like this?"

Olivia laid a gentle hand on Irwin's arm. "We're not laughing because this situation is at all funny, *ha-ha*, but because we all deeply loved and cared about Cornelia, and this whole trip thing she's got going on is, well," she drew in a large breath. "—it's just like her to conjure up something as crazy as this for us to do together."

Irwin winced at Olivia's depiction of Cornelia *conjuring up anything*. "What exactly are you saying, Olivia?"

Olivia didn't back down. "You know full well Cornelia's a—*was* rather—a first-class nurturer."

"Meddler, part-time snoop..." said Harper.

"Blabbermouth, busybody," added Darren.

"Let's not forget matchmaker," reminded Christopher.

Yes." Olivia nodded. "All of that, but also the glue that kept us joined at the hip and grounded."

Growing impatient, Irwin stood up and walked over to the sink to fill himself a glass of cold water from the tap. From a small plastic pill bottle, he shook two headache tablets onto his palm. Then one more for good measure. "Your point being?" he asked, willing the medicine to inundate his bloodstream.

"My point is this," said Olivia, calmer. "Cornelia knows us, and rightly assumed we'd fall apart after she died. Which, if you think about it, wasn't all that far off, am I right?" she asked of the room.

Everyone but Irwin nodded in agreement.

"Therefore, I think it's pretty safe to assume that Cornelia purposely designed this so-called trip to help heal us through our loss."

Irwin's jaw dropped. He'd never once thought of Cornelia's request as anything but a final way to commemorate her passing. With one eyebrow raised, he leaned both hands on the table, impressed by Olivia's intuitiveness. "Elaborate."

"My pleasure." Olivia smiled. "This road trip, last hurrah, soul journey, whatever you want to call it, is as much for us as it is for Cornelia."

"*Ahhh*, I'm not so sure, Liv," said Darren.

"And why would you say that?" Olivia's face jerked toward Darren in a challenge.

Darren shifted in his chair under his wife's unwavering glare. "I mean, it's not like Cornelia's been all up there these past few months," he said. "It would have taken a gargantuan miracle for her to plan this whole thing to this detail—if you get my drift." Darren shot Irwin a supportive, *I'm with you buddy*, head nod.

Irwin, in turn, rolled his eyes.

"Who's to say Cornelia did it recently?" Christopher pointed out, sounding exactly like the lawyer he was. "She could have very well made these arrangements a while ago."

Darren conceded. "True."

Irwin *tsked*.

"Knowing Cornelia, she probably did it the day she got diagnosed," said Harper.

This time, everyone—including Irwin mumbled in agreement.

"Harper is correct, going by what her attorney, Mr. Davenport, told me." Irwin plopped down in his seat, exhausted, and unable to process much more. "And if we accept this as truth," he went on to say, the hammering in his head starting to clear. "—then Cornelia, fighting the symptoms of dementia, had the forethought and wherewithal to plan this so-called adventure in advance of her diagnosis. That, or this could simply be what she described in her letter, a last escapade and final wish."

"Hurrah," corrected Harper sighing, the bout of earlier giggles all but dissipated. "Cornelia called it 'our last hurrah.'" Cupping her face, Harper bowed her head. "Cornelia could do anything she put her mind to—dementia or not." Harper's words tumbled out in a forced bravado, but it sounded closer to a choking wheeze. "She was one of the most amazing, most brilliant, most talented people I have ever met in my life."

"I wish I knew a way we could know for sure," muttered Irwin, unexpectedly overcome by sorrow.

"Well, we're about to find out." Olivia reached across the table and plucked a postcard from the smallest pile. "Lady and gentlemen. May I introduce Exhibit A."

CHAPTER 3

THE FULL MOON had the night sky alight and twinkling by the time everyone had left Irwin's home. After a steamy, much-too hot humid day, the cooler evening air felt like a gift. A good time for Irwin to take a short walk to clear his head.

Upon returning home a short time later, Irwin climbed the stoop. It took all the energy he had left to unlock the side door and drag his tired body inside.

"Oh, for heaven's sake," he shouted after flipping on the kitchen light switch, cupping his eyes against the piercing glare of the overhead light. "*Argh*," he growled—mad at himself, madder at the world, and now, infuriated with light-bulbs in general.

"I did it again."

He'd meant to change out the 100-watt lightbulbs sprinkled throughout his house months ago, preferring a more low-lit aesthetic as opposed to the inquisition lights he now lived with. But then life happened, and he always seemed to get sidetracked or forget. In retrospect, Irwin should have been impervious to this nightly light-assault by now, a change that came about as a result of how often Cornelia had complained about his dimly lit kitchen.

"Honestly, Irwin. How can you see a thing in here?" she'd pout whenever over, her nose creased into an exaggerated frown.

"It's not that bad," he'd tell her for the hundredth time, failing to be amused by her exaggerated eye squints and hand-tapping routine.

"It's horrible, and frankly, dangerous. Especially for us, old folk," Cornelia would complain, making a point to glance around the room with her thin lips pressed together in a grimace. "Then again," she'd trail off, insinuating her distaste for his admittedly outdated, ascetic kitchen. "Here's a novel idea. How about changing it?"

"The light?"

"No, you ridiculous old sod, the entire kitchen. An update would do wonders. A gut job would make this dreary place brighter and feel eons cheerier. Night and day."

"I like it just the way it is," he'd tell her, refusing to concede.

"Of course, *you* do."

One evening during one of Cornelia's repeat performances, Irwin caught her tapping around his kitchen table with her eyes closed, ready to collide into a disaster.

"Be *careful*," he yelled—albeit a bit too late.

"Oh, sugar-muffins," stammered Cornelia, stubbing her toe against the chair leg for real. "See! I told you so."

After the toe debacle, Irwin gave in. He had grabbed his ladder and dragged it around the house, changing out every single bulb.

Irwin sighed.

I'd happily change a million lightbulbs if Cornelia would only come back.

IT TYPICALLY DIDN'T TAKE LONG for Irwin's eyes to adjust. And as usual, he made his hundredth mental note to change the lightbulbs back to low and gloomy.

Just not yet.

Irwin leaned against the doorframe, anticipating another long night. He closed his eyes, wondering if and when the memories would ever stop.

A chill suddenly coursed up his spine. Irwin shuddered, deathly afraid they would.

Enough.

Irwin lowered himself onto a small wooden bench kept by the side door. He sank down, kicked off his shoes, peeled off his socks, and slid his tired, sore feet into a pair of well-worn house slippers.

"*Ahhh*. Much better."

In true Mr. Roger's style, he stood, slipping on an old V-neck cardigan, fastening every last button. Then he strode over to the kitchen table, resigned to tackle the task of sorting through his latest batch of accumulated mail—mostly junk and bills. Irwin barely scanned each piece before finally separating them into three neat stacks—toss, recycle, and pay.

"I hate this," he grumbled, recalling how his aversion to mail had stuck in Cornelia's craw.

"*Sheesh*, Irwin. What the hell are you saving it for?" she'd harp, referring to the mound of unopened posts in the middle of his kitchen table. "A bonfire?"

Cornelia, as her dementia symptoms worsened, would

ask Irwin the same questions over and over again as if for the first time. She'd even ask using the same faux-appalled inflection in her delivery. But none of that bothered Irwin. In fact, he preferred the redundancy. For him, repetition meant less thinking, and less thinking meant less sadness—a fair enough tradeoff under the circumstances. Irwin lifted one of the piles and dropped it on the table, recalling how, much like two seasoned actors vying for the leading role in a play nobody wanted to see, they executed their parts to perfection until the final curtain call dropped.

"*Jeez*, Irwin. You've got enough mail here to wallpaper your guest bathroom," she'd harass him, poking her way through the pile until Irwin snatched it out of her hands.

Over the ensuing months that had unbearably turned to years, Irwin watched his closest friend—one of the wittiest and smartest people he ever had the honor of knowing—deteriorate before his eyes. He observed in horror the way her eyes often turned vacant and afraid. He listened as her lips strangled simple sentences, spewing learned scripts which propelled her hopelessly into a prison of redundancy. Losing Cornelia to dementia had torn Irwin's spirit in two at every single opportunity.

"*Sheesh*, Irwin. What the hell are you saving it all for?" she'd repeat. "A bonfire?"

"I'll get to it," he'd tell her, keen to suppress any hint of impatience from slipping into his reply. "Most of its junk anyway."

Irwin's replies never satisfied Cornelia, who would then, without fail, come back with, "Well, how would you know unless you plow through it?"

That's when Irwin would look for the most inconsequential piece of mail in the bunch—usually in the form of an advertisement or flyer. Something ridiculous, like the obnoxious postcards he received congratulating him on winning some obscure contest no one had ever heard about.

—Congratulations, Irwin Abernathy! You are the lucky winner of a seven-day, all-expense-paid cruise to—?

A cruise? The place never mattered.

Irwin, a man dangling precariously on the precipice of recluse would never have been so easily enticed simply because of a half-baked marketing scheme.

"Need I say more?" he'd ask, waving the oversized post-card in the air at her.

"Point taken," she'd reply, her diminished attention beginning to fade, already drifting off elsewhere until the next conversation, for now, all but forgotten.

Not so for Irwin, who never got to forget anything.

Exhausted, Irwin gave the pile a less than cursory once-over, before chucking the worthless junk to the side, only to restack any remaining bills into an even neater new, still left unopened mound.

Once completing that task, Irwin stood fixed, vacillating. Uncertain as to what to do next and worn out from the monsoon of decisions left on his plate. He covered his face and exhaled into his palms, feeling the rise of trepidation beginning to creep back in.

This is all too much.

Even the simple act of opening an envelope had left Irwin feeling spent, so he left the bills exactly where they were, ready to call it a night.

"*Whoa!*" he shouted as he turned the corner on his way upstairs, almost ramming straight into three large covered plastic bins, one stacked up on the other, completely forgetting he had asked Darren to leave them by the steps.

You have got to be kidding me.

There, heaped in a pile, sat Cornelia's belongings reclaimed from the adult center. Irwin shifted the containers

39

enough to be able to pop open their tops for a look-see. As expected, one box contained articles of clothing. The rest looked filled with a mixture of gifts one is inundated with when convalescing, along with other, more useful items, likely brought by Harper or perhaps, Olivia.

Irwin sneaked a look at the second container, and to no surprise, found it filled with many items he recognized from Cornelia's home. In all likelihood brought in batches by Harper, the one responsible for packing up Cornelia's things. Small trinkets, a loose stack of photos held together by a rubber band, a few photo albums, and the usual hodgepodge collection of souvenirs and keepsakes one might accumulate during a lifetime.

The last container held a single row of folders, smartly stacked, and filled with what Irwin assumed were private documents.

I can't.

He snapped closed the lids but got only as far as two steps up the stairs before the rein of curiosity kicked in, making him backtrack. Back to facing what secrets awaited him inside and contemplating what to do next.

I can't do this.

Irwin never wanted to be the one made responsible for going through Cornelia's personal effects. At the time, she'd told him she understood. And yet, here they were. In his house, by his stairs, filled with answers—or possibly more questions.

Irwin stretched his arms, cracked his knuckles, and pushed the containers flush against the wall for support. He snapped open the lid from the one perched on top and got to work, elbow-deep, using his fingers to grope around. This box held photos albums and a collection of framed pictures. Curious, Irwin yanked out the largest frame first.

"Oh." The old photo showed Cornelia, and presumably,

her new husband, taken on what appeared to be their wedding day. Irwin recalled seeing something similar to this photograph displayed in her house when they had first met.

"Beautiful," Irwin had told her, staring closely at the two handsome young faces smiling wide-eyed for the camera, their expressions full of hope. "I never knew you were married."

At the time, Cornelia hadn't wanted to discuss it, and snatched the frame out of Irwin's hands, referencing her husband only as *him*.

"Yes, well, that's from another lifetime," she had told him. "Nothing but two stupid kids, rushing into a life we had no business living."

Irwin watched her stare at the photo clutched in her hands. At the time, he would have sworn her hand had trembled, but to this day, he couldn't be sure.

"We thought we had all the answers." Cornelia had spoken in barely a whisper, never bothering to conceal the resurfaced anguish.

"It still hurts," he had said aloud, not meaning to. A bad habit Irwin indulged whenever confronted by an uncomfortable social situation.

Cornelia shot Irwin a harsh glare. "Since when does heartbreak have an expiration date?" she snapped.

Ouch. —I, the King of Misery, deserved that.

"I apologize," he said. "What happened?"

Cornelia flipped the photo over and placed it face down on the hall table. "Vietnam happened. End of story," she answered him curtly.

In retrospect, it had been odd how Cornelia, as somebody who took pleasure from being in everyone else's business, suddenly hadn't been too keen on anybody being in hers.

"I'm sorry, again," Irwin said, unwilling to push her any

further. He walked over to Cornelia's bookshelf, unfocused. Lost under a mountain of his own painful memories.

IRWIN REMEMBERED the day when he had foolishly marched into the recruiters' office to volunteer for service at eighteen years old—less than one full month after graduating high school. By that time, the Vietnam War had been waging for sixteen long years. His grandmother, who Irwin had been staying with at the time—hated the war and thought the United States had no business being there, and she let him and the rest of the world know it.

He recalled the posters and the marching in the streets. His grandmother had also joined the peaceful *Vietnam War Out Now* rally on the National Mall in Washington D.C., and came back determined to write weekly scathing letters to her senators.

As an ardent anti-war protestor and peace advocate, Ethel Chamberlin had cried inconsolably upon hearing Irwin's plans to join, going as far as to locking herself in her bedroom for hours and refusing to speak to him, except when addressing him as an 'Idiot.'

The next morning, his grandmother woke early and got dressed in a tie-dyed tee-shirt and jeans. Around her neck, a peace sign necklace. Without a glance or a single word to Irwin, she grabbed her cane, handbag, car keys, and hobbled straight out the door. Less than an hour later, Irwin found her parked in a lawn chair obstructing the front entrance of the recruiter's office—blocking him or any other young man from entering.

"Don't any of you dare try to pass me," warned the snarky five-foot-one, seventy-two-year-old Ethel Chamberlin Abernathy, brandishing her cane in Irwin's face. "I mean it, buddy. Back it up!"

This showdown went on for a bit. No one in their right mind was anxious or stupid enough to toy with a semi-armed rancorous senior. Eventually, however, Irwin, with the assistance of another young man needing to get inside, decided to take matters into their own hands—figuratively as well as literally. On the count of three, the two gently lifted her chair a few feet in the air, with Ethel still in it cursing up a blusterous storm. When a group of guys waiting off to the side saw the coast clear, they made a beeline for the front door, one piling in after the next, and moving as if not sure how long the sudden reprieve would last.

Ethel, however, remained adamant and ready to fight to her last breath. She stayed rooted in her lawn chair with her arms crisscrossed defiantly over her chest, and the cane propped between her knees, unwilling to budge or concede defeat. With little recourse, Irwin bent over and planted a soft kiss on top of her head. "I love you," he whispered before heading inside.

"Idiot," she hissed after him as a stream of tears slid down her soft, dewy cheeks.

Despite his grandmother's appeals, endless protests, and colorful threats, Irwin joined the military. Less than a full month later, Irwin, along with thousands of other young men from around the country, many of whom were nothing more than babies like him, were sent off to boot camp.

Irwin's cheeks burned with shame. "Such an awful, pointless war," he had lamented, remembering the sheer terror scorched across his grandmother's face on the day she watched her only grandchild board the military bus. The day she swore she'd never see him alive again.

Irwin had been forced to stand alone on the sidewalk, waiting to board. Unlike other families who came to say their last tearful goodbyes, Ethel declined. Instead, she parked across the street, refusing to speak to him, but strangely, also not driving away.

He remembered how nervously he had gripped the strap to his duffel bag, the butterflies in his stomach, the dread pulsing in his heart. Every few seconds, he'd glance over his shoulder to steal a peek across the street where his grandmother remained fixed. And each time, without fail, their eyes would lock for a brief blink of a second before she would jerk her face away in disgust. This same scene repeated itself until right before Irwin's turn to board for good. He remembered taking one last glance, but this time, much to his surprise, he caught his grandmother's tear-filled unwavering eyes glued on him.

Trying hard not to tear-up, he gave her a slight, tentative wave, and in return, she mouthed, 'Idiot,' before blowing him a long, final kiss. Then, as if it never happened, Ethel rolled her window up in a huff, revved the engine, and sped away. Irwin watched in hopeless dread as his grandmother peeled away from the curb a bit too fast, causing the tires to screech.

"*Psssst.*" Cornelia snapped her fingers in Irwin's face, reminding him she was still standing there, waiting for an answer. "Are you okay?"

"*Huh?*" Irwin blinked, startled.

"I asked if you were okay. You looked as if you zoned out on me there," she had teased. "Lost in your thoughts?"

"*Ahem,*" Irwin cleared his throat, then turned his face away to wipe his moist cheek. "Sorry. The war...far too many young lives were lost."

"Yes, far too many. Death, unfortunately, is one hell of a nasty byproduct of war, Irwin," Cornelia lamented, all evidence of her prior jesting gone. "Much like the legacy of decimated lives back home—the ones forced to wait for their boys and girls to return. Putting shattered lives on hold while keeping a watchful eye open for the familiar military car pulling into your driveway, coming to deliver the bad news. Or watching the evening death toll, all the while begging God to keep your loved one safe." Cornelia bit down on her quivering bottom lip. "I'm afraid everyone served back then. Soldiers, their families, and friends—sweethearts and wives. Everyone irreparably damaged forever."

Unable to add anything of value to the wall of agony pitched between them, Irwin said nothing.

"No winners, I'm afraid," Cornelia muttered angrily, "but plenty of losers."

Irwin remembered watching Cornelia's face, already drained of color, turn an awful ashy white against the backdrop of amassed, painful memories. But unlike Cornelia's husband, who hadn't made it back alive, Irwin had been one of the luckier ones. For whatever reason, they never shipped him overseas—selecting Irwin to serve out his deployment stateside at a military hospital doing administrative work. Irwin never saw combat—only the limb-missing, war-torn, traumatized aftermath of the still breathing walking dead.

Irwin completed his military duty and returned home officially unscathed. At least that's what his honorable discharge paperwork indicated. His guilt for not serving with his best friend overseas, however, spoke volumes to the contrary. Their separation of duties had left a dark stain on Irwin's soul that continued to haunt him to this day.

Cornelia then shoved the wedding photo into a drawer, slamming it shut with her hip. "Did you serve?" she had inquired, barely making eye contact with him as if his answer had the power to hurl her back into an even darker place from which she came.

45

"Not really," he had replied, pokerfaced, shrugging to convey a halfhearted denial.

And for once, Cornelia hadn't bothered to pry.

Although curious, Irwin had chosen not to pursue this conversation and had let it drop. But now, as he stood staring down at Cornelia's framed photo clasped tightly in his fist, he had to wonder if he had made the wisest decision.

"COME ON, ALREADY." Irwin struggled to wedge the frame back inside the box. It had been a long day, and he was more than ready to call it a night, but for whatever reason, the darn thing refused to slip in without him possibly damaging it. Instead, he yanked out another frame to make room. Unlike the wedding photo, this one looked more recent, perhaps taken in the late nineteen seventies—going by the snazzy outfit.

After the war, and anxious to shed his fatigues, Irwin had tried his hand at wearing button-down shirts paired with corduroy flare pants, or paisley open-necked shirts tucked in with a flashy rhinestone belt. He'd felt—*and looked* appalling. Irwin couldn't help but bemoan the memory of his flamboyant getups, thankful beyond measure that cellphone cameras had not yet been invented.

He drew this next photo closer, wanting to get a better look. The young woman smiling for the camera had long, straight hair severely parted down the middle, hanging carefree but way past her shoulders. She wore what looked like a white fitted tank top tucked inside a pair of high-waisted bluejeaned bellbottoms—the unspoken 'cool' uniform of the times. She also appeared to be standing in the middle of some kind of meadow, surrounded by tall, wild grass. He brought the photo closer, attempting to place her face, but drew a blank.

Irwin flipped the frame over and undid the tiny latch on the back. He then gently slid the photo out, hoping to find a name or something helpful inscribed on the back. Anything to give him a hint as to who these people had been to Cornelia, but nothing. Disappointed but not surprised, he returned the photo to its protective casing, relocked the latch, and placed it back in the bin.

"We've been friends for over twenty years, Cornelia, and I still know so little about you," he mumbled to his empty house. He reached down to grab the next photo. "And who, pray tell, might you be?"

As before, Irwin undid the back latch and tugged the photo free of its casing. This time, however, he was in luck.

Dearest Cornelia,

I never thought I'd make it here, but I did, Home at last. I can barely believe it myself.

Thank you for believing in me and in my dreams and for everything you did to help me make them come true. I'll never forget you.

Missing you and your beautiful smile.

Yours always,
Love, Elle

"ELLE... ELLE..." muttered Irwin, recognizing the name as one listed in Cornelia's letter. He reached into his pocket and pulled out the letter to confirm the spelling. He ran a finger down the list of names and plucked the paper. "And there you are. Miss San Diego."

He glanced back at the slightly faded photograph, whose signs of aging did little to refute the captivating smile. Irwin couldn't help but stare forlornly at the stunning woman, maybe then in her late thirties, early forties. She posed, waving at the camera, presumably from in front of a large body of water. A beach or shoreline, most likely.

Wide awake, Irwin lifted the containers and placed each one on the floor, using his foot to slide all three bins closer to the steps. Resting on the second step, he continued to admire the photo, his imagination speculating as to what could have happened to this woman to cause Cornelia to intervene?

For the next few hours, Irwin remained entranced, perched on the bottom step and scrutinizing every photo, keepsake, slip of paper, or note—willing himself to commit each face to memory, and anxious to learn more. He compared faces to names, jotted down copious notes, and highlighted observations—listing them in columns. By the time Irwin had pulled out the last frame, he had more questions than answers. Questions he should have asked while Cornelia had been alive. Answers she should have provided to him willingly.

Besides the questions, Irwin felt an inexplicable resentment beginning to brew towards his newly departed dead friend, a person he would have sworn only days ago he knew well. Now, Irwin wasn't so sure.

He sat, feeling overwhelmed, reading letters written from strangers who had evidently had a meaningful past with Cornelia. There were photos with faces but no names. And those that contained names had no apparent history. Irwin couldn't understand why on earth Cornelia, his closest friend, had kept so much of her life a secret. It hurt. Deeply. And yet, just as intensely, Irwin felt an unbearable sense of guilt for feeling that way. Confused, beyond wearied and flat out irritable, he stopped and put everything away.

Irwin made his slow ascension up the stairs and into his bedroom to rest. But as he lay on the bed, enveloped by dark, he couldn't fall asleep. His mind much too triggered to sleep. The next onslaught of unwelcome memories decided to show and wrench him back in time. Back to the day he last saw his best friend—or what was left of him—tagged and zipped up in a black body bag—draped ceremoniously with a flag in preparation for its final journey home. The same day Irwin vowed never to get that close to anyone ever again. A declaration he had since broken a dozen times over.

September 1971

"FOR THE LOVE of what's left of my sanity, kick the damn ball, Irwin," shouted Jimmy, frantically waving his hands. "Come on, man."

The two young men had been best friends since first grade, and neighbors with a single brownstone house planted between them for most of their young lives. Jimmy lived with his parents and two sisters. Irwin resided with his bossy, protective grandmother.

"Time's a ticking," yelled Jimmy, kicking a pebble with his sneaker. "We don't have all day, you know."

A few neighborhood guys had decided to throw together one last impromptu tag football game for the boys shipping out. At least four from their block were headed to basic training any day now. Another batch were set to leave over the coming weeks. The mood, at least during the game, had been a mixture of friendly competition and outright rivalry. Still, the undercurrent of apprehension and raw nerves never lingered too far away.

Unlike Irwin, most of the guys had refused to sign up, preferring to take their chance on the lottery. Reggie's number got drawn first. Louie's next, Jimmy's last. Irwin decided to sign up once Jimmy's number got pulled.

"Why in the hell did you do that?" shouted Jimmy lounging on his stoop, staring at Irwin like he had two heads. "Just answer me, why?" Jimmy shook his head. "I-I can't believe you would do such a stupid thing."

Irwin picked an acorn off the sidewalk and rolled it between his fingers. "Because we're friends."

"Because we're friends." Jimmy ran a thick hand through his overgrown, curly hair, still shaking his head in utter disbelief. "Yeah, that part I get, asshole, but friend or not, you don't go volunteering to die next to me. For crying out loud, man, I can pretty much guarantee there's nothing in the friendship handbook to support that level of stupidity."

Irwin tossed the acorn into the gutter and picked up another. "They would have pulled my card sooner or later," he countered, his voice strained from having the same argument with his grandmother long into the night before.

Irwin had tried to explain how he had no choice. All men, ages eighteen to twenty-six, were required to register at the local selective service board. Then they used a container holding three hundred and sixty-six balls listing every birth date for an entire year. Once picked, you were drafted and ordered to report to the induction center for further processing.

"Or maybe not." Jimmy leaned back, pressing the small of his sweaty back against the cement step. Feet crossed at the ankles, he threw his head back, staring into the sky as if contemplating what to say.

"You could have gone to college and applied for a college deferment to finish your studies. Granted, that's not necessarily a guarantee they still won't yank from you, but it's a whole lot better odds than volunteering, you schmuck. Then you could have at least served as an officer after graduation if you had to go in." Jimmy rubbed his forehead, plainly disgusted. "Shoot—who knows? The war could have been over by then."

This had been almost word-for-word what Irwin's grandmother had screamed at him the night before, minus the part when she flung a towel at his face and called him an idiot.

"What a shitshow," said Jimmy.

Irwin's face went blank. "What do you mean?"

"You. This damn forsaken war. Signing up. It ruins everything."

"What do you mean?" Irwin looked baffled. "We'll go to basic together. I got your back—you got mine."

Jimmy scoffed. "It doesn't work like that, Einstein," he barked back, red-faced. "I got drafted. Conscripted. Whatever you want to call it. But unlike you, guys who get drafted like me don't get to pick and choose which branch they'll serve with. Hell, I gotta serve two years on active duty while you, Mr. Stupid Volunteer, now have to do three."

Irwin's eyes grew large, surprised by that information. "Then I'll just ask to get sent where they send you," he said, plopping down next to Jimmy on the stoop.

Jimmy slid over to give Irwin room and rubbed his eyes. "Grow up, will you? This isn't some freaking sleepaway camp. We don't get to bunk up and pick tents. This is war, for cripes sake. People are dying and coming home in body bags, not sleeping bags."

More humiliated than angry, Irwin tossed a pebble, almost hitting a parked car. "You don't think I know that?" he snapped, face flushed with resentment.

The two friends sat on the stoop, trapped in an elongated silence neither one appeared anxious to budge from until Jimmy, no longer angry, threw a drowning-in-self-pity Irwin a life jacket.

"*Mmhm,* but the thing is, I was kinda hoping you wouldn't get called," explained Jimmy, eyes downcast, his voice barely audible. "I wanted you to be here to look out for my family until I got back, or in case I—" He paused, drawing in a forced breath. "—and to make sure my old man lays off the sauce."

Irwin's mouth dropped.

Overcome and feeling like an imbecile, Irwin had wanted to run and hide. Find the closest overpass and hurl his body straight into oncoming traffic. Anything to make the rage and shame bursting inside him subside.

He had messed up.

Big time.

Although Irwin's intentions had been right for all the best reasons, it had been his arrogance of youth and the curse of infallibility, which had determined his erratic course of action. He had been too overconfident in his conviction that he and he alone stood between Jimmy and certain demise. But at the time, Irwin, incapable of tapping into his growing arsenal of snarky retorts couldn't rationalize any of this to his friend. Nor his grandmother, for that matter. So instead, Irwin did what Irwin always does whenever confronted by misfortune—especially that of his making.

He shut down.

The street grew busy. People strode past, anxious to get where they were going, paying Irwin and Jimmy little attention. Cars honked and sped by, while trucks lumbered past—their tires screeching behind rusted brakes. Harried mothers pushed prams while older children skipped and frolicked ahead without abandon—each person playing their part to perfection.

Jimmy, not usually the type to hold a grudge, spoke first.

"I'm almost afraid to ask, but how did our esteemed local anti-war resister handle your news?" Jimmy had always liked Irwin's grandmother, and she him. The two enjoyed many a conversation about local politics and the crumbling state of the world. They often solved world crises over tall cups of iced tea and healthy slices of homemade pie. Unbeknown to Irwin's grandmother, Jimmy agreed with most of her antiwar sentiments, except the part about burning his draft card to take permanent residence in Canada.

Irwin's brows drew together. "She wants to kill me," he said, the corner of his mouth twisting into a faint but discernible lopsided grin.

"Yeah," Jimmy laughed. "That makes two of us."

TWENTY-ONE-YEAR-OLD ARMY FIELD INFANTRY OFFICER, Private James Conroy McFadden landed in Vietnam on August 14, 1973. He died on August 12, 1975, during his second tour of duty, two days before slated to return home. Upon hearing the news, Air Force Staff Sergeant, Irwin Abernathy requested to accompany his best friend's casket back home to his grieving family.

Jimmy's death marked the starting point of Irwin's career in losing the people in his life he cared about the most.

CHAPTER 4

Seven days until departure.

BEFORE ENDING their impromptu meeting the other night, everyone decided they wanted to leave on their assigned road trip as soon as all the final arrangements were made. Today's assignment consisted of Irwin and Harper taking a short trip into town.

"Excellent choice," said Mr. Fitzgerald, owner of *Fitzgerald & Sons Funeral Home* on Main Street, a quaint white colonial building with black shutters and an impressive manicured lawn.

After much discussion, Irwin and Harper decided to go with the pewter Grecian cremation urn crafted from solid brass with a brushed finish and a top-opening secured with a threaded lid.

"You have the option of having it engraved in a variety of fonts," explained Mr. Fitzgerald. "Engraving can be up to four lines with a total of thirty-five characters on each line."

Irwin handed Fitzgerald a small sheet of paper. "We would like Cornelia's full name and the date of her birth and death."

"Very good." Mr. Fitzgerald jotted down the information. "Would you perhaps wish to add a brief description under her name?"

Irwin squinted. "For example?"

"Some people write beloved wife, daughter, mother..." explained Mr. Fitzgerald.

"How about beloved meddler and snoop?" grumbled Irwin.

Harper sharp-elbowed Irwin to the ribs. "Beloved friend works fine, Mr. Fitzgerald, and if possible, I'd like to add a short poem. Something I wrote."

"You wrote a poem?" Irwin asked.

"More like a haiku, but not a haiku," whispered Harper, her eyes staring straight ahead at Mr. Fitzgerald.

"We customarily offer ten poems to choose from," said Mr. Fitzgerald, "but for a small added fee, we can substitute that for your personalized message."

"I understand." Irwin, hands clasped in front of him, nodded. "May we have a moment alone to discuss this?" he asked, not really asking.

"Why, of course." Mr. Fitzgerald stood. "Take all the time you need," he said as he strode across the carpeted office, leaving Harper and Irwin to talk in private. The two chose to sit on the small damask sofa off to the side of the room.

Irwin dove right in. "I don't see why we need to have anything engraved on the urn," he said, his voice barely above a strained, snarky whisper. "Especially since we're driving across the country to dump her ashes into the ocean."

"So, what?"

"So, why all the unnecessary added expense?"

Harper gasped. "I can't believe you."

"What?"

Harper furrowed her brows. "What if something unexpected happens, then what, *hmm?*"

"Something unexpected, like what?"

"I don't know," she shrugged, voice cracking. "—like an unfortunate incident."

Irwin sneered. "What kind of unfortunate incident?"

"Well, *umm*—Oh, okay. For example. Let's say Cornelia's urn gets lost—or worse, *stolen*." Harper clutched her throat. "Having it engraved could help police identify it."

Irwin tipped his head skyward, throwing his hands in the air in an *I give up* gesture. "Who in their right mind goes around stealing urns?"

"I don't know, Irwin, but I can't just dump Cornelia into some plain, old ugly metal pot and call it a day. This is Cornelia we're talking about." Tears streamed nonstop down Harper's stressed, blotchy face.

Irwin's posture crumpled. His lips pursed into an embarrassed frown. "I'm sorry," he said, reaching out to touch her shoulder, but then yanking it straight back. "You're right. This is Cornelia. Please forgive me." He handed Harper a tissue. "We'll have anything you want engraved on it," he said, awkwardly trying to comfort Harper by tapping her on the shoulder.

Harper blew her nose, leaned her head gently on her friend's bony, stiff shoulder and whispered. "Thank you."

LATER THAT EVENING, the group reconvened around Irwin's kitchen table. Their mood mimicked the overbearing heat—dismal. Nevertheless, they all plodded along.

To make planning for the trip go smoother, everyone took over a different related task. Olivia, the official cook of the group, notwithstanding Irwin's incessant sass and grievances, agreed to manage food preparation. Christopher said he'd handle renting the van and, without much prodding, volunteered to do most of the driving. Darren offered to get the bookshop ready to make it easier for Roger to navigate.

Irwin insisted on riding shotgun as the self-appointed point person between them and Cornelia's various contacts. As he spoke, he orbited the kitchen table, interjecting ideas and opinions here and there while bear-hugging an accordion-style file folder over-stuffed with papers.

"Why don't you let me deal with Cornelia's people?" offered Harper, anticipating a disaster. "Besides, don't you have enough on your plate dealing with the lawyer and all the *um*, *ah*, other important stuff you need to get done?" she clumsily added, unable to describe what exactly this man did all day.

"Thank you, Harper, but I have everything under control," Irwin replied, right before dropping his folder filled with papers, postcards, envelopes, along with a single book skidding across the floor.

Harper bent to help retrieve Irwin's stuff. She grabbed the book, but Irwin snatched it out of her hands just as she started to sift through it.

"If you don't mind," he said, tugging it out of her grasp and stuffing it and everything else back inside his packet.

"Was that a map book?" Harper asked.

Irwin nodded.

"You have an entire book filled with maps?"

"That's a redundant observation," Irwin had replied.

"Anything past one map is redundant."

"Until we get lost," he snapped back.

"Have no fear." Harper wiggled her cellphone in the air. "It's called, G-P-S." Harper made sure to enunciate each letter, finding Irwin's weird attachment to antiquated paper maps bizarre. Anyone else—besides a stodgy old troglodyte like him, would already know that digital online maps were inherently more accurate.

"M-Y-O-B," replied Irwin, equally as brash.

"S-S-D-D." Darren plopped his head onto the kitchen table.

"Which stands for what?" asked Irwin.

"Same shit, different day," he groaned from beneath his folded arms.

"Enough already with all the acronyms," yelled Olivia. "This situation is difficult enough without all this ridiculous back and forth." She glared at Harper, then at Irwin. "We're going to have to work together to get through this. Irwin, bring your map book if it makes you happy. Harper, you've got your phone. I'm sure we'll have occasion to use both during this trip."

Little did Olivia know at the time how true her passing prediction would turn out.

Six sweltering days before departure.

Christopher and Harper's stuffy one-bedroom apartment above the bookshop felt hotter than a brick oven. Every surface tacky to the touch, much like melting spat-out gum on a city summer sidewalk.

Harper padded sluggishly across the room barefoot, the soles of her damp feet squishing against the wood floorboards with every step. She dabbed at her neck and hairline with a tissue, while the thin cotton sundress she wore clung limply against her clammy body. Desperate for relief, she crossed the room to tug, curse, and yank every available windowpane as wide open as possible. However, without even the slightest hint of a breeze, the air inside her apartment remained suffocating and dead still.

"It's like a sauna in here," she moaned, fanning herself with her palm. "What we need is a new air conditioner."

The old one had conked out on them only days before, leaving the couple nothing for relief except an old cranky ceiling fan fitted with four lethargic, barely moving blades, doing almost nothing to assuage the oppressive summer heat.

Sticky and miserable, Harper plopped down on the sofa, but before she had a chance to get comfortable, Bones leaped onto her lap, spreading his furred body across her legs, sandwiching Harper between him and two dank pillows.

"No, you don't." Harper attempted to jostle the cat off by shifting her weight to a more cooling, less stifling section of the couch, but Bones went rigid the second she dared touch him. "You're killing me, here," she implored the stubborn cat, but Bones wouldn't budge, instead outspreading his plump, overfed body flush across Harper's overheated belly.

"You must be so hot with all that fur."

Bones stretched across Harper's lap, flicking her face with his tail while casually licking his paws, panting.

"Aww, you poor, poor kitty." Harper reached for a magazine to fan him.

Bones, enjoying the rush of cooler air, tilted his head, purring in unmistakable appreciation for Harper's loving attention and much-needed reprieve. Unfortunately, his fanning only continued for a solid thirty seconds more before Harper called it quits.

"Sorry, buddy, but I'm way too hot and bothered to keep this routine up," she grumbled, letting the magazine slip to the floor as her soaked-to-the-skin clammy body flopped back against the faux leather couch. "I-feel-so-gross and this stupid couch feels grosser."

Bones mewed and nudged under her chin.

Harper chin-nudged him back.

"I don't know, Bones. Call it a sixth sense, or maybe it's just a standard case of paranoia, but I keep feeling like I forgot to do something seriously important."

Harper let out a deep-weighted sigh. She reached over, snatched her phone off the coffee table and scrolled through her to-do list, checking and rechecking what she had left to do.

The dying fan made one last dismal spin before coming to a complete grinding stop.

Harper stared up at the ceiling and punched the pillow. "Are you freaking kidding me right now?" She closed her eyes and tossed the pillow at the fan, but her throw made it only halfway up before plopping down on the floor with a dull thud.

"*Argh!*"

Ignoring the sweat pooling under her dress, she searched for places to stay after Columbus, Ohio—the group's first designated pitstop to meet someone named Mildred. Harper next plugged in the woman's address and the word 'hotel,' and a list popped up on her screen.

"*Mu-ha-ha,*" she muttered, rather pleased with herself. "You might have your fancy map book and printed out directions, Irwin, but I got something a whole lot better." Harper clicked SAVE and filed the information in a folder under *In Case Irwin's Plans Become a Shit Show*. Harper glanced down at the photocopy of Cornelia's list. Besides the name and address, there wasn't much else to go on.

"Mildred."

The instructions read:

'Please deliver the attached letter to Millie. She'll have something to give to you as well. And do me a favor—remind her I said, 'I told you so.' She'll know why.'

Strange. Most of Cornelia's instructions were equally as vague —*Bring this to so-and-so, make sure to tell whoever whatever.* Not so much as a clue as to who these people were and what they had meant to her. Almost as if Cornelia was leaving out pertinent information on purpose.

Harper shrugged.

On second thought, knowing Cornelia, that might not be such a bad thing.

Harper checked the time. Still early.

"What do you think, Bones? Is Cornelia sending us on a wild goose chase or what?" She scratched the top of the cat's head, thinking about how much she adored her strange but loveable, extended family. How she relished the evenings spent together breaking bread, swapping stories, or discussing books and movies.

Harper looked forward to helping her mother prepare the meals or assisting Irwin with setting up a new book display. She especially cherished the afternoons spent with her dad during their lunch break, munching on sandwiches and talking about a host of different topics. Despite what often sounded like cynical nitpicking and sarcastic volleyball, they all really got along well—forever laughing over something.

At times, it had been awkward living down the hall next to her parents, but not totally awful. However, being crammed together in a minivan for days on end and subjected to nothing but Irwin's constant grumbles and complaints for thousands of miles did seem particularly horrendous. Not to mention the proximity to her mother's reoccurring hot flashes and over-the-top mood swings—undeniably set off by her father's less than perceptive remarks. Harper imagined long hours of silence coupled with mind-numbing scenery—

days of crossing sleep-inducing plains, offset by occasional bickering and the occasional protest. By her calculations, she imagined boredom settling in around mile marker five—and that estimate seemed overly generous.

Harper, a self-proclaimed foodie, couldn't imagine having to eat days of premade cold meals kept barely bacteria-free, stored in Dad's leaky old cooler. The darn thing looked older than Irwin and in worse shape.

No way.

She gripped her stomach, wincing.

Not in this life.

Harper flopped back against the cushions. "I can't do this." She typed in 'restaurant' along with their designated route, and a long list of possibilities popped up on her screen. "Thank you, food gods—"

A little more than an hour passed before Harper shut down.

"Well, that's done," she said, feeling sweaty but accomplished. After reading through hundreds of reviews, some highly entertaining and spirited, Harper managed to compile a fairly impressive list of food spots to try along their way should their rations, or Dad's cooler, go bust.

Why does Irwin get to be co-pilot?

Harper pictured the long, tedious hours stuck in the back of the van with her parents, watching poor Christopher, typically an easygoing sort of guy, turn into a frazzled lunatic, and all because of Irwin and his ridiculous timeframe. Which, knowing Irwin, meant stopping only for necessary bathroom breaks and intermittent fill-ups.

Harper sighed, hoping what she anticipated would not come to fruition.

However, there still remained one irrefutable and undeniable truth—whether they decided upon a coffee can or traditional urn—they were about to embark on a critical mission.

And this mission entailed making sure their precious cargo arrived safely to its final resting place. This, of course, left them little to no wiggle room to accommodate the group's usual, run-of-the-mill penchant for screwing everything up.

Harper typed in 'hotels'—searching for inexpensive, decent places to rest, instead of the anticipated shady motels Irwin would undoubtedly select, seeing that the man didn't give a fig about customer ratings or reviews.

"I keep my own counsel, thank you very much," Irwin had stated snippily at their last meeting. "And therefore, do not incline to solicit the opinions of strangers."

No surprise, Irwin wasn't kidding.

Harper also checked into possible touristy places to visit along Irwin's inflexible route, something to look forward to other than the boredom. As she compiled her list, she made *extra-triply* sure nothing picked dared veer off Irwin's path to perdition. No use inviting mutiny on their group's first maiden voyage.

A LOW POWER MODE message flashed across Harper's screen.

"*Uh-oh*." She'd been so engrossed in notetaking she hadn't noticed the tiny charge icon in the corner of her screen slipping into blood-curdling red.

Harper, ignoring Bones' disapproval, slid him to the side far enough to extend her arm over the couch ledge to plug in her phone charger. As luck would have it, she had been recently gifted a new ten-foot cord—a non-altruistic present from Christopher after she almost choked him to death with her last, way shorter version.

"It's not my fault the only available bedroom socket is on your side of the bed," she had tried explaining to him as she crawled over his resting, prone body, the taut cord stretched across his larynx.

"*And*, we're back in business." Harper leaned back,

anxious to finish gathering her notes. However, no sooner had she reclined on the cushion did Bones re-squash his entire big self onto her lap, this time draping his whole furry body over both of Harper's hands.

"Oh, no you don't, lazy boy," she informed him in no uncertain terms. "I'm going to need these."

Although situated at a higher elevation, July in the Pocono Mountains could still become unbearably humid. This summer, a succession of muggy scorching days followed by even hotter, hard-to-breathe sticky nights had been particularly brutal, and they were only half-way through. It hadn't helped any that their apartment had nothing but ceiling fans to keep them comfortable. Something Christopher had complained about often ...

"JUST ONE AIR CONDITIONER," he had pleaded one evening, his chest drenched in sweat. He spread his body across the bed, his back sideways as if willing the fan's barely warm moving air to bring much-needed relief. "Is that too much to ask for?"

Harper, sitting up against the headboard, fanned herself with a rolled-up magazine. "I went to the store yesterday to buy one, but they were sold out. No surprise there."

Christopher grinned and reached his hand out to grasp her thigh. "Then there's only one thing left we can do to get comfortable," he teased, his hands mischievously working their way up her leg, caressing her back.

Harper, although feeling sticky and uncomfortable, liked the direction her man's mind was heading.

"I'll beat you there!" In one rapid bound, Harper tore from the bed to the shower, giggling, with Christopher, already stripped down to his boxers, trailing not far behind.

BONES NUDGED his head against Harper's leg once more.

"Bones! Seriously, dude," she implored. "I need to work here," but Harper's pleas fell on deaf, *couldn't-give-a-meow* cat ears.

After a bit of creative fidgeting, Harper managed to slide her hands free but didn't have the heart to jostle her four-legged pal again, despite having lost feeling in her lower extremities over an hour ago. Instead, she stroked the top of his head, and in return, Bones purred louder, nuzzling his furry face lovingly against her belly. Then he dragged himself into a crooked sitting position, continuing to smoosh his human friend playfully beneath her chin with his head. His feline way of letting Harper know to keep showing him the love.

Harper nudged him, coaxing him to the side, but Bones still wouldn't budge. "Move," she groaned. "*Please.*"

In response, Bones flicked his tail, clipping Harper beneath her nose.

"*Achoo!*" Harper sneezed, taking advantage of the sudden shudder to stretch her stiff feet coaxing much-needed blood to flow.

"Would you give me a break already?" she begged, but Harper already knew the stubborn cat wouldn't comply. He'd become her constant shadow ever since Cornelia's abrupt departure to the assisted living center last year. While at times annoying, Harper couldn't blame him. Cornelia's absence had been difficult on everyone, and Bones, despite his naturally ornery disposition, took it especially hard, barely eating and wallowing under Cornelia's favorite store chair for hours at a time, declining to leave.

After a few weeks of mourning, the grief-stricken tabby

started acting weird—weirder than usual—even by Bones' standard of strange.

Harper remembered one afternoon finding him in her apartment perched in front of a turned-off TV, staring at nothing. At other times, she'd hear him yowling whenever one of Cornelia's favorite show tunes came on the radio. This operatic blood-curdling, hair-raising routine of his would last until the song finished, with Bones mewing to the final bitter end. Then, as if his tiny feline heart had shattered in two, he'd slink back under Cornelia's empty chair to await her return, his head curled morosely on his paws, and his dark eyes glazed over, eerily vacant.

Irwin drove himself and everyone else nuts trying to coax Bones to eat, but he wouldn't do more than nibble. As a last resort, Irwin brought Bones back to his house, hoping the familiar surroundings would help yank him out of his funk. Irwin even plied the cat with copious amounts of Shrimp Lo Mein—his favorite. And for a short time, it seemed to do the trick, until one morning when Irwin awoke, jarred awake by Bones licking under his armpits.

"STOP THAT!" he roared, swatting the cat with his pillow.

That little ditty had been Irwin's last straw.

Irwin had arrived at the bookshop a few hours later beyond disconcerted. "I'm not sure how much more of this cat's antics I can take," he announced, stomping toward Harper. "Here. He's all yours," he said, shoving Bones into Harper's arms.

"*Aww*, he's not so bad," Harper countered while cuddling him, amazed at how effortlessly the white lie sprang off the tip of her tongue. She scratched behind the cat's ears. "He just needs more time to process his loss. Right, my whittle-little buddy?" she cooed, in that grating baby-kitty-talk cat fanatics do.

"Time to process?" Irwin scowled. "That's rich. Next you'll tell me he needs cat psychotherapy."

"Don't be ridiculous." Harper cuddled Bones. "But he's got feelings too, you know. Poor little whittle, boo-boo." Harper glared at Irwin. "Don't be so hard on him. Bones lost a lot of people he loved, too, you know."

Harper had been referring to Gilly, Irwin's deceased fiancée, and Bones' first Kitty Momma, as well as Dakota, Gilly's daughter and first legitimate playmate. And now, Bones had lost his best crime partner-buddy and snack benefactor, Cornelia.

"How do you expect him to act?"

Bones turned his head and hissed at Irwin. Then, as if attempting to shut out the world, covered his furry head with both paws.

"*Aww!* Now, look what you've done! You've hurt his feelings."

"His feelings?" Irwin snarled. "*Gah!* May I remind you, young lady, that you weren't the one startled awake this morning having under your armpits orally excavated!"

Harper nose wrinkled. "*Ewww.*"

"Precisely." Irwin raised a winning brow and scowled. "And how do you suppose that unsettling ordeal made me feel?"

"Flattered?" she managed to blurt out, barely stifling a giggle.

Irwin ground his jaw. "Like I said, he's all yours." Irwin hoofed it as far away as possible before Harper had a chance to protest. "And I strongly suggest you find some way to counter his nonexistent lack of etiquette."

"Oh, Bones," she muttered. "What am I going to do with you?"

Harper couldn't blame Irwin. It wasn't like he was the only one getting irritated with Bones.

On one particularly petrifying occasion, Olivia entered

the kitchen to make herself a cup of tea and found Bones perched on her counter using his paw to move the knobs on her gas burner.

"Stop!" she had screeched, swatting him away with her slipper. "You're gonna get us all killed!"

The second final last straw.

That's when Harper decided to step in and take over, and Bones hadn't left her side since.

DESPITE THE RAIN clouds suddenly appearing and threatening to burst, the air in the apartment continued to suffocate.

"Come on, buddy," Harper pleaded, her back damp from sweat. "Scooch over. Just a smidgen for me, okay?"

Harper massaged the back of her neck and then thighs, relieved to gain feeling in her body again. "Now that wasn't so terrible, was it?"

And then it hit.

Like a Mack Truck hits—full force.

"*Ahhh*!" Harper bolted straight up as her mouth dropped open.

"Oh, no! Bones!" she yelped, clamping a sweaty palm across her lips, causing the cat to flinch. "I *knew* it! I knew I forgot something important! Stupid, stupid, stupid me."

Harper had been so busy searching for hotels and gas stations along their route that she'd completely forgotten about what to do about Bones. The cat, who, for all his pretentious attitude and ostentatious snobbery, suffered from extreme motion sickness. Irwin swore he watched him get woozy trotting too fast to his food tray.

Bones would never make it across the country.

Her eyes watered as she glanced over at Bones—her lovable, naughty, rebellious-as-all-hell—Bones.

Harper typed 'What to Do About Bones?' at the top of her To-Do list. Then added Roger Ledbetter and Regan Vanhorn's names next to his with an even larger, bolded question mark.

CHAPTER 5

"Is everything okay?" Olivia had been down the short hall, busy folding laundry when she noticed Harper through the open apartment door, sprawled out on her couch. "I heard you yelling about something," she said, glancing over a folded stack of towels.

"I'm fine. Melting, but fine," responded Harper, her phone clasped in both hands.

Olivia headbutted her bedroom door open and disappeared.

"Ma?" Harper called after her.

"You rang?" Olivia poked her head out of the bedroom.

"I have a question for you." Harper toddled out of her apartment and leaned inside her parent's open bedroom door. "Do you think Bones would do okay with Regan Vanhorn?"

Both Regan Vanhorn and Roger Ledbetter were friends of

Irwin's from his librarian days. Irwin described Regan as 'kind but mildly eccentric,' and Roger as 'terminally insufferable.' But deep down inside, Harper knew he cared deeply about them both.

When Cornelia's dementia towards the end had caused her to deteriorate rapidly, those two stepped in to watch over the bookshop. This, of course, freed the rest of them to rush off to the hospital whenever necessary. Who better than to watch Bones in their absence? Besides, Harper had always suspected Bones of carrying a bit of a crush on Regan, especially whenever she sang or brushed his furry belly—something he didn't allow just anybody to do.

Olivia stepped out of her bedroom, both hands resting around her svelte waist. "You mean for the entire two weeks? Maybe longer?"

Harper gave a half-nod-shrug. "Unless you can think of somebody else better?"

Olivia's eyes rolled and she laughed. Not a 'ha-ha, that's funny' laugh, but more of a shrill like *'you've got to be out of your mind'* laugh.

"Not you, too," Harper groaned. "But I get it. Bones is still on Irwin's hit list, too."

Olivia snorted. "And for good reason!"

By this time, Bones had followed Harper down the hall. Tail high, he circled her legs, nuzzling his nose against her ankle. Harper bent over and scooped him up, caressing his tiny head. "He's not that bad."

Olivia wagged a red-painted lengthy fingernail in the air. "Not that bad? That crazy cat almost blew us up," she snapped, apparently still pretty heated about the gas stove incident.

"He's a curious kitty is all." Harper never failed to defend Bones, ignoring his less than affable behavior. "But I don't think he'll do well on the trip."

"Not with his motion sickness." Olivia leaned her frame against the hall wall. "Trust me. I've cleaned up my fair share of that cat's throw up to know that won't work."

Harper agreed.

"I don't know, Harper. Do you think Regan could handle our four-pawed pyromaniac for that long without having to call the fire department?" Olivia liked to act as if she still had it out for Bones, but Harper knew better, catching her on more than one occasion scooping pricy albacore tuna fish into his bowl.

Harper kissed the top of her purring cat's nose. "What other choice do we have? It's not as if we can leave him with just anybody."

Regrettably, Bones wasn't all that fond of Roger. On those rare occasions when Roger stopped by, he'd flat out ignored the man, and in truth, Roger barely acknowledged Bones' presence either. In Harper's opinion, the two didn't make for the greatest fit.

Harper patted the top of Bones' furry head, now jammed under her left rib. She felt his comfort purrs rumble beneath her tee-shirt, and his hot short breaths rush against her skin, but as hot as she felt, she didn't have the heart to push him away.

"Well, I guess it couldn't hurt to ask," said Olivia, shouting from somewhere inside her bedroom. "But if she agrees, she's crazier than I thought."

FIVE DAYS until departure and so much left to do.

"TWO WEEKS?" Regan used the back of her wrist to inch her over-sized purple glasses back up her pointy nose before ramming another children's book into the overstuffed library's shelf.

"At the most, if Irwin has anything to say about it," explained Harper, handing Regan the next book off the top of the stack.

The two women had met years back when Harper, then a troubled teenager, had locked herself in the library's women's bathroom, refusing to come out. Regan had offered to stay in the restroom with Harper until Irwin came to the rescue. Since then, the two had bonded over books and their mutual admiration for their curmudgeon pal.

"I'm not sure how well he'll do on a car trip."

Regan paused. "Are we talking about Irwin or Bones?"

Harper chuckled.

"No, seriously," Regan said. "I need to know which because I adamantly refuse to watch Irwin for two minutes, no less two weeks."

"Noted. No worries. I meant Bones. And we'll make sure to leave more than enough cat food, kitty litter, and money to cover his occasional petition for Shrimp Lo Mein."

"I love Shrimp Lo Mein." Regan tried making more space on the shelf but failed. She grew increasingly frustrated the more she attempted to cram the book into the too-small space. After a bit of huffing, puffing, and snarling, Regan gave up. Face flushed, she stood and dropped the remainder of displaced books in a metal book cart. "Have you spoken with Irwin about any of this yet?"

"Not exactly." Harper bowed her head, staring down at her sneakers.

"*Harper—*"

"In my defense, I figured I'd speak to you first. See if you were okay with this before I hit Irwin with it."

"I see." Regan wheeled the small stack of remaining books over to her desk, her flowy, ankle-length skirt trailing behind her. "Hey! Don't do that," she shouted at a small boy ready to dip his entire arm into the turtle tank. She softened her tone. "I wouldn't do that if I were you. Shakespeare loves to nibble the fingers of little boys he doesn't know."

The little boy, eyes wide and mouth agape, whipped his tiny arm out of harm's way. "He bites?"

"He can, but not me." Regan hiked over to the tank, reached in and lifted the box turtle out of his glass cage for the little boy to see up close safely. "Allow me to make the proper introductions. Shakespeare, this is—" Regan tilted her head. "I'm sorry, I forgot to ask you your name."

"Billy," answered the bashful child, eyes cast down.

"Nice to meet you, Billy. Shakespeare, this is my new friend, Billy. He'd like to say hello and possibly feel your shell." Regan lifted the turtle to eye level. "Are you cool with that?"

The turtle twisted his head, nothing to indicate he understood, but enough for Regan to continue her routine.

"Here, Billy, old Shakes here say he's cool with a light pet." She held the turtle forward but gave the child enough space to change his mind.

"Hi, Shakespeare," Billy said, petting the turtle's shell with quick timid strokes. "He's really cool."

"He is super cool," agreed Regan. "Did you know the study of turtles is called cheloniology? It comes from the Greek word meaning turtle. Makes sense, right?"

Billy nodded. "Does Shakespeare the turtle know his name?"

"Now that's an excellent question! You must do super well in school."

Billy shyly nodded. "Science is kinda my favorite subject." "I can tell," winked Regan. "Now, to answer your brilliant inquiry, turtles don't hear too well. Scientists say they only respond to a few sounds made by other turtles or their hatching eggs. However, between you and me, I don't believe it." Regan tipped her head to the side as if delivering highly confidential information. "This guy knows full well who I am, and I'd swear on a stack of *National Geographic's* that he loves my purple glasses but only pretends he doesn't."

Billy giggled, his bashfulness rapidly fading away. "Can I hold him?"

Regan pursed her lips. "Sorry, my new friend, but not this time. I know Shakespeare is super cute, but to be honest, he really doesn't like being handled and petted like, let's say a puppy or kitten." Regan smiled and turned the turtle head to face hers. "Okay, sir. Time for you to go back in."

Regan placed the box turtle carefully inside his glass tank, but this time, positioning him near the front panel so Billy would still be able to see him up close. "You know what? I have an idea." She rose to her feet. "How would you like to learn more about Shakespeare and his other turtle friends?"

"Okay," Billy nodded, excited.

"Awesome sauce. Stay put and keep Shakespeare company. I'll be back in a snap."

Off Regan went, returning in less than a minute, holding not one, but three books about turtles. "There you go, my new friend Billy. Lots and lots of super cool information here. Anything you need to know about turtles."

Billy smiled, clutching the turtle books to his chest like a newfound treasure.

Regan bent down on one knee to look at little Billy at eye level. "I think Shakespeare really digs you, so the next time you come back to the library, make sure to bring him some romaine lettuce or a few pieces of overripe fruit, and he'll love you forever and ever," she said, winking.

Little Billy, grinning from ear-to-ear, nodded, his three turtle books still hard-pressed protectively to his chest.

Billy's mom, who had been watching the entire interaction from the side, mouthed a grateful *thank you*.

Regan nodded, *"Anytime,"* she mimed back before returning to Harper, waiting near her desk.

"Now...where were we?" she mumbled, looking lost. Then, without missing a beat. "Ah, yes, now I remember. Listen, Harper. I adore Mr. Bones, and you know that. And I have absolutely no issue watching him for as long as you guys need me to. Matter-of-fact, he's more than welcome to hang out at my apartment instead of staying at the bookshop alone. He could have the run of my place, and I could sure use the company. However, my 'yes' remains solely contingent on Irwin agreeing."

Harper nodded. "Understood."

Regan patted Harper on the back, then lightly squeezed her shoulder. "Look, I know how important this trip is, and if I can do anything to help, I will. You can count on me." She walked behind her desk, tugged the handle on her drawer, and handed Harper her card with her cell phone number stamped on it. "Should Irwin agree, then all's good—call me. But if Irwin doesn't, I'm afraid the answer is an emphatic, no."

CHAPTER 6

FOUR DAYS LEFT UNTIL DEPARTURE.

"'HEAR YE, hear ye. Know all men by these present.' The meeting of The Abernathy & Crane Family, plus one, has now officially convened," Darren's voice thundered across the small, cozy kitchen as he clunked a long-handled wooden spoon against Olivia's table like a mallet. "Will everyone kindly take their seats."

"Give me that," snarled Irwin, snatching the spoon out of Darren's hand. "For once, could you stop goofing around? We have less than a week until we leave, and there are still quite a few pressing matters to discuss." Irwin handed Darren's pretend gavel to Olivia. "Please put this someplace where your child-husband can't reach it." Irwin then busied himself gathering a stack of papers, handing out a stapled packet to each person present. "One for you, Christopher, one for you, Harper, and one for you, Olivia." Irwin stopped and glared down at Darren. "...and this is for *you*," he said, handing Darren only a single sheet of paper. "Now, if the rest of you would turn to page one."

"*Uhm*, Irwin?" nudged Darren, peeking at everyone else's substantial packets, confused. "I only got one page."

"*Quiet*," admonished Olivia, perched at the edge of her chair with her posture upright and stiff like a turn-of-the-century schoolmarm. "Go ahead, Irwin. Ignore him. The rest of us are listening."

"I'm listening," muttered Darren, slightly miffed. He glanced around the table, eyes wide open as if appealing for support. "It's just that Irwin said to turn to page one, which doesn't make a whole lotta sense when there's only one sheet."

"What are you talking about now?" Olivia brandished her packet and thumbed the pages in her husband's face. "There are multiple pages."

Irwin, still standing, leaned in and rested his palms on the table. "Children. If I may interrupt?"

Olivia and Darren continued to quibble, while Irwin jerked his head back, imploring the lightning god to strike him dead.

"Nothing painful," he instructed Thor, "but don't miss either."

The noise in the small space turned instantly deafening with everyone talking at once. Irwin watched as *The Abernathy & Crane Family* meeting dissolved into its usual cockup.

Irwin's head began spinning. Between the constant exchange of sharp-traded retorts, Darren's all-too-frequent unrelated questions laced with redundant observations,

Olivia's erratic hot flashes, and Harper's less than amusing sidebar comments, he had a hard time keeping up.

"People!" Irwin rapped the table using his knuckles. "Please." He leaned over and whispered to Darren, "I only gave you the first page," he clarified, exercising a pained forbearance he honestly didn't feel.

Darren rose half-way out of his chair, vindicated, "See!" He slapped the table. "I told you so."

"Hush, anyway." Olivia pursed her lips and pressed the shut-up finger to her mouth. "And sit down, for goodness sake. It's too hot for all that jumping around, hon."

"Now I'm hon, again," grumbled Darren. "You're all seeing this, right? It's not my imagination. She's making me crazy."

"You make yourself crazy," teased Olivia.

Harper, already slumped in her chair, slid down lower. From the corner of his eye, Irwin watched as she kept glancing in Christopher's direction, trying to provoke from him a response. Christopher almost chuckled aloud when she mouthed, *I told you so*. Nevertheless, to Christopher's unflagging credit, he didn't respond, but instead twisted his face in the complete opposite direction so as not to be seen laughing.

From across the table, Darren and Olivia faced one another, their two clammy foreheads almost touching. They started bickering about something else entirely, exchanging what sounded like a heated, semi-hushed squabble. Meanwhile, Harper, never one to give up easily, none too discreetly prodded Christopher in the thigh with her toes under the table.

Out of everyone present, it was Christopher's determination to maintain some sense of decorum that Irwin appreciated the most. He cleared his throat. "*Ahem*," but nobody noticed. "Excuse me," Irwin yelled, his jaw visibly tight, but everyone kept talking and goofing around. He then clapped his hands loudly, but this time, only Darren glanced up.

"Bet you wish you had my wooden spoon now," Darren goaded, slumped in his chair crossing his arms triumphantly over his chest.

Irwin rapped the table again, using his entire fist to accentuate each word. "Are-We-Quite-Done-Yet!" he shouted in his most librarian-ish dressing-down intonation.

The noise abruptly stopped.

A solemn collection of heads nodded.

"May I say something?" asked a poker-faced Harper leaning both her elbows on the table.

"If you must," agreed Irwin.

"I gotta admit, Irwin." Harper slapped the stapled paper on the table. "You've outdone yourself this time. This is one *long* and exhaustive, yet, somewhat still shockingly impressive list you've compiled here."

Irwin's mouth twitched as he mentally picked apart Harper's veiled compliment, waiting for the catch.

"I mean, look at this," she said, flipping through each sheet. "Page after page after page. You seem to have covered everything."

"I tried," he agreed, staring down at her, waiting, and waiting...

Harper shrugged. "Almost."

Splat!

And there it was.

Everyone turned to watch the two lock eyes in a standoff.

Harper's nose twitched, but to her credit, she'd didn't reach up to scratch it.

Irwin, meanwhile, struggling to match Harper's calm, ignored the vein pulsating on the side of his neck. Neither one dared move a muscle.

"Would you care to elaborate?" Irwin asked, feigning

composure, his angular stubbled chin lifted ever-so-pointedly in Harper's direction.

"Almost," she repeated, noticeably enjoying herself, "as in, what do we plan on doing about him?" Harper cocked her head in Bones' direction.

Ah ha! Victory!

Irwin grinned. "Page six, paragraph three," he said, tapping at Harper's papers with his long bony finger.

Only the subdued sounds of papers turning could be heard.

"Oh. My bad," shrugged Harper in feigned defeat. "My, my, how could I have ever missed that?" she teased, doing her best southern belle imitation, but Irwin didn't care. He'd won.

"Why is it so unbelievably hot in here?" Olivia tossed her head back, stretching her damp neck, groaning. She cranked her head up and glanced around the table. "Or is it only me?"

Darren's opened his mouth to answer but caught Irwin's warning scowl just in the nick of time.

Olivia reached for another napkin—her third or perhaps fourth. Irwin had lost count.

"I feel disgusting. Man, do I hate humidity." Olivia wiped her forehead. "It's nighttime. The sun is down. It shouldn't be this hot anymore, and yet here I am, still pooling sweat. I can't stand it." Olivia sprung to her feet and stomped over to Irwin's freezer where she plunged her head deep inside. "*Ahhh*, this is much, much better."

The room watched in stunned silence, but no one dared speak.

"This is nothing," Darren finally whispered, hiding his mouth behind his hand. He slid his chair closer to the table and let out a long, suffering sigh. "She had the AC on full blast last night. Froze me out," he complained, rubbing his throat. "Come to think of it; it still hurts when I swallow. I might be coming down with pneumonia." Darren felt his forehead and coughed twice.

"I can hear you talking about me, Darren," said Olivia, the sound of her discontent somewhat muffled by the icebox.

Darren had confided in Irwin about his suspecting Olivia of going through the change. He had explained how one minute she'd be complaining about the overbearing heat, and the next, screaming about how freezing it was. Happy and cheerful one sec, then *poof*—off the deep end.

Olivia poked her head out. "Can we get this meeting over with, already? I'm burning up over here."

"See," muttered Darren, under his breath.

Olivia trudged to the table, snatching a paper plate on her way back. "I'm hungry. Anybody else hungry? I could go for some cookies." She paused, fanning herself with the plate. "No. Not cookies. I don't feel like cookies. Maybe potato salad—and not that German potato salad or the vinaigrette style one they sell at the store." Olivia wrinkled her nose. "I like the one with the mayo, eggs, sweet pepper, and onions. Anybody else want potato salad?" she asked, not waiting for an answer. "No? Okay," Olivia kept talking a mile a minute. "Maybe later then."

Irwin, his eyebrows pinched together, stared at Olivia, utterly confused. Watching her hormonal meltdowns was the human equivalent to a train derailment on speed dial.

—*Jekyll or Hyde sure have nothing on this woman*, he thought, almost feeling bad for Darren.

Olivia slid into her chair and picked up her packet, while Darren, still nursing page one, peered over her shoulder to see what he was missing.

"Stop that," Olivia snapped at him, too hot and irritated to put up with any more of her husband's shenanigans.

"What?" Darren protested. "I only have page one, remember?"

"Play nice, you two," teased Harper, savoring the chaos to continue prodding Christopher playfully under the table.

"I've got a question," interjected Christopher, fighting to keep his face serious while twisting his upper body further away from a now giggling Harper.

Irwin nodded at Christopher, thankful for the momentary Romper Room reprieve. "Go ahead."

"It says here, *umm,* still on page one on the very bottom, that you are allotting a total of one-hour stops to deliver each of Cornelia's specified letters. Am I reading that correctly?"

Irwin nodded. "That is correct."

Christopher glanced around the table. "Well, are you sure that'll give us enough time?"

Irwin frowned. "Why wouldn't it?"

"*Ah*...okay." Christopher ran his fingers through his damp hair, continuing to securitize the timeline. "Let's say for a moment that one of the people on Cornelia's list feels like talking—or maybe they start asking us questions. It's not like we can toss the letter at them and leave."

"We most certainly can," disagreed Irwin, head wagging. "I checked and rechecked. I found nothing whatsoever from Cornelia requiring us, specifically me, to schmooze."

"No schmoozing required," Harper muttered under her breath, jotting Irwin's comment down just to cross it off her list with a flourish.

"Furthermore," interjected Irwin, ignoring Harper's quip. "We have a tight schedule to adhere to largely because we still have a bookstore to run here. Need I also remind you our customers will not appreciate our being gone for too long."

"Irwin does make a good point," agreed Olivia.

"Yes, the bookstore is a concern. I agree as well," said Harper directed to her mother. "But let me get this straight, Irwin. You expect us to drive clear across the entire country, stopping only for one-hour handoffs, and then continuing on to San Diego to stand on some bluff we've never been to, where we unceremoniously dump Cornelia's remains in the ocean? Then, God forbid, without a single minute to spare, to, you know, mourn or anything, we have to hop on a plane back to Pennsylvania, all—by the what? Ninth, tenth, eleventh, twelfth day?" She exhaled, her eyes never wavering from his.

Irwin shifted his weight to his other leg. "Although an unnecessarily crude description, it is fairly accurate."

"This is insane." Harper balked, looking around the table. "Don't you all agree?"

At first, Darren nodded, then caught wind of Olivia's stern expression and stopped dead cold, clamping his mouth shut before his wife shoved him permanently off the menopausal cliff.

"Not if we stick to the itinerary." Irwin whipped out a small map from out of his folder and pointed. "It takes approximately eight days, maybe nine with necessary stops, as Harper has already pointed out, to drive from coast to coast. As you can see from the timetable provided, I have allotted a full, extra twenty-four hours to our trip to compensate for any unforeseen breaks and delivery stops. This addition should prove more than sufficient."

"Well, I stand corrected," Harper whistled, not impressed. "A full twenty-four hours. How generous of you." She leaned back in her chair, visibly annoyed.

"I assume I'll be doing most of the driving?" asked Christopher, noticeably trying to stay focused on the bottom line, despite the distractions.

Irwin nodded. "Yes, if you wouldn't mind."

Christopher nodded. "Not a problem. I happen to enjoy long-distance driving." Christopher shuffled through some of his paperwork. "At first, I thought about renting us an RV, something to drive, sleep, and cook in, but it got pretty pricey."

"How pricey are we talkin'?" asked Darren.

"Typically, a hundred and seventy-five to two hundred and seventy-five dollars, but those were for the ones ten years and older. I checked a few of them out and didn't think they would work. The newer models were great. They had all the latest amenities, but those would run us anywhere between three hundred and fifty to four hundred and fifty a night—still fairly comparable to what we would be paying for all our hotel rooms, if not the same amount."

"That's not terrible," said Olivia.

"I agree, but on some nights, I figured we would be driving straight through, so no need for a hotel." Christopher paused. "Besides the gas costs being astronomical, my biggest reason for not wanting to rent it, to be honest with all of you, is I'm just not entirely sure how comfortable I am driving one of those things. They're massive."

"And the van?" asked Darren.

"I got a deal for less than eighty dollars a day," answered Christopher. "—with unlimited mileage. It still means paying for hotels, gas, and tolls, but at least in a hotel, even I get to rest. Plus, the use of their amenities."

"Let's not forget to factor in our return plane tickets," mentioned Harper.

"Yes," Irwin agreed. "I had planned on purchasing those a few days before we're ready to return to Pennsylvania."

"Waiting that long is going to run a pretty penny," whistled Darren. "I say we should all cover the cost of our own tickets. It seems only right."

Irwin shook his head. "Thank you, Darren, but no, I'd rather purchase them after we have completed our..." Irwin searched for the right word. "...tasks—in case we find ourselves delayed for whatever reason. And in regards to the cost of hotels, gas, van rental—Cornelia already factored that in and left a check that will more than cover the amount. Which reminds me," he snapped his fingers. "—Does everyone have either a passport or a Real ID? We'll need them to fly back, even on a domestic flight since our illustrious state of Pennsylvania hasn't seen fit to upgrade our driver's licenses to federally compliant identification cards."

Flushed, Olivia grabbed for another napkin. "I don't know about the rest of you, but I'd rather just get the Real ID card. I'm glad Pennsylvania refused. I read somewhere, I forgot where, but it's some kind of national ID system."

"So?" asked Darren. "What if it is?"

Olivia's pupils flared in Darren's direction. "So, genius, let's say someone hacks into any of the state's database—they'll gain total access to everyone's personal information. Talk about identity fraud!"

"Don't you think that if someone wanted your information, they could already get it?" countered Darren, inching his chair a safer distance away.

"*Ahem*," Irwin cleared his throat, tired of playing referee. "Be that as it may, my question stands—albeit slightly revised. Does everyone have a passport, then?

Everyone around the table exchanged glances.

—Yes.

—Yeah, I have one, someplace.

—I do, too.

—I think so.

"Excellent. Please remember to pack them for the trip. However, I'll need a photocopy from each one of you before I'm able to purchase the tickets," Irwin explained.

"Makes perfect sense," said Harper, toying with her pen.

Irwin raised a brow, prepared for the proverbial second shoe to land. He didn't have to wait long.

"Except...," mumbled Harper.

Clunk.

"Except what?" asked Irwin guarded.

Harper's eyes ran down the list. "Well, for example, you have here, 'Each person is allotted one small soft duffel bag sized luggage.'" She peered her pretty eyes over the top of the paper. "And 'one carry-on'? —I hate to be the one to inform you, Irwin, but this isn't a plane."

"Do we have a weight limit?" interjected Darren, not trying to be funny, although this time, Christopher did laugh. Olivia's face contorted in disgust.

"No, but we will be flying back," said Irwin.

"That's true," Harper conceded.

"The rest, I think, is pretty self-explanatory," added Irwin. "There are five of us traveling and one minivan. Space will be limited. Soft luggage of a lesser size will make our trip feel less crowded."

"Except we have a roof rack," interrupted Christopher.

"Perfect!" beamed a triumphant Harper.

"What about my cooler?" asked Darren, concerned.

Harper stifled a laugh while Olivia, who hated Darren's sieve-like old cooler and had wanted it thrown out for years, rubbed Darren's arm a bit too affectionately. "Let's see how it does on the trip," she cooed. "It's old, sweetheart, and sometimes leaks. You know that." She paused. "Maybe it's time to retire it."

Darren nodded and shrugged, visibly defeated. "I guess."

"*Ahhh*—Irwin?" signaled Harper. "Maybe we ought to continue?" she said, tugging his shirt.

"Yes," Irwin replied, all too happy to get this meeting over with. "Harper? You were saying something?"

"What about this part here?" She tapped her finger against the paper. 'Pack enough clothes because laundry stops will be limited.'"

Irwin shrugged. "I'm not seeing a problem with that."

"The problem, Irwin, is that it's not necessarily true. Most of the hotels I found along our route offer laundry service or have machines available for guests to use—and before you say anything, I already checked. All we need to do is remember to bring small containers of laundry soap and softener."

"And coins," offered Darren, trying to be helpful.

"Sorry, Dad, but welcome to the twenty-first century where cards are cash." Harper's previous unflappability was starting to wane. "But you know what? Let's push past all that for the moment and concentrate on this one," she grinned. "My all-time favorite." She cleared her throat. 'The radio will be kept off at all times—allocated solely for news or traffic updates. The only exception: group selected audiobooks."

"Hence, why I added this section here," Irwin interrupted, leaning over to point to the line that read, 'Each person is responsible for bringing earphones.'"

"Yeah, I saw that," Harper laughed. "As if anybody would ever want to listen to a song or audiobook you selected. But right here, this is the part that got me." She pointed at the bottom of the page. "What do you mean by 'no humming, gum chewing, popping, slurping, smacking, loud yawning, snoring, unnecessary squeezing of plastic bottles, or the incessant rustling or crinkling of plastic or paper bags—Since when did you become misophonic?"

"I'm not," humphed Irwin, reluctant to admit a strong aversion to the sounds of plastic or paper bags opening and closing—especially snack bags. Although frankly, he wouldn't go as far as to equate his disfavor to that of an actual phobia. "Also, self-explanatory," he added with false bravado.

"Not really." Harper shot back, "but before we get off-track debating the finer points of your *misophonia* when the truth is you're the only one who needs to bring sound-reducing headphones, humor me for a second." Harper wiggled in her chair to sit up straighter. "Skipping past all of the predictable Irwin-induced drivel," Harper winked at Irwin. "I'd like to direct your attention to the so-called timetable. Specifically—revisiting the part about purchasing the tickets to fly home once we're done in California. I mean, Irwin, we can purchase them now and add travel protection. That way, it's way cheaper, and we won't be financially penalized if we have to change dates."

Irwin bit his bottom lip. "That wasn't something I was aware of," he reluctantly admitted.

Harper smiled. "Yeah, well, I'm full of surprises."

"As well as a few other things," Irwin grumbled. The room grew still. "If there's nothing else? He waited a moment longer. "No? Good. Everyone, please turn to page two."

"I would if I could," bemoaned Darren, his arms flanked across his torso.

"Here. Take mine. I've already finished reading it," said Olivia. She pressed her packet into Darren's chest and raised her hand. "Question—"

"You don't have to raise your hand, Mom," groaned Harper, rubbing her eyes.

"Oh. Right," Olivia blushed. "Silly me." She slinked her arm down and slipped her hand into her pocket. "Some old habits are hard to break, I guess." She leaned forward. "So, here's my concern. Has anyone spoken to the people we're supposed to be meeting on Cornelia's behalf?" Olivia began reading their names off Irwin's list. "Ohio, Mildred Loxley. Next, Amarillo, Texas, to see a guy named Martin Newman. Old boyfriend, maybe? Third stop, New Mexico, and that's Luna, no last name provided. Cool first name, though. Means the moon, I think. And there's one more—a woman named Elle Reed. She's the one in San Diego at our last stop."

Irwin's mind wandered off to the photo he discovered the other night of Elle. His ears reddened as his face colored. "All taken care of," he said, dabbing his forehead as if sweating.

"I've already informed each person on Cornelia's list as to when to expect us. I also mentioned we would phone once we got closer." Irwin finally sat down. He bowed his head and lifted a pen to write. "Is there anything else we need to discuss?"

"Yeah. I got a question." Darren lifted a finger in the air to say something but hesitated.

Of course, he does.

Irwin sighed and placed his pen on the table.

Everyone waited.

Olivia, turning madder by the second, glared toward the ceiling and started counting to ten, backward.

Darren's face reddened. A tiny bead of sweat dribbled down the side of his cheek. He glanced around the table as if looking for answers. After a few seconds elapsed, Irwin, whose waning patience had all but evaporated, exploded.

"If you would please—" he roared.

"Sorry," apologized Darren, almost in a whisper. He leaned against the table and steepled his fingers, crouched over so low as if what he had to say equated to the secret encryption to a Swiss bank safe. "I love Cornelia, and I've got no problem doing what she's asked, but, *umm,* well, here's my issue." He hesitated. "Well, the thing is this—"

"Spit it out, Dad."

Darren exhaled. "Right. I'm just gonna say what we're all thinking. Who exactly are these people?" he waited. "I mean, it's not like we know diddlysquat about them."

"We know they were important to Cornelia. Isn't that enough?" asked Olivia.

"No," interrupted Harper. "Not necessarily. I mean, I think Dad's right this time. We don't know anything about them, and it feels kind of weird, you know? And kind of macabre if you ask me." Harper glanced at Christopher. "Am I wrong?"

Christopher shrugged. "I'm not sure if there's a clear-cut right or wrong in this kind of situation, but this trip doesn't seem macabre to me at all." Christopher held everyone's attention. "I can remember before my mother died. At the time, she had been anxious about leaving stuff undone, as she'd put it. She wrote me a list, something similar to what Cornelia did, but not nearly as elaborate. No trips or anything of that kind, but Mom did spend her last few weeks dictating a bunch of instructions to me. Stuff she wanted to do but never got around to doing. 'Make sure you give your Aunt Regina the soup bowl with the birds on it. She's always admired it.' And 'don't forget to pay the light and water bill. Look in my top drawer in my bedroom for a cardboard box. I kept some money in there since no thief would dare look in a box labeled 'tampons' she'd tell me." Christopher's voice seemed to drift further away. "Mom stayed a full-time worrier to the end. She practically fretted about everyone and every-thing until her last dying breath—even about people she barely knew."

Harper's eyes glistened. "She sounds a lot like our Cornelia." She softly stroked Christopher's arm.

"For sure," he nodded. "I guess that's why this last myste-rious request trip doesn't bother me. I mean, in many ways, it makes perfect sense." Christopher drew in a deep breath before continuing. "Think of it like this," he said in a voice he must have used to plead a case before a jury. "How many people suddenly die and never have the opportunity to tell the people in their life how much they meant to them? Or they die before revealing their last wishes. Maybe there were apologies to be made, secrets to share, or just personal stuff needed to be said. Not being able to do those things leaves those left behind feeling confused...unsettled, —Left always having to guess what their loved ones would have wanted in the end. But that's not what's happening here, is it? People like my mom and Cornelia— they were blessed with an opportunity. A gift, really, of time to set things right. A last chance to let us all know how they feel and what they needed or wanted." Christopher peered around the hushed, tear-filled room. "Sorry. I didn't mean to go off on a tangent."

"Darn you, Christopher," sobbed Olivia, her bottom lip quivering. She leaned over and buried her head into Darren's shoulder, weeping. "I can't believe she's gone."

Harper yanked a thread escaping from the worn ribbing on her stained with sweat tee-shirt. "Christopher's right," she sniffled. "We gotta do this. We have to honor Cornelia's last wishes, no matter how weird it gets," muttered Harper, her voice cracking as she wiped her tears away with the back if her hand. Christopher drew her in for a long hug.

Without further discourse, a pact, as vast as the universe and as deep as the ocean, solidified between the friends.

"Perhaps the heat is getting to all of us," said Irwin, wiping his eyes and struggling to find the right words to say. However, the resolve etched across his craggy face told it all. For all his constant nitpicking, he held no pretense concerning the gravity of this trip.

Unquestionably, what lay ahead would most certainly be a journey like no other. Not only putting to test their private reserves, but also the depth of their friendships—the bonds they had all so carefully built together over the past few years. Traveling in such close proximity, he assumed, would most assuredly expose everyone's shortcomings, some sooner than others, and to varying degrees. Yet, apart from his usual cantankerous demeanor, Irwin silently prayed for the four people gracing this table...friends he had grown to love and treasure. He hoped they would not walk away from this trip disappointed, or *worse*—hating him with an unbridled passion. He cleared his throat. "If there's nothing further, will everyone please turn to the next page."

Only a faint sound of stifled snuffles and pages slowly turning were heard.

Irwin's voiced cracked. "Ahem. Olivia?"

"Yes, Irwin?" she sniffled, lifting her head off Darren's shoulder.

"As the only person amongst us who can adequately prepare anything close to digestible, how has the meal preparation been going?"

Olivia's jaw dropped open. "Adequately digestible?" She flashed Irwin the dirtiest look. "Tell me he just didn't say that," she said to the rest of the group.

Darren squeezed Olivia's hand and smiled. "Remember the source from whence it came. 'Adequately digestible' is Irwin-speak for delicious and appreciated."

"It had better be," Olivia sneered, balanced high in her chair.

Irwin waited for the side chatter to halt before continuing to address Olivia. "Have you, by any chance, decided which foods you intend to pack? We should probably stick to sandwiches or other nonperishable portable food items for easier transport."

Eye's narrowed, Olivia dug her nails into her thighs, glaring long and hard at Irwin before answering. "No, Irwin. I have not. However, I can assure you, anything I do *prepare* will most certainly travel easily. Most especially my *tolerable* chicken salad, my *barely palatable* macaroni, my *easy to masticate* potato salad, and my *marginally edible* tea cake."

"That's the spirit!" said Darren, his grin warping into an exaggerated goofy smile.

"Oh, shut up," snapped Olivia.

"This just keeps getting better." Harper tossed her latest balled up napkin at the trashcan and missed.

"Are we closing the bookshop while we're gone?" asked Christopher.

Irwin shrugged. "Without anyone to take over, we may have to."

"I thought you were going to ask Roger?" asked Darren, sounding disappointed. "I've been working all week to get the storeroom ready for him. Besides, knowing books, he's helped out in the shop before."

"But doesn't he still work at the library?" asked Olivia.

"He does," said Irwin. "I have to go to the library tomorrow to return some books. I'll speak to him then. I'll see if he'd be willing to cover at least a few days while we're gone. I wouldn't want our customers to think we've shut our doors for good."

"That's the last thing we need." Olivia went back to fanning her face with her mangled, bent paper plate.

"I can stay behind to run the shop if you want," offered Darren.

Irwin, Olivia, and Harper exchanged the fastest *Do NOT let that happen* face amongst themselves.

"No, Dad," spoke up Harper, doing her best to make her dad look away from Irwin's incredulous stare. "Cornelia made it clear, she wants you on this trip as well. Right, Irwin?"

Irwin's face, while not entirely deadpan, had softened impressively, transforming from outright skepticism to his fairly standard, *not in this lifetime* scowl.

At this, everyone began talking at the same time again, tossing other ideas around. Irwin clapped for silence, directing his attention to Christopher. "Any final update on the van rental?"

"Yes, sir." Christopher yanked a piece of paper from his back pocket. "I've got it secured for Saturday. It's a large minivan, seats eight, so we should be pretty comfortable. If needed, we can remove the second-row seats for maximum cargo space. Plus, there's the added roof rack." He winked at Harper.

"Why do you sound like a commercial," she teased. "So, come on down and grab yourself and your filly a minivan at Billy Bob's—Catch 'em While You Can Car Symposium."

"Pick up time?" asked Irwin, his eyes downcast, his voice droll, and his pen ready.

"Nine in the morning," said Christopher. "Drop off is in San Diego. They did say they'd only bill us for as long as we keep it."

"I don't think we will need it for all those days, but fine." Irwin continued jotting down notes.

Christopher snapped his fingers and turned to face Harper. "I put your name down as the secondary driver."

At this, Irwin's head snapped to attention so fast it caused everyone but Harper to flinch. "Halt," he roared.

Christopher stared at Irwin, dumbfounded. "Sorry?"

"You will need to amend that. I will be the designated secondary driver," Irwin said, "—and Harper," he grinned, tilting his head slightly in her direction, "will be the backup driver of last resort."

"Oh, hilarious," smirked Harper, more exasperated than entertained. "Look, everyone, Irwin's got all the jokes tonight." She spoke to Christopher. "You know what? I've got an idea. How about we tie Irwin to the roof rack? That should make us feel less crowded."

"Page three," Irwin repeated, gathering his papers into a neat pile.

"Maybe bring a crate of duct tape," said Harper. "—for the complainers."

"Page three," Irwin's voice boomed, wishing he could put some people on mute.

Spreading his squat, muscular legs wide apart, Darren slunk further back into his chair. Tossing his head back, he began kneading his throbbing temples. "And to think..." he groaned. "We haven't even left Pennsylvania yet."

CHAPTER 7

Three hot, miserable days left before departure.

Despite the unbearably hot, sticky summer temperatures threatening to make her lose her mind, the last few days whizzed by in a frantic, albeit chaotic flurry of activity. Olivia busied herself shopping and preparing various meals for the trip. She also made sure to finish any last-minute washing—packing her single-sized duffel to adhere to Irwin's imposed size limitations—*on top of everything else*. And of course, Olivia continued to spend an excessive amount of time downstairs in the bookshop behind her desk, placing last-minute book orders, counting the day's receipts, or happily helping customers. Anything not to think.

Olivia preferred life this way. Keeping busy had always

been her go-to coping mechanism during stressful times, most of all, to avoid feeling. Keeping busy provided for her a ready-made viable excuse to shove the grief from losing Cornelia temporarily to the side. Most of all, *busy* provided Olivia a ready-made excuse to deflect, since she wasn't at all close to ready yet to face the growing uncertainty brought on by the new life-altering, perplexing change happening inside her body. Change Olivia didn't appreciate, couldn't seem to regulate, and failed to comprehend. She needed help—and soon.

Olivia checked the time.

"Damn!" With no time to waste, she snatched her car keys and headed for the door. She would have to hurry if she wanted to make it to her doctor appointment on time.

"ARE YOU SURE? LIKE SURE-SURE?" Olivia asked, stumbling over her words as she spoke with her gynecologist for the second time a few days earlier. "At my age?"

Dr. Leseberg, a young, attractive woman whose body type mimicked that of youth-perfect, nodded. "Perimenopause commonly starts a few years before menopause. It's when your ovaries are gradually beginning to make less estrogen. For most women, it begins in their forties."

The doctor's office, despite the intentionally placed comfortable furniture, warm woods, and polished surfaces, felt constrained. A bit too flawless. Much like the lovely Dr. Leseberg.

Olivia tugged at the waist of her tight jeans, wishing she could stretch the dungaree material an extra two sizes instead of feeling it pinch-digging into her newly attained roll of flab protruding from the side. She shifted in her chair, hoping to take some of the pressure off, but nothing worked, so she leaned back determined to ignore the lack of oxygen reaching her lungs. "And how long does this peri-whatever you called it, —hell, last?"

"Up until menopause begins."

Olivia frowned at her doctor's ambiguous answer, wishing she could smear the impeccably applied frost-tinted lip gloss off the woman's heart-shaped lips without going to jail.

"I know—clearly not the answer you wanted to hear." The doctor's expression softened. "The technical answer is menopause begins at the point your ovaries stop releasing eggs. In layman terms, once you've gone a full twelve-months without menstruating, you are considered in menopause."

My God. Olivia nodded slowly. "So, perimenopause has been the reason for all the missed or late periods?" She slunk into her chair, feeling even more depressed.

Dr. Leseberg nodded. "Missed, late periods, and the infamous hot flashes."

"I. Hate. Those," exclaimed Olivia, ignoring the pools of sweat pilling under her drenched armpits despite the office's cooler temps.

"Most women do. Patients can also experience unexplained weight gain, a disruption to sleep patterns, vaginal dryness, not to mention the overall changes taking place in their body. It can be disconcerting, but it's perfectly normal." She paused. "You certainly are not alone."

Olivia blushed, one-quarter embarrassed, one quarter powerless, and the rest utterly fed up. Despite everything she'd heard up to now, she still felt inexplicably alone. She watched Dr. Leseberg's perfectly manicured fingers jot down the next whatever in her file. Olivia twisted her neck, wishing she had better harnessed her ability to read upside down.

"What about mood swings?"

"Guilty as charged," announced Olivia, wriggling her non-manicured fingers. "I'm what you would call a mess. A first-class basket case. Close to certifiable." Olivia felt near to tears.

"I strongly doubt that." Dr. Leseberg handed Olivia a tissue. "The inability to feel in control of your emotions can be extremely frustrating."

"Tell me about it."

"Are you experiencing other symptoms?"

"My breasts feel slightly tender. Not swollen or sore—just tender, and not all the time, either."

"Well, if you find you are becoming swollen or too uncomfortable, let me know right away, okay? If you like, I can write you out a prescription for hormone medication or a topical cream. Either one will at least provide some relief."

"I'll let you know if it gets worse." Olivia bowed her head, twisting her fingers on her lap. "I feel kind of stupid asking this, but is there anything else on this uninvited top ten menopause parade I should be looking forward to? I mean, don't get me wrong, so far, it's been an absolute blast. I'm having the time of my life over here."

Dr. Leseberg leaned back in her chair and nodded, her eyes glued on Olivia. "Have you experienced an increase in headaches, specifically migraines?"

"No," Olivia shook her head. "No headaches, yet." *Only homicidal thoughts.*

"How about a decrease in your sexual drive?"

Why did she have to ask that? Olivia's cheeks turned a darker shade of pink. "Just the opposite. I feel—I don't know what to call it..."

"Frisky?"

Did Doctor Perfect just say frisky? ... What does she know about frisky...

"Yeah. *Um*, you could say that—" Olivia rolled her eyes then paused, not wishing to sound rude. Darren had been right the other night when he commented about how snarky she'd been acting lately. "Let's just say I think I'm wearing my husband out." Olivia's bold admission turned her face from a slight blush to a stark beet red as she thought back to exactly how *frisky* she'd been.

The doctor laughed. "Also, perfectly normal." Dr. Leseberg tossed her pen on the desk and leaned in closer to Olivia as if the two were old friends sharing a juicy secret. "Listen, I'm not going to pretend to know your tastes or aversions, and I certainly don't want you to think for one minute that I'm asking you to disclose anything to me, but let's just say, for the sake of argument, that some of my patients have admitted to me in passing experiencing a heightened sense of sexuality during perimenopause." Eyes wide open, she bobbled her head up and down like, *get my drift?* "And to satisfy that unexpected heightened arousal, some have opted to supplement these urges by using other options," she added. "—beneficial, always available options."

"Beneficial, always available options," repeated Olivia patently confused, and half expecting the good doctor to wink and click her heels. Olivia squinted, trying her darndest to get a read on the doctor's secret agent grin when all of a sudden, the veiled implication clicked. "Oh, I get it now. You mean options *with batteries!*"

"Exactly. Specifically, vibrators." The doctor reached into her desk and pulled out a pamphlet. It read: 'The Benefits of Self-Care for the Perimenopausal Woman in You—In and Out of the Bedroom.'

Olivia suppressed a giggle. "Catchy title," she muttered under her breath, slightly tilting her head sideways to grasp the full effect of one of the more detailed illustrations in particular, and stunned by the variety of shapes, sizes, and colors available.

Olivia cleared her throat before returning her attention to the conversation. "I can't wait for this whole perimenopause thing to be over," she said, her hand automatically rubbing her soft bloated belly. "I've been feeling self-conscious lately. Especially because of the way my stomach gets all distended and bloated for no reason. It's ugly as hell." She winced at hearing how whiny she sounded and quickly added, "Not to imply my husband has said anything negative to me about it, but still..." *Why am I defending Darren to her?*

Olivia wanted to stop talking, but lately, words of all shapes and sizes kept pouring out of her mouth in a steady stream. "Is that normal? To, *um*, be *frisky* while at the same time feeling totally gross?"

"Perfectly. The hormonal changes I spoke about earlier can also contribute to feelings of depression, undesirability, or for some, a heightened or lack of interest in sex. If you like, we can try testosterone hormone therapy to help regulate some of those emotions for you."

Olivia shook her head "No. I'd rather go the natural route for now, if that's okay?"

Dr. Leseberg closed her file, propped her elbows on her blotter, and clasped her tastefully well-manicured fingers together. "Olivia, this is your body. As your doctor, and as a woman, I want my patients to feel proactive about their care. Which means you and only you get to call the shots here. While I am here to support you in whatever it takes to make you feel whole and healthy again, you are in charge of your body. Full stop."

"Thank you." Olivia smiled, relieved—mentally taking back most of the petty assumptions she held against this lovely creature. "Really. I mean that." She tucked the pamphlets into her pocketbook for later reading.

"My pleasure." Dr. Leseberg smiled back. "Are there any other concerns you'd like to discuss, or something you're not sure about?"

"I, *umm*, yes. Well. *Huh*." Olivia groaned. "This is sort of embarrassing." She leaned in closer, careful to modulate her voice almost to a stage whisper. "Whenever I sneeze or jump up and down, I feel the sudden urge to urinate."

"Also, perfectly normal."

"Really?" Olivia jerked her head back. "This is part of this perimenopausal thing, too?" Olivia wondered if her mother, now gone, had also experienced any of these symptoms as well.

"Most definitely. Bladder changes are typical during peri-menopause. As estrogen in your body decreases, it leaves the pelvic and bladder muscles weaker than normal."

"Great," groaned Olivia. "Adult diapers are us—"

"The leaking's that bad?"

"No...not really. Just a tiny trickle sometimes, but it's still disgusting."

Dr. Leseberg nodded. "Understood. Then, for now at least, you may want to wear a pad for extra protection. Meanwhile, how about trying some Kegel exercises to strengthen the muscles of the bladder and pelvic floor?"

Exercises? Olivia grumbled aloud. She despised exercise.

"I promise. It's not *that* bad," laughed the doctor, wearing a knowing smile. She reached into her magic drawer again and plucked out another sheet of paper, this one also filled with illustrations. "Here. Take a look at this." She allowed Olivia a moment to read the article. "And what's neat about these exercises—they can be done discreetly while sitting down or standing up, and nobody is ever the wiser."

Olivia stared down at the instructive drawings, her mouth flopped wide open in amazement. "And they work?"

"That's the rumor," said Dr. Leseberg. "My patients swear by them. Mind you; it's still up to you to find the time to do them."

Olivia's former frown perked into what could only be described as a naughty grin as she mentally calculated the hours she'd soon have at her disposal to spend covertly exercising. "Oh, this I can do," she muttered to herself, grinning ear-to-ear.

THE DRIVE back to the bookshop gave Olivia the time she needed to think. It had been good speaking to Dr. Leseberg. Their strange conversation had satisfied most of her concerns and put to rest quite a few others. However, as good as their chat had been, it had done little to alleviate the heavy sadness once again creeping back inside her. For those emotions, Olivia would have to dust-off and practice the age-old art of *masking* once again; hiding behind a well-practiced wall of fake smiles and false cheeriness—a skill she had been forced to master over a lifetime ago. Still, Olivia couldn't seem to keep from breaking down in tears at the oddest times or swallowing down a sudden rise of panic, or even becoming irritated over the stupidest things. This erratic behavior had become her new unwelcomed norm, most especially whenever she assumed no one was watching.

"Grief and perimenopause be damned," she mumbled, determined to plow forward. She still had a ton left to do to get the store ready for Irwin's friend to take over—if Irwin got Roger to agree. But no matter how much Olivia did to prepare, she still didn't feel comfortable leaving the bookshop for any extended period.

Funny—it hadn't been all that long ago when the thought of her running a bookshop had made her crumble to her knees.

When Irwin first offered Olivia the job as bookshop manager years ago, Olivia had initially viewed his proposal as temporary...a kind gesture that in the end, wouldn't go anywhere. Back then, despite her love for reading, Olivia couldn't remember when she had last read for pleasure. Being offered a job to work around books all day had sounded like a dream, and a much-needed rescue from a life seemingly determined to slam its doors repeatedly shut in her face.

Irwin, true to form, had not only provided Olivia with a generous lifeline back to routine but managed through his unwavering trust to help her make the slow trek back to believing in herself—which, for the record, had been no small feat. Particularly for a woman who had up to that point made a career out of making some piss-poor decisions. Nevertheless, from day one, Irwin never hesitated once in handing Olivia a set of keys and turning the entire bookshop operation over to her. Nor did he ever question her capabilities. Soon enough, the safe space she had needed to heal had turned a nine-to-five job into a passion.

Since then, admittedly, there had been days when Olivia found herself feeling drained as she climbed the stairs up to her apartment above the bookshop after a long, demanding day. The bottoms of her swollen feet would throb, and the back of her calves would burn. Nevertheless, she never once begrudged those difficult days. Even during the shop's busiest season, Olivia never minded taking on tasks not necessarily part of her job description. Instead she welcomed them as a reminder. Her cue to remain grateful for second chances— and in her particular case, third chances. Tired or not, Olivia welcomed the opportunity to do her part to keep her special happy place afloat and prospering.

—*Her happy place.*

It had taken a long time, but Olivia could now freely admit, albeit only to herself, that over the past few years, she'd slowly become a better version of the person she'd always known she could be. Living and working in a place free of judgment and overflowing with encouragement had inspired her to mature. She had begun to forgive herself for stupid past indiscretions, but equally, also demand of herself the challenge to aspire to new ambitions. Olivia no longer people-pleased to survive. Nor did she hide behind partitions of shame. This new, stronger version of herself refused to be tethered any longer to a suffocating past encased by distant, painful memories.

But working at the bookshop hadn't merely brought stability into Olivia's life, but a revitalized passion for words. Reading had unearthed in her an uncompromising thirst for stories, and a ravenousness hunger for history. Most of all, a sense of self-determination and self-awareness—veering her off the once bumpy and dysfunctional road most traveled toward a journey of recovery and self-forgiveness. Here in her happy place, this wordily delicious, safe haven, Olivia felt appreciated. Wanted. Needed. Respected. Surrounded by those she deeply loved and who loved her. For once, she held the total package in her grateful hands, hot flashes, mood swings, night sweats, and all.

Cornelia had also been a large part of Olivia's radical transformation, never allowing Olivia to indulge in guilt or humiliation.

"I don't think I can do this," Olivia had complained to Cornelia one evening after a few months of working at the shop. She had been tallying the day's receipts after a particularly difficult day. "*Ugh!* This is ridiculous. I'm usually good with numbers, but I keep coming up short by a few cents. It's driving me insane."

"Non-*cents*, my dear. Take your time. Remember, it's only money."

"But it's not *only* the money," Olivia grumbled, ignoring Cornelia's play on words. "It's the people, the vendors, this township—somedays I can barely figure out what I'm doing."

Cornelia leaned on her cane as she rose from her chair. She was a bit unsteady at first but recovered her balance soon enough to adjust her sweater without toppling over. "Oh, phooey. You're doing fine, Olivia." Cornelia hobbled closer to the register and plucked a butterscotch from the 'Feel Free to Take' candy dish Olivia kept filled for customers. "Stop being so hard on yourself."

"I can't help it. I feel I'm in over my head."

"You're not even close."

Olivia sneered. "I wish I could believe that."

"*Staap!* Life's about change. It can't exist in stagnation. We all have learning curves and emotional landmines to traverse and endure. Even those of us who make it look easy." Cornelia winked. "Listen, I'd be the last one to interrupt your highly entertaining pity party, but just so that you know, your daughter is extremely proud of you."

Olivia stopped counting and glanced up. "What?"

"You heard me. Harper admires how you faced your problems, rebuilt your life, and taken this business and turned it into a success in ways neither Irwin or I could have anticipated." Cornelia grimaced and spat the candy into a tissue. "*Ewww.* I hate these nasty things. They taste like hand sanitizer." She wiped her mouth with the back of her hand and tossed the balled-up tissue in the trash. "Listen, Olivia, without exaggeration, you have singlehandedly surpassed everyone's expectations—including Mr. Chuckles—and Lord knows, that's saying a lot."

Olivia's eyes watered, and her mouth dropped open. She hugged her arms, stunned by the sudden rush of emotion threatening to take over. She wracked her brain, unable to recall whether Irwin had ever said a word about the matter, pro or con. Nor Harper, for that matter.

"She told you that?" asked Olivia. "In those exact words?"

"Yes. From Harper's lip to my ears, and not only once, either." Cornelia ambled toward the front of the store and peered out the window. "We are all proud of you, Olivia. Me especially."

Olivia returned her attention to the receipts. Still, her thoughts wavered, remembering all too clearly the numerous dreary jobs she had held in the past. How she'd have to wake up before the butt-crack of dawn Monday through Saturday, plodding through countless hours of work, only to still be financially strapped and overstressed on payday. But what choice did she have back then? It wasn't as if she could up and quit. Harper had been a baby, then soon enough a toddler and a teen. Olivia had been what? A recovering drug addict— and Darren? While Olivia had managed to stay out of jail, her husband hadn't, doing time behind bars for almost six years, while cold turkey kicking his drug habit. It hadn't been easy for him either, consumed by anger and resentment. Nevertheless, much to Olivia's bitterness, Darren had played the role of the absentee misunderstood parent to perfection. Olivia honestly hated him back then, frightened he'd return home and drag her back into his dysfunctional world. A world Olivia barely had the tools to resist herself.

No. The pursuit of happiness had not been a choice or a consideration back then, and any goals or aspirations Olivia had to self-improve were flung off to the far recesses of her mind, upended by the day-to-day pressures of earning enough to buy food, paying for substandard lodging, and keeping the lights and heat on. Olivia had done back then what she had to do to survive, to make ends meet—despite coming up short more often than she ever cared to admit. Yet, somehow, she learned to make do. As Harper got older, she had helped wherever she could, and when Darren returned, he arrived only half the mess he had been before he left.

Together they scraped by. Until they didn't. Enter Irwin Abernathy and Cornelia Parish, stage door three—the human equivalents to duct tape.

OLIVIA PARKED the car behind the bookshop, turned off the engine, and buried her damp, tear-stained face inside her wrapped arms on the steering wheel. Her body trembled as she wept.

"I miss you, Cornelia," she sobbed, almost to the point of heaving, drowning in a thousand memories of Cornelia rushing to the surface.

Why, why, why did you have to go?

"I'm back," she announced, marching into the bookshop and tossing her handbag dejectedly behind the register. It took a bit, but the blotchy-faced Olivia eventually regained her footing—rushing around the bookshop, busy getting stuff done until she made the awful, stupid mistake of glancing toward Cornelia's empty chair.

And that's all it took.

A loud, pain-filled sob from the darkest depth of her soul escaped amongst a cacophony of sniffled back tears. She couldn't help it. The customers all began staring at her, but this time, Olivia didn't care.

I can do this.

I. Will. Do This.

As with most everything else, Cornelia had been right about this part of Olivia's life as well. Within a short time, Olivia had not only learned the ropes and excelled, but she came to the startling realization about how much she adored being the conduit for dispossessed stories in need of finding a good home. She especially enjoyed watching her customers, young and old, fall madly in love with a new book. What would start as guarded excitement quickly turned to excitement as they inevitably would flip the book from front to the back—their eyes intent on absorbing all the provided details in the hope the author's words would speak to them and draw them in. Then finally came the last test, the reverent touching of fingertips against the cover and pages as if the intimate contact had the power to create an invisible kinetic energy exchange, taking on the form of proprietorship—the finalizing bond between book and humbled explorer.

And children—or the 'little people' as Olivia preferred calling them, were her absolute favorites to observe. Possibly because of their innocence and wonder, or maybe because the world hadn't wholly nullified their natural curiosity or their innate ability to show unbridled joy. Children didn't know yet how to pretend or put on airs for acceptance. If something spoke to them, their answers remained authentic and pure. If the call came in the form of a book, Olivia would see the children latch onto their find for dear life—carrying it around the bookstore like a long-lost friend.

However, there were also circumstances when Olivia had to be the bad guy responsible for prying their newfound treasures from their tiny fingers, just long enough to ring it up. This undertaking seemed almost too cruel. That's when Olivia, a mother herself, would break the rules by walking around the counter to scan the barcode in the back, unwilling to separate a sobbing little person from their next awaited adventure.

Regrettably, there were also those unfortunate times when a little person would fall head over heels in love with a book, but a parent, for whatever reason, would order them to put it back on the shelf.

That's usually when Cornelia, unable to contain herself, would jump in, declaring the book free.

"You did it," Cornelia would exclaim to the sobbing, now terror-filled, baffled child. "We have a winner, Olivia. Look!" Then she'd bow down low to speak directly to the crier. "You must be extremely clever to have found the extra book I hid." Then, without the slightest hint of remorse for bold face lying, Cornelia would turn to the equally as confused parent and whisper. "That's an extra book sent from the warehouse. I must have forgotten to box it and left it on the shelf. No biggie. We always give those copies away anyway since we can't sell or return them. Right, Olivia?"

"Yes," Olivia would nod, her head bouncing up and down on cue as any good, lying coconspirator would do. "Absolutely."

More often than not, the parent would relent. The hysterical child would stop crying, and another cherished book would find a new home.

Olivia gave up a long time ago trying to figure out how many so-called 'free books' the two of them had given away, thankful Irwin had never found out.

OLIVIA TURNED the sign on the door over to CLOSED. It had been a long day, but she couldn't help but wonder how Irwin made out with Roger and what the two had finally decided. Although she hadn't said anything to Irwin, she didn't want anyone—including good old Roger Ledbetter—a highly skilled librarian—to come into her domain and start fussing around with the system she'd worked so hard to create.

From day one, Olivia organized the shop into various sections: non-fiction, fiction, romance, classics, poetry, the arts, children, and more. However, unlike the library, she alphabetized by title as opposed to the author, and to her delight, her customers seemed to like it that way.

Her customers.

More like neighbors and friends now. People Olivia had come to know and interact with over the years—and not just in conversations solely concerning books either. As trust between them grew, discussions about books morphed into conversations about their families, their children, their hopes and dreams. Sometimes, she even found herself lamenting with them about their unfortunate losses...something Olivia understood all too well.

Like Mr. Weinstein, for example—one of Olivia's weekly visitors, who came every Friday evening without fail. Rain or shine, sleet or snow could not keep the man away, and oddly enough, he always managed to arrive an hour or so before the shop closed for the night.

Olivia would watch him stroll around the store, up and down the aisles as if seeing the many shelved options for the first time. Olivia liked it when he'd zero in on a potential pick, flipping reverently through the pages. If the book passed muster, he'd read the back. This process continued for a good few minutes until he finally decided upon the winner. He wasn't terribly picky, just thoughtful. Whatever selected had to be perfect since Mr. Weinstein never came to the shop for himself, but for his wife—something he had done faithfully since ***Abernathy & Crane*** first opened its doors almost five years earlier.

"I met my Sybil in a bookstore," he had once shared with Olivia as he got ready to pay for his book. "I had been living in New York City at the time, studying to be a doctor, and close to starting my residency. I needed to order a textbook. I can't remember which one, but that doesn't matter," he said, shaking his head. "What does matter is who I saw when I arrived." His lips lifted into a grin.

"Oh?" Olivia couldn't help but feel intrigued.

"*Oy vey*, is right," Mr. Weinstein agreed, smiling. "I can remember it like it happened yesterday. There she stood," he said, spreading his arms. "The most beautiful girl in the universe." He shook his head at the pleasant memory. "I couldn't take my eyes off her."

"Love at first sight?" asked Olivia, practically swooning from behind the register. By this time, she had stopped ringing up the book to lean her elbows on the counter; her chin cupped in both palms.

Mr. Weinstein chuckled. "What love at first sight? She saw me staring at her, gave me the once over, rolled her eyes to the heavens, and walked away."

Olivia gasped. "No way!"

"Oh, yes. She left me crushed, but not discouraged," he said, wagging his crooked finger in the air. "Not when I knew I had found the right girl for me."

Olivia's mouth opened in wonder. "So, what did you do next?"

"Well, naturally, I refused to give up. I followed her, like a—" Mr. Weinstein pressed a finger to his clean-shaven chin, thinking, "—whadda you call it these days? When a guy follows a girl...?"

"Follows a girl..." Olivia pondered, stumped. "You don't mean a stalker, do you?"

"*Bah*. They're nutsy-coocoo," He said, circling his temple with his finger. "Anyways, let's just say I left the store and followed this stunning woman for blocks from a respectable distance. *Oy vey*, you should have seen me. Young, strapping, strong with a constitution like an ox. Not like now," he chuckled, his voice taking on a melancholy tone. "Anyway, there I was, trailing her home, hiding behind garbage pails and stoops so I wouldn't frighten her." Mr. Weinstein lowered his voice. "I must have looked like such an imbecile, but I didn't care. Not one single solitary hoot. Nothing, and I mean nothing, was going to stop me from learning her name."

"Go on," prompted Olivia, her open palm cupped over her heart.

"Yes, well, my *following* her finally paid off. I not only found out her name but where she lived. Every day for the next few months, I'd make up any excuse to be in her neighborhood, hoping one day to bump into her again." Mr. Weinstein let out a hearty laugh this time. "Now mind you, Miss Olivia, I had no idea what I would say to her *if* she had actually spoken to me, but love can make you do some crazy, off-the-wall things—and I was most definitely smitten." He sighed and took a deep breath.

"When did you two finally meet again?" asked Olivia, thoroughly enamored and carried away by Mr. Weinstein's tender story.

"Oh, not for a while, and not until I saw her again in that same bookstore. Turns out, she went there every Friday after work to treat herself to a new book. Can you believe it? She told me sometime later on she read to carry her through the long weekends."

Olivia finally exhaled, unaware of how long she had been holding her breath. "What did you do to finally win her over?"

"*Ahhh*, well, that, I'm afraid that took time. I gotta tell you, although no doubt a looker, my Sybil hadn't dated much back then, although I had always suspected there might have been a few suitors before me who tried." Mr. Weinstein's eyes clouded for a moment as if rekindling a memory. "You see, Miss Olivia, times were different back then." He shrugged, drawing his bony shoulders up to his ears. "Different times, different expectations. Different strokes for different folks, if you get my meaning."

Olivia nodded as if she did, but she didn't. Not entirely.

Mr. Weinstein noticed Olivia's quizzical expression and expounded. "Unlike me, my Sybil came from a strict religious family. Her bringing home some strange man she'd met at a bookshop would have been severely frowned upon."

Olivia noticed his hand tremble and reached out to hold it. After a moment of waiting for him to finish, she squeezed his fingers lightly to prod him along. "Mr. Weinstein, please, you're killing me over here—"

Mr. Weinstein continued. "What could I do?" He shrugged, pausing for effect. "So—I did the only thing I could think of to win her heart."

Olivia groaned, "—*which was...*"

"I bought her a book, of course," he mumbled, feigning exasperation with Olivia. "Whatever book her heart desired. I didn't care—but on one condition."

Olivia waved him on.

"She had to let me write her a little message inside."

Olivia giggled. "I can only imagine what you wrote."

This time Mr. Weinstein blushed. "Oh, no. Nothing untoward. Merely a simple proclamation: "To the most beautiful girl in the world, who one day I hope to make my wife. Respectfully yours, Harry J. Weinstein."

"You didn't!" exclaimed Olivia, in awe.

"I did, indeed. And I wrote the same exact thing in every book I bought for her until one day she looked me straight in the eye and said, "Harry J. Weinstein—when are you going to ask me properly?' And I said, "'If I do, Sybil Rosen, what will be your answer?' And she pecked me on the cheek right here," he pointed to his face, "smiled, and said, 'Ask me and find out."

"This is so romantic," gushed Olivia, blinking back happy tears.

"You think so, *tsk-tsk*?" Mr. Weinstein shrugged, but his face was all smiles.

"Are you kidding me?" Olivia dabbed her eyes with a tissue. "So how long did this dreamy cat and mouse routine of yours go on for?"

"*Oy*, every single Friday evening for almost an entire year until Sybil finally agreed to have lunch with me." Mr. Weinstein chuckled.

"That's a lot of books!"

"It sure was, but that's my Sybil—hard-to-get, and worth every penny." He winked at Olivia. "And look at me. I'm still buying this crazy, loveable woman a book, although now, she needs me to read them to her." Mr. Weinstein's voice lowered again. "I'm afraid my Sybil's eyes aren't so good now. It's the glaucoma, you see. It took over, and unfortunately, we caught it too late." Mr. Weinstein sighed. "Such is life."

"*Aww.* I'm so sorry."

Mr. Weinstein brandished a stern, crooked finger in Olivia's direction. "No. No, Miss Olivia. No, sorrys about it." He held up his Sybil's next book selection. "*This* is a privilege. Not many are as blessed as I have been to love for as long as I have and enjoy a life with such a beautiful woman. So, I gotta be her eyes, now. Big deal. Who am I to complain? The good Lord knows she's put up with me for over fifty years. Not too shabby. Am I right?"

THAT EVENING, before turning in for the night, Olivia took her time to jot down a long, detailed list for Roger about every do and don't concerning the shop she could think of. At the tippy top of her paper, she added in bold print, 'Please make sure to take extra good care of Mr. Weinstein for me.'

CHAPTER 8

Two days left until departure.

Closing the bookshop for any stretch of time could prove tricky. One couldn't just lock up and split. There were assorted tasks to finish, responsibilities to take care of, vendors to contact, and deliveries to postpone. Most of all, there were loyal customers and friends to notify.

Although the bookshop saw a fair share of foot traffic, everyone—meaning everyone besides Irwin—agreed it could still use a bit more promotion. Having relied solely on outdoor, handwritten signs propped near the shop's entrance or the occasional online post to keep their customers in the know hadn't been at all enough. Nor were the rare sponsored community events or the sporadic local author readings,

Irwin under duress, agreed to host. The ***Abernathy & Crane Bookshop*** needed to do more. They needed to keep up with the times—if they wanted a functional bookshop to come home to when this all ended.

"Trust me," implored Harper, peeking out from behind her nest of long, wild curls bouncing in place with her plea. "Social media will be an important added component to our now lackluster marketing. Having an online presence will not only help us keep in better contact with our customers, but we can promote our books and advertise upcoming sales as well. In this instance, we could use it to fill clientele who knew Cornelia, about why we won't be having her memorial locally."

"My signs accomplish the same thing," said Irwin, not entirely sure what Harper meant by 'lackluster.' "We're a small-town shop with a select clientele," he managed to contrive a comeback, working double-time to sound remotely as if he knew what he was yammering on about. "Word of mouth has worked before, and it can work again. Moreover, I prefer we know who our customers are, and provide a more personal touch, especially when informing them about personal calamities," he added. "Don't you?"

"Fair enough, and for the most part, that doesn't have to change," agreed Harper. "There's no reason why we can't do both, while still maintaining a viable social media presence to provide potential new customers with our location, hours, and any other pertinent information. For example, let's say we decide in the future to invite an author to speak again. Making these small changes could better us highlight their book online—or post a short book review—or even an author interview. Something to whet reader appetites. Of course, I would take over writing those things up." Harper waved her palms in the air and nodded her head yes, as if by her doing so, Irwin would follow suit and do the same.

However, Irwin did the exact opposite. His eyes glazed over, his mouth turned taut, and his veined hands interlocked in an interstellar death grip against the front of his bony body, much as they usually did whenever he felt in close proximity to information overload.

Sensing she was losing him, Harper spoke even faster, but this time she crammed every last single point she'd been planning to make into the tiniest, most minuscule allotted Irwin-nanosecond she had left. "Nothing fancy to start, but upbeat. Fun and entertaining. But we must also keep the focus on making our webpage something our customers can trust and appreciate—as well as a means by which they can reach out to us if they need to."

Irwin tapped his foot, getting antsy. "And what would something upbeat, not fancy but entertaining and fun cost me?"

"Now that's the beauty of what I'm proposing," replied Harper. "To start, not much. There's a ton of free social media sites to tap into, and a few we already have. I can work to grow those, but to do what I'm looking to do, we will need something better. Something way more attractive. Specifically, a web host which can provide better fonts and visuals, and that, I'm afraid, will cost us a bit. But remember, Irwin, in this day and age customers expect businesses, even small-town bookshops like ours, to stay current. Nobody uses the phonebook. They're obsolete. People want what they want available on social media at the press of a button."

"*Ahem*," Darren cleared his throat, waving a hand. "Sorry to interrupt, but where do we keep those big black markers? The ones we use to make our signs with?"

"They're in the storeroom on the second shelf, way in the back in the cardboard box labeled 'markers,'" answered Harper, her expectant eyes locked onto Irwin's unimpressed face.

"And what about oaktag?"

"In the storeroom closet, bottom shelf, propped on the side," Harper snapped.

"*Sheesh*," Darren muttered in response, stomping away. "Sorry to have interrupted. Feel free to resume your bickering."

"See that?" Irwin, wearing a sardonic grin, clasped his hands. "Case in point: You were able to answer not one, but two utterly annoying questions in less than four seconds, and without all the added fancy-schmancy stuff. Well done."

"Come on, Irwin. —Apples and oranges. What just happened wasn't close to the same thing, and you know it." Harper crossed arms. "At least let me put together a customized website, nothing overly expensive, but something where we can update customers about any promotions we're having or possible events—or like now, letting them know we have to close for an emergency."

Irwin, brows rutted together, gripped his elbow with one hand to support the other arm while his finger tapped-tapped away at his pointy chin in deep deliberation.

Harper waited and waited—and waited for an answer, nibbling on her bottom lip. "Well?" she almost shouted.

Irwin gave one of his noncommittal half-shrugs. "Frankly, I think what you're proposing is a colossal waste of time and expense." Then he added, "Didn't we try something like this a few years ago?"

Irwin's memory had been only marginally accurate. The bookshop did, in fact, have a web page which Irwin himself had put together. And it wound up looking like something Irwin put together. Dull, lifeless, and standoffish. And since nobody bothered to regularly attend to keeping it updated and fresh—including its original creator—it went unviewed.

"I wouldn't exactly call what you made a website," Harper grumbled.

"Be that as it may, we seem capable of providing the same services you're describing using our already proven and dependable sidewalk notices and by word of mouth. Why fix what isn't broken at this juncture?"

Harper shook her head. "You're impossible, you know that?"

While Irwin and Harper continued their back and forth, Darren took it upon himself to do his part. Snatching a marker off the shelf and a large piece of oaktag from the storage closet, he began composing a sign. Nothing elaborate—just a little something to inform their customers in advance about when the shop would be open and closed for the next few weeks. When finished, Darren carried his creation, along with a roll of tape, and marched his way toward the front of the bookshop, right past the debating dynamic duo.

"What do you think you're doing?" asked Irwin after catching Darren fumbling to tape the large oaktag flat against the store window.

"I made us a poster, Boss."

"A poster?" asked Irwin, his face fixed in concern. "What kind of poster?"

Pressing down firmly on the corner of the oaktag with his entire arm, Darren ripped off a piece of tape using his teeth. "I heard you and Harper discussing the importance of letting our customers know certain stuff, so I figured I'd help out." After a few more moments of struggle, Darren taped the last corner semi-straight to the glass. "There!" he announced triumphantly, his hands gripped at his waist. He took a small step backward to admire his handiwork. "Not too bad, if I say so myself."

Irwin shot Harper a look, then slowly moseyed over to where Darren stood and stared at the crudely handmade notice.

"So?" asked Darren, evidently feeling proud of himself. "Whaddya think?"

Irwin stared at the crudely made poster for a long, hard minute. "I think you misspelled this word over here," he said, pointing. "As well as this one. And for the life of me, I can't decipher what this sentence even means."

Darren leaned in and winced. "*Jeez.*"

"And right here," Irwin waved a finger, "there should be a semicolon after this word, not an em dash."

"A what dash?"

"An em—," Irwin paused and sighed. "Just forget it."

Darren squinted, stretching his neck. To take a closer look. "Oh that?" he laughed. "That's just a smear. One of those annoying gnats flew by me and I squashed him."

Irwin's face contorted. "Smear or not, it doesn't belong there," he hissed, visibly grossed out. "But nothing a little whiteout can't repair." Then something else caught Irwin's eye. He bent closer, this time his nose practically touching the window and *tsked*. "And while you're at it, whiteout this word. It's crass and redundant." Irwin continued to read—his lips moving but devoid of sound. "And you might as well amputate this unintelligible, barely passing as an English sentence as well." Irwin rubbed his chin, then stepped backward next to Darren. "I think that should do it," he said, slapping Darren on the shoulder. "But other than that—good job."

Harper bit her bottom lip as she watched her mortally deflated father tear own his poster to drag it off to the backroom. "Do you always have to be so damn flippant? He really tries, you know."

Irwin's chin dipped down. "I know he does," he mumbled contritely, grabbing for the doorknob. "In any event, I'm off to the library to speak with Roger should anyone need me." Then before yanking the door completely open, he added,

"Fine. You win, but I'm pressed for time right now. Feel free to make whatever changes you wish when we get back—but Harper, whatever you decide, for goodness sake, keep it classy."

As AGREED, Irwin headed off to the library to speak with Roger Ledbetter. He found his former library colleague working behind the front desk, stamping books.

"I appreciate you doing this," said Irwin, standing off to the side, out of the way. Roger had not only agreed to keep the bookstore open on his days off, but also for a few hours during the weekday before his evening shift at the library began.

"Not a problem. Glad to help." Head bent, Roger kept his eyes focused on his task. "I loved Cornelia, too, you know." His voice cracked. "I mean, what wasn't to love about her, right?" Roger coughed to clear his throat. "Sorry."

Irwin nodded. It never ceased to amaze him the effect Cornelia had on people. Everyone who met her loved her. Even those she had just met. People gravitated to her, speaking with and divulging their entire lives to Cornelia as if they had been long time friends instead of mere strangers standing on a grocery checkout line, waiting for their turn.

"How are you doing?" asked Roger. "I mean, with all of this?"

Irwin knew Roger meant Cornelia, but Roger, like most people, avoided using words like death and dying, and instead relied on casual, less socially awkward euphuisms such as *passing, expiring, fading, vanishing,* and *loss.*
—*I'm sorry for your loss.*
—*Did you hear that so-and-so expired last night in their sleep?*
—*So sorry to hear of [insert name or title] passing.*

—In the end, she took her last breath and faded gently away...

Not that Irwin minded because he honestly didn't. Not in the slightest. Merely one of many cloaked observations. In truth, Irwin didn't care much for fatalistic verbiage any more than Roger did. Especially if and when referring to Cornelia.

"Irwin?" Roger stamped another book. "Earth to Irwin."

Irwin snapped to attention. "I'm sorry, Roger, I apologize. I've had a lot on my mind recently. Please repeat what you said."

"I asked you if you were okay."

Irwin gave a non-committal shrug, not having given much attention to his being okay or not. With a full plate, plans still in the making, and a long list of things left to do, the opportunity to process his heart-wrenching loss and all it entailed hadn't quite manifested. In truth, Irwin had been mentally preparing himself for the physical body of Cornelia to *pass* for over a year, when her mind and all she had been previously had *vanished* long before. However, now, much to Irwin's astonishment and angst, he had never imagined Cornelia having the fortitude or mental clarity left to be up to her old tricks. It had taken sheer genius to devise such a harebrained, cross-country last hurrah as a wake. Then again, *shame on me*, he chastised himself.

I should have anticipated something along those lines. This was, after all, Cornelia.

Mercifully, the preparations for this latest escapade had kept him too busy during the day to think, and much too exhausted at night to dwell on his grief, but this wasn't a topic Irwin felt comfortable discussing. He knew from past experience how the culmination of a lifetime of buried emotions would ultimately catch up to him, much as they had with previous, devastating losses. How they would revisit his dreams and become the framework of his nightmares. And true to form, they would, in all likelihood, burst onto the scene at the worst possible time.

"I'm fine," he answered Roger, voice flat, his face devoid of reaction—*or so he thought.*

Roger, staring at his old friend, tossed the hardcover book he'd just finished stamping on the precariously tilting pile, and darted around his desk to the other side.

"Oh, no." Irwin groaned a primeval grunt as he saw one of his ten worst fears materializing right before his eyes—in the form of one, Roger Ledbetter. "No, no, no-No, NO—" Irwin jerked his shoulder sideways attempting to deflect Roger's embrace, but his spastic maneuvering had little effect.

Dreading the looming onslaught of human contact, Irwin's face scrunched into the sourest, most unattractive cringe. Panicked, he managed to take a long, exaggerated step back, endeavoring to create a wider berth of room between him and the incoming lunatic hellbent on lunging for him. But instead of getting away, Irwin wound up somehow banging backward into a library cart crammed with returned books—knocking off the complete upper row upon impact.

"*Grrr,*" Irwin grumbled, but the loud crash of books did little to deter Roger Ledbetter—whose pursed thin lips made for one of the saddest, most pathetic dour frowns—from rushing toward him like a man with a mission.

With nothing but centimeters left between them, Roger did the absolute unthinkable. Deftly stepping over the fallen pile of books, he lunged at Irwin hard, bearhugging the literal breath clear out of him.

"Get Off Me!" Irwin gasped, his long, lanky arms locked flat against his body, powerless to wiggle free.

Realizing Roger wasn't about to let go on his own, Irwin tried to shimmy his way out of his tight grasp but failed. Then Irwin did a wild wiggle-waggle, head bobbing, full-body jiggle, bordering on the obscene, using the pressure from his shoulders to force-release his upper body from this crazy man's embrace, but that too, failed. Trapped and cocooned, Irwin stood fuming—practically snorting, while everyone loitering around the lobby enjoyed a front-row seat to Irwin's melting composure.

"Irwin, Irwin, Irwin," Roger lamented far too loudly, his heartfelt sincerity punctuating each consonant. "You can't keep your emotions all bottled up inside like this. It's not healthy."

"What on earth do you think you're doing, Roger?" he snarled through clenched teeth.

Roger tilted his head to the side as if studying Irwin, his face brimming with worry and concern. He gripped his buddy, old pal, squarely by the shoulders and sighed. "Poor, poor Irwin," he mumbled, drawing Irwin in closer for the next suffocating cuddle, and killing any chance Irwin had to bolt. "There, there, old friend," Roger muttered, clapping Irwin on the back. "Everything's going to be okay."

"*Roger*—" Irwin couldn't bear another second. "Would you *kindly* release me," he yelled at the top of his lungs, startling a few of the newer arriving library patrons standing around with their mouths wide open. But Roger, too caught up in his feelings, didn't budge.

"That's it." With little to no recourse left, Irwin lifted his leg as high as possible and stomped Roger's shoe hard, at the same time tugging his body free from the other side.

"*Ouch!*" Roger howled, releasing Irwin to grip his damaged foot. Irwin saw Roger's face morph straightaway from compassion to a crumpled ashen red glare, overcome with agony.

"*Oww*," moaned practically everyone else in the lobby, commiserating with Roger's pain but unable to look away, entranced by the howling man hopping and springing riotously about like somebody had set his ass on fire.

One mom, not finding any of this amusing, tried to block her inquisitive toddler's view, but the agile, curious youngster managed to squirm his way forward.

"Why's that old mean man kicking Mr. Rogers?" the child howled, his tiny round eyes filled with concern for his 'bestest' library buddy.

Irwin snatched a thick oversized book off the cart and held it in front of him like a shield, just in case Roger got any more good ideas, but Roger, consumed with pain, never noticed and continued groaning and bouncing.

"What in the —" Roger stammered through gritted teeth, probably ready to yell out a colorful collection of expletives when suddenly his voice tempered, probably after realizing he had an audience. "HECK—why did you do that for?" Roger seethed, bending over to massage his throbbing foot.

"You left me no choice," answered Irwin, stoned-faced, lowering the thick novel-buffer, but only a smidgen. "I had to do something."

"—and by *something* you mean stomp the bejesus out of my foot? *Ouch*, —I think you broke my toes!" whimpered Roger, dangling on the precipice of a full-blown breakdown, glaring hard at Irwin, his now flushed facial features contorted in anguish.

"I apologize," Irwin said, but only half meaning it. "However, in my defense, I sent out more than enough nonverbal touch-avoidance predisposition signals to avoid this kind of unfortunate event from ever occurring."

Clearly in agony, Roger, eyes bulged, could only manage to glare at Irwin. "I didn't catch a flippin word of what you just said."

"Evidently." Irwin clasped his hands to his front. "—but

that's my fault as well. I should have considered how impervious to subtlety you tend to be around others."

Irwin handed Roger a tissue "It's nothing against you personally, Roger. I merely prefer not to be manhandled." He paused. "—by anyone." Irwin waited again. "*Ever.*" Compelled by Roger's look of disdain, Irwin felt the unexpected need to explain more. "While most people feel perfectly fine making close physical contact, I am evidently not one of them."

"No fooling," moaned Roger. "*My toes...*" Roger stood up, struggling to return to his desk, but in a sudden onset of clumsiness, stumbled.

Irwin moved forward to help, but Roger battered his hand high in the air toward him "Don't you even!" he yelled. Roger attempted to step forward, putting his full weight down on his aching foot. "*Oww,*" he winced, mouth covered with his palm, muting any escaping yelps.

Irwin scrutinized Roger's awkward hobble back behind his desk, impressed by the man's ability to maintain a rhythm with his catalog of silent curses spewing under his breath.

"You still didn't need to do *that*, Irwin," Roger managed to finally spit out, almost in a normal voice.

"Perhaps," Irwin agreed. "But I did say, albeit not as bluntly as I should have, not to touch me. Under duress, I felt an immediate need to—"

"Break my foot."

"No. Certainly not that." Irwin shook his head, offended. "More like get your attention. In the future, I will, without reserve, take the sole responsibility to position myself farther away from you to prevent this kind of mishap from ever retaking place, lest you forget."

Roger's eyes nearly popped out of his head. "Oh, believe me, Irwin," he groaned, lowering himself into a chair, his damaged foot propped up on a pile of fallen books. "One does not easily forget having their foot bones smashed to smithereens."

ONCE IRWIN RETURNED HOME LATER that afternoon, he sat in his office, reviewing their intended route. He compared his directions against the map book he'd appropriated from the library before Roger's public meltdown. In an age when most people relied solely on cell phones and GPS devices, Irwin preferred paper directions. No signal to lose or batteries to change. He leaned back in his chair, satisfied with his plans.

Harper can turn her patronizing little nose up at my paper map all she wants, he decided, *but a book is far more reliable.*

Once finished, Irwin revised his list, checking off anything completed, while highlighting in bright yellow marker anything still pending.

He sighed. Despite the rough start and differences of opinion, everything seemed to be falling into place. This realization should have had him feeling good, or at the least, accomplished, but not in Irwin's *woe is me world*, where everything falling neatly into place typically equated to imminent pending disaster. Nevertheless, Irwin dismissed his rising dread and jotted down a few more ideas on the growing list, ignoring the overall sadness looming just beneath the unstable surface ever since they had begun to make plans.

Outside, the summer sun continued to shine, despite it being late in the day and almost time for dinner. As if on cue, Irwin's stomach growled, prompting him to recall the last full meal he'd eaten. His appetite these last few weeks had declined, leaving him picking at his plate and finding the bulk of his meals tasteless and a chore to chew. Olivia, taking on her new role as the main meddler in his life, had noticed and kept sending him home with readymade meals.

"All you need to do is pop the container's top off and put it in the microwave when you get home," she'd instruct him every single time. "Three to five minutes tops. You don't want it to dry out."

"Should I use a fork or a spoon," he'd ask, bristling.

But tonight, instead of Irwin's mind being on eating, his thoughts drifted far and wide, racing from subject to subject. This time landing on the matter of friendship and how quickly relationships could change. He deliberated about how, over time, some friendships grew stronger, easily spanning decades, while others that may have started strong and perhaps endured many a challenge ultimately ran out of steam, only to fizzle out and slowly fade into something barely recognizable.

Perhaps, he thought, *those relationships, when faced with changes too enormous to navigate, became disjointed and polarized.*

Conversations that had once flowed easily began to turn stilted and strained, flailing to an eventual and abrupt halt. Each party, misled by miscommunication, attempt to nurse their open-hearted wounds by collecting their hurt feelings to wear like a badge. Unable to find a fix, they instead choose to litter the highway to hell, paving their excursion with false assumptions. Ultimately, smothered with hurt, barely a survivor will endure amid the emotionally charged carnage— an impact akin to a head-on, fatal collision.

Irwin sighed. He missed those friends, but not the drama.

He walked to the window and pulled the curtains closed while the sun outside began to set.

Then again, he decided, *there are also those friendships that cease to exist due to an extenuating circumstance—perhaps an event so cataclysmic, so life-altering, that when it occurs, it spins out of everyone's grasp and control.*

Sometimes those kinds of earth-shattering trials sneak onto the scene, gradually trickling droplets of suffering and petty jealousies. Much like how a slow-moving hurricane, whose formidable gusts of wind hover in one place, rotating at a slow—almost torturous pace. At other times, an imminent change can happen, its impact on a friendship akin to an unexpected tsunami, crashing onto the shoreline of one's soul with an unrivaled force, matched only by its sheer power to destroy everyone and everything in its path in a blink of an eye and without reason.

Those were the hardest losses to rationalize. To come to terms with. To accept.

Much like death, for example. For Irwin, death marked the ultimate change—a forever and never-ending change. An uncompromising painful kind of transformation that guts a person down to their core, shredding any hope discovered along the way, and debasing dreams never before realized.

Irwin had experienced countless gut-wrenching deaths over the years. Too many to count. He had tried talking himself into believing how, with ample time and experience, he'd become better at handling the next devastating loss. However, Irwin, in his infinite wisdom, had once again severely underestimated his unceasing capacity to feel.

CHAPTER 9

ONE DAY LEFT BEFORE DEPARTURE.

"IF POSSIBLE, I'd like to be on the road tomorrow morning by nine, as agreed," Irwin announced, bolting the bookshop's front door. "Christopher has informed me the van will be ready for pick-up by eight, which gives us ample time to load up and be on our way no later than half-past nine—at the latest. I'm hoping this timetable works for everyone. If not, speak up now or forever hold your peace."

"It works for me," said Harper. "My bags are already packed, except for a few last-minute incidentals," she added.

Bones rubbed his purring body against Harper's calf, blissfully unaware of his impending future. Harper leaned over and scooched him behind his ear. "*Um,* so that you all know," she jerked her head specifically at Irwin to avoid saying Bones' name out loud. "Regan should be here within the half-hour to pick-up *you-know-who*." Wink-wink. "I have all of *you-know-who's* stuff packed and stashed," —more neck spasms, — "behind the counter."

Irwin glared at Harper, his mouth wide open, seemingly spellbound by her use of various eye, hand, and neck movements.

"Impressed?" she asked, giving him a double wink-wink.

Irwin joggled his head as if trying to recoup his concentration. "Before you go off and dislocate your neck, did you remember to grab his water bowl?" he asked. "The tiny one with the red and blue fishes from my place?"

"Check," replied Harper.

"What about his Tom & Jerry car blanket?"

"Already washed and packed," said Harper, her head nodding along as Irwin spoke.

"His teaser wand? The one with the torn-up feather dangling by its last thread?"

"Packed."

Irwin crossed his arms. "How about that stupid cat tunnel? He loves that thing."

"Got it."

Irwin pointed across the room at his furry nemesis, now napping under Cornelia's empty chair. "We should probably make sure we send his collar—the one with the medical information printed on it so that—"

"Already in the bag, Irwin," Harper laughed, exhaling as her eyes stared up at the ceiling. "I packed everything." For all Irwin's constant carping and complaining about how much he couldn't stand cats, particularly Bones, she knew Irwin adored him almost as much, if not more than she did.

Darren, who had been leaning against the counter, not paying attention, reached into his back pocket and pulled out a few mangled travel brochures. "I have something I'd like to discuss."

"Oh?" As if preparing to be annoyed, Irwin let out a long, weary breath. "My heart vaults with trepidation."

"I don't know what that means." Darren handed Irwin and Harper each a pamphlet, "But what I have to say concerns the trip."

"I'm listening," replied Irwin, looking hesitant to open the brochure.

Darren rubbed his palms together. "Let's say we're all in the van, driving along, minding our business—"

"What else would we be doing?" interrupted Irwin, his impatience already rising exponentially. However, Darren, forever the optimist, kept right on talking, ostensibly unfettered by Irwin's interruption.

"—when all of a sudden, we notice something, I don't know, let's say, super interesting. I mean, like out of this world mind-blowing, right?" Darren paused, his eyes darting back and forth between the stoic pair staring him down, waiting.

Harper jammed her hands into her pockets and rocked slightly on the back of her heels, her eyes fixated on the floor.

Meanwhile, Irwin, who never learned to conceal his exasperation, glared straight at Darren. "And," he motioned with one hand at Darren for him to get to the point.

"*And* ... let's say, we all decide we wanna go see this awesome, incredible, mind-blowing thing, whatever it is." Darren slapped his hands together, grinning ear-to-ear.

"*And*—," Irwin bellowed this time even louder, appearing ready to yank what little hair left on his head out by the roots.

"Can we?" Darren proposed, with a lilt of optimism. "Can we do it? I mean, like, is it possible to extend the timetable?"

"Extend it?" Irwin *tsked*. "Why would we want to do that, exactly?"

"I don't know," shrugged Darren. "Like I said, to see something cool. Go somewhere. Give our legs the chance to stretch for a bit. *Sheesh*, Irwin. You can't expect us to sit in a van for hours on end without doing anything."

Irwin stared at Darren while Harper flipped through her father's brochure.

"*Aw*, come on you two," Darren implored, drawing them into a big group hug which Irwin deftly squirmed out of upon impact. "I know why we're making this trip. That goes without saying, right? But seriously, this doesn't mean we shouldn't make the most of an opportunity?"

"*Ahem*." Irwin cleared his throat, indicating his readiness for this conversation to come to an end.

Darren disregarded Irwin's throat clearing and continued to press his point. "We're heading across the country, this beautiful land of ours. Which, if we're honest, I haven't seen a lot of due to extenuating reasons best not revisited right now."

"Thank you," muttered Irwin.

Darren grinned. "But I, for one, would like to do something other than stay trapped in a van like a sardine. This trip is as much a celebration of Cornelia's life as it is her wake. And for what it's worth, I don't think Cornelia would mind."

"We will not be trapped in a van like sardines," Irwin curtly reminded Darren. "We have four people to deliver letters to."

"But you know that's not what Dad means, Irwin," said Harper, beginning to soften to the idea.

"I say we put it to a vote," proposed Christopher upon entering the room.

"I agree, but it should be a unanimous vote. Otherwise, it wouldn't be exactly fair," clarified Harper, not wishing to give Irwin an out. "Since we're all in this together."

"In what together?" Olivia shouted as she came barreling

through from the shop's backdoor panting, her arms weighed down by packages. "What did I miss now?"

"Hold on." Darren sprang to attention, ready to relieve his wife of her heavy load. "Let me get that for you."

"Thanks, but be careful, this bag and that one both have glass in them," she warned. "They were having a sale on salad dressing, olives, and tomato sauce, and I couldn't help myself. I practically emptied the shelves." Olivia paused. "What are we discussing now?"

"Whether or not we should deviate from Irwin's iron-clad itinerary to fit in some sightseeing along our route," explained Harper.

"Oh, I'd love to do that," agreed Olivia. "but only if we can squeeze it in."

"My idea," announced Darren, looking pleased to see his wife happy.

"I'm cool with it as well," agreed Christopher. "However, as a heads up, I can't be gone from the office for too long. I told them two weeks, tops. At the same time, it might be good for us mentally to break up the monotony with a few stops as we go."

Harper nodded. It had been a long while since she and Christopher had any extended time to spend alone together. Between his increasing job responsibilities and long hours, and her studies and Cornelia's waning health...well, it hadn't been easy. And now this trip wouldn't be either. *At least we'll be together*, she kept reminding herself.

Everyone turned to face Irwin, who, by the dour, stubborn look on his face, left little to the imagination about where he stood on the matter.

"Come on, Irwin," implored Harper, lightly tugging his shirt. "Don't be such a party-pooper."

"I'm no such thing," Irwin replied. "I'm just not sure we will be able to fit this all in."

"Why not?" asked Darren.

"First off, this is not a vacation trip. We have been tasked to deliver letters and make sure Cornelia's ashes are respectfully dumped in the Pacific Ocean," said Irwin. "And secondly, we all have a strict schedule to adhere to. As Christopher has already pointed out, we can't be away for long, nor can we just go off willy-nilly every time one of you sees something they'd like to indulge in."

Harper fluttered her eyelashes as she weaved her bare arm through Irwin's. She leaned in and pecked him on the cheek. "Oh, sure we can. We're five adults here, perfectly capable of weighing the pros and cons." Although everyone knew Irwin's aversion to touch, it had warmed Harper's heart how he no longer flinched or balked whenever she kissed or sidled up close next to him. For some time, she had suspected that Irwin made a special allowance where her cuddles were concerned and did his best to ignore her preoccupation to exasperate him. "Listen, let's agree to do this, but only if time permits. All we need to know from you is if you're on board."

"In terms of?" Irwin asked.

"—in terms of the group deciding whether or not they want to do something off the beaten path. We can put it to a vote if you agree to remain open-minded," said Harper.

Irwin humphed. "I take exception to what you are implying. I am perfectly capable of remaining objective, no matter the circumstance." He fixed his posture, standing a bit taller. "Should a time arise for a decision to be made, I am more than qualified to weigh whatever pros and cons before rendering my final decision."

"What did he say?" asked Darren.

"*Au contraire mon ami,* not a final decision—but a vote," corrected Harper, trying not to laugh when she noticed Irwin massaging his temple—his way of coping with incoming stress. "We all get a say in this, but fine. If Irwin says he can be objective, I'm cool with that," she announced to the group, "—a vote it is."

"Wait," Irwin interjected, looking quite flustered. "I don't think that's at all what I implied—"

"So, to recap," Harper continued to speak over Irwin's protest. "If we as a group decide to extend our trip or stop somewhere to do a little sightseeing, we put it to a vote. And if everybody agrees, it's a go." She squeezed Irwin's arm and leaned in to give him a big warm grin. "Thanks, Irwin!"

Irwin pressed his thin lips into a tight, strained line.

For a second, Harper felt kind of bad, knowing how crushed Irwin must have felt watching his beloved, well-thought-out itinerary get chipped away into a thousand and one unrecognizable pieces—and in less than thirty seconds.

A light urgent tapping at the shop's front door startled everyone. Peering through the window, waving, was a smiling face sporting an obnoxiously large pair of purple-rimmed glasses.

"It's me," shouted the pleasant, familiar voice. "Regan. Open up."

Harper did a double-take, then rushed to unlock the door. "Oh, Regan—Hi!" she exclaimed, having forgotten all about her coming. "Sorry about that. I didn't realize you were here."

"Not a problem," Regan glanced down at her watch. "I know I'm a few minutes early, but I'm double-parked out front. I'll need to get—*you know who* and his things before I get hit with a ticket."

"Sure thing." Harper walked over to Cornelia's chair to retrieve Bones. She half-expected him to make his usual mad dash upstairs to hide, but instead, Bones allowed Harper to coax him out. Harper coddled her living furball close against her heart, missing him already.

"Dad, do me a favor and grab the bags I left behind the register and bring them out to Regan's car for me?"

"You got it, kid," he nodded. Darren reached an open hand out to Regan. "Keys?"

Regan ran a finger through her lengthy hair piled high upon her head, pushing loose strands back into place. "It's not locked."

Harper watched her father's expression change from helpful to curious to amused when he saw Regan's haphazardly stabbed ladybug hairclips popping out of her bun, failing to do even a half-decent job of keeping the mass of her unruly strands in place. Still, nothing rivaled Regan's long, flowing off-orange-brownish caftan, or the Roman-style sandals she wore strapped up to her calves, looking like something dragged forward in time from a Woodstock dumpster fire.

"Good enough," chuckled Darren, shooting a wink in his daughter's direction.

Regan inched nearer to her charge. "Hey there, buddy," she murmured, letting Bones sniff and lick the tips of her fingers. "Remember me?" Regan moved slightly closer and then opened the rest of her palm. Bones nuzzled his nose against her skin. After a few moments, Regan outstretched her arms. "Ready?" she said, and much to everyone's astonishment—especially Harper's, not only didn't Bones put up a fight, but he sprang willingly into Regan's welcoming warm embrace—purring and rubbing against her chin and greeting her like a long-lost friend.

"What in the—" Harper stood, mouth opened and stunned. *That little*— "*Eh*? Like, wow," she muttered, flummoxed. "I've always known Bones liked you, Regan, but I sure wasn't expecting that kind of reaction." Harper heard her voice take on a strange combination of being thoroughly impressed and downright offended.

Irwin stood off to the side of the room, visibly relieved. "At least we won't have to chase or wheedle him off the top of some bookshelf." Irwin handed Regan a long, sealed white envelope. "This should be enough to, *uhm*, cover anything extra *you-know-who* may need. If not, let me know what I owe you when I return."

"Cool breeze," uttered Regan.

Harper bit her lip to stop from laughing at Irwin's horrorstruck expression as he watched Regan stuff the envelope into her brassiere.

"Okeydokey people," said Regan. "We're off, right, Mr. Bones?"

"Wait. Don't you want me to put you-know-who in a travel carrier or something?" asked Harper, still half-expecting a complete kitty meltdown to happen any second now.

"*Nah*, I don't think that's necessary. I live only a few minutes from here. As far as I'm concerned, Bones is perfectly welcome to my lap while I drive. Besides, this separation is going to be traumatic enough for him to deal with. I don't want to make it any harder on him. Best to keep him calm and happy."

Irwin snorted. "Good luck with that."

"Okay...if you think so." Harper half-smiled. "Although, I gotta be honest, I'm still having a hard time believing he came to you like that. I thought for sure we'd have to drag him out of his hiding places. One of these days, you'll have to let me in on your secret."

"Shrimp Lo Mein," Regan blurted out matter-of-fact. "I picked up a quart for my little buddy and me on the way over. Thought we'd get off to a yummy good start." She nuzzled her face against Bones. "I'm sure that's the reason for his sudden adoration of me."

Harper smiled again, albeit this time feeling a whole lot less wounded. "Thanks again for agreeing to this. I knew he wouldn't make it across the country with his motion sickness." Harper bent over and burrowed her face into her cat's fur one last time. "Be a good boy for Regan," she whispered. "I promise to be back as soon as I can."

Bones raised his furry head off Regan's shoulder and pressed his tiny forehead lovingly against Harper's cheek and purred.

LATER THAT EVENING, while everyone else busied themselves with last-minute preparations and packing, Irwin went to visit Gilly. It had been difficult finding the time to go to the cemetery with everything else going on demanding his attention. Still, Irwin refused to leave Pennsylvania without saying goodbye to his heart.

He parked in his usual space and walked over. The uncomfortable humidity plaguing him most of the day had finally lifted somewhat. The approaching evening air felt warm but much more pleasant. In the far-off distance, high up in the sky, stars faintly twinkled, awaiting twilight's canvas to arrive. However, the day's blazing sun remained vigilant, anchored stubbornly to the horizon. Not yet willing to conclude to its final descent.

Irwin took the cement path through the now all too familiar grounds towards Gilly's plot, something he had done faithfully almost every week for the past eight years.

Eight years. Eight long years.

An entire lifetime. So much had transpired since Gilly's passing. Since the day Fate ripped Irwin's heart out and trampled over it without the slightest hint of remorse. The day Fate left Irwin's dreams shattered and discarded—along with any hope of a shared future.

On that day, when word reached Irwin informing him his fiancée had been killed in a car crash, and her daughter,

Dakota, left in a coma, Irwin could hardly breathe. Grief and anguish seemed to take turns throttling the air out of him, bringing him to the point of collapse when the doctor warned him not to expect the child to make it.

That awful, rotten day, when Fate robbed Irwin of every modicum of joy in his life—and when Happiness stopped dead-cold in its tracks.

The promise of a future with Gilly, which had once fueled his very existence, had now vanished. After her death, Irwin self-quarantined his heartache, confining the most considerable portion of himself into a self-imposed locked cage of loneliness. No matter how hard he tried to make sense out of the tragedy, desperate to hold onto what little sanity he had left, he couldn't. This kind of vicious, senseless loss made no sense. There were no hidden virtues to hold onto. No do-overs. No nothing.

Each day forward, Irwin found himself tumbling deeper and harder into a pointless abyss. He'd spend long days in a seamless blur, one after the other until every last minuscule droplet of joy he had created to insulate him from his miserable, now meaningless life disappeared.

Except for Cornelia, Irwin's closest friend in the entire world, and his last link to Gilly and Dakota.

A woman who flat-out refused to allow Irwin to indulge forever in his unhappiness, often battling him down to the core, and refusing to give up on him no matter how low and wretched he became. The more Irwin tried to close her out and push her away, the harder Cornelia pursued him, dragging him back to life, kicking and screaming.

Eventually, Cornelia's relentless love and devotion had won out, compelling a semi-broken, irascible Irwin to collect the pieces from his loss and heartbreak to push past. It had been a lengthy and arduous battle from the start, but

Cornelia never wavered and plowed stubbornly forward, determined to help her friend heal.

And now she was dead. Forever. Irwin no longer had Cornelia to talk to, to bounce off ideas, or dilemmas, or even concerns. He could no longer laugh with her to the point of tearing up or lean on her for support when life pulled the chair out from beneath him again.

"SHE'S GONE, GILLY," he said, standing next to her gravestone. "Cornelia passed away last week. Her body couldn't take another minute." As he spoke, his shoulders slouched. In one hand, Irwin held a bouquet while he rested his other hand on top of Gilly's flat headstone, something he'd do whenever faced with the burden of delivering more bad news.

"I want to apologize for not coming sooner. Unbeknownst to me, your friend and mine had been busy those first few months right after her diagnosis, plotting, and planning. Since her passing, I have been tasked as her Executor, expected to attend to all her last wishes. Some requests I had expected, while others, not so much." Irwin grinned. "Let's just say I am now duty-bound to take Cornelia's ashes cross-country. I am expected to stop periodically during this trip to deliver letters she had written to a collection of people from her former life. People who, mind you, I don't know, nor can remember ever hearing her speak about, although she may have mentioned a friend named Mildred once or twice. I can't be positive."

The surrounding evening's light grew dim as dusk loomed. The earlier clatter of birds flittering across the sky quieted and calmed. Off in the near distance, Irwin could faintly detect a low grumbling hum from nearby highway traffic zooming past, but here, inside the cemetery grounds, not a single voice aloud spoke but his.

"And before you ask, Cornelia requested I scatter her ashes in La Jolla Cove, some seaside community within the city of San Diego, California, which runs along the Pacific Ocean coastline. My exact instructions are to stand on a cliff surrounded on three sides by ocean bluffs and beaches, and without falling in myself, 'pour her in.' Her words, not mine." Irwin rolled his eyes. "Why there and not here? I'm not entirely sure, but like most everything else Cornelia has tasked me to do, this too remains an enigma."

He shifted the beautiful full bouquet in his left hand. "You may find this interesting. According to legend, at one time, bootleggers favored La Jolla Cove to funnel whiskey during the Prohibition. Later on, smugglers took over, using the cove to stow illegal immigrants. Now, presumably, the area is a haven for many artists and creatives. I suspect this may have been Cornelia's motivation." Irwin shrugged. "But what do I know?"

Irwin shrugged. "To be honest, Gilly, I don't know what to make of this trip or the fact Cornelia has me now meeting all these strangers—people from her past. A past she failed to let anyone here, me included, in on. I'm still trying to process why and coming up short."

Irwin shook his head, feeling the rise of his anger and confusion getting the better of him. Instead of standing still, he opted to pace around the grave, never realizing how many times he pointed or waved the bouquet in the air when punctuating his scattered thoughts as he spoke.

"Bones? No. We aren't taking him. —Not with his motion sickness. Regan's agreed to watch him. As a matter of fact, she swung by the shop early this evening to pick him up, reeking of Shrimp Lo Mein. Needless to say, your spoiled rotten cat couldn't have been happier."

Irwin, tired of carrying the load, placed the blooming yellow daffodils in the small cylinder vase located by the front of Gilly's grave. He then lowered himself to one knee to pluck at a few weeds daring to sprout around the stone's sides.

"I should be back in about two weeks or so, although realistically, taking into account my abysmal track record with death and destruction, I wouldn't count on it." Irwin tossed the collected weeds to the side and stood, brushing the dirt off his knees.

"Listen, although I look the part of the walking crypt keeper part two, I'm still not sure how any of this, 'alive one-minute—dead the next' stuff works. Frankly, I'd like to imagine Cornelia is with you now, this minute in heaven, and the two of you ladies are listening to me and having a raucous good laugh at my expense." Irwin's voice cracked. "I can't explain why, but that's what I'd like to believe." He glanced down and clapped the remaining specks of dirt from his hands.

Irwin let out a long exhale, his eyes closed as if trying to process what next he felt compelled to say.

"I'm not entirely sure what—*or who*—lies in store for me or why making this trip feels so necessary, but this is something I have to see through." The image of Elle's pretty smiling face flashed through Irwin's mind, and he blushed. "But no matter what happens, I hope you will always know how much I always loved you."

Irwin stepped away from Gilly's headstone, his hands clasped behind his back. "We leave tomorrow, rain or shine. And despite all the uncertainty and trepidation, I have to believe deep down inside Cornelia had a darn good reason to keep me in the dark about her past, but for the life of me, Gilly, I can't figure out what it is."

CHAPTER 10

MILDRED TRIED IGNORING the nervousness building up inside her as she paced the length of her one-floor house like the Mad Hatter.

One more day...

"*Gah,* why oh, why did I ever agree to meet with these people?" she moaned, cocking her head in the direction of her dozing kitty.

Upon hearing her voice, Horatio stretched his long, tiger-striped body along the rear of Mildred's sofa. Although technically still considered a kitten, Horatio had taken to basking in his new mommy's bay window like a seasoned feline, relishing a bit of mid-morning sun worship in-between his many quizzical and often naughty endeavors. Despite his penchant for misbehaving, Horatio seemed to have adapted nicely to his newly adopted home, where he stayed fortified by an onslaught of cuddles, bowls of tasty vittles, and fresh, cold water—not to mention an ample supply of welcomed central air.

Mildred was heading toward the kitchen, but by chance, happened to glance down the hall toward the front door when she noticed her handwoven Aztec runner, a colorful handmade piece gifted to her years back from Cornelia, now slanted off to the side and flipped over at a single corner.

Again.

"Thanks, Horatio," she called, before bending over to straighten it out. After a bit of fidgeting and sliding back into place, Mildred stood, unexpectedly out of breath. Puffing, she gripped the sharp crimp traversing the hollow of her lower back and winced.

"*Whoa*, that hurt." She staggered backward. It took a few seconds for her to catch her breath. Then she glanced down and cocked her head to the side. "Would you give me a break," she groaned, after realizing with great annoyance how the darn rug still looked slightly uncentered. However, refusing to become a cripple over a throw rug, Mildred used the heel of her bare foot this time to inch the runner properly into place.

"I wish you would stop messing with this thing," she complained to her snoozing, unsympathetic kitty.

"*Hmm*," Mildred squinted her eyes, and tilted her head again. "I think that looks a whole bunch better." Keeping busy meant less time to think.

Tomorrow's the day.

Her stomach lurched while the knot stuck in her gut fired off a healthy new round of acid reflux.

Mildred had been dreading the arrival of this visit since Cornelia's decline. Despite agreeing to help finish whatever ridiculousness Cornelia had put into motion before her death, there was something inexplicably unsettling about this impending visit.

Cornelia's friends.

She didn't know any of these people, except from whatever Cornelia had shared with her over the years, which only added to Mildred's growing apprehension.

It's just nerves—

However, the same *just nerves* were presently having a field day somersaulting against the wall of her gut.

But why?

Perhaps because tomorrow's visit signaled finality—a premature closure on what had been almost a life-long friendship, still too raw to forcibly digest. Not that Mildred hadn't had enough forewarning.

Looking back, Mildred had to admit, Cornelia's declining health hadn't been the world's greatest kept secret. And in truth it had been Cornelia herself who had phoned Mildred on her way home from the doctor's appointment on that unforgettable, dreadful day.

"What's wrong?" Mildred had practically yelled into the phone, sensing something off the second she heard Cornelia's voice.

"I just left, and it's confirmed."

Mildred remembered how her heart pounded and her pulse raced, bracing against what inevitably would come next.

"I have Alzheimer's."

Alzheimer's?

Cornelia's diagnosis left Mildred gut-punched. Not because she hadn't expected to hear something serious, the signs had all been there, but because this illness's particular comportment seemed especially brutal. Of all the diseases for Mildred's full of life and adventurous friend to suffer from— memory loss seemed the cruelest.

"We'll get a second opinion," Mildred had blurted, grasping at straws, clutching the phone in her hand.

"*Ah*, Millie, that, I'm afraid, was the second opinion." Cornelia's tone had sounded more shattered than weepy. "I-I...oh, I don't know what I'm trying to say. For once, I'm at a loss for words, if you can believe it. And honestly, I didn't mean to dump this all on you." Cornelia paused. "I probably shouldn't have called, but, well, I just didn't know what else to do."

"*Pffh*. Don't be ridiculous. I'm glad you told me. I mean, how many times have I called you with my problems?" Mildred sniffled, trying to conceal her sobs by clearing her throat. "Listen, why don't you come and stay with me?"

"I can't."

"No, stop. Listen, we've talked about this before, you and me, living together. That way I can be there to help you during this—" Mildred combed her mind, searching for the right word to say.

Cornelia, perhaps sensing Mildred's discomfort, cut her off before she had the chance to continue. "I appreciate that, Mill—I do, but you know as well as I do, I just can't up and leave. Not now, and certainly not with everything else happening." Cornelia had sighed into the phone. "Besides, I don't have a lot of time left to get stuff straightened out. I'm on the clock."

"But Cornelia—"

"No, Mill. Don't say it. There's no use pretending this isn't happening. Not anymore, and not with my mind slipping away by the second."

Cornelia's memory lapses were legendary. Something the two old friends had chalked up to old age. But now that the evil, malignant disease had been given an official title, it no longer felt like an episodic irritation, but more of a dire one—a foreboding warning of what tomorrow promised to bring.

"By things, I assume you mean Irwin and Harper?" Mildred cringed, knowing how petty that sounded, but Cornelia, for whatever her reason, didn't seem to take notice.

"Yes, but also Olivia, Darren, and young Christopher. I consider them all my family now. And before you say it, and as crazy as it sounds, despite my forte for self-sabotage, I've made a good life here."

"I know that."

"Do you?" Cornelia's breathing labored.

"Cornelia?" Mildred heard Cornelia struggle for air. "Are you okay?" she stammered into the phone.

Cornelia coughed, fighting to clear her throat. "Anxiety," she announced as if that one-word descriptor explained everything. "Listen, Mill, I may not be able to get out your way, but that doesn't mean you can't come to Pennsylvania. You know that. There's always room for you here. Heck, I've told you this for years how much I'd enjoy having you stay with me."

Mildred did know, but like Cornelia, she, too, had worked hard to make a life for herself in Ohio. Admittedly not as full and exciting as the one Cornelia had scraped together, and indeed a hell of a lot more isolated, but a life, nonetheless. She couldn't—*no*—she wouldn't just pick up and walk away.

"I know, Cornelia, and I appreciate it."

"Anyway, I should dry my eyes, fix my lipstick, and head back home. I gotta find some way to digest this protracted death sentence." Cornelia then hesitated. "I'm assuming there's a bunch of legal crap I'm going to have to tie up before I..." Her unfinished sentence had hung heavy in the air. "I'll probably need your help with some of it—if you're up to it."

A pool of hot tears rose in the back of Mildred's eyes, ready to burst. "Anything you need."

"Thanks." Cornelia paused. "I also gotta figure out a way to dump all of this on Irwin without him falling to pieces."

Irwin again.

Instant loathing replaced Mildred's sorrow. "How is the illusive Mr. Irwin Abernathy holding up these days?" she had asked, her bitterness and jealousy resurfacing to the top, seeping once again through the cracks of her hardened, usually better-behaved heart.

"He's doing the best he can," Cornelia answered, again disregarding Mildred's voiced resentment.

Once again, the two old friends had reached that same emotional roadblock, much as they had done many times before whenever the topic of Irwin Abernathy came up. And Cornelia, much to Mildred's utter disappointment, never budged. For whatever reason, that erosive man held a prominent and permanent place in Cornelia's heart, something Mildred could never compete with.

"What's that supposed to mean —'He's doing the best he can?'" Mildred hadn't bothered to mask the snark in her voice. "He's a grown man, for goodness sake."

"Losing Gilly for one," Cornelia answered as if they'd never had this conversation before. "Losing her so suddenly has been awfully hard on Irwin. A shock. Broke his heart and closed him down for the longest time. Then when her daughter..." Cornelia paused. "*Uhh...umm*...Oh, dear."

"Dakota," Mildred answered flatly.

"Yes. Thank you—*Dakota*. When Dakota died next...what a mess. *Jeez*, to be honest, Mill, Irwin's just starting to become a fully functioning human again." Cornelia coughed. "Dry throat. I'm sorry, where were we?"

"Irwin."

"Yes. Irwin. I credit most of Irwin's recovery to Harper. And of course, the rest of the crew, and the bookshop. Lord, Irwin loves that dusty old place. Such a bibliophile."

Mildred thought she heard Cornelia's sob, catch.

"And to think, just as life around here had started to resemble something close to normal—or as normal as we seem able to manage—I now have to dump this on him."

This time, there was no mistaking Cornelia's voice cracking.

"Hey, Irwin, old pal. Guess what?" Cornelia had mimicked as if trying aloud what she would most assuredly never say. 'It's time to face death again. That's right, old grump. Ironically though, only one of us will be burdened to remember." Cornelia choked.

"You worry about him too much," Mildred had interjected, not sounding as compassionate as she should have. "This is about you now—not Irwin, not Harper, no one else, including me."

"No, Mill, darlin', that's where you're wrong. This is most assuredly about Irwin, just as much as it's about you, Harper, Olivia, Darren, and Christopher—and me. Also, don't forget, I still need to inform Martin, Luna and Jax, and..." Cornelia faltered, her memory slipping again. "Hell's bells!"

"Elle," prodded Mildred.

"Yes. —and Elle." Cornelia's frustration at her growing inability to instantly recall names made her angry. "Bottom-line, I have to do this my way, Millie, and I'm going to need your help."

There had been countless opportunities since that awful conversation for Millie to tell her best friend how much she would need her, too. How what she was expected to face alone terrified her. How being usurped felt almost as humiliating as dying alone. Mildred almost let slip, 'No worries on the dead and gone thing, Cornelia. I'll be joining you soon enough, my old friend.'

Instead, Mildred told her dearest friend what she needed to hear.

"You know I'll always be here for you, Cornelia," she had replied tenderly, despite really wanting to scream and smash the phone against the wall, breaking it into a thousand unrecognizable pieces. "Tell me what you want me to do."

THE INITIAL RESENTMENT Mildred felt after Cornelia's diagnosis eventually subsided, only to be replaced by unimaginable heartache. It had been hard enough with Cornelia living a state away, but at least she had the option to pick up the phone whenever she wanted to chat. Then, as if a light switch turned off, Cornelia began slipping into an unfathomable bottomless abyss so deep that even Mildred could no longer reach her.

Towards the bitter long last days, Mildred had reached for the phone continuously, only to slam it back in its cradle a split second later after remembering her friend, the woman she knew and loved, would no longer be cerebrally on the receiving end—Cornelia's memories had all but vanished.

So unfair...

Mildred never meant to hold Cornelia accountable for either her dementia or her death, yet, in some absurd way, that was precisely what she did, and all because she couldn't get past feeling slighted. Disheartened with how Cornelia replaced her needs with those of a far-distant, cantankerous former librarian neighbor, saddled with an unnatural and frequent association with the Angel of Death.

And then, there were the letters.

Dozens of them in all shapes and sizes.

Since the diagnosis, Cornelia had made it her life's final mission to write Mildred countless letters packed with years' worth of stories. Her stories. Their stories. Strangers' stories. Recollections from the past. Predictions for the future.

Early on, Cornelia wrote at a fever's pitch, almost as if by her transcribing these events onto paper, she could somehow preserve the remembrances her mind remained determined to erase.

Mildred found a couple of Cornelia's earliest voiced stories downright hysterical, while others did nothing but torment. Later on, Cornelia wound up dictating more extended tangents—a random compendium of disparate names, dates, and places—whose sole purpose as a list, it turned out, was simply to exist.

As Cornelia's memories continued to slip and deteriorate, and her far and few moments of clarity collided and blurred, it was Mildred who had to sift through the bombastic, hazy recollections—more like half-stories than actual events. Nonsensical, incensed ramblings Mildred attributed more to Cornelia's illness and fear than to any one person's real faults or shortcomings. Many diatribes were missing whole beginnings and others, entire endings. Mildred struggled to make sense of these as well but with little success. By far, these were Cornelia's angriest accounts—laden with fantastical debatable descriptions, too cruel to be true. Nevertheless, accurate or not, nothing Cornelia concocted or shared could ever be confused with boring. However, upon Cornelia's passing, whether right or wrong, Mildred felt she had no choice but to destroy those illusory accounts.

Then, out of nowhere, thicker mailers began showing up at Mildred's doorstep, arriving every few weeks or so, complete with detailed instructions in regards to the sealed, labeled letters Mildred had been instructed to deliver.

'Don't open.' 'Hand this letter off to...' 'Remember to tell so-and-so this and that—'

True to her word, Mildred did whatever Cornelia asked of her, but her unwavering commitment did little to sway Cornelia from deflecting on topics she deemed too uncomfortable to discuss. Cornelia's impenetrable defense left Mildred resentful, wracked with guilt, and drowning under more unanswered questions than answers.

Maybe tomorrow's visit will bring closure. And if not, she mused, *at least I'll get to meet the insufferable Mr. Irwin Abernathy face-to-face.*

Mildred's stomach did another little flip. Social anxiety. A chronic mood disorder that had made leaving the house feel nearly impossible, except in short, well-planned, anxious bursts. While not considered technically agoraphobic, Mildred got mighty close, worsening since her retirement. With no place to be, she'd often lock herself away behind the safety of her walls, sometimes for days or weeks—anything to avoid the predictable surge of disquiet whenever faced with the stressors of the outside world.

But even Mildred didn't consider herself a total recluse. She enjoyed an active online life—over a thousand plus friends from all over the world. People she recognized by their catchy thumbnail faces and public snatches of their lives she felt privileged to share.

Mildred especially liked the cozy, sometimes witty banter, the shared photos of glorious exotic vacations, recent births, or pending nuptials. Graduations were one of her absolute favorites—all those young, smiling faces—ready to take on the world.

Mildred valued these interactive, albeit brief interactions which let her feel connected to a bigger, outside world, while still allowing her to maintain the illusion of a safe and controlled life.

But not so with Cornelia, with whom Mildred had made and nurtured a genuine, real human connection. Cornelia had not only understood her limitations, but had gone out of her way to make sure Mildred felt wanted and happy—as if a state of happiness was something one could experience while living inside their head twenty-four hours a day, seven days a week, 365 days a year.

"Oh, Cornelia," Mildred sighed, missing her friend more than ever, and feeling the familiar compulsion to begin pacing the length of her home all over again.

Theirs had been a friendship spanning decades, and it had endured at least through Cornelia's lifetime. Now, with her only real anchor to a healthy life gone forever, Mildred wasn't sure what to do next.

FINDING herself back in the hallway, Mildred ignored the still off-centered rug, and lifted a stack of neatly hand-labeled sealed envelopes fastened together with a broad rubber band. She tucked them into a drawer for safekeeping, glad this final request would end soon, and yet saddened it had come down to this. The unbearable loss of Cornelia had caused Mildred to grieve in ways she couldn't quite comprehend—not only for Cornelia's death, which had been devastating enough, but also for her own pending mortality.

As if by reflex, Mildred reached up to touch the small raised welt where the doctor had implanted the tiny reflector—a radar device used to help identify a tumor's location. The unhealed scar protruded ever so slightly from beneath her shirt.

"We have you scheduled for surgery two weeks from today, making that a ..." said the oncologist's nurse, a middle-aged woman named Kerri, sporting a head of patchy gray roots peeking out from beneath a head-full of too bottle dark strands, as she scrutinized her computer's calendar. "Ah, yes. August seventeenth. That's a Monday morning. Dr. Fields prefers to schedule all surgeries for Mondays," she'd informed Mildred a few days earlier. "And don't forget, we'll need you at the hospital by five in the morning. Remember, nothing to eat or drink after midnight." Kerri had reached into a drawer to yank out a sheet of paper. "Here's a list of all the pre-op procedures. If you have any questions, feel free to call me. My extension is here." Kerri highlighted her number with an audacious pink marker.

"That'll work," Mildred had replied, only half-paying attention, and more focused on importing the date and time onto her phone calendar, except her shaking hands made the task ridiculously impossible.

"How long until I'm back on my feet? Give or take." Mildred still hadn't figured out how to manage the recovery period alone, if one didn't count Horatio, who, for all intents and purposes, would be utterly useless, notwithstanding his abundant cuddles and delicious canoodling.

"With this procedure, patients can expect to resume normal activity after a day or two." The woman paused. "Oh, wait." Kerri glanced down at her notes, frowning. "You're undergoing a sentinel lymph node biopsy at the same time as the lumpectomy, correct?"

Mildred nodded in the affirmative as the nerves vaulting around her innards refused to settle.

"*Hmmm,* then I'd say to expect to resume regular activities about two weeks after surgery." The nurse gazed at Mildred kindly. "I assume you will have support at home during the recovery period, correct?"

"Yes. Absolutely," Mildred had lied, unwilling to let the Kerri's of the world know how ridiculously alone she'd be, especially since her best friend was gone forever.

No, not gone. Dead. Cornelia is dead.
  As in never coming back.

To calm the battalion of thoughts marching around in her head, Mildred puttered about her already pristine home, rearranging the pillows on her sofa, plucking dead leaves from hanging plants, and dusting previously dusted surfaces. This, of course, only served to make waiting on the arrival of her *dead* best friend's so-called family feel all the more surreal.

However, unlike Mildred, Cornelia had never been alone. One of the perks of having a small coalition of family and friends. 'A compendium of acquired misfits,' Mildred liked to tease, but in truth, they had honestly loved Cornelia, and were there when her time to exit arrived.

Not so for Mildred, who had only just begun to accept the awful truth that her aloneness—the insulated, cloistered world she'd lived all these years, meant nobody, with perhaps the exception of Horatio, would even notice her gone.

"No, no, no!" Mildred shook her head.

"I have to get through this," she told herself. *I promised.*

On the verge of crying, Mildred started to pace.

I'll give them whatever is theirs, and that will be that.

"Simple enough, simple enough, simple enough," she repeated with every stomp of her foot in the hope of actually one day believing it.

CHAPTER 11

*And so, **it begins**.*

"Babe—" shouted Harper through the open bathroom door, poking her soap-soaked head out from behind the shower curtain. "Do me a favor?"

"What's up?" asked Christopher, making his way down the hall.

"Would you grab my bag on the way down? But not the backpack. Leave that on the bed. I still have more stuff to add."

"You got it." Christopher hoisted the strap of his laptop bag over one shoulder. He headed into the bedroom to grip not one, but two duffel bag handles.

"Before you go downstairs, make sure my parents are awake," shouted Harper. "Bang on their door if you have to."

"Sure thing. Rouse girlfriend's parents with loud, obnoxious banging," muttered Christopher, struggling under the weight of Harper's bag in particular. "What could go wrong?"

"Oh—and before I forget—ask Irwin if he remembered to give Roger the extra set of shop keys. If not, we're going to have to drop them off on our way out of PA."

"Extra set of keys...Irwin, shop, Roger, drop off," Christopher mumbled, letting both duffel bags drop to the floor in a loud thump.

"Did something just fall?" Harper yelled. "Chris? I think something just fell."

Beads of sweat trickled from Christopher's hairline down his cheek, only to pool around his neckline. He leaned his sweaty back against the tiny kitchen's door frame to catch his breath. "One of these days, this gorgeous woman is going to be the end of me," he grumbled, huffing and puffing against the oppressive heat.

"Chris?"

He didn't answer.

"Hon?" she yelled again, a bit more forcibly.

He chuckled, picturing her scrubbing the soap quickly out of her hair, growing annoyed.

"Are you still here?" she called out.

Instead of replying, Christopher decided to have a little fun at Harper's expense. He grabbed one of her thicker textbooks off the kitchen table and held it high in the air.

"Chris?" she called out again.

Thump!

—Christopher swiftly returned the book to the table, then bolted full-speed to hide behind one of the semi-opened closet doors. Harper, dubiously wrapped in an oversized towel shot from the bathroom, looking like a startled gazelle, unaware of the small puddles of water and suds left everywhere she stepped.

"*Ick*—" she griped, spitting long strands of thick wet soapy hair out of her mouth.

Although he had his body pressed hard against the wall, Christopher could still observe Harper through the door's narrow open crack. He watched as she scanned the living room high and low like a skilled wildlife tracker, searching for any sign that something had gone amiss.

"What in the heck was that?"

He had to suppress the urge to laugh as she scampered right past him. Back and forth she ran through their apartment, utterly confused.

"Oh well," she shrugged upon failing to determine the source of the strange noise.

Nevertheless, Christopher, knowing his girlfriend's tenacious personality, didn't dare budge an inch and a good thing, too, because as soon as Harper started sloshing her way back to the bathroom, she abruptly stopped and spun around in his exact direction.

Christopher held his breath, not wanting to attract her attention by any sudden movement. He only hoped she couldn't hear his heart hammering in his chest.

Harper didn't move, but remained pin-point silent, and information gathering. Not a muscle twitched except those in her eyes as they meticulously scrutinized and scanned her tiny patch in the world. At one point, Christopher half-expected her to drop down on all fours to search under furniture, maybe on her stomach so she could pull herself forward with her elbows.

After what felt like an excruciating eternity, she gave up.

Yes! he soundlessly fist-pumped from behind the door.

"That's so weird," he heard her mutter. "I could have sworn I heard something."

MEANWHILE, in the apartment next door…

A bead of sticky sweat trickled down the side of Olivia's cheek as she rushed into the kitchen to pack the last of the condiments into an oversized hand tote. She had purposely woken up early to be ready on time, sick of hearing all the snide jokes about how late she always was, but now, as the morning sped by, her mild irritation turned to outright frustration.

I forgot something. I know it…

Olivia glanced around her tidy-to-obsessive, perfect apartment for a hint, any hint, but noted nothing out of place or missing. She walked into the hall, nothing but Darren's decrepit old cooler parked by the front door, needing to be taken downstairs.

But that's not it, or is it?

Olivia heard Darren in their bedroom, drawers being slid open and slammed shut. She had pleaded with him to pack the night before, but as usual, Darren had his way of doing things.

"Don't worry. I got this," he had informed her.

Zzzzz—ip —

Finally! —the welcomed sound of her husband's bag closing. Just as she was about to shout for him, a loud knock at the door startled her.

"Olivia?"

Christopher!

"It's not locked," she answered, heading back into the living room.

"Just me." Christopher entered with his hands full. "I've been instructed by your progeny to make sure you two are up and getting ready to go."

"Almost." Olivia checked the time. "But by my watch, I

still have fifteen minutes." She swiped her damp chin with the back of her hand. "It's unbearably humid this morning. I'm already sweating like a pig."

"You and me, both."

"I hope that van of yours has good AC," she warned. Olivia rechecked the time. "I gotta hurry. I want to rinse off again before we leave."

"Harper's in the shower also, so," Christopher shrugged and glanced down at his load then over at Darren's cooler. "Anyway, I'm headed downstairs to start loading up the van. I'll be back up to grab that and whatever else you need me to take down."

"You're a doll, thanks. I'll let Darren know. He should be done soon and will be able to help." Olivia turned and stopped. "*Uhm,* Irwin isn't here, yet, is he?"

"I'm sure he is. If I know him, he's already standing by the van at attention, his clipboard, directions, and maps ready to go. Chin up, chest out, shoulders back, stomach in," Christopher teased imitating Irwin. Giving Olivia a mock salute, he hoisted the computer strap higher on his shoulder, then bent at the knees carefully to retrieve the duffels. "I'll be back."

"I thought I heard voices," said Darren, entering the living room, dragging two bags with him. "What did you pack in here?" he asked, glaring accusingly at Olivia, flipping him the one-finger salute.

"Never you mind," she chastised, raising a perfectly plucked eyebrow. "And that was Christopher you heard. Apparently, our spawn, who is currently still showering, mind you, had the audacity to make him check in on us—the nerve."

Darren dropped the bags and reached for the cooler.

"Don't worry about that. Christopher already said he's coming back for it."

"I got it!" Darren looked miffed as he struggled to lift the cooler up by its corner. "Man, that thing's heavy."

Olivia smirked, ready to respond with something snarky, but then, out of nowhere, a surge of deliciously hot naughty thoughts about their previous evening burst through her body, igniting an energy inside she couldn't explain.

A tide of ravenous heat spread to her cheeks as she envisioned thinking about how easily Darren had lifted her onto their bed. *The feel of his broad, muscular arms laying her down gently upon the crisp, inviting sheets...his soft dewy kisses planted lightly on her lips, down her neck, along her—*

"Hold up." Darren snapped his fingers, causing Olivia to flinch.

Swooning from a mixture of head fog and yearning, she watched the man she desired and loved sprint into their bedroom, only to reappear moments later holding an extra pair of folded socks.

"Socks?"

"Can't have too many," he explained, shoving them into the outside zippered compartment of his duffel. Then he paused, and poof—off he went again to grab a few more pairs.

"Are you sure you're going to have enough?" She thought about her battery-operated pink friend and lubricant packed in the bottom of her bag and blushed.

"Go ahead, make fun of me all you want," said Darren, "but I bet you won't be complaining when I have to kick off my sneaker after sixteen hours in a van."

"Point taken." Olivia's hands kept fidgeting. She started to pace to suppress the uncontrollable heat building inside, moving with her back turned toward Darren, trying to avoid his eyes.

Darren watched his wife circle the room. His head cocked to the side in confusion. "Liv? Are you okay?"

"I'm fine," she snapped, hugging herself.

Darren frowned. "You don't look fine. To be honest, you look kinda funny."

Funny? Olivia stopped pacing.

—*I'll show him funny*.

Olivia nodded, unable to answer. She didn't trust the unbearable churning making her dwell on all the unthinkable things. She fanned her neck and blew out a long breath. "Right." She tapped her watch-less wrist. "Well, I better hurry up. You know Irwin, and I've got less than seven minutes to rinse-off."

...and the she blushed.

Darren wiped off his forehead. "It's too hot in here," he said, harmlessly enough, while gathering the luggage.

You have no idea.

Olivia nibbled her bottom lip, her eyes taking in her husband's glistening body. On the brink of losing all sense of dignity, she spat a strand out of her mouth as she stomped past her husband, yanking her sweaty tee and clingy shorts off on the way. As she dared a glance back, Olivia laughed when she saw Darren's mouth drop wide open.

Darren swallowed hard. "Liv?" he whispered, the duffels falling into a pile on the floor.

"Six minutes and counting," she purred, gliding seductively down the rest of the hall, her eyes urging him to join her.

"Oh, hell yeah." Darren couldn't shove the old cooler out into the hall and lock the apartment door any faster. He hopped and stripped down the hallway until he arrived wearing nothing but a big goofy smile.

TEN MINUTES LATER...

"I'm gonna bring the rest of this stuff down," said Darren, indicating Olivia's duffel.

"No. Leave it. I'm not done," she said, reapplying her lipstick. "I'll bring it down with me."

"Are you sure? It's pretty heavy."

"I'll be fine."

Darren shrugged. "If you say so." He bent over, ready to take the rest of the stuff, but paused mid-grab. "*Uhm*, Liv? Is there anything else you want me to do before I go?"

Olivia poked her head out the bathroom door.

"Nope." Olivia shook her head. "That's everything," she teased. "Go ahead. I'll lock up and be down in a few minutes."

"You're sure?"

"Positive. You're officially in the clear."

"Yes, ma'am." Darren grabbed the rest of the stuff and started to leave.

"Oh, wait!" Olivia rushed past him into the kitchen. "Take these bags with you, too," she said, returning with two over-filled food totes. "Here you go." She lifted and hung each strap over one of his shoulders and pecked him playfully on the cheek.

Darren winced under the added heavy load. "Any-thing-else?"

Slightly out of breath, Olivia leaned in, cradled his face, and kissed him on the lips. "Nope," she purred, pecking him on the ear. "You're good, Mr. Crane. *Real good.*"

THE BOOKSHOP...

Irwin paced the length of the store, along the hot side-walk with his clipboard wedged securely under one arm. Although early in the morning, the sun's rays had already begun to aim down oppressive heat. Irwin checked his watch for the umpteenth time and sighed. Only a few more minutes until the *Abernathy & Crane* Traveling Sideshow hit the wide-open road. *Hopefully—*

He lifted his duffel off the curb and moved it near the back of the van.

"Hey, Irwin," greeted Christopher, dragging his collection of luggage and totes toward the trunk. He jiggled the keys until he found the rental's fob and clicked the doors to unlock. "Might as well start cooling it off while we pack," he said, jacking up the AC to full blast. He peered down. "Is this all you're taking?" he asked Irwin, pointing to the lone, small bag.

"Indeed," said Irwin, lifting his head in surprise as to why Christopher had asked such a ridiculous question. "What more do you think I require?"

"I don't know. It's a long trip." Christopher balanced himself on the van's step, more like a lip, and opened the cargo bubble on top. "Can you hand me your bag?"

Irwin complied, followed by the other bags.

"No, not my computer bag. I want to put that in the back for safekeeping."

Irwin popped open the trunk. "We should put the cooler in here as well."

"That's what I was thinking." Christopher climbed down. "I'll be back. I told Olivia I'd get the cooler."

"Please check on the stragglers while you're at it. Feel free to toss them out the window if necessary."

"Will do."

Once inside, Irwin shimmied his bony bottom across the still uncomfortably searing front passenger seat. Unable to help himself, he twiddled with the van's dials, adjusting the air-conditioner and moving his chair back just so. Once satisfied, he busied himself organizing a few of his belongings. One Chapstick, an unopened pack of breath mints, a small travel-sized packet of tissues, one small writing pad, and an extra ballpoint pen. He tucked his paperwork and directions inside the door's side pocket, then proceeded to empty all loose change and singles from his pocket, filling one of the available cup holders. Lastly, he removed the small felt box he'd been carrying around in his pocket since that last day at the hospital. He had meant to leave it with Cornelia that day, either press it into her palm or clip it around her neck, but with the way everything had happened so quickly—he didn't. Irwin placed the box in the far back of the glove compartment, careful to tuck it under the vehicle's paperwork. "That should do it," he mumbled, and then checked the time. Less than four and half more minutes before they were officially late.

In his peripheral vision, he noticed Darren and Christopher staggering out from the bookshop's front door, laughing about something. Christopher carried the cooler in front of him as if it weighed nothing, while Darren, weighted down by a collection of bags, lagged.

Christopher popped the hatch open and easily shoved the cooler inside. He climbed up on the van's lip and unzipped the cargo bubble. "Hand me the rest of the bags." Christopher shoved the last duffel to the back and accepted the next one from Darren. When done relieving Darren of all his stuff, he asked, "Is this everything?"

"I wish, but no. Olivia still has one more bag."

"Harper too, but only a backpack. I think she intends on keeping it inside the van with her."

"Did I hear my name?" asked Harper, strolling up to the van with one hand gripping the strap of her trusty backpack slung casually over one shoulder while using the other to hold the handle of an infant baby carrier. A small receiving blanket had been carefully draped over a strange-shaped object.

"What in the name?" Despite the suffocating heat, Irwin

couldn't roll his window down fast enough. Leaning his head out, he couldn't stop gawking.

Darren, seemingly equally as confused, ran a hand through his damp, sweaty hair.

Christopher, foot braced against the van's step, glanced down perplexed.

Since neither Darren or Christopher dared ask, Irwin took it upon himself.

"I know I'm going to hate myself for this, but why are you carrying *that thing?*"

"This *thing* is called an infant baby car seat," corrected Harper.

"What's in it?" asked Darren.

"*Who* is probably a better question, Dad." Harper lifted the corner of the blanket revealing Cornelia's small urn.

"*Whoa,*" muttered Darren.

Christopher looked away.

Irwin, who had almost half his body protruding out of the window, went to speak. His lips moved, but no sound came out.

"And before any of you say a word, this is staying in the seat next to me," retorted Harper, leaving no room for argument.

Mr. Fitzgerald from the funeral parlor had delivered Cornelia's urn last evening. Prior to any discussion about what should be done, Harper had jumped in, offering to be its caretaker for the duration of the trip. At the time, Irwin had readily agreed, never once considering how exactly Harper planned to carry out such a responsibility. Admittedly, a baby carrier never showed up on his radar of bizarre choices.

"But it's an urn," he mumbled. "—in a baby seat."

"*Woo-hoo!* There's no getting over on you, Irwin." Harper replaced the blanket and gingerly tucked it in on all sides. "Specifically, Cornelia's urn," Harper turned her head toward the three men, apparently braced for a confrontation. "What of it?"

A trifecta of heads cocked and nodded in mock understanding.

Irwin leaned his head farther out of the window. "*Hmmm.* Perhaps I should rephrase my question. Why do you, in particular, have an urn strapped inside an infant baby car seat?"

Harper's shoulders slumped forward. She tilted her head and squinted at Irwin as if he was senseless. "Well, what would you suggest I do with it? Toss it in the hatch? Chuck it in the cargo holder? Oh, I know—I'll keep it in the car under the seat so that every time we come to an abrupt stop, it can roll around on the floor. It'll be a blast."

Irwin yanked his head back slightly and blinked, trying to reply, but again, he found himself unable to respond.

"Harper—" warned Darren, his hands clasped tightly on his waist. "I think that's enough."

"But is it, though?" she snapped, losing her cool. Harper angled her head first in her father's direction, waiting for a reply, then back at Irwin, still looking somewhat befuddled. "I apologize, but honestly, what would you two suggest I do with Cornelia's remains until we get to San Diego? Hold it on my lap for twenty-seven hundred miles?" Without warning, she lowered her head and began to sniffle, her head bobbing on the precipice of tears. A thick strand from atop her messy bun fell free, concealing her eyes.

Irwin saw Darren shoot Christopher a cautious, pleading stare.

Christopher, who, up to that point had remained quiet, shook his head an emphatic, *not me.* Then chin-nodded in Irwin's direction.

Irwin, no longer pretending to be in control, threw his hands in the air, giving up. Without uttering a single word, he leaned back in his seat and rolled the window only partially closed, leaving it down a slight crack, but enough to still hear. When done, he folded his hands on his lap and stared straight ahead, crestfallen.

"Good. Glad we're all in agreement," mumbled Harper between choked sniffles. "Now, if you would excuse me."

Irwin watched through the side view window as she lifted the carrier and pushed it gently across to the far end of the van's long seat, directly behind the driver's side. After buckling it in, Harper fixed the baby blanket over it one last time. Teary-eyed and spent, she fell back and blew out a long, winded breath.

"Okay then," Darren rubbed his palms together. "I'm going across the street. I need a ridiculously strong extra-large cup of coffee. Anybody else want anything?"

"I could use a honey-glazed donut and an apple juice." Christopher reached into his back pocket for his wallet, but Darren waved it away.

"Irwin?" Darren asked through the open van door.

Irwin checked his watch, frowning, and shook his head no. *Over eight minutes late.* "Nothing for me, thank you."

Darren softened his voice. "Baby girl?"

"I'm good, Dad, but Mom's going to want a large tea, light, extra sugar—and a cruller."

"Good idea." Just as Darren made the mad dash across the main street, Olivia, carrying her duffel and pocketbook, used her knee to shove open the bookshop door.

"I'm coming, I'm coming." Olivia lowered her bag onto the scorching cement sidewalk, turned, and locked the store's door behind her. "Where'd your father go?" she asked Harper after leaving her duffel behind the van.

"Making a donut run."

"Oh, darn it—" Olivia pouted, climbing into the seat

behind Harper. "I wish I woulda known. I'd have told him to get me something."

"He is," said Harper.

"Thank the Lord." After more huffing and puffing, Olivia finally settled in her seat. "For the love of all that is good and pure, Christopher, AC—Now!"

"On it." Christopher cranked up the van's air conditioner to the highest it would go, much to Irwin's discomfort.

Moments later, Darren, hands full, reappeared carrying drinks and an entire bag of donuts. Harper jumped out of the van to slide the door open for him.

"Thanks, kiddo," he said, handing off the bags to Olivia while climbing into the backseat next to his wife.

"*Man*, this AC feels great." He handed Olivia her tea, then reached into the paper bag for her donut. "They're still warm."

"You're a lifesaver." Olivia swigged a long mouthful of tea. "*Yum-o.* Thank you," she moaned revived, letting out a small, satisfied groan with each bite. "This is exactly what the doctor ordered."

"Here." Darren took his, then handed his daughter, now back in her seat, the rest. "Pass this upfront."

Harper handed off Christopher's juice and donut to Irwin.

"Thanks. Thanks, Darren." Christopher jammed his straw into his juice container. "Everyone buckled up back there?"

"We're good here," shouted Olivia, busy attacking her donut.

"Ditto," replied Harper, her earbuds already in place.

Irwin yanked the seatbelt strap taut across his chest. He reached down for his map book and the directions. "For the bulk of this first part of this trip, it's fairly straightforward. We'll need to get on Interstate I-80 West and take that straight for three hundred and ten miles."

Christopher nodded. He glanced over his shoulder, ready

to pull out when he realized the cars ahead of him parked too close. To make the sharp left to pull away from the curb, he had to first backup. Christopher started to back up when a loud CRUNCH startled everyone.

"What the hell was that!" yelled Christopher, slamming his foot down on the break. Irwin lurched forward, as did Harper, Olivia, and Darren.

"Whoa, what the heck did we hit?" shouted Darren, his tee shirt now sloshed with hot coffee.

Christopher threw the van into park and rushed out to see, with Harper and Darren right behind him. Olivia, her hands full, stayed inside, chewing. Meanwhile, Irwin, jaw clenched, unbuckled his seatbelt, muttering something incoherent under his breath.

"Oh no," muttered Darren. "She's going to kill us."

"Not us, cowboy—you," said Harper. "I hope nothing broke inside." She bent over and unzipped the duffel bag covered with tire tread marks on the outside. Harper lifted a flat broken blow dryer in the air, then handed it to her father. "This looks like the only casualty so far. She sniffed the bag. "No perfume or soaps seemed to have broken."

"That's because your Mother packed most of her crap in my bag," complained Darren, wiping the nervous panic off his brow. "*Man*—I can't believe I forgot to put this in the truck, but I honestly didn't see it."

"Apparently, Captain Obvious." Irwin tossed the smallest broken dryer bits into the nearby trash can. "However, time is ticking, and we are already running late. Christopher? If you wouldn't mind?"

Darren ran both hands through his damp hair. "Wait until Olivia sees this."

Harper flinched at the steps approaching. "*Uh-oh*." Harper attempted to close the bag fast, but the zipper wouldn't catch.

"When I see what?" Olivia shoved her way between Darren and Irwin, her expression mortified to find her bag open and flattened. "Oh no." She bent down and scooped it possessively into her arms. Turning her back to the group, she peeked inside and paled.

"*Phew.*"

"I'm sorry, Liv. It's all my fault," said Darren. "I didn't see it when I came back with the donuts. I totally forgot about your bag."

Red-faced Olivia moved a few items around, zipped the duffel closed. and then whirled back around. "It's fine. Really." She waved and shooed the group forward and away. "It's just a bag. Nothing's broken."

Harper dangled the flattened blow dryer in her mother's face.

"*Ah-huh.* I see." Olivia shrugged it off as if it meant nothing. "Well, almost nothing. I can always buy a new one of those." She tossed the dryer, what was left of it, into the trash can. "Easy come, easy go," she shriek-caroled, her face contorting in the weirdest smile. "Okay, everybody, shows over. Let's get a move on."

"I can run upstairs and get that other bag if you want," offered Darren. "It would only take a few minutes to repack everything."

"No. This is fine." Olivia gritted her teeth into the biggest fake smile. "Let's go."

"Want me to put your bag in the cargo holder?" asked Christopher.

"No, damn it, I do not," Olivia screeched, losing it. She vaulted backward at the same time, still hugging her duffel bag protectively against her sweaty bosom. She stopped and exhaled. "Gosh, I'm sorry, Christopher. I-I didn't mean to yell at you like that." She stumbled back a step or two, raising a shaking hand high between herself and everyone else. "Maybe I'll, um, keep this under my seat for now?"

"Sure, Liv. Whatever you wanna do," said Darren, "but I...*err, um...*"

"What?" she glared at her hemming, hawing husband. "Spit it out already."

"I think your bag's leaking."

"What!" Olivia's eyes widened in sheer terror. She flipped the duffel over, and there on the bottom was the biggest, stickiest wet stain. "Oh." Her eyes darted from face to face. "Would you look at that. I, *err,* must have left a tube of hand cream in there," she stammered, pressing the damp spot against her shirt. "No big deal. I didn't like that hand cream anyway. Who needs to walk around smelling like a morning's orchid?" She sorta meant to chuckle, but her chuckle came out sounding more like an unhinged cackle. "Time to all get back in the van. Spit spot. Time to go."

"Spit spot?" Harper jerked her head back. "Great. Now we have Mom channeling Mary Poppins."

"At least let me get you some paper towels to clean it up so it doesn't get all over your clothes," offered Darren, clambering closer.

"I said it was NO-BIG-DEAL!" thundered Olivia, her initial shock transforming into unleashed fury in an instant.

The stunned group stood with their arms dangling from their sides, staring at Olivia, transfixed and speechless.

The morning was turning out much as Irwin expected it would.

"I need air conditioning," grumbled Olivia, on the move.

Irwin side-stepped just in time to give the seething Olivia enough room to pass.

"Well? Olivia tucked a wayward strand of damp hair behind her ear. "Don't just stand there, let's go," she yelled, clenching her duffel, panting.

The chastised group did as commanded, filing quietly back into the van.

Christopher, ahead of everyone else, slid into the driver's seat. He turned his keys and cranked the AC to full blast. Meanwhile, Irwin, not sure what had just happened, returned to his place, eyebrows furrowed in deep deliberation. A stunned looking Darren reclaimed his spot in the far back of the van by the window, while Olivia, sitting next to him, planted her sticky-bottom bag with black tread marks diagonally over the top securely between her feet.

Harper climbed in last, sliding the van door firmly closed. Nothing but the sounds of the engine rumbling and the AC blasting filled the uncomfortable airspace between family and friends. Once buckled in, she leaned over to the infant carrier, peeled the blanket back ever-so-slightly by its corner, and whispered, "Well, I hope you're enjoying yourself."

CHAPTER 12

SEVEN HOURS and one fill-up later.

"Turn, turn, *TURN*," shrieked Harper, practically springing out of her seat. "——Not that way!"

Still buckled in, she pressed her body frontward, pulling against the restraint but it barely budged. "Slow down! Give me a second to get the directions." Body swaying and head bouncing, Harper managed somehow to glide her fingers across the small cell screen, tapping and swiping at an impressive speed.

"We need to stay straight," said Irwin. "The map says nothing about 'turn, turn, TURN.' By my guestimate, we have at least two more miles to go before we turn anywhere."

"Except that staying straight will take us almost four miles out of our way," Harper snapped back, displaying her phone's GPS page as proof. "What sense does that make?"

"Four miles. Absurd," Irwin countered. "We're almost there."

The van hit a pit and sent everyone bouncing.

"*Argh*, Chris—do we need to hit every bump known to humankind?" Harper yelped through gritted teeth."

"Sorry. Pothole city here." Christopher gripped the steering wheel harder. "Plus, this van's got poor suspension to boot. On the next fill-up, we'll need to check the tires. Sometimes a bumpy ride indicates poor tire alignment or incorrect air pressure."

"Fascinating." Irwin twisted around in his seat. "And why the sudden rush?" he asked Harper. "Aren't you the one who demanded we take the scenic route? 'Behold the sites, Irwin.' 'Grasp nature in all its breathtaking beauty, Irwin.'"

"I'm rushed, Irwin, because my bladder's ready to explode like Mount St. Helens," she snapped, slamming her back hard against the seat in protest.

"Too much information," Irwin turned forward, covering his ears.

"You asked." Harper squeezed her thighs tight, pressing her palms against her lap while one leg pumped up and down. "Seriously. I think I'm leaking."

Irwin traced their intended route with his bouncing finger. "Christopher, please disregard the ill-informed, uncouth blatherings ruminating from your one and only, and continue straight ahead until we reach," he glanced back down at the map to make sure. "Ranger Avenue."

"Ranger Avenue it is," repeated Christopher.

"Hold up," Harper shouted, her eyes glued to her screen. "What street did Irwin just say?"

"I didn't. I said avenue. We turn at Ranger Avenue."

"Really now." Harper snickered. "Because by my accurate directions, there is no Ranger Avenue."

"There most certainly is and I'm looking right at it," Irwin twisted around and shoved his map under Harper's nose. "Right here!" he said. "In black and white."

"Guys—" Christopher yelled, attempting to interrupt the fray. "Hey, stop it a minute and look—"

Harper and Irwin, their voices raised, didn't hear Christopher, so Christopher raised his voice another two volumes.

"I really need you two to stop arguing and look at this—"

Harper leaned in, flat out ignoring Christopher. She glanced down at Irwin's map, then back at her phone. "Nope. No Ranger Avenue listed. No Ranger Avenue, no Ranger Street, and no Ranger Drive. It. Does. Not. Exist."

"*Uhh*, guys," Christopher interrupted louder. "I really need you to—"

"It's right here!" Irwin plucked the paper. "Keep going straight."

"I don't care what that thing says," shouted Harper, head shaking. "There's NO Ranger, anything!"

Christopher slammed his foot on the brake, sending everyone inside lurching forward.

"Holy cow—what in the hell?" screeched Harper as she pitched forward, her one hand extended protectively over the strapped-in urn.

"What just happened?" yelled Darren seated in the back, his arms wrapped tightly around a sleepy but stunned-awake Olivia.

Christopher, in an unbridled fit of frustration, slapped his palms against the steering wheel. "Look for yourselves!" he said, pointing furiously at the playground located directly in front, overrun with small, young children playing, baby-filled strollers decked out in all the latest parenting gadgets, and harried, anxious parents traipsing in every direction after their unruly spawn.

The fairly large metal sign bolted onto the chain-link

fence ahead of them read, 'Welcome to Ranger Park—Where Children Are Free to Roam on the Range.'

"There's your ranger," mumbled Harper.

Irwin slunk lower in his seat, the sting of humiliation scorching his sallow cheeks. "Oh," he mumbled with hooded eyes cast down in the direction of his map book.

Harper unbuckled her seatbelt and shimmied forward. "Irr-win?" she said, tugging his sleeve. "Hand me your map book, just for a minute," she asked sweetly.

Irwin fingered the coil-bound spiral spine of the book.

"Irwin?" Harper wriggled her fingers. "Come on. Just hand it over."

Everyone waited and watched while Irwin, not yet ready to acquiesce, shifted around in his seat as if weighing his options.

"Seriously," said Harper. "I'm not trying to harass or embarrass you. Just let me see the map." She wriggled her fingers again, coaxing him to give it up.

Irwin exhaled. He closed the book and handed it over his shoulder to Harper.

"Thank you." Harper glanced first at the cover, then read the inside front page. Within seconds, she began to giggle. "I'm sorry. I don't mean to rub it in, but seriously?"

"What now?" Christopher, his face taut with stress turned around, his expression a muddled cross between aggravation and puzzlement.

"This is great." Harper handed Christopher the opened book to see for himself. She pointed to the book's date of publication.

Christopher glanced down and glared at Irwin. "*Gah*, you are something else."

Darren unbuckled his seatbelt. "Let me see." he demanded, stretching over the seat ahead of him.

"Nineteen eighty-five." Christopher glared at Irwin.

"You've been giving me directions based on a map book created over three decades ago."

"Affirmative," chuckled Harper, having a wee bit too much fun at Irwin's awkward expense.

Irwin continued to stare out the window twiddling his thumbs, apparently not ready to engage.

Christopher couldn't stop shaking his head. "I can't believe this." He handed the book back to Harper

Harper shimmied closer to Irwin. "Just out of curiosity," she said in a low conspiratorial whisper, the opened book raised high in the air. "—you do realize this so-called dependable map book you are so fond of still shows Russia as being part of the Soviet Union?"

"Fine," admitted Irwin over the groups loud, incredulous groan. "I can admit it the maps might be a little outdated."

"Just a tad." Harper squelched a giggle.

"But I would also like to point out that up to this point, it has gotten us this far without a single glitch," countered a flustered Irwin, not ready to fully concede to his blunder.

"That's only because we had one highway to take until the Ranger Avenue escapade," reasoned Christopher. "And not for nothin, Irwin, but our almost driving straight into a playground filled with children could be considered by most civilized people as something more than a 'single glitch.'"

"Harper handed Irwin back his book. "I have to ask, how long have you had this thing?"

Irwin's chest rose, then sunk. "A few days."

"You bought an outdated map book?" Harper asked.

"No. I saved it."

"Saved it?" said Olivia, joining the cross-examination late. "What do you mean you saved it? Saved it from what?"

Irwin glowered. "If you all must know, I found it in the library's donation bin."

Christopher's head dropped and he began banging his forehead against the steering wheel.

Harper screeched.

"Priceless," said Olivia, fanning herself.

Darren leaned back in his seat. He crossed his arms looking perfectly content to watch this drama playout from a safe distance. "For what's it's worth, at least it's not me this time," he added.

At this, Irwin slapped his thighs, ready to face the music. "They were going to toss it—a perfectly good book. What would you have had me do?"

"One, not rescue it, and two, not use it on this trip." Harper jiggled her phone. "I motion from this point moving forward, I'm in charge of directions."

"I second," mumbled Darren. "Liv?"

"I'm good with that."

"Christopher?"

"Yeah, sure." Christopher glared at Irwin. "Whatever."

"I concede to that decision," said Irwin, "However, I should probably warn you, I, like Bones, suffer from acute motion sickness, exacerbated when seated in the back of any vehicle."

"Fine," agreed Harper, crossing her arms defiantly across her chest. "Stay in the front."

"Fine," repeated Irwin, jamming his obsolete map book into the van's side door pocket.

Christopher waited for everyone to settle down. Then he started the engine and slowly backed the van away from the playground.

"I'm going to need you to make a U-turn at the end of this road and then a sharp left," said Harper, leg still bouncing. "That will bring us back to the main road. And FYI, I wasn't kidding about needing to pee."

"Still too much information," grumbled Irwin, sulking.

Olivia, her eyes squeezed shut, steepled her hands in earnest prayer. "God, I know you're busy, but if you're seeing this disaster unfold, and have even a single, unused nanosecond to spare from protecting the world from flash floods, global poverty, famine, war, plague and protests, please do whatever you can to save us from ourselves. As always, much appreciated."

"Amen," chorused everyone—Irwin included.

A FEW MINUTES LATER, Christopher turned onto Mildred's block.

"We're here, ladies and gentlemen. Welcome to Columbus, Ohio. Local time, 6:36 pm. The temperature is currently eighty-eight degrees. For your safety and comfort, please remain seated with your seatbelts fastened until I turn off the engine sign." Christopher turned his key. "At this time, you may use your cellular phones or antiquated maps. Please check around your seat for any personal belongings you may have brought on board with you, including wrappers, urns, or other paraphernalia. Lastly, please use caution when opening the door to disembark, as many of you are not all that coordinated."

"He's talking about you," Olivia teased Darren, who in response, laughed and nibbled her neck.

"If you should require further devanning assistance, please remain in your seat until all other passengers have devanned. One of our crew members, *specifically me*, will then be pleased to assist you."

Olivia laughed.

"On behalf of Abernathy & Crane and the entire crew, *again me,* I'd like to thank you for joining us and look forward to seeing you onboard again soon."

"Like in the next five minutes," mumbled Irwin.

"I really, really need to use a bathroom," repeated Harper.

"I'm starving," said Darren.

"We should have stayed at the park," said Olivia. "They had nice benches. We could have had a picnic. I love picnics."

"I still need to pee," Harper whined, crossing and uncrossing her legs.

"And y'all have a nice day," concluded Christopher, popping two headache tablets, and swallowing them dry.

CHAPTER 13

THE DOORBELL BUZZED. Mildred rushed from the kitchen down the hall, practically stumbling into the counter on her way to grab a quick peek out the front door's side narrow window.

There, standing on her stoop, were the five people she had been waiting a long time to meet. Mildred did a quick headcount—three men and two women, as expected. And by Cornelia's all too accurate accounts, she assumed the oldest gentleman with his face pressed against the window, fogging up her glass and staring back at her to be the one and only, Irwin Abernathy.

With a gracious smile, Mildred peered through the window and mouthed 'one-sec' while ignoring the unsteady body tremors having a field day with her limbs. She first unlocked the front door, followed by a screen.

"Hello, hello," she exclaimed, sounding tons cheerier than she felt. "I'm so glad to finally meet you."

The entire group replied with the same enthused courtesy, except for Irwin, who stood fiddling with the envelope he intended to hand over. He lifted his arm, ready to shove the letter at Mildred when Olivia audibly gasped. In one giant leap for humankind, she dashed forward, wedging her entire body in the middle of them, while using her one free hand to yank Irwin's arm back down.

"So nice to meet you as well," said Olivia, pumping Mildred's hand with her one free arm like a politician on crack.

Harper, doing a little up and down jig, pursed her lips in evident embarrassment, while her father, his eyes locked onto the ground, inched away, leaving a wider berth between him and Irwin.

Mildred, no slouch herself in the weird people department, picked up on the odd exchange, although not entirely sure what to make of it. "Yes, well, me too," she grinned, again wondering what she had gotten herself into.

Mildred held the front door wide open. "Please, everyone, don't stand out there, baking." She moved to the side, giving everyone enough room to pass. "Come in where it's much cooler."

"You don't have to tell me twice," said Olivia, fanning herself. "Sorry we're late."

"Did you have a hard time finding the place?" asked Mildred, not to anyone in particular.

Irwin, with the social grace of a toddler weighted down with a full diaper, blurted out a resounding 'Yes!' but the group's louder, 'No, not at all' and 'The directions you gave were easy to follow' immediately drowned out his perfunctory gripe.

"I'm Mildred, by the way, but feel free to call me, Millie."

She reached out to shake everyone's hand, starting to her far left.

"I'm Christopher. Nice to meet you."

"Nice to meet you as well, Christopher."

"Hi. I'm Darren, and you've already met my wife, Olivia." Darren extended his hand for a shake, while Olivia gave a cutesy wave.

"Hi." Mildred smiled. She glanced toward the beautiful young woman who she assumed to be Harper, still doing a strange slight hop from foot-to-foot, but just as she went to say hello, her attention fell to Harper's hand, clutching what appeared to be a—?

"It's an infant carrier," droned Irwin, filling in the uncomfortable blanks. "And no, there's no baby. Only a —"

"Hi! So nice to meet you. I'm Harper, and this—" Harper chin-nodded toward the infant car seat, deftly interrupting Irwin in mid-sentence, "is a *super* long story which I would be more than happy to retell, but for the moment, I am in desperate need of your lavatory."

"Down this hall and to the left," Millie instructed Harper, already toddling on her way.

Millie folded her arms over her chest, then, feeling the ache from the stent, slid them down around her waist. "A baby carrier which contains no baby. I'm looking forward to hearing all about it," she replied, amused, and starting to understand why Cornelia always sounded so entertained by this group.

"Trust me, you really don't," said Irwin as if reading Millie's mind. "I'm—"

"Wait! Don't tell me. I think I know who you are." Millie recalled Cornelia mentioning Irwin's aversion to touch and kept her arms folded, offering him only a slight head bob of acknowledgment. "Glad to finally meet you, Irwin Abernathy."

I've heard so much about you." She noticed Irwin wince and wondered why.

Irwin offered Millie a feeble nod and a polite, "Nice to meet you as well, Mildred."

"Please," said Mildred, no longer overcome with angst and finding this bunch of strangers as charming as Cornelia had made them out to be. "Why don't you all follow me to the screened-in porch. I fixed us something to eat. I figured you must all be famished after your long ride."

Christopher, Darren, and Olivia murmured a collective yes and thank you and proceeded to follow Millie through to the porch.

Irwin, never happy to have his schedule slide into oblivion, hung back long enough to shoot Olivia a piercing glare, tapping his finger hard against his wrist.

Olivia scrunched up her nose and mouthed, 'Don't you even dare' back at him and marched away, apparently delighted to catch up with the group.

IRWIN CLOSED his eyes in defeat—"I should have known this wouldn't work," he grumbled.

Meow

Irwin popped one eye open and glanced down to find a tiny, gray-striped kitten resting near his leg, staring up at him.

"I'm Irwin," he said by way of formal introduction. "But perhaps I should forewarn you. I don't particularly get on well with your species."

The kitten cocked his head to the side as if in feline contemplation before baring two rows of tiny pearly white fangs.

Hiss

"Trust me, small creature. I don't wish to be here as much as you don't want me here," Irwin responded, unfazed.

The cat glowered for a second or two longer before skulking back toward the sofa, his small tail set high in the air—a response known in cat circles as an '*up yours, human*'.

"Good. Glad we were able to get that out of the way. Now, if you would excuse me, it's time I found the rest of my group." Irwin glanced left, then right, not entirely sure which direction to go, so he passed the bookshelf and headed through Mildred's kitchen in the hope it would lead him in the right direction.

The nice-sized room appeared spotless but inviting. Not a speck or a crumb to be found, much like the rest of Mildred's home. Everything in its designated place. Yet, surprisingly, while the house seemed organized to obsessive perfection, Irwin couldn't help but notice a sheet of paper, more of a form, haphazardly stuck on her refrigerator smack dab in the middle. It's unaligned, off-centeredness seemed out of place in such an orderly space.

Irwin took a quick glance over his shoulder before setting the paper straight. His initial intention had been to fix it, however, without exactly meaning to, his eyes rolled over the page, absorbing the disturbing information held within his fingertips.

"What are we doing now," taunted Harper from behind Irwin, causing him to jolt.

"I wish you wouldn't do that," he seethed, one hand cupping his pulsing throat, while his voice—no louder than an agitated whisper—let her have it. "One of these days, Harper Crane, you're going to be responsible for giving me a heart attack."

"Then perhaps, Irwin Abernathy, you should take whatever necessary measures to stop spying on people," she teased.

"I am doing no such thing," Irwin countered, his fingers fumbling with the refrigerator magnet.

Harper plucked the form out of his hand. "Oh, really?"

"Yes, well."

Harper, a super reader extraordinaire, read across the paper in record time. "Holy macaroni, Batman," she muttered. "She's got—"

"Lower your voice," Irwin admonished, waving his fingers in her face like a spastic spider. "I can read, too."

"What are we going to do?"

"Do?" Irwin's head juddered. "Do about what?"

"What do you mean—do about what? This, obviously." Harper plucked the paper again.

"Stop that," he hissed, peeking over Harper's shoulder. "There's nothing for us to do but mind our business. Are we capable of such a feat?"

"Millie may need our help."

"Then, she'll ask for it."

"Not necessarily."

Irwin sucked his teeth at Harper the same way she'd done to him a hundred times before. "We don't even know her."

"We know she's Cornelia's friend. Isn't that enough?"

"We know that *now*," he snapped, determined to nurse his bruised ego from Cornelia's growing list of subterfuge. "Listen, we should get out of here and join the others."

Harper, however, not one to let anything go that easy, disagreed. "She may not have anybody to ask."

"That, too, is none of our business."

"Oh?" Harper cocked her head. "Because I distinctly remember you making my problems your business."

"Not the same thing."

"And my mother's, and my father's—and, oh wait, and Christopher's."

"Again, an entirely different situation. Let's go."

"How?" Harper returned the form to the fridge.

The sound of loud laughter resonating from the porch startled the pair.

"I'm not going to have this conversation with you right now," seethed Irwin.

"Fine. Then we'll have later," Harper snapped a photo of Mildred's appointment form behind his back.

"Fine."

"Double Fine."

"There's no such thing," quipped Irwin.

"Let you tell it."

HARPER FOLLOWED Irwin into Millie's airy sunroom and over to the long wooden farm table covered with a crisp white linen tablecloth boasting an impressive spread. A large wicker basket lined with a checkered cloth napkin overflowed with savory smelling rolls, baguettes, croissants, and bagels had been placed in the middle of the table within everyone's reach. Next to it, a tray of sliced deli meats on one round serving tray, and various hard and soft cheeses filling the other. Millie had provided them three different types of salads—tossed, potato, and macaroni, alongside an ample side of coleslaw. A small plate containing a variety of pickles, olives, and an assortment of dilled sliced vegetables sat next to a mason jar filled with freshly squeezed homemade lemonade.

Harper squeezed past her father, taking the seat next to Christopher. Irwin, meanwhile, plunked his bony body down on a cushioned ladder chair, the only available chair at the far end, which coincidently or not, seated him directly across from Millie.

"Look who finally made it," said Olivia, her mouth twisted

in a mock —*what are you two up to now* accusatory smile of hers. "Nice of you two to join us. We were ready to send out a search party."

Harper chuckled. "Ah, still timing my potty visits, *huh* Ma?"

Although Olivia's mouth lifted into a pleasant enough smile, her mother-trained stare never left her daughter's face.

"While waiting for Harper, I had the opportunity to meet your kitten," said Irwin.

"*Ah*, you've met my new housemate, Horatio," cooed Mildred. "Such a cuddle bug. I found him under my front stoop a few weeks ago. Possibly abandoned. No idea, really, but he was such a tiny, terrified little thing. Starving for equal amounts of food and affection."

"He's got a fine set of fangs," muttered Irwin.

"Irwin also has a cat," explained Harper, speaking over him. She sipped her lemonade. "*Mmm,* yum."

"Incorrect," said Irwin. "The cat Harper is referring to belonged more to Cornelia, and now he's Harper's charge."

Mildred smiled. "This must be Bones you're talking about. Cornelia adored that cat. She always had some hilarious anecdote to share about him."

"Yes. Utterly hilarious. Unfortunately, Bones has been pining away for Cornelia ever since she—" Irwin hesitated. "and now he's latched onto Harper."

"We actually wanted to bring him along," explained Harper, reaching across the table for the breadbasket. "but the poor thing suffers from motion sickness.

"No, we didn't," corrected Irwin, shaking his head, looking at Mildred. "I know I certainly didn't."

"Ignore him," said Harper, scrunching her nose at Irwin. "Anyway, Bones is with a friend of ours. She's watching him until we return. I just hope he's behaving himself. He can be a real handful sometimes." Harper plucked a still-warm roll from the basket, and took a long, steady whiff, swooning. "*Mmm*, this bread smell sinfully delicious."

"They taste even better than they smell," replied Mildred, taking one for herself and passing the basket. "We have a lovely bakery right around the corner, right across from the new playground. Both opened up sometime last year." Mildred tore the tiniest piece, no bigger than a postage stamp, and popped it gingerly in her mouth.

"Yes, we passed the playground on our way here." Harper winked at Irwin. "Dad, could you pass the butter, please?"

Darren handed off the small etched glass bowl.

"Thanks." Harper dug her butter knife into the dish. "Millie, your home is beyond beautiful—and your garden, truly gorgeous. I can't imagine how much work you must do to maintain it all. Is this something you do all by yourself, or do you have help?"

Irwin, his fork midway to his lips, halted, cutting his eyes at Harper.

Harper, a frequent recipient of Irwin's disapproval, knew not to make any prolonged eye contact with him. Instead, she kept her focus solely on Millie, ignoring the glower busy drilling an invisible hole in her perfectly shaped skull.

"I agree. This spread is incredible," exclaimed Olivia, lightly kicking Irwin in the shin from beneath the table.

Harper saw Millie's eyes dart between Irwin and Olivia, and then back to her as if catching something in their exchange.

"I, *uhm*, do it all myself. I'm retired now and pretty much a homebody," said Mildred. "To be honest, although not a large home, the upkeep has become a bit more than I bargained for. Still, I enjoy getting outside in the garden." She handed Olivia a bowl. "Here. Try the salad. All the vegetables came from my backyard, except, of course, the olives." She passed the tray. "Cornelia once mentioned to me that you were all partial to her Baked Ziti, a recipe I actually gave her many moons ago," Mildred, explained, "but I figured with this oppressive heat and your traveling, a meal that heavy wouldn't exactly be the wisest choice. I decided on lighter fare. I hope you don't mind."

"Are you kidding? No way. Everything is beyond perfection," said Harper, rearranging her napkin across her lap. "Thank you for going to so much trouble. I just hope we haven't put you out."

"Not at all." Mildred looked more relaxed. "I'm only sorry we had to meet under such—difficult circumstances."

Within an instant, everyone's polite smiles faded.

"But enough of that," said Mildred, breaking the awkward silence. She lifted the bowl of potato salad, dug a serving spoon in, and handed it off to Darren. "Please, don't be shy. Eat up and enjoy."

"You don't have to tell me twice," said Darren, already filling his plate.

CHAPTER 14

FOR THE NEXT FEW HOURS, Irwin listened while the group exchanged information about themselves, shared tidbits about their trip, including a bunch about the missing star of the show.

He studied Mildred, seemingly unable to help herself, laughing without abandon at the sidesplitting and often hilarious stories everyone joyfully shared about Cornelia. He noticed how frequently she used her napkin to dab away tears, which Irwin sincerely hoped were of the happy variety.

"Why doesn't any of this surprise me?" Mildred finally said between fits of giggles, trying not to laugh again. "That sounds so much like the Cornelia I knew."

"That's nothing." Darren reached for another roll. "Matter-of-fact, once while visiting in her the hospital, Cornelia decided she wanted to watch some movie in the lounge area—I think a murder mystery." Darren sat hunched over in full story mode. "You gotta picture this, Millie. The room we're in is big, right? And they got it playing on one of those gigantic screens, the same kind we had back in the day at school but only much bigger." Darren spread his arms wide for emphasis.

"Darren," Olivia coaxed sweetly.

"Right. Sorry. I tend to go off on tangents sometimes," Darren conceded.

"Sometimes?" Irwin snorted.

"Moving on. So, when we got there, the place was already packed with patients and staff, but somehow, we managed to find two empty seats smack dab in the middle. I, of course, didn't care, but Cornelia wasn't happy. She preferred being closer to the front and—"

"Darren... —Honey?" Olivia coaxed.

"Right." Darren flushed and shrugged. "Sorry again. Anyway, everybody gets seated, they dimmed the lights and started the movie. Everything's going fine until we get to the part when the main character— a lady—some realtor or something, I can't remember exactly now, but she's inside this old house getting it on with the bad guy pretending to be a client, but she doesn't know he's the killer. And, of course, she's doing her, you know," Darren glances around at the blank faces. "—the moaning and screaming thing."

"Thank you, Darren," interrupted Irwin. "That's quite enough."

"But I'm not done yet," replied Darren, shooting Irwin a confused stare. "Where was I? Oh, right, the woman's getting her thing off, and of course, all her screaming and moaning triggers one of the patients who yells out, clear as day, "What's happening to her? I don't understand what's happening!"

Mildred, balanced at the edge of her seat, pressed her napkin against her lips. "Then what?"

"Well, that's when Cornelia decides to stand up and shout for everyone to hear, "She's getting her rocks off, you dunce! Now sit down and shut up."

"Oh, no," shrieks Mildred.

"Oh, yes, and then she turns to me and says clear as day, "The first time I had an orgasm I didn't know what was happening either. Scared the living shit out of me, and I couldn't wait to do it again."

"She did not!" snorted Mildred, consumed in fits of laughter.

"She sure did. Cross my heart. And, even though they had the room sorta dark, I could have sworn I saw the director in the corner, cringing."

"I love it," said Mildred, clapping her hands.

Irwin, having heard this embarrassing story before, lowered his eyes, keeping both hands busy nursing his lemonade, wishing he had been granted the power of Thor to give Darren a good, strong zap. Nothing lethal, but certainly enough to shut him up.

"My turn, and believe me, that's nothing," giggled Harper.

"I don't think Mildred wants to hear any more of this nonsense," interjected Irwin.

"No, I would, actually," said Mildred. "This is fabulous. Please continue, Harper."

"Sure thing." Harper shot Irwin a big toothy grin. "I don't think any of us can ever forget the time when Cornelia started answering the adult center's phones, using a thick Slovenian accent. 'Hel-lo. Mel-an-ia's Magical Massage Parlor. How may I assist you today?'

At the time, no one had a clue as to what Cornelia had been up to until a bunch of weird-looking guys started showing up at the front desk, demanding in hushed tones to speak to Melania, and *only* Melania. Melania, the real center's receptionist, told me how creeped out she'd been by the sudden deluge of men coming to her desk, asking to speak to her, and swearing they had an appointment!" Harper chuckled.

"Did this Melania person—the real one I mean—did she ever find out what they wanted?" asked Mildred, unconsciously rolling her napkin into a ball.

"She sure did, and when she did," giggled Harper, "You'll just have to trust me when I tell you, it *vasn't* pretty. Practically gave the old girl a coronary."

Mildred laughed. "This is hilarious."

"Sidesplitting," muttered Irwin.

"It really was," said Harper, sticking her tongue playfully out at Irwin.

"However, what Harper's not saying is how intensely the center didn't share in Cornelia's hilarity," added Christopher. "And demanded I draw up a written agreement for Cornelia to sign—as if that would've held any legal weight—making her promise to cease and desist or risk being asked to leave."

"And did Cornelia ever fess up to her delinquencies?" asked Mildred, undeniably overcome with affection for her long-lost nutty friend.

"*Meh*." Harper shrugged. "The place isn't that big, and Cornelia's stunts were already legendary, so it didn't take them long to track down the culprit and phone us."

"Phone, me," corrected Irwin, frowning.

"Then me," said Christopher, smirking.

"And of course, when Irwin confronted her, Cornelia acted as if she didn't remember a thing," said Harper. "She just kept pretending to be shocked and appalled by the director's allegations until we got back to her room. That's when she dropped the air-head act and tossed me one of her mystery books, winking. —*The Case of the Missing Masseuse*."

Harper paused and sighed. "Good times. Seriously good times."

Everyone basked in the levity until Irwin spoke.

"There's no denying Cornelia enjoyed nothing more than making light of her disease. Disconcertingly so, using humor to downplay her fear. Toward the end, right before all her memories had fully dissipated, we could see her frustration and resentment mounting. Almost as if in a sudden flip of a switch, she changed. —Dementia, Alzheimer's. Not all laughs, I'm afraid."

"How do you mean she changed, Irwin?" Mildred asked, looking critically somber now. "Besides being afraid, which I would think would be a normal response for anyone losing their memories and body functions."

"I agree," said Irwin. "However, Cornelia, who had been the world's loudest cheerleader for anyone trying their best, suddenly turned hypercritical, and it never took much to set her off. I had to regularly stop her from berating the other patients or verbally harassing the staff. One time I walked in on her accusing the cleaning crew of stealing her stuff," recalled Irwin, stone-faced. "Now, bear in mind, Cornelia couldn't help herself by then, and the staff understood, but still." Irwin lifted his cup for a sip. "I remember once hearing someone describe dementia as a 'ruthless mistress.' I can't say I disagree."

"Neither can I." Mildred nodded, her saddened eyes downcast.

"Millie?" Christopher asked. "I hope I'm not being too forward, but I'm curious. How did you and Cornelia meet? That is if you don't mind sharing."

Irwin thought Christopher's timing couldn't have been more perfect.

"Do you want the long or abridged version?" she asked.

"Any version you feel comfortable sharing," replied Harper, the group's resident empath.

Mildred nodded and began to tell her story, not bothering to spare the awkward details.

He'd seen the same reaction in Cornelia, making Irwin wonder if perhaps Mildred's breast cancer diagnosis had somehow provided her a modicum of freedom from the need to temper her feelings or disguise her truths in order to make other people feel less uncomfortable.

"I had been attending school at Ohio State at the time," said Mildred. "My Dad's Alma-Ata; full-time student majoring in English—in my last year. What a time to be alive; 1969. I was twenty-one years old and full of myself. You couldn't tell me anything." Mildred grinned. "The anti-Vietnam War movement had swept across our nation with a vengeance—my university included. We held massive protests and sit-ins all over campus. You may have read about how we occupied one of the halls to protest the war? I had been one of the demonstrators. A total crazy scene, magnified when the police ordered us out. They said we had five minutes to vacate the premises, or they'd arrest us all, so we left." Mildred lifted her glass, taking measured small sips of her lemonade.

"But the protests didn't stop and only intensified. By late April 1970, people were not only arrested but getting seriously hurt, and shot. We were not only protesting the war, but also the university's rejection of a list of demands we had given to them demanding to add Black and women studies to the university's courses. Can you imagine over five thousand students chanting and picketing? A dangerous scene and ripe for disaster."

Irwin's jaw tightened.

Mildred must have noticed because all at once, she stopped talking, until Harper, in all her youth and wisdom, prodded her gently on.

"And did it?" asked Harper. "Become a disaster?"

"It did indeed," said Mildred. "The campus and surrounding towns turned into a hotbed of unrest, and it didn't take long before everything became chaotic. That's when the National Guard showed up, marching towards us decked out in riot gear. I remember standing near to a few kids pelting them with small rocks or pebbles, calling them names, and they, in turn, responded by launching tear-gas grenades at us. Complete and utter mayhem."

"*Jeez*," murmured Darren.

"For sure. Anyway, I saw things were spiraling down fast, so I tried to make a run for it. By that point, people were everywhere, but I knew with the way things were escalating, that I needed to find someplace safe to wait it out. I couldn't afford to get kicked out of school. My parents, especially my dad, would have killed me."

"Because he went to the same school?" asked Christopher.

Mildred nodded. "That, and the fact he had served in World War II as a plane mechanic. Our politics had clashed on more than one occasion, but my joining the Vietnam War protests really soured my father toward me. Getting kicked out of college a year before I graduated would have permanently sealed the deal."

As Mildred spoke, Irwin felt his own tangled-up, embittered memories from that time assaulting him from the inside-out.

"I ran, in what direction, I honestly to this day couldn't tell you, but I'll never forget the way my heart pounded in my throat, making me afraid and unsure of what to do next. The mind plays tricks. I thought I had run far, but even at a distance, I still heard people chanting— 'Pigs Off-Campus' and 'Pigs Go Home.' But I kept running, never once daring to stop or turn around—not with the National Guards all suited up for action." Mildred paused. "I recall turning a corner around a brick building. I think it may have been the science center at the time. I don't know, I just remember needing a minute to catch my breath, but soon enough realized I had company."

Olivia gasped and clutched Darren's hand, squeezing it hard. "Oh, no."

"Two men were already there. The stench radiating from their unwashed, alcohol-infused bodies told me they were two sheets to the wind. I later found out—people talk—that one had served in Vietnam, and I assume now, in that alley to self-medicate. The other — a friend or cousin, I don't know, something.

Anyway, the cousin, that's how I refer to him, approached me from the front, while the other one loomed from the back. I tried to move away, but the one from behind shoved me forward, knocking me off-balance so hard I tripped and fell against the side of the brick building. I remember being winded and gasping for breath."

While trying to catch my breath, I heard the cousin slur, 'Look at what we got here—a real live, gen-u-ine protestor.' God, his breath smelled stale. Then he said, 'Get a load of this,' and he pointed to my armband. At first, I didn't know what he meant," explained Mildred. "But then it hit me: In all the noise and confusion, I'd forgotten to take off my red armband. The one that said, 'Bring all the GIs home now!' stamped in big, bold black letters. That must have infuriated him because then he said, 'Well, ain't that somethin'?'"

"I don't want any trouble," I told them. That's when the one standing behind me, who had a hand on his zipper, said, 'Oh, sweet thing, it's a bit too late for all that.'"

"Oh, my Lord," murmured Olivia.

"I begged them to leave me alone, but the guy behind me shoved me hard, this time sending me face-first, smack against the same brick building." Mildred paused. "You know, it's funny what one remembers." She shook her head. "For example, besides the stench, I remember how this guy had the grungiest hands I'd ever seen. I mean, nails caked with dirt and grime."

"Living rough," said Darren.

"Quite true," agreed Mildred. "Soldiers returning from the war, many with serious physical and emotional issues, had been given a rough time in this country. Not welcoming or supportive at all."

"Then what happened?" asked Harper, the taskmaster.

Mildred winced. "That's when he reached out and started to fumble with my jeans, trying to tug them down. I screamed my head off for help, but with everything else going on around us, nobody could hear me."

"This is horrible," muttered Olivia, her fingers gripping Darren's arm. "You must have been so frightened."

"Absolutely terrified." Mildred lifted her eyes to the sky, the tiniest of smiles tugging at her lips. "But then, like something straight out of a movie—the cavalry arrived."

"The military came?" asked Darren.

"No, something even scarier," laughed Mildred. "A small woman, not taller than five-two, marched around the corner roaring and looking madder than a hornet, brandishing a closed umbrella like a sword."

"Cornelia?" shouted Harper, balanced precariously at the edge of her chair.

"You bet," smiled Mildred. 'Get off her,' Cornelia had yelled at them, stomping over."

That's our Cornelia," said Darren. "Fearless."

"Insane is more like it," muttered Irwin.

"You bet," said Mildred, "but fearless or insane—something in Cornelia's expression made those two drunks stop dead in their tracks, especially when she smashed a glass bottle with her umbrella handle and grabbed the broken, jagged neck in her other hand. 'I'll slice and dice the next fool who dares lay a finger on her again,' she yelled at them.

"Hot diggity damn," shouted Darren, slapping his knee. "Firecracker."

"Now granted, they were drunk, but the distraction was enough for me to get away, and I booked toward Cornelia, running with everything I had and scared out of my wits."

"What did Cornelia do next?" asked Harper enthralled.

"She continued to threaten them like a woman possessed. They stared at her more confused than scared, but it worked."

"You got away!" shouted Olivia, clutching her heart and fanning her flushed face with her open hand, puffing.

"We sure enough did." Mildred shrugged. "But, to be honest, they were probably too plastered and stunned to go after us."

"Man—what a story! And to think, Cornelia told me she hadn't been a war protestor," said Harper.

"Oh, but at the time, she wasn't," corrected Mildred. "On the contrary. Cornelia had been married to a soldier serving in Vietnam when that happened."

"Then why was she there?" asked Olivia.

"To apply for classes. Cornelia wanted to finish her degree in case..." Mildred hesitated, "—in case her husband didn't return home. Cornelia later confided that the war never made any sense to her, but at the time, she didn't feel comfortable as a soldier's wife joining the protests. She just wanted her husband home in one piece, safe and sound."

"Did her husband make it back?" asked Darren.

"Yes and no. He returned home less than a year later, physically intact, but psychologically," Mildred shook her head, staring down at her hands. "Suffice to say he suffered from a severe case of post-traumatic stress disorder, or what the military then referred to as shell shock or combat fatigue."

"Even so, Cornelia must have been relieved to have him home," said Harper.

"Yes. Without a doubt, but you have to understand Harper, back then, soldiers who carried the war home with them didn't always find the kind of help they needed at their disposal."

Irwin shifted in his seat, not sure how much more of this conversation he could take.

"A lot like today," muttered Harper sharply.

"No. Much worse, if you can imagine. Much, much worse." Mildred sighed. "Long story short, despite Cornelia's love and devotion—because I have to tell you, she truly did love that man—but when he came home, he was a total mess. He needed way more help than she could provide. Between his anxiety attacks, the heightened startle reflex, the severe and sudden mood swings, and long bouts of insomnia," Mildred shrugged, "...it didn't take Cornelia long to realize how damaged and dangerous he'd become. Then one day, I'd say about six or seven months after he returned home, he snapped. Totally lost it. And he scared Cornelia enough to make her pack and leave him for good."

"So, they lived apart?" asked Harper.

"Yes. A mutual decision. I hated to see Cornelia go and move so far away, but I understood, and in hindsight, it had been the best decision. Pennsylvania became her home. She felt safe and loved there." Mildred glanced at Irwin.

"Did her husband stay in Ohio?" asked Harper.

"In the beginning, but within the year he left for Michigan. I believe Cornelia once mentioned him having family out there. I'm not sure how long he stayed, but eventually, he retired. Last I heard, he settled down in Amarillo,

Texas. Found work with one of the agriculture plants down there." Mildred glanced toward Irwin, again.

Irwin's head pounded. When he looked up, he saw Mildred's eyes locked onto him.

"Wait," interrupted Harper, blinking. "Are you saying Cornelia's husband is still alive?"

"Very much so," confirmed Mildred, her hands clasped together.

Irwin grimaced, pinching the sagging skin at his throat.

"Okay...," said Harper. "Wow. This sure is news to me."

"To all of us," muttered Irwin.

"I still don't understand—" pushed Harper, her brows narrowed in confusion.

Mildred's shoulders slumped. She placed her napkin gingerly on her plate and leaned back in her chair. "I should apologize. I thought you all knew."

"Knew what?" asked Irwin, gripping the edge of the table, looking like a condemned man bracing for the next heat-seeking missile to target his heart again.

"Martin Newman—" Mildred gazed around the table at the dumbfounded faces staring back at her. She swallowed hard before speaking. "The man next on your itinerary to give a letter to?" She paused, her face inflamed. "He's Cornelia's husband."

"*What?*" screeched Olivia, choking on her lemonade mid-gulp.

"You mean ex-husband, right?" Darren shot his gaze ping-ponging around the table in search of confirmation.

"Oh no," corrected Mildred with a soft head shake, her voice quieter and less animated. "Martin and Cornelia never got around to filing for a divorce."

All at once, five heads turned toward Mildred, pitched at the identical tilt in one shocked, synchronized motion.

"Well, I'll be," muttered Darren, blowing a hefty breath out his cheeks.

No one else spoke. Instead, a weighted heavy silence permeated the shared space.

In one swift move, Irwin snatched his mug of lemonade and chugged the remaining half-cup down in one long, angry guzzle. When done, he slammed the empty vessel onto the table.

"This just keeps getting better and better, doesn't it?"

It was late, and time to go. Everyone gathered in the hall by Mildred's front door to say their goodbyes.

"Thanks again for everything." Harper guided Mildred into a soft, gentle embrace. "Keep in touch, and don't be a stranger. We would love for you to come to Pennsylvania, and see the bookshop, hang out for a while."

Mildred squeezed Harper's upper arm. "Thank you. I would like that."

"This is for you, Mildred." Irwin handed her Cornelia's letter.

"Oh, sugar! I almost forgot!" Mildred turned and tugged open the hall drawer. She pulled out the stack of envelopes, undid the rubber band, and began handing them out. "Cornelia sent these to me for you as well."

After letters and final farewells were exchanged, the group filed back into the van, each clutching their respective envelopes.

Christopher started the engine and twisted the AC dial to full blast. "Next stop—Amarillo Texas—where we will meet the undead, never-divorced husband of one recently deceased Cornelia Parish. Buckle up, everyone." Christopher used the time it took for the van to cool down to peruse his letter.

"It's late. Nearly nine. Would you like us to stop or are you good with more driving tonight?" asked Irwin glumly.

"I'm fine," Christopher nodded. "A little caught off-guard by the news, but it's whatever. I would like to get in a few more hours of driving in before we call it a night, though. Make up for lost time."

Irwin nodded. "If you're up to it. Let me know when you need to call it quits and we'll pull over for the night."

Everyone else remained quiet, much too fixated on reading their letters by the light of their cell phones, except for Irwin, who tucked his sealed envelope into his folder.

Irwin stared out of the passenger side window, resentment and disappointment tussling back and forth in his mind, unable to come up with a good reason as to why Cornelia had kept him out of the loop. On the one hand, he couldn't imagine how hard, how exhausting it must have been to conceal this other part of her life the way she had. Having always to stay extra careful not to let anything slip or reveal too much. He shook his head at the irony.

Poor Cornelia—years spent guarding her secrets to the end, all while battling a disease ready to extinguish what memories she kept protected.

Irwin reflected on the thousands of conversations they'd shared over the years. He wracked his brain, eager to recall if he had ever remembered Cornelia deliberately acting evasive or dishonest, but against the backdrop of each memory, he drew another blank. Sure, there were times when he knew she hadn't wanted to talk about certain subjects, and Cornelia, never one to cower, said as much. And Irwin, wanting to be the good and loyal friend, never pushed.

Irwin's fingers twisted and recoiled as his frustration increased.

Pfft!

This wasn't some one-off, some innocuous gray area of a

supposed harmless untruth or a fabricated innocuous little lie crafted to keep the peace. Nor were these unfolding ambiguities a product of Cornelia's incessant need to protect him from his social defects and embarrassing lack of people skills. These weren't people who had evolved from some irrelevant, isolated event from years ago, or even a remote embarrassing incident Cornelia may not have wished to divulge.

No. These were, *are*, all people from an entire other lifetime.

—Cornelia's other life.

Real and current relationship, she had kept to herself—most of all, from me.

Irwin failed to fathom how his best friend had managed to divide one existence, while simultaneously living the other, without at least one side, me—not knowing a thing about the other.

Why did this hurt more?

—Furthermore, did Cornelia truly owe him or anyone else an explanation?

Did I have the right to expect one?

Irwin understood secrets and the necessity sometimes to take them to the grave. He also appreciated the unmistakable harm caused to the person forced to live and conceal them.

But an entire other life kept a secret?

Hard to fathom, and yet, here they were.

Irwin rubbed his eyes, exhausted. None of this made any sense, and with Cornelia now gone and unable to provide clarity, it probably never would.

We were friends. For years. We talked about everything, or at least I thought we did.

His mind drifted to Mildred, who, by all accounts, seemed more than kind enough. Her home had felt welcoming, and she certainly had treated their intrusion with nothing but consideration and grace, going out of her way to be friendly and thoughtful.

Why keep her a secret?

Irwin's thoughts drifted to Elle's photo again. *Her pretty smile...*

Perhaps this latest letter from Cornelia's would explain her reasons if, in fact, Cornelia had any. Nevertheless, unlike everyone else in the van, Irwin didn't feel close to ready or compelled enough to know what those reasons were, nor did he wish to make peace with its author, just yet.

No. For now, Irwin chose to wallow unimpeded in his annoyance, and bask in his offense.

Irwin heard papers rustling from behind his seat, most likely one of Cornelia's letters. He didn't need to turn around to know its reader required a moment of privacy.

He sighed and closed his eyes, clasping one gnarled hand inside the other.

Cornelia Parish—you got some serious 'splaining to do...

CHAPTER 15

Six and half long hours later, a weary Christopher turned off the freeway under Irwin's orders to 'pull into the—'*Look, there's a place we can stop at right off the highway*'—what could go wrong' —Bates Motel, located somewhere in St. Louis, Missouri.

In truth, the semi-dilapidated, two-floor, U-shaped, twenty-four-room unsightly edifice had the appallingly over-confident title of 'The Bentley'—a much too hoity-toity name for such a mind-blowing dump.

To the side of every room's door, each painted a red-blood curdling color, hung a dim yellow light that seemed to appeal to a wide variety of ravenous insects. Irwin shuddered, already feeling itchy.

Upon entering 'the office' Irwin found a scruffy-looking older man, three weeks past a good shave, and presumably the proprietor, hunched over behind a desk, either sleeping or reading—hard to tell.

The lobby, a space best described as a dull-lit fishbowl surrounded by bullet-proof glass, should have been Irwin's first of many red flags, but fatigue had won out, and here they all were.

"Are you sure this place hasn't been condemned," asked a heavy-lidded Harper, bravely leaning her forehead against her room door as she wriggled her key into the lock.

"If not, it should have been," said Christopher, displaying what Irwin thought of as a herculean effort as he gallantly swatted away mobs of aggressive moths, insatiable mosquitos, and possibly a few murder hornets—some almost the size of a hummingbird.

"For once, we are in full agreement." Irwin used the end of his shirttail to grip the doorknob as he, too, courageously battled with his lock. "On the bright side, our brief stay here should provide us lifetime immunity from all air-borne diseases, and quite possibly the bubonic plague." Irwin slapped a bug feasting on his neck. "Not sure about murdering hornets, though."

"I'm honestly petrified to go inside," groaned Harper. "*Gah!* This thing refuses to work. Are you sure I have the right key?" she grumbled, fiddling with the lock. "It's gotta be bad when nobody's bothered to update their passkey."

"Less talking, more opening," snapped Christopher, swatting a blood-thirsty mosquito who had foolishly landed on his forearm. "These bugs are eating me up alive out here."

Click.

"Finally," said Harper. "Okay, Chris. On the count of three, we run in and slam the door shut. Ready?"

"Ready as I'll ever be. Hold up." Christopher hovered his hand midair by the side of his neck and then— *slap.* "Got it."

Harper gripped the door handle, ready to push. "One,

two—screw this." Harper shoved the door open with her hip, and together the pair barreled inside, slamming it closed behind them.

Less than two seconds later, Irwin heard Harper roar, "GROSS."

Like a man stuck on a sinking ship, Irwin jiggled his key faster inside the lock. "Come on..." he muttered. However, if being eaten alive by ravenous insects hadn't been enough, out emerged an unsightly woman of indeterminate age, popping out of her room three doors down, wearing nothing but a questionable pair of black panties, a worn-out black bra that had seen better days —*and probably nights*—and a garter belt, unhooked at one thigh. She toddled over holding a glass, presumably filled with some kind of alcoholic beverage mixed with melting, once cubed ice.

"Hi there, honey," she slurred at Irwin, wobbling on the back of her heels.

Irwin watched as the woman's bony hand quaked, causing her drink to splash onto her ultra-long, chipped, red-painted toenails jutting out like rabid claws through open-toe shoes.

"Whoopsie-daisy," she burped.

Irwin recoiled just as the woman's faded blonde Dolly Parton knock-off wig started to slip precariously to one ide.

"Wanna party?" asked the doused silly woman, slurring all too loudly.

Harper's door cracked open a bit, then wider. "Friend of yours?" she asked Irwin, her inquiry bristling with sarcasm.

The woman's head spun toward Harper. "You wanna par-day, too?" she hiccuped, stumbling over her own foot when she attempted to flash Harper a toothless, flirty smile. "Opps, ' es-cuse-me."

"What's wrong now?" asked Christopher, peeking his head out. "Oh, no."

"Oh, no is right," replied the drunk woman, doddering on

one shoe. "I don't *fink* I ever did a foursome before," she slurred while slurping at her glass. "That'll cost ya extra."

"Good night," laughed Harper, yanking Christopher inside, slamming her door closed.

"For heaven's sake." Irwin twisted his body so as not to face the drunk Dolly directly. "Every single day. My life is like something out of *Laugh-In*." He jammed his key in the lock harder, beyond overjoyed when it finally decided to cooperate, popping open with a surprising *swoosh*.

Against his better judgment, Irwin rushed inside the dingy room, anxious to get away from doused Dolly, when all of a sudden, a rancid stench tore through his nostril cavity—a fetid type odor one would envision if say, the room had been chosen by a serial killer to store dead, mutilated bodies way past their prime.

Irwin shoved the door closed and flicked on the light.

As if the stench hadn't been bad enough.

Irwin took in his temporary abode, spotting random spots of chipped paint, a nice-sized hole in the bathroom door the shape of a fist, the hanging sullied curtains which had presumably, at one time, been white, perhaps at the turn of the century. Most disturbing, however, was the questionable comforter with the caked-on, off-white stains splattered across the top.

"I will never again complain about Harper's lack of tidiness," he grumbled loudly, too afraid to touch anything.

"I heard that," Harper shouted back through the motel's paper-thin walls.

Irwin stood frozen in place, glimpsing around the rest of the room and running a mental calculation as to when last he had a tetanus shot.

"I hate my life."

218

NEXT MORNING...

"My eyes sting, my head is pounding, and I think I may have slipped a disk in my neck from sleeping in a vertical position."

"And you're all bit up," said Harper, giving Irwin a probing gaze.

"Correct. My body, or what is left of it, is inundated with bug bites, no doubt courtesy of the chair I fell asleep in," groaned Irwin, leaning his wiry frame against the motel's handrail to get a better look below at the obscenely sozzled man struggling to unzip his pants while swaying in front of a sort of greenish, kidney-shaped swimming pool enclosed by a rusted metal fence—*conceivably Drunk Dolly's boyfriend.*

"Is he going to—?" Harper pointed.

"I believe he is."

Harper sucked her tongue, aggressively hacking gobs of phlegm into a tissue. "I can't be certain, but I'm pretty sure I swallowed a dynasty of live moths last night," she said, wiping drool from her lips.

Irwin cringed. "I'm sure your mother will be relieved to know you have fulfilled your protein requirements for the year."

"Hardy-ha-ha." Harper rested her head against Irwin's shoulder. "Did your bed have a coin-operated massage machine thingy, too?"

Irwin shrugged. "I have absolutely no idea. I refused to venture close enough to find out."

"Smart man."

Irwin rolled his sleeve to expose the constellation of bug bites riding up his arm. "Yes. Absolutely brilliant."

"*Oww*," muttered Harper, lifting her head to take a closer look at his arm. "That's gotta itch something fierce."

Irwin rolled his sleeve back down. "I shamefully admit to getting nipped in places I didn't even know existed."

Harper leaned into Irwin. "This trip is getting more complicated by the day."

"No argument from me." Irwin turned his head from left to right. "Have you noticed the parking lot?" he paused. "It's littered with cans, food wrappers—at least I hope they're food wrappers—and Lord knows what else, but barely another vehicle in sight. That should have been our first red flag."

Harper laughed. "Hey," she nudged his arm. "I want to apologize for the hard time I've been giving you recently. Being a smartass is my way of coping with loss. I hope you know I'm mostly messing with you, right?"

"You're fine, Harper. You're a self-confessed smartass, and I am an obsessive complainer." Irwin let out a wearied sigh. "It's more everything else," he said, feeling strained to the limits. "Everywhere I turn these days, I find myself confronted by yet another insurmountable hurdle. It also hasn't helped any how Cornelia set this whole nutty excursion of hers into motion—hoodwinking us all into discovering one shocking revelation after the next."

"You have a point." Harper fidgeted. "Maybe this trip wasn't such a good idea after all."

"Possibly, but what would have been the alternative?" Irwin stared straight ahead out of two puffy eyes, his interest no longer preoccupied with the inebriated pissing man below. He turned to face Harper. Clasping his veined hands together, he spoke no louder than in a strained, exhausted mutter. "I'm afraid I no longer know what is or isn't a good idea anymore. What I had once thought resembled a close friendship has turned out to be a relationship fraught with secrecy and omission, orchestrated by a woman whose life choices and motivations continue to confound me."

"What do you mean, confound you?" Harper tilted her head, scowling. "—This isn't and has never been about you."

Bewilderment spread across Irwin's face. "I beg to differ. Cornelia and I have been close friends for years. Decades. In fact, we were more like family."

Harper's chin lifted as she stared right through him, her gaze steady and penetrating. "And, as a result, you're now pissed-off to holy hell because she didn't confide in you about her old friends or the undead husband."

Irwin's eyebrows knitted together causing the crease in his forehead to widen. "Careful."

"Noted. However, can I at least assume, in your opinion, Cornelia not informing you has somehow nullified decades worth of friendship, laughter, and adventures? And whatever else you two shared?"

"I never said that."

"But you can't deny you were thinking it." Harper gave Irwin a curt nod. The two stood in silence, the tension building. "It doesn't, you know. Nullify anything."

"I. Trusted. Her." Those three words left a sour taste in his mouth.

"Then trust her now."

Irwin cackled. "Despite everything that has come to light?"

"No. Because of it. *Sheesh,* Irwin. Stop viewing people as one-dimensional, homogenized beings. They're not. We're not. We're complicated, and sometimes we make choices that don't always pan out." She elbowed him gently in the ribs. "Why am I the one having to explain this to you?" Harper released a theatrical, appalled snort. "Granted, Cornelia did keep a large portion of her past life a secret. —But big hairy deal. And, before you ask, I don't know why, and in the scheme of things, does it actually matter anymore?"

Irwin bowed his head, not saying anything, but still listening.

"Look, we may never know what motivated Cornelia to

do this, but if you can stop acting holier than thou for one hot minute, I think we can both agree, something about her past made it too hard for her to share—whatever the reasons." Harper shrugged. "Who knows, maybe after a long time all this stuff became too painful for her to face, or maybe too humiliating to reveal. Or maybe she was protecting somebody? I don't know." She sighed. "But whatever her reason, don't you think Cornelia, who has never once turned her back on you—despite your sterling disposition—should get a hall pass for privacy?"

Irwin, not about to let that one go, responded. "Privacy— I understand. Pain and humiliation—*jeez*, my middle name. But where does that leave trust?"

"In your ballcourt," Harper shot back. "But I think, even positioned from high up on your tainted horse, you can admit there are probably a whole lotta things from your past life you haven't been all that anxious to tell us about."

Bullseye.

Irwin flinched.

I hate it when she's right.

Irwin thought back to his grandmother and to the legacy of pain his youthful decisions had caused her. He remembered his old friend, Jimmy McFadden, and the countless other war-ravaged dead, whose bodies had been left in his care to sort out. They, too, had all once been whole human beings with a future ahead of them. People who had a soul, countless dreams, and aspirations—and yes, secrets as well, he had to admit.

Harper continued as if reading his thoughts. "We've all got secrets and reasons for not wanting to drag painful shit up, but before you go condemning Cornelia to 'worst duplicitous friend of the century,' why don't you at least allow her to show you now all she's been protecting? Open up that old cranky heart of yours and accept this trip for what it is—

warts and all. Don't get angry—but instead, treasure whatever's in her letters. You know, the ones she spent the cherished last few moments of her mental clarity working on."

Irwin's shoulders drooped.

"And, not for nothing, but you might want to give Cornelia's way a try. See how it goes. Of course, that will mean having to actively suspend all of your standard Irwin myopic knee-jerk reactions." Harper smiled. "In other words, my dearest, grumpiest man, you'll have to give Cornelia your absolute, uncompromising trust."

Irwin hated to admit it, but what Harper said made sense. He elbowed her gently back. "When did you become so smart?" he asked, feeling the weight of the world begin to lift.

"Back when a grumpy primordial librarian-guy wearing a stupid hunting cap decided to open up his cantankerous heart to welcome, accept, and adore me with every fiber of his being, instead of demanding I morph into some version of what everyone else thought I should be."

Touché.

Irwin half-smiled. "This adventure she has us on, it hasn't been exclusively about me."

"Nope. And for better or worse, *worse* being the operative word, I'm on this crazy Cornelia ride with you." Harper squeezed Irwin's arm and pecked him on the cheek. "You're not alone."

Just as Harper said this, her foot brushed against the baby carrier much too close to Irwin's leg. Harper attempted to shift forward, twisting her shoulder ever so slightly in an all-too-obvious attempt to block Irwin's sight of the urn.

Irwin glanced down at the ground, shook his head in defeat, and sighed.

"Okay," Harper mumbled sheepishly. "I probably should have stressed metaphorically not alone. Ashes don't count. Sorry."

"It doesn't matter."

The two stood in compatible silence until Harper blurted out, "This motel sucks."

"Yes." Irwin scratched his itching arm. "Yes, it does."

"You checked the ratings, right?"

"Ratings?" Irwin repeated. "Don't be ridiculous. I saw a billboard last night while we were driving and said, "Let's go there.'"

"I should have known."

Irwin chuckled. "Did you manage to get any sleep?"

"Maybe an hour, two tops." Harper yawned. "You wouldn't happen to know how far we are from the undead husband?"

"By my loose, entirely unreliable calculations, Amarillo, Texas is a good eleven or so hours away. It doesn't matter though, I told Mr. Newman not to expect us until tomorrow morning. By the way, I meant to ask you, how's Christopher holding up? He pushed himself hard last night."

"Bug manifestation or not, he's still knocked out cold. If it's all right with you, and it doesn't totally screw over your timetable, I'd like to give him another hour or so before we get on the road."

This time Irwin could tell Harper wasn't messing with him. "What timetable?"

She smiled.

"Perchance, are your parents awake yet?" he asked, pretty confident he already knew the answer.

"Dad is. Not sure about Mom." Harper looked over the railing, smirking. "But look who is awake," Harper pointed to their sozzled neighbor from the evening before, busy kicking a soda machine with the heel of her barefoot. "Are you ready to meet this undead husband of Cornelia's?"

"You really should stop referring to him as 'the undead.'"

"Duly noted."

"And what is there to be ready about? We knock on the

man's door, hand him Cornelia's letter, wish him a renewed long lease on life, and leave."

Harper chuckled.

"What?"

"Nothing."

"No. Spill it," Irwin urged, quick to employ one of Harper's favorite euphuisms.

"It's just I thought you would have figured out by now that nothing Cornelia ever did went as planned."

Irwin nodded. "Maybe *that* was the plan."

"Maybe."

Sir Pisser from Drunkville reappeared. Harper and Irwin watched in rapt interest as his wiry frame oscillated to and fro, looking ready to tip right over, but oddly able to remain semi-upright.

"I see his mouth moving," said Harper. "I wonder what he's saying?"

"I have absolutely no idea," mumbled Irwin. "Although I find it fascinating how this ostensibly well-oiled man is able to sustain the most animated conversation with a stop sign."

"Well, I, for one, am intrigued." Harper stretched her arms high and wide, unable to suppress another yawn. "I have to admit, I'm more than curious as to why Cornelia led us to believe Martin died."

"I'm sure she had her reasons," though Irwin, who had spent a good portion of last night straining his exhausted brain cells and staring off into nothingness, couldn't come up with one.

"Did Cornelia happen to mention anything about the undead husband in your letter?"

"Again, no idea."

Harper shot Irwin an incredulous stare. "Why not?"

"I haven't read it yet."

"You haven't read it yet? Why?"

"Because frankly, I'm terrified what more it might reveal."

Harper hesitated. "Well, do you ever plan on reading it?"

"I do."

"Well, that's good, I guess." Nose creased, Harper didn't look entirely convinced. "Still, I wonder what he's going to be like."

On this point, Irwin concurred. He'd been wondering the same thing. Martin Newman had been polite but curt on the phone, and at the time, Irwin hadn't given it much thought. After all, how should the man have acted after hearing that someone he'd known and been close to had died? The fact that the dead person had been the man's estranged wife had never occurred to Irwin, leaving him to wonder what Martin knew about him. "Hard to imagine going through life still married to someone you don't live with anymore."

"It's a lot more common than you might think," said Harper. "We were just discussing this in my sociology class a few months ago. It's called *living apart together*. The couple is still committed but chooses not to cohabit."

"That's assuming they remained committed."

Harper shrugged. "They must have, to some degree. Cornelia has us delivering one of her letters to him. Why else send us all the way there, then?"

"To deliver the divorce papers she hadn't gotten around to mailing him for the last umpteen decades."

"Funny, *har-har*." Harper gasped. "Hold up—are you jealous?"

Irwin's head cocked at the most peculiar, if not uncomfortable angle. "Jealous? Not in the slightest."

"*Yu-huh*." Harper sneered.

Irwin sneered back. "I am not jealous."

"If you say so." Harper stretched. "You know, don't get mad at me for saying this, but maybe Cornelia wasn't keeping

226

any of this stuff from you in as much as she was protecting you from it."

"Protecting me?" Irwin snorted. "I don't need protecting. I'm a grown man, and you're not making any sense."

"Maybe she explained it to you in her letter."

"Not reading it yet."

"You should."

"Not ready." Irwin paused. "And why, all of a sudden, are you pushing this point?" He stared at Harper, trying to get a read. "Is this your way of saying Cornelia told you her reasons in your letter?"

"She might have," answered Harper sounding rather coy.

"Harper—"

"No. Relax. My letter didn't have anything to do with this situation, I swear." Harper crossed her heart. "My letter dealt strictly with me and Chris."

"Oh. I see," Irwin said, but didn't. "Is there a problem brewing?"

"Not at all."

"If there is, you don't have to talk about it."

"I don't?" Harper said, feigning shock. "You mean there's something left in this vast universe I can still keep to myself? Will wonders ever cease?"

IRWIN SPENT most of the long drive yesterday trying to decide what to say to Cornelia's estranged—unknown, thought to be dead husband, but not dead or divorced husband at all, to be exact. He spent the short drive from their latest flee-bitten motel to their next stop, forgetting practically everything he wanted to say.

"We've got about five minutes until we're there," announced Harper. "What's the plan?"

Good question.

I think I should handle this face-to-face and on my own," said Irwin, although that hadn't been anything close to the strategy he had contemplated for the last umpteen hours on the road. He had even toyed with the idea of taking the coward's way out by leaving the letter in his mailbox and driving away.

"I agree with Irwin," said Olivia. "Who knows how this man feels. Five strangers on his porch might be a bit too much to handle."

"Are you okay with that?" asked Harper. "Because I'm more than happy to go with you."

"I can do it," insisted Irwin.

"But if you're going to be the one to do this, Irwin, be nice," Olivia reminded him sternly, her reproach only missing a cat of nine tails to round out her delivery. "Don't just shove the letter in his hands like you tried to do to Millie and leave. Make some small talk. Ask him if there's anything we can do to help. In other words, be open and empathetic—you know, a human being."

"Okay."

"I mean it, Irwin. This is probably just as uncomfortable for him as it is for us."

"Okay."

"So, what are you going to say?" asked Harper as she read-justed the baby blanket over the urn.

"Everything your mother just enumerated."

"Good luck." Harper nodded. "I think we need a signal."

"For what?"

"In case you need help."

Irwin rolled his eyes. We don't need a signal and I don't need your help. Need I remind you of my grown man status?"

"Still, if it gets to be too much, clasp your hands behind

your back. Like this," Harper showed him. "And I'll come out."

"This is ridiculous."

"You never know."

"And we have arrived." Christopher pulled the van up to the curb in front of Martin Newman's light blue ranch house, whose well-kept exterior screamed pure Americana. It had the standard *Leave it to Beaver* white picket fence, a painted porch with a rocker, and the American flag anchored to a pole on his lawn at full mast. Martin's lush green grass carpet, complemented by red and white flowerbeds, looked well-tended, and cut to military precision. Even the man's shiny red, unscratched, no-rust to be found, pickup truck in the driveway supported this cultural amalgamation.

"You probably shoulda shaved," muttered Harper, peering through the window.

Irwin rubbed his hand over the two-day stubble jutting from his chin. "I'll be back."

With Martin's letter firmly in hand, Irwin marched to the front of the house, careful to stay only on the devoid of weeds brick path, and climbed up three well painted wide-plank steps leading to the man's impeccably maintained porch. Inhaling a deep breath, Irwin pushed the doorbell and waited, never bothering to glance over his shoulder at the four nosey faces pressed against the van's windows, and in all likelihood, fogging up the glass.

No answer.

Irwin pressed the doorbell again. This time he heard faint footsteps coming closer. His pulse raced as the locks began to turn and unlatch.

The door opened.

There, standing tall behind a screen stood a hefty, clean-shaven man, sporting a full thick head of steel-gray hair but no smile. Many years had passed, but Martin still mirrored the younger version Irwin remembered from the framed wedding photo displayed prominently at Cornelia's.

The two men stared at the other in silent summation.

"Mr. Newman?" said Irwin first.

"I'm Martin Newman." The older man's voice sounded neither harsh nor welcoming.

"Sir, I'm Irwin Abernathy. I spoke to you last week...about Cor—*ah, umm*, about your wife's passing. I've come to deliver the letter she requested I bring to you."

Martin nodded.

Irwin caught the man's eyes dart for a split second from him to the van.

"Yes. I remember," he said, grim-faced. "I appreciate you coming."

Irwin replayed Olivia's strict instructions over in his head. "Sir, I'm terribly sorry for your loss. If there is anything you'd like to know or ask, please feel free to do so. I will try to address any and all of your concerns to the best of my ability."

Martin, his expression unreadable, merely nodded as he opened the screen door just a crack—only enough to stick his arm halfway out.

While not the optimal of greetings, Irwin understood he could do nothing but press Cornelia's letter into Martin's open, waiting hand. The screen door shut immediately afterward.

Irwin watched Martin glance down at the envelope, as if his eyes were scrutinizing the handwriting on its front.

"Thank you, Mr. Abernathy. I wish you and your family a safe rest of your journey. Good day." And with that, Martin went to shut the door.

"Wait," said Irwin. "One more thing." He pulled a tiny tissue-wrapped packet out of his pocket.

"Yes?"

"Cornelia wanted you to have this."

Inside the tissue paper lay Cornelia's wedding band.

"You should probably know, Mr. Newman, Cornelia never took it off."

Irwin caught Martin's lip quiver.

Martin gripped the packet in his clenched fist and closed the door, leaving Irwin standing on his porch, dumbfounded. Irwin lifted his hand, half-tempted to knock again, but on second thought, turned around and walked back to the van.

"What happened?" they all asked him at once.

"In truth, not much of anything." Irwin slid into his seat. "I introduced myself. Mr. Newman, as you all observed, opened the door, retrieved the letter, and thanked me. He then wished us all a good rest of the trip and shut the door."

"Oh, no. What did you say to him?" asked Olivia, her tone accusing.

"Nothing."

"You must have said something," Olivia pushed.

"Nothing."

"How rude," muttered Harper.

"No," Irwin disagreed. "I wouldn't necessarily call Mr. Newman's response rude at all. On the contrary." Irwin stammered. He had understood the man's reaction, having responded in the same manner on more than one occasion. "He wasn't being impolite." Irwin paused. "To me, his actions felt more like a man—" Irwin faltered again, at a loss for words.

"—like a man trapped and needing to be alone with his thoughts and grief," said Darren stoically from the backseat.

All heads turned in awe.

Darren lifted his chin, his expression serious. "It's obvious that whatever transpired between him and Cornelia in the past is complicated and none of our business. We did what Cornelia asked us to do. We delivered her letter. So, let's go and let the man be." Darren paused and swallowed hard. "We're done here."

Olivia's eyes glistened, most certainly under the spell of her own long-ago painful memories. With the gentlest of smiles, she laid a tender, knowing hand on her husband's shoulder and squeezed.

Harper continued to stare at her dad with renewed admiration, her big brown eyes shimmering with pride.

Irwin, shocked speechless for the second time in less than two minutes, turned himself completely around in his seat to confirm the identity of the speaker.

"Irwin?" Christopher murmured. "It's your call. What do you want us to do?"

Irwin leaned back in his chair as an onslaught of mixed competing feelings raced through his mind, one more confusing than the last. He had so many questions still left unanswered. He happened to glance out the side window, catching sight of Martin Newman in his backyard, digging— the delivered, visibly opened letter protruding from the man's back pocket.

As if somehow sensing Irwin staring at him, Martin stopped and lunged the tip of his shovel into the soft earth. He placed one cupped hand protectively over his eyes, presumably to protect them from the sun's intense glare.

Martin's eyes locked onto Irwin's, and within an instant, two men from vastly different worlds, never before having set sights on the other, but who had deeply loved the same woman in their own special way, pooled between them a lifetime of soundless admissions. Still gripping the shovel, a stone-faced Martin covered his heart with his free hand, mouthing the words, *thank you,* before turning his full concentration back to exhuming the rich earth beneath his feet.

And then, as if a light flicked on, Irwin understood all he needed to.

"*Ashes to ashes, dust to dust.*"

Irwin had his answer.

Irwin fixed his attention forward and buckled his seatbelt, then clasped his hands on his lap, his chin jutted high and onward. "You heard the man, Christopher. We're done here. Let's go."

CHAPTER 16

DESPITE AN UNFORTUNATE SERIES of small malfunctions, the drive had, thus far, gone remarkably smooth. Two letters successfully delivered, which left only two more. The monotony of the actual ride, however, didn't seem close to ending. To combat the boredom, Christopher ran a bunch of numbers off in his head, a game he played to keep himself alert. This time he calculated how long it would take to reach New Mexico to make their next delivery stop—barring any unforeseeable upsets, probably within the next few hours.

A slight pulsing, like maracas, thumped against the inside of his skull, making concentrating on the road difficult. Part of the problem had to do with his sunglasses. He'd forgotten them in the motel room and hadn't realized it until already on the highway.

Christopher cupped his forehead to shield his unprotected, strained eyes from the sun's intense midday glare. He pressed his fingertips just above the eyelid where it ached the most, kneading away at the eyestrain, discovering soon enough that his insistent rubbing served only to pain him further.

Pain or not, he started to feel tired, so he reached for the radio, but jerked his hand from the tempting dial when he remembered Irwin's 'no radio rule.'

Christopher, no longer able to contain his exhaustion, belted out a drawn-out but soundless yawn, and in doing so, stretch out any underlying kinks in his aching, stiff neck. When that failed to yield the expected results, he shifted positions. An inch to the left, a smidgen to the right, sit up higher, lower—crouch. But nothing helped, so he slumped in his seat, beaten, his shoulder blades hurting as much as they had when he first started this morning.

When will this trip end?

Even Christopher, a proud, self-proclaimed enthusiast of long drives, had to concede—there was only so much barren open highway one should be expected to endure.

"*Ahhhh-hhaaaaa.*" Christopher yawned again. He couldn't help it. They just kept on coming, one right after the other, but this time, he didn't feel inclined to stay quiet.

Last night had been a disaster. Harper, not the least bit happy about their accommodations, had them sleeping on their beach towels after she drenched the bed with enough disinfectant to kill a rhino. But one night's lack of sleep hadn't been the lone issue. The weeks leading up to Cornelia's passing had taken their toll, both physically and emotionally, leaving everyone on a short fuse.

Olivia began fussing more than her usual, biting off the head of anyone at the drop of a dime. Darren, usually a talker, kept more to himself and out of his wife's line of fire. Harper, ordinarily a cup half-full personality, broke down at the mere mention of Cornelia's name. Christopher had lost count how many times he'd come home from work to find her curled up on the couch with Bones dutifully curled beneath, or the nights he held her for hours at a time, or at least until his arms got numb.

Irwin, meanwhile, remained his usual stuffy, stoic self, at least on the outside. Except upon closer inspection, it became glaringly apparent that even he had lost interest in life. Quieter than usual, spending more time alone, and no longer indulging in the lost art of busting chops or zinging those in close vicinity with his sarcastic witticisms—Darren, his favorite target, included.

Then, adding to Christopher's strain—were Cornelia's letters. What she had shared now weighed heavily on his mind—not that everything she'd written didn't make sense because it did...a bit too much. And, in all honesty, it wasn't like he hadn't been contemplating doing the same things she pushed for. But thinking about what needed doing and making it happen were two distinctly different animals. And as each day blurred into the next without any tangible, fore-seeable end in sight, the less sure of himself he became—as if somehow, he had lost his emotional footing somewhere.

Christopher wasn't accustomed to states of indecision. Now, he second-guessed everything he did or said. He patted his jean pockets to make sure the tiny felt box was still there.

This past year had centered primarily on surviving Cornelia's last days emotionally intact. No small feat, but as Cornelia's letter had so surgically pointed out—*ad nauseum*—indecision over these past few months had been the least of his problems.

That's it. Christopher pounded the steering wheel. *Once this is over, I make my move.*

He peered into the rearview mirror to look at Harper and exhaled.

Or maybe not.

Just then, Harper, presumably listening to music—her head bouncing and earbuds in, glanced up, her soft brown eyes meeting his. Her smile zapped the remainder of Christopher's heart in two.

"Are you okay?" she asked, tugging out an earbud. "You look distressed."

"I'm fine," he lied, forcing down another yawn. "It's this blasted sun. It's like it's burning a hole into my head." He rubbed his eyes. "I can't believe I left my glasses at the hotel."

"You're free to borrow mine." Harper pointed playfully to the rainbow, cat-eyed, sassy pair perched on her pretty face. "But fair warning, I think there's a rest stop coming up with a gift shop in about, oh," she peered down at her GPS, "in about two-hundred miles. They should have something more your style," she teased.

"You think?" he laughed softly, not wanting to stir Irwin from his slumber.

"How about you let me take the wheel for a bit?" Harper whispered, tucking her earphones into a side pocket, not waiting for an answer. "Your copilot is out cold, and you need a chance to rest anyway."

Christopher, using a hand to block the sun, nodded. "That's not a terrible idea. Are you sure?" he asked, side-eying his napping, long-suffering copilot. Christopher vacillated.

"What is it?" Harper asked.

Christopher knew Harper could manage the van, but unless the directions were stamped to her forehead, she wouldn't be able to find her way out of a paper bag.

"It's not like I'll get us lost, you know," she shot back as if reading his mind. "We've got a straight run for the next umpteen hundred miles."

Christopher gave a hesitant nod.

"I'll just drive us to the next visitor center, and then you're more than welcome to take over again, once you buy a pair of shades." Harper bounced in her seat. "Come on. You know I'm right. And unlike you, I'm wide awake and bored out of my mind."

Christopher couldn't argue with that. "Fine."

He checked the rearview mirror for any oncoming traffic before pulling off, then chuckled, unable to recall when he'd last seen another car. Nothing ahead for miles except towering saguaro cactuses popping out from the landscape in the far-off distance. He slowed down, steering the van onto the side of the dusty desert road, its tires crunching against sand, pebbles, and gravel.

"We should be in New Mexico soon," he mumbled mid-yawn, turning off the engine and stepping out of the van to fully stretch his achy back and legs.

Harper slid the door open as soon as the vehicle stopped, making a beeline around the front to the driver's side, but her speed did little to protect her from Christopher's playful butt tap as she passed.

"Your chariot awaits you, Mademoiselle," Christopher said, extending a hand to help Harper climb in. He leaned in and planted a soft, gentle kiss against her dewy strawberry-flavored glossed lips before slamming the door closed.

Irwin lifted his disheveled head. "Wa—wait, why did we just stop? What's going on?" Globules of saliva ran down his stubbled chin.

"Never you mind, my petulant slumbering friend." Harper shimmied the seat forward and adjusted her mirrors before buckling up. "I got this."

Irwin's head shot straight up like a meerkat. "Got what?" he asked, rattled. "What does she think she's got?" Irwin shouted at Christopher. "I mean get? —has—*argh*. You know what I mean."

Christopher slid the van door closed and buckled in.

"Ready when you are." His elbow accidentally brushed against the urn still buckled into the seat next to his. It took everything he had not to toss the entire contraption out the window—*No offense, Cornelia*.

On the night of Cornelia's passing, he had held a sobbing Harper, wracked in crushing grief until her body, no longer able to keep up the intensity, gave in, sending her off into a fitful, tortured sleep ... a sleep consumed by heartbreaking agony. Yet, Christopher had never seen a more beautiful, kinder, or gentler woman in his life. He pledged then and there to be supportive, even if it meant traipsing across the country to see this rolling circus wake through.

Nevertheless, as much as he missed and loved Cornelia, Harper's introduction of the baby carrier had concerned him, adding a new level of absurdity he couldn't quite wrap his head around.

Just a few more days, he reminded himself, inching his body as far away from the urn as possible—*just a few more days*.

HARPER TURNED the key into the ignition and slowly pulled onto the highway, while Irwin, fully conscious now, sat high in his seat.

"I'm the designated copilot and listed second driver," he said, none too happy. "Pull over and let me take the wheel."

"Not on your life," replied Harper, all smiles. "There's absolutely no traffic, we have almost a full tank of gas—and in a few, we'll be in New Mexico. What could go wrong?"

Irwin hated that question. He squeezed his eyes shut, shaking his head as if in denial. "Stop saying that 'what could go wrong' thing. There's no need for you to challenge the Universe to a duel." He glared at Harper, her shades on and humming, looking happier than she had for days. "Fine. You can drive, but no speeding, no deviating, and absolutely no madness," he informed her, his arms crossed over his chest.

Harper shot Irwin a curt head nod. "Right-o, because you know me, I might drive us into a cactus just for shits and giggles."

Irwin snorted.

"You worry too much, and it's not good for your health."

"This entire trip is not good for my health," Irwin retorted, recognizing a sudden compulsion to flee.

Harper grinned. "Yeah, well, worry produces stress, stress creates acid, and acid burns holes into the lining of your stomach. And that, my cantankerous old chum, is called an ulcer."

"Thank you, Doctor Kildare."

"Who?"

Irwin tipped his head in disbelief. "Don't tell me you've never heard of Dr. James Kildare?" Irwin's mouth fell open in disbelief. "Dr. Kildare came from a tv medical drama. It ran from 1961 to 1966, but don't quote me on that."

"How do you remember this stuff?" asked Harper, sounding impressed.

"I am a former librarian," he spat, jerking his head back, insulted. "It comes with the territory."

"Well, excuse me." Harper pretended to be offended. "But why call me Dr. Kildare?"

Irwin recalled watching the show with his grandmother. They'd sit huddled together on her long, well-worn damask sofa, the one protected in annoying plastic, and laden with one too many throw pillows. She, of course, would chatter away throughout the entire show, droning on about how handsome and smart 'the good doctor' was, and how Irwin, no slump in the grades department, should go to medical school straight out of high school.

"Kildare played the part of an intern." Irwin stopped to think. "Oh. I remember—at Blair General Hospital. A fictitious place. Anyway, the show centered primarily on the way Kildare dealt with his patients and their problems, along with the general ups and downs of being a doctor."

"Did you like it?"

"Very much, and believe me, I wasn't alone. It hit the top ten in its first season." Irwin grinned. "Although, not the most complicated plot. It had more of a soap opera quality to it, except for the later episodes when the storyline shifted from Kildare and began to center on the lives of his patients and families." Irwin chuckled.

"What's so funny?" Harper looked briefly at him.

"Just memories." He tapped his chin before continuing. "Here's a piece of history. I think you'll appreciate it."

"Go ahead."

"At the time of the show's release, it had gained so much popularity that people wrote to Richard Chamberlain, the actor who played the part of Dr. Kildare, asking him for real medical advice."

"That's crazy!"

"I agree. I can remember reading once that the network, I'm assuming to promote the show, decided to have Dr. Kildare paged over various train station, airports, and bus station intercoms across the country."

Harper beamed at Irwin, seemingly enjoying his moment of nostalgia, but in a flash, her cheerfulness turned to fear.

"What was that?" she screeched, eyes riveted on the windshield.

Irwin, busy enjoying the view out his side window, turned. "What was what?"

"I think I saw something move."

"Where?"

"On the window. There," she pointed.

"Hallucinations shouldn't be an issue, thanks in part to your father's dilapidated cooler."

"I'm being serious, Irwin. I saw something move."

Irwin could always tell when Harper was playing with him, and by golly, this wasn't it.

"What did this something look like?"

"I-I don't know. It moved too fast for me to be sure." Harper shifted around in her seat, getting antsier.

Just as Irwin turned to ask if anyone else had seen anything, Harper let out a blood curdling scream.

"*EEK*! ——Did you see that? Harper bounced and squirmed in her seat, her cheeks turning a bright red. "Did you see it! It's a freakin' snake!" she yelled, teetering at the brink of hyperventilation. "What do I do?"

Irwin's head whipped back.

No way.

Then forward.

Yes, way!

"Mother of——" he groaned just as the thick tip of the rattle-shaped tail smacked against the glass.

Somehow, unbeknown to anyone, the snake must have lodged under the van's hood, quite possibly during their last stop, and now it had decided to slither the rest of his long, massive body across the van's windshield, semi-blocking Harper's view.

"Irwin! What do I do?" Harper screamed again, the knuckles on both her hands turning white with fright.

"Stay calm," he shouted, not at all feeling calm himself. He fumbled frantically around, digging into the glove compartment, then under the seat, and finally in his folder, searching for anything to swat the snake away. So far, he'd only came up with a ballpoint pen.

"*Aww* great," Harper screeched, on the other side of irrational. "Why don't you lean out the window? Stab him in the eye! That should do it."

Irwin tossed the pen and grabbed for the map book.

"Oh. Even better."

The snake slithered the bulk of its body across the entire window.

Harper recoiled in her seat. "I think it's trying to come inside."

"What's coming inside?" shouted Olivia. "Holy macaroni —is that a snake?" She elbowed Darren awake. "There's an anaconda on the windshield!"

"A what?"

Christopher, still belted-in, leaned as far forward as he could, gripping Harper's shoulder. "Okay, baby. Stay steady. I want you to ease up on the gas and pull to the side of the road, nice and easy."

"How? I can't see!" she screamed.

"That's because he has his tail wrapped around the wiper," hollered Irwin, slapping the glass with an open palm. "Go!" he yelled at the snake. "Get off!"

"Harper, focus on me. Pull over to the side of the road," ordered Christopher.

"I'm trying!" Harper's hand, drenched in panic, slipped, causing the van to veer and swerve. She arched her back, stretching her neck to peer around the beast's intrusive body. "Get off!" she screamed, inadvertently turning the wheel with each screeched syllable. But instead of dislodging, the snake jutted his tongue at the glass, causing an already freaked out Harper to crank the steering wheel too sharp to the right. She switched the wipers on, but because of the snake's position, it allowed for only one wiper to move freely, doing nothing more than bopping the reptile repeatedly on his head.

"It's not working," she shrieked. "He's still stuck and now mad."

"Who cares if he's mad!" Irwin reached over and turned the knob. "Put it at full speed!"

"Stop that!" Harper slapped Irwin's hand away. "I did that already."

"Harper, let me just—"

"Move, Irwin." Harper held her hand poised protectively over the knob. "Would you leave it alone already!"

Rebuked, Irwin went to shift away, but somehow, either a knee or elbow—some appendage—managed to knock into the shift, throwing the van into neutral.

"*Argh!*" everyone screamed while Harper valiantly fought for control of the wheel as the van began to spin.

"*Ahhh!*" yelled everyone, bracing for impact.

And—

Boom.

The van smashed head-on into a sign pole, coming to an abrupt stop. The snake, unable to hang on, released its hold and shot forward, its lower body now pinned between the metal pole and the hood of the van.

"Gross," whispered Harper, shook up but not hurt. "Everybody okay?"

—"Yeah."

—"I'm okay."

—"I'm good."

"Alive," grunted Irwin, his head pressed against the back of his seat, pointing at the windshield. "Unlike him."

Harper turned the key, but the motor only skittered and coughed to a dead stop. "Now what?"

"Now, I get to call the rental company and see where we need to go from here," snapped Christopher. He shook his phone. "Great. Barely any reception." He slid the van door open and stepped out. "I need to see if I can pick up a better signal."

"What about the snake?" asked Darren. "Are you sure it's dead?"

Irwin, unable to contain himself a single second longer, spun clear around in his seat. "The reptile," he bellowed, "has been severed into two distinct, no longer breathing parts." Irwin's voice took on a strange if unnatural stillness. 'I think it is safe to assume, he's **DEAD**! However, my inquisitive, dolt of a friend, feel free to venture outside and check for yourself."

Harper plunged her face into her cupped hands, sobbing. "I'm sorry," she sniffled. "This is all my fault."

"No it's not," soothed Olivia, now seated closer to her daughter.

"Oh, yes, it most certainly is," countered Irwin in a huff.

"Besides the snake, obviously, what exactly did we hit?" asked Olivia, wisps of hair strewn across her cheeks.

Irwin rolled down his window and stuck his head out to take a better look.

"It's an enormously large orange-yellow sign," he said. "It reads...

**"'WELCOME TO NEW MEXICO.
THE LAND OF ENCHANTMENT'"**

CHRISTOPHER TRUDGED BACK to the van, his feet kicking up clouds of dust wherever he stomped. "Okay. Do you want the good news or the bad first?"

"Is there a difference?" Irwin snarled, barely looking up.

"In this case, there is."

"Then by all means, the good news first."

"Right. Good news it is. Spoke to the rental company. They're sending out a tow truck to pick up the van. They also told me our insurance should cover the damage, minus the deductible."

"Okay, that is good news," admitted Irwin, somewhat less irate.

"I agree. They also said that if we didn't manage to damage the pole and only the vehicle, we shouldn't get charged with the destruction of public property."

"I didn't even think about that." Irwin bounded right back into fuming. "And what about us?" he asked, massaging his temples.

"They agreed, after much threatening on my part, to loan us another vehicle for the duration of this trip."

Irwin stiffened. "As a former librarian, Christopher, and wordsmith, I am well acquainted with ambiguous word selection. You specifically said vehicle as opposed to a specific kind." Irwin paused, giving Christopher a deep probing glare. "What specific kind of vehicle are we talking about?"

"A regular four-door car." Christopher frowned. "It was all they had left. It was that or nothing."

Irwin shrugged. "Okay. That's not so bad. A sedan, then."

"No. Not exactly."

"Christopher," implored Irwin. "Take me out of my misery. My blood pressure can only take so much."

"We've been given a compact car."

Irwin nodded slowly. "How compact is compact?"

"— as in small and cramped," admitted Christopher.

"How are we gonna fit all of our stuff in it?" asked Darren, on his knees, rummaging through the cooler in search of something to eat.

"I'm afraid it's going to be a tight squeeze, but it's not like we have much choice," shrugged Christopher. "With limited trunk space and now no additional storage on top, we're probably going to have to give up the cooler."

"*Ahhh*, man," sputtered Darren. "Don't say that," he groaned, mouth half-full. "Not my cooler."

"I'm afraid so," nodded Christopher.

"*Aww* honey, that's such awful news," said Olivia, doing a lousy job of masking her delight. "But such is life. When faced with catastrophe, we must all do our part and rise to the occasion. You know, sacrifice for the greater good." She wrapped her arm around Darren's shoulder and gave him a supportive squeeze.

Harper, tears streaming down her face, grabbed for another tissue, and blew her nose. "Can this day get any worse?"

Christopher, leaning on the door frame, scratched his head and drew in a long, labored breath. Then he tapped Harper on the shoulder.

"What?" she bemoaned, a glazed wary expression of alarm stamped across her face.

"I'm afraid it can."

"What's that supposed to mean?"

"It means there won't be enough room for the baby carrier, either."

To everyone's surprise, Harper merely shrugged. "Fine," she said. "I'll just hold it."

Irwin, who had up to now remained moderately quiet, went to say something. Then on second thought, closed his mouth. He shook his head and counted to three before addressing Harper directly. "You intend on holding the urn the entire rest of the way to San Diego?"

Harper slid the van door open and stepped out in a huff. "All. The. Freakin. Way."

Darren, who had wedged an open can of soda between his knees to free up his hands, chuckled. "Well, we should at least get better gas mileage with a smaller car."

Irwin let out a strangled, exasperated yelp.

"What? Am I wrong?" Darren asked as he offered Olivia a bite of his sandwich, which she, in turn, smooshed in his face.

CHAPTER 17

PRECISELY TWO HOURS, twenty-seven minutes, and six seconds later, an old rusty, formerly red tow truck, followed by another much smaller car, parked alongside the road near the van.

"That," Christopher slapped his knees, "should be our tow and rental." He pulled himself to his feet slowly...drained by the day's unfolding events and scorching heat. "I got this." He walked first toward the man climbing out of the tow truck and gave him a slight half-wave.

"Well, I'll be damned," said the truck driver, blowing a loud whistle through two slightly fissured front teeth. "You weren't kidding about the size of that thing." With crowbar in hand, he slid the slant under the dead snake's head and tilted it up for a closer look. "Yawp. Looks like a Coiled Prairie Rattler."

"Are they poisonous?"

"Hell, yeah." The driver twisted his head and spat a wad of chewing tobacco phlegm onto the hot pavement, which shriveled before the man could break out into a stained astounded grin. "Looks to me like a venomous pit viper."

"How can you tell?" Christopher leaned in, curious.

"By the diamond-shaped head and thin neck." The man angled his head to the side, air-measuring the dead snake's size. "Yawp. These things can easily get up to five feet in length, like your guy right here." Without missing a beat, the man picked up and raised the snake's head higher for Christopher's perusal. "Come here. See this here small pit on its head?" He pointed. "It's what they call heat sensitive. Once they've injected their venom into you, they lay back and chill. Leave you be to suffer. Of course, you're gonna think you got time to escape, but trust me, city boy, you ain't gonna get far. And if by chance you do, these sly vipers can track you down by your scent and ingest you. Nasty business."

Just then, a tall, wiry man, dressed in a crisp white collar short-sleeve shirt tucked into a pair of barely wrinkled khakis sauntered over.

"Still scaring the tourists, Bill?" said the clean-shaven man gripping an efficient-looking clipboard with one hand while extending his other to give Bill's hand a friendly shake. "I thought I'd catch you out here."

"Ramsey," Bill nodded, returning the greeting and shake equally as warm. "Who else you think they gonna send?"

The men shared a laugh. Then Ramsey turned to Christopher. "Greetings, traveler. I'm Taye Ramsey." He held out a hand to Christopher. "But you can call me Taye. Everybody else does, except good ole Bill over here."

Bill ignored the comment. Too busy leaning into his cab, reaching for the control to lower the tow bed.

"I'm Christopher James. I spoke to you on the phone, and

boy am I glad to see you two." He swiped his forehead with his sweaty palm. "It's hot as hell out here."

"Speaking of which," said Ramsey, "I wasn't sure if you folks had ample supplies. Lots of travelers come through here ill-equipped, expecting to see a rest stop or corner store every other mile. If you would kindly follow me back to the car, I can offer you and your—," he hesitated. "—friends?"

"Family."

"Family. I stand corrected," chuckled Ramsey, good-naturedly. The man had a natural calm about him, which had already started to work its charm to put Christopher at ease. "Feel free to grab enough ice water for everyone. I think there's even a few bags of chips and whatnot, in case anyone's hungry. You and me can talk while we walk. I'd like you to catch me up on exactly what transpired here." Ramsey looked for Bill and shouted over the truck's engine. "All right, if I grab a ride back with you when you're done?"

"Sure thing." Bill wiped his hands on an oil-stained rag, then shut the engine off to address the group. "You folks have everything you want out of the van 'cause once I get her on the bed, it's a done deal."

"We already cleared it out," replied Darren, resting on top of his cooler, casually munching on a sandwich between inter-mittent gulps of lukewarm water to help get it down. "But I'll take one of those waters."

As Bill stuck his rag in his back pocket, he caught a glimpse of the covered baby carrier resting on the pavement by Harper's feet and frowned. "Ma'am, you don't want to leave your baby all covered up on the ground like that. It's close to ninety-eight degrees out here." As he spoke, a dribble of sweat slid down his chin, landing with a plop on the rib of his tee-shirt. "I got the air blasting in my cab. Feel free to sit in there with your baby."

"Kind of you, but it's not a baby," announced Irwin.

"Whaddya mean it's not a baby?" Bill cocked his head to the side, his stare narrowing in confusion. "Ain't that a baby carrier?"

"It is, but it's contains no baby." Irwin bent over and tugged the blanket back. "And, as you can clearly see, these particular contents have already been exposed to way hotter temperatures than anything either you or I are experiencing here."

"Whoa." Bill paled.

"Exactly."

Harper gave Irwin one of her exaggerated eye rolls before snatching the blanket out of Irwin's hands.

Bill, with pupils dilated as wide as half-dollars, stuttered. "That's a-a—"

Irwin nodded. "Indeed, sir, it is most assuredly is."

Bill pitched both of his greased stained hands high in the air in surrender. "You know what?" He shook his head. "—I don't even wanna know." He spun and staggered away, mumbling to himself.

"Smart man," muttered Irwin.

THEY ARRIVED in Las Cruces by nightfall. Tired, hungry, a bit disheveled, and dreadfully disheartened.

Their next stop: Luna and her son, Jax, who lived in Doña Ana County, 225 miles south of Albuquerque, but still considered within the Chihuahuan Desert. Along with the anticipated standard desert climate, they noticed the city surrounded by interesting vegetation, like tarbush, creosote bushes, soap tree, broom dalea, and various other desert grasses, including black grama and tobosa. Dotted across the lower slopes, Irwin pointed out the cacti and an assortment of shrubs that dominated the range, much like those found in the areas of the grassland uplands.

"As you can see," said Irwin, sounding like a much less friendly Rick Steves tour guide, "The Mesilla Valley is surrounded on both sides by dry streams called arroyos. These streams are lined with small scattered trees and are home to many wildlife creatures who customarily make the short jump from the undesirable urban areas to adjacent mountains and suitable deserts."

While driving through the historic district, a lovely looking town made even more vibrant by bygone days olden buildings, the group passed several water tanks, each artistically ornamented with stunning painted murals.

"I despise graffiti," grumbled Irwin, nonplused.

"That's not—" Harper snapped, then sighed. "What's the point."

"We're here," said Christopher talking over them. He turned right to park in front of a lovely and inviting hotel. "Why don't you all get out here and I'll meet you inside."

"Excellent suggestion." Irwin undid his seatbelt and gathered his things. "I suggest we take our bags with us. Christopher, pop the trunk, please."

"Now, this place looks wonderful," said Olivia, impressed. "Much, much better than that other place we stayed in."

"Alcatraz would have been better than the other place we stayed in," grumbled Harper, the first one out of the car.

The rest disembarked, collected their belongings, and followed Irwin inside, while Christopher drove off in search of someplace close to park.

"Let me do the talking," whispered Irwin as they approached the front desk.

"Fine by me," said Darren, walking at Irwin's side. "All I know is, I need a hot meal, an even hotter shower, a soft bed, and eight hours of uninterrupted, blissful sleep. Preferably in that order." Darren ran a hand over the back of his head and yawned. "What a day."

Olivia clapped him on the shoulder. "Hot meal, I think we can find that. Hot shower and soft bed, your chances are looking up. However, eight hours of uninterrupted sleep?" She winked. "—from your mouth to God's ears."

Darren drew Olivia in close, grasping her by the waist, whispering something in her ear that made her giggle and blush like a schoolgirl.

"Get a room," Irwin barked, picking up his pace so as to march as far past the amorous couple as possible.

"Waiting on you," countered Darren, apparently a bit too brash for Irwin's taste, although the retort did provoke another round of favorable giggles from Olivia.

While Irwin spoke to the young man at the front desk, the small group dragged their tired bodies and luggage over to the lounge area to grab a comfortable seat. Irwin returned minutes later and handed out the room passes before bidding everyone a good night.

"Remember," he said, "we need to be downstairs and ready to leave by ten. No later."

"Aren't you coming out to eat with us?" Olivia asked Irwin, concerned. "We've been on the road all day, and I haven't seen you eat since..." she paused, glaring at him. "When have you last eaten?"

Irwin tugged at his earlobe and sighed. "Olivia, thank you for your concern, but I'm exhausted, filthy, and want nothing more than to shower and sleep. I promise, if I get hungry, I'll call for room service."

Olivia scowled, looking not at all appeased by Irwin's answer. "*Hmm*. Okay. You go get cleaned up, and do whatever it is you do, and I'll pick you up a plate of something when we go out. What room are you in?"

"I'm fine."

Olivia, her brows knitted together, stared at Irwin, waiting for an answer, but realized soon enough he wasn't going to give in that easy, so she snapped her fingers in his face.

Irwin, looking too bushed to put up much of a fight, lifted his passkey to show her.

Olivia beamed. "Good. I'll see you soon. And Irwin," Olivia called out as he walked toward the elevator. "Don't you dare pretend to be asleep when I knock."

Irwin dragging his feet to the elevators, lifted a weary hand indicating he heard, but never turned around or stopped.

"Liv. Look at this." Darren waved an open pamphlet he had been reading at her. "Free continental breakfast served from six to ten. I'm down with that."

"That's nice," replied Olivia, her mind on other more pressing matters. "How about less talking and more walking, Mr. Crane?" She nudged Darren forward, hiking her duffel's stained shoulder strap proprietorially over one arm.

There's a little friend I want you to meet.

Harper stepped across the ceramic floor into the shower, positioning her body under the hot water, willing the steady pulse to massage away the day's aches and stiffness from her worn-out limbs. She inhaled deeply.

Why am I such a screw-up?

Steam filled the room. She bent her neck and stuck her entire head under the nozzle, allowing the water to rain down, saturating her long, wavy locks.

—How could I have been so stupid? Christopher must despise me.

Harper readjusted the showerhead to a more robust setting, angling her head just right against the heaven-sent pulse so it worked its magic against the crick in her neck. But the water couldn't stop her thoughts from racing.

First, the urn. Then the whole getting lost debacle—which technically was more Irwin's fault than mine, but still. And now the van.

Harper sniffed the hotel's complimentary body soap. "Oh." She sniffed again. "That's really nice," she squeezed a generous amount of the peach-scented liquid onto a washcloth while sudsy bubbles trickled down her back.

She closed her eyes and leaned back on the shower wall, crossing her soap-slathered arms over her stomach in a protective huddle, rocking slightly and ready to burst out into tears.

I wouldn't blame Chris if he breaks up with me after this trip.

OUTSIDE THE BATHROOM, Christopher sat at the edge of their king-size bed hunched over, his head dropped, and wearing nothing but the hotel's plush white towel wrapped and knotted around his waist, waiting for Harper to finish. It had been a long, draining day. The unexpected loss of the van, while problematic, hadn't been anything earth-shattering. He placed the blame for the accident more on himself than either on Harper or Irwin. He should have just pulled over, rested, and then continued. Besides, how could he be mad at either one of them for reacting the way they did?

A poison viper? Who wouldn't have?

Christopher swallowed, wincing at the lump forming in the back of his throat.

Dread. The lump was dread, plain and simple.

It could have easily turned out worse. Harper could have been hurt, or—

He pounded his fist into the mattress, limbs shaking mad. No. He wouldn't let his mind go there again.

Christopher inhaled and blew out a long, shaky breath.

Bottom line, nobody got hurt except the snake, and that he could live with.

He folded Cornelia's letter and carefully tucked it in his duffel's inside pocket out of sight, not that he believed for one second Harper would poke around in his stuff. Respect for each other's privacy had never been an issue between the pair. If anything, Harper's total unwavering trust in him at times felt a bit undeserving, like nothing he had ever experienced before. As such, Christopher went out of his way to earn and keep that confidence, making sure to pay extra attention to what brought Harper happiness and what made her feel secure, never willing to take either her or their relationship for granted. Christopher had learned over time what made Harper withdraw inside herself and what made her feel unsafe, staying vigilant and careful never to become either of them.

And now, after everything, and despite how she may react, Christopher needed to face Harper once and for all. He had waited long enough. Vacillated long enough...and had made enough excuses.

"*Stop being afraid of your shadow,*" Cornelia had written to him in his letter.

"*I know, I know—you have experienced your fair share of loss. And frankly, that can make anyone a bit over cautious about taking more chances, especially where matters of the heart are concerned. Take it from me, Christopher, Life is too short to play games, or to put off until tomorrow what the heart needs today—and certainly not for propriety's sake. Or even stupider, "Until the time is right' nonsense. The time will never be right or perfect, and maybe my dear, dear boy, it's not supposed to be.*

"*Fact is, by the time you get around to reading this, I'll be dead. Long gone and never coming back. That's not to say I haven't appreciated all you have both done for me these last few months, what I still can remember of it anyway. And I should probably take this opportunity to say an even bigger thank you to you for all the stuff I probably won't remember down the road. Just know I love you both. Never forget that.*

"Listen, it's no use letting Harper or yourself for that matter, continue to sink into ugly vats of grief when there's so much darn beautiful living left to do. So, get on with it, already! Cast all your apprehensions and worthless uncertainty to the wind—me along with it if you please—and step up to the plate.

"Trust yourself. And don't choke, for goodness sake. No more over-thinking or dilly-dallying. No more using me as your excuse. Knock any and all lingering doubts straight out of the park and out of your life. You don't need them.

I have faith in you."

CHRISTOPHER'S HAND TREMBLED.

Good old Cornelia.

A strange melodic sound resonated from inside the bathroom. A familiar tune Christopher recognized as something Harper hummed whenever she felt unusually sad or mournful.

Enough of this.

He wouldn't let her beat up on herself for things out of her control. He loved Harper with every fiber of his being and wanted to be with her for the rest of his life. Nobody or nothing would ever change that, and it was about time he told her.

Christopher rose, no longer willing to wait, or put off for

one-second longer what he needed to do—*what he should have done long ago.*

I have faith in you.

He reached for his jeans, slid his hand inside the pocket, and pulled out the box he'd been carrying around with him for months, always waiting for the perfect time that never seemed to arrive.

It's now or never.

He stood at the bathroom door and peeked inside, almost able to make out the alluring silhouette of Harper's body veiled behind a steam-filled curtain. He heard her whimper and cringed.

Don't choke.

Don't hesitate.

No more over-thinking.

Christopher popped open the box, removed the ring, and tossed the empty container onto the counter. He slid the curtain over, letting his towel fall unceremoniously to the floor.

"Harper?" he whispered.

Harper turned, her cheeks flushed from crying.

"Hey, you," she murmured, her long wavy hair wet and slicked back. She wiped her tears and pretended to smile. "Something I can do for you?" She looked down and away.

Pulse racing, Christopher inched forward, the diamond engagement ring hard-pressed inside his fist. "Well, now that you mention it."

Harper moved back giving him room to join her. "I'm so sorry," she sobbed. "I've made a mess out of everything."

"No, *shush*. Stop."

"I wouldn't blame you if you hated me."

"Hate you? No baby, not even a little," he tried to assure her. He held Harper's waist tight under the shower's hot, steamy spray. "I need you to listen to me, okay?"

Harper whimpered.

"Baby—" Christopher pulled his head back, lifting her chin so her eyes met his.

"Ye-ah?" Harper whimpered again, her voice choked with tears.

"I, *err*, I... I've wanted to *umm*, I need, *ah*, I mean I want to ask you something," he finally fumbled out, his practiced words stumbling and tripping over the other. Christopher held Harper's hand in his, the ring between his fingers hovering at the tip of hers.

"Harper Leigh Crane, will you do me the honor of becoming my wife?"

Harper gasped, her sniffles from seconds before nothing more than a faded memory. She flung her soapy arms around Christopher's neck and pulled him in closer until their bodies meshed.

"Yes, yes, yes, yes, oh yes," she murmured into Christopher's ear, down his neck, on his cheek, across his lips. Standing on her tiptoes, her face close to his, she leaned in and planted the sweetest, softest, saltiest, soapiest kiss upon his lips.

Christopher slid the ring the rest of the way on. Then, without pause, he closed the curtain behind him, no longer afraid, no longer uncertain, and smart enough not to wait to be invited twice.

THE GROUP ASSEMBLED in the hotel lobby the following morning as agreed, well-rested and refreshed—Irwin included.

Irwin placed the list of names on the table. "Next stop, Luna and Jax," he announced.

Harper, sitting next to him, leaned over and conspicuously laid her left hand on the paper, her fingers spread wide.

Irwin didn't notice at first, but Olivia sure did, and jumped to her feet, belting out a mother's joyful shriek heard around the world.

"Oh, my goodness!" she squealed, leaping to her feet to run around the round table to hug her daughter. "Congratulations, baby girl!" Olivia held Harper's hand, the two of them jumping up and down and swooning. "Look, Darren, our baby girl, is engaged."

"Well look at that," Darren said, rising from his chair, his chest puffed out like a proud papa.

Christopher, grinning ear to ear, pushed out his chair and stood, looking grateful to welcome his future father-in-law's firm handshake and proud bear hug.

Flummoxed and feeling way beyond his realm, Irwin remained seated, his hands resting flat upon his lap. He knew he should react—do or say something appropriate—but he wasn't sure what. So instead, he sat stiff, his head rotating from the elated women to the proud men. Irwin wasn't exactly smiling, but he wasn't frowning either.

"Look, Irwin," said Olivia, bursting with excitement. She wagged Harper's ringed finger into his face. "Would you look at this ring—it sparkles!"

"Yes. It is quite enchanting," Irwin agreed, projecting what he hoped mirrored Olivia's enthusiasm.

The other hotel guests filling the bustling breakfast room soon picked up on the reason for all the happiness and began cheering and clapping when Christopher, face beaming, embraced Harper by the waist and thrusting his fist into the air, hollered, "She said yes!"

The room burst into hoorays, and tons of clapping, shouts of congratulations, *oobs*, and *ahbs* —and even a few cat whistles.

Everyone seemed to be enjoying themselves when unbeknown to Harper, the urn she had so carefully hidden under the table, somehow dislodged, rolling straight into the pathway of a man carrying a full food tray.

"*Whoa*," the man yelped, clad head-to-toe in the American, 'I'm a tourist' approved khaki-colored Bermuda shorts, along with the standard awful, horizontally striped collared shirt, forever unfashionably belted in at the waist. Around his neck, a pair of sunglasses hung on a blue lanyard.

The man somehow managed to jump successfully out of the way and remain upright with his food tray securely in hand, ignoring the inconsequential bit of oatmeal that had sloshed and dribbled off the side of his bowl.

"Oh, no!" Harper dashed to retrieve Cornelia's urn, which by this time had rolled under the next table. "Oh gosh, I'm so sorry," she blathered, wrapping her arms around the urn as the old stunned couple in their booth looked on, somewhat amused.

"Are you, okay, sir?" Harper asked the man with the tray, who seemed somewhat disorientated, and didn't hear her at first—seemingly more concerned with what part of his meal did and did not make it.

"Are you all right?" she asked again.

"*Uhh*, yeah. I'm fine, I think." When he glanced up, his eyes locked onto the urn in Harper's embrace.

"Is that an urn?" he asked, stunned, but before she could answer, yelled, "Why in the hell would you bring that thing in here?" The angry timbre of his raspy voice was loud enough to make everyone in the restaurant stop talking.

"I'm really sorry, sir," Harper barely choked out, embarrassed. "I can't believe this is happening."

Irwin saw the rosy flush of exuberance from only moments before drain from Harper's face. He watched in dismay as she withdrew back into a mushy pool of misery.

Not today, Satan.

Irwin rose to his feet and snatched the urn from Harper's arms. "Give it back!" he shouted at Harper, cradling the jar in his arms like a baby. "It's mine." And then, in a voice close to that of a five-year-old boy, he began scene two. "It's okay, Grandma," he blathered loudly enough for everyone in the back to hear, swaying on his heels as if ready to belt out a lullaby. "I won't let anything bad happen to you ever, ever, ever again." Irwin sucked his tongue, blew out his cheeks, and let out the loudest raspberry. "I promise."

The man, who moments before looked ready to argue, glanced back at Harper, his face softened and apologetic. "I-I didn't know. I'm, *ahh*, sorry," he implored.

Harper, trying not to laugh at Irwin's whacky performance, shrugged and leaned into the man. "He thinks it's his long-lost grandmother," she whispered conspiratorially loud. "Poor thing, he takes it everywhere he goes."

The man's mouth dropped open in stunned disbelief.

"She's right," added Olivia while making a show out of guiding Irwin out of the restaurant. "We've tried to make him leave it in the car, but he refuses and starts to cry."

Irwin cut his eyes at Olivia, letting her know he didn't entirely appreciate her added layer of crazy, but then remembered his role and expelled a loud pathetic wail.

"See what I mean?" Olivia said, pretending to console Irwin. "There, there, Grandpa."

The room watched in uncomfortable silence as Darren and Christopher moved around their table, shoving chairs back into place and collecting luggage. Christopher grabbed as many bags as he could, chin nodded Harper to follow him, while Darren, thoroughly enjoying himself, felt the need to land one last imparting quip.

"Sorry about that, everybody, and please excuse the disruption," he said, giving the spectators a lighthearted knowing head shrug. "Enjoy the rest of your breakfast, and don't you worry, we're on our way to bring old Pops back right now to the," Darren paused long enough to cross his eye and make an exaggerate circling motion with his index finger at his temple.

The room gave a collect gasp at his crudeness—which became Darren's cue to split. He quickly grabbed whatever bags were left and shouted over his departing shoulder, "Have a good day now."

The group rushed toward their car, not daring to look back. No one uttered another word until all the bags got packed in the trunk, and all windows were securely rolled up. Then, and only then did they burst into fits of uncontrolled laughter.

Still clutching the urn, and not precisely joining in, Irwin snarled. "Well, that was completely humiliating," he said, drawing more raucous laughter from the group.

It took a bit before everyone settled down, but once they did, Harper, situated behind Christopher, leaned forward and whispered into her fiancé's ear. "I warned you years ago. We come as a package deal."

Christopher, his cheeks flushed from laughter, whispered back, "I wouldn't have it any other way."

CHAPTER 18

THE GROUP PARKED by the side of the highway. They decided to hike the remainder of the distance rather than chance a possibly jarring carnival drive across rocky terrain in a rental hooptie with already spotty AC. They walked in single file down a lengthy man-made trail, which could have been easily dismissed as nothing more than a footpath imprinted upon dust-filled earth from years of repeated human use more than actual design.

No one spoke, but instead, kept their heads cast down and their eyes peeled open, on the lookout for anything snake-shaped, wiggling, and with sharp fangs possibly ready to lunge.

Irwin, now the unofficial 'Urn Keeper,' led the pack, with Darren taking up the rear. Both men stomped ahead as if ready to hightail it back to civilization—at warp speed—at the first sign of any trouble.

A faint trace of something fragrant but smoke-smelling drifted through the air, its scent more robust and pleasant the closer the group came to the large clearing. After less than a sweaty minute's hike, they arrived at their destination. An impressive oasis of life and creativity. An artist colony consigned to a stretch of once-barren land and safeguarded by nothing more than a wall of ideally situated tiny houses. Somebody had gone to the trouble of staking into the clay earth a single, colorfully hand-painted bright sign to greet them as they entered.

Long wooden picnic tables that had seen better days were intentionally placed about and covered with a wide array of clay pots and other kinds of handmade earthenware of all different shapes and sizes. Elaborate macramé and tinkling windchimes hung on every available hook or peg, giving each of the small unique-shaped dwellings a warm, welcoming feel. Large easels could be seen propped up here and there, ready for their next patrons' attention, but currently unmanned.

Something caught Harper's eye, and she couldn't help herself. Without saying a word, she drifted away from the group to one of the tables filled with a collection of still-wet painted, small clay birdbaths, each supporting two delicate love birds perched on a rim. She reached down to hold one but stopped herself. She instead used her finger to trace the smooth edge of a dried piece that reminded her so much of the one Cornelia had cherished and displayed back home.

"Harper!" called Olivia.

"I'm coming." Harper quickly snapped a photo before returning to the group.

A door to one of the tiny houses, located by the makeshift entrance, opened. The group turned to see a slender, some-what tall, striking woman approaching them. Her worn work boots kicked up dust with each deliberate step. She looked every bit the part of the free-spirited hippie desert dweller, replete with torn at the knee faded blue jeans and a crisp white tank top. She wore an old, soft leather cowboy hat over her exceptionally long, ultra-straight, sunlit brown hair, speckled now, Irwin noticed, with hints of gray. Around her bronzed neck hung a collection of sterling silver chains, one sporting a large violet amethyst teardrop, the other an old, no longer in use patina colored New York City subway token. To describe the lady merely as beautiful would have been a terrible disservice.

Irwin stole a quick peek at Harper, not at all surprised to find her staring with unmitigated admiration at the woman. A commonality of spirit flashed between the two that even Irwin couldn't deny. Perhaps in a different time and world, they could have been friends.

A young, handsome preteen boy with jet black long hair pulled into a ponytail accompanied her. They strode together toward the group, but unlike the smiling woman, the boy wore an unwelcoming grim expression. Clearly, he thought this group of new visitors wasn't as appreciated as the entrance sign professed.

"Warmest welcome to Falcon's Nest. I'm Luna, and this is my son, Jax."

The stony-faced Jax stood silent, but under his mother's direction, offered the group a feeble, less than pleasant nod 'hello.'

Irwin started to make the introductions, but Harper jolted forward, clasping his forearm. "Let me," she murmured, stepping forward, clearly energized by some invisible yet highly transmittable creative spirit. "These are my people."

"So nice to meet you both. I'm Harper Crane, and this is Irwin Abernathy, the person who contacted you. This is

Christopher, and my parents, Darren and Olivia. We're Cornelia's family."

Jax's face, at the simple passing reference to Cornelia's name, morphed from deeply somber and suspicious to excited and animated. He tugged his mom's wrist, his dark brown eyes glued to her lips—looking to her for confirmation.

She signed back, "Yes. This is Auntie Cornelia's family."

Now all smiles, Jax's hands signed, "Welcome, family. Please, follow me."

Harper, who had taken three levels of American Sign Language in college, understood enough to translate Jax's request aloud to the group, and together they followed him and his mother toward the center of the compound.

"Feel free to sit and relax here," invited Luna, pointing to a wide variety of wooden chairs and lively painted benches nestled in a circle around an unlit, but well-used firepit.

Irwin, entirely out of his element, stood rigid and stiff. Nothing about the weathered wood furniture indicated comfort to him. As everyone moved to sit, he remained where he stood, hands clasped in front of him.

"Thank you," Harper said to Luna and Jax, pulling Irwin's arm to join her. "Give me that," she pried the urn from his arms and shoved it into her backpack.

Everyone sat, waiting for Luna to continue, but before she spoke, the energy in the air seemed to turn oddly still and quiet. Even Irwin detected the shift, feeling as if they were being watched.

Luna picked up on the group's discomfort and made a show of waving to the others milling about, observing. A few of the onlookers offered tentative waves, but nobody ventured any closer, choosing to remain at a respectful, and probably what they considered safer distance away.

"I'll be right with you," said Luna to the group before turning to sign to her son. "Jax? Give me a hand."

Jax, the former sullen, glowering boy, followed obediently after his mom, almost with a skip. But instead of going into the house marked 'office,' Irwin noticed they entered the building next to it—a lovely, picturesque cottage-style tiny home with lace hanging from open windows in place of screens. Crisp, recently laundered white sheets hung on a clothesline between two erected poles. Nearby, an impressive variety of vegetable plants surrounded a huge metal drum, presumably used to store water. More windchimes hung from the corner of the small, neatly painted white porch, tinkling, and chinking ever so slightly in the almost nonexistent breeze.

Moments later, Luna and Jax reappeared. Luna carried a tray filled with cups and a pitcher, and Jax held a serving plate, its unidentified treats covered with cheesecloth.

"I hope you like lavender iced tea," Luna said, placing the tray on one of the benches. She poured each person a glass while Jax went person-to-person, offering homemade oatmeal raisin and lavender sugar cookies.

"I love lavender iced tea," said Harper, sipping. "And this is beyond delicious. Thank you."

"*Hmmm*," agreed both Olivia and Christopher, politely sipping.

Darren bit into his sugar cookie and let out a loud pleasure-filled moan. "Man, I've had sugar cookies before, but this is out of this world good."

"Thank you," said Luna, looking pleased. "They're simple, but we like them." She pointed to another sizeable garden on the far end of one of the other houses. "We grow most of what we use, and we buy or trade the rest with local farmers."

"Even the lavender?" asked Harper.

"Yes. Even the lavender," answered Luna.

"Incredible. The cookies, the tea, this place." Harper sat with rapt attention. "Can you tell us more about Falcon's Nest?" asked Harper as she glanced around, releasing an appreciative sigh. "Everything here feels so peaceful."

Irwin scowled. Peaceful wasn't exactly how he would have described it, almost positive he could identify the smoky smell from before as cannabis.

Luna poured the last cup of iced tea for herself and sat on a large rock fixed between Harper and Irwin's chairs. "We call this continuous circle of tiny homes around you, 'The Peace Train.' Every tiny house you see here represents not only a shelter but a safety net for those who have had to escape unimaginable and often dangerous living conditions. It started when Jax and I moved here over fourteen years ago. The actual community you see before you began to grow approximately three years later—the brainchild of your friend and mine."

"Wait," said Harper. "You mean, Cornelia?"

"The one and only," replied Luna, sipping her tea.

"And who are the rest of these people, if you don't mind me asking?" asked Olivia. "Friends or family?"

Luna shook her head. "I like to describe our small-knit community as a group of unlikely friends who eventually became family. Falcon's Nest is special because, unlike other shelters, it offers a safe place for creatives to feel protected and understood. What originally started as a vision eventually turned into a community. All the subsequent units you see here were built with the help of the community. We pooled our funds and bartered for what we needed through the sale of our art. And, as the needs of our community increased and changed, so did the size of our circle. To date, we have twenty acres we call home."

"That's incredible," said Harper.

"Thank you."

"Do you get many visitors?" asked Irwin.

Harper shot Irwin a snarl, but Luna never noticed.

"No. Barely ever. We do have the occasional neighbor or farmer stop by when making deliveries, but for the most part, we're on our own, and I prefer it that way."

Irwin nodded, but as soon as Luna looked away, he poked his tongue out at Harper, making Jax, sitting across from them and watching them closely, laugh.

"What was the motivation behind you and Cornelia for creating this place?" asked Christopher.

"Excellent question." Luna shifted on the rock to get more comfortable, her voice taking on almost a philosophical intonation. "Each person comes to us with a backstory and plenty of baggage. There's no getting around that. It takes time and space to heal, and we can offer that. However, with that said, we also share many commonalities. One of which is to avoid danger and recrimination at all costs."

"Are you referring specifically to domestic violence?" asked Olivia, her cookies balanced on a napkin on her knees.

"Yes. Domestic violence, sexual assault, stalking—bigotry, racism, sexism, classism—you name it. Each person here escaped from some form of an abusive relationship or situation. Falcon's Nest offered them refuge."

"I noticed each house is named differently," said Harper. "Do you decide on the names or the visitors?"

"*Ah*, yes. The names." Luna beamed at her son. "They were actually Jax's idea."

Jax, sitting off to the side, nodded and blushed, but his mother continued.

"Although I know who everyone is, no real names are used. We ask everyone when they come to take on an alias. We do that for their protection—as well as ours. Nevertheless, having to lose one's identity, even for safety purposes, is difficult enough. Then, to have to live someplace out in the middle of nowhere?" Luna shrugged. "It's rough. We believe a person's name is the most important connection to one's identity and individuality. To be asked to leave that behind can feel daunting and lonely. That's when my sweet Jax came up with the idea to let everyone name their tiny house with something that held meaning to them. For example, my name Luna means 'the moon.' The moon is considered the universal representation of time. However, as a feminine symbol, its phases embody points symbolizing eternity, immortality, and enlightenment, only from a darker side of nature. Accurately appropriate, wouldn't you say? And hence, why I named my tiny home *The Crescent House*."

Jax walked over and tapped his mother's shoulder. Everyone watched as his fingers danced.

Luna smiled and nodded. "Jax wants me to tell you he named his tiny home, *Stargazer*."

"What!" Harper signed back, albeit a whole lot slower. She needed to fingerspell the majority of her reply. Jax politely watched Harper sign as she spoke, nodding intermittingly as encouragement, "After Jean-Luc Picard's first captaincy? *The USS Stargazer?* Right?" signed Harper.

Visibly excited to be in the presence of another Star Trek fan, Jax nodded and signed back, "*Yes!* —*it's the model Captain Picard kept on his desk in the ready room.*"

"I thought so," exclaimed Harper aloud. Then she contorted her fingers in Mr. Spock's 'Live Long and Prosper" symbol.

Jax giggled and returned the famed Trekkie greeting, much to his mother's amusement and Irwin's exasperation.

"May we continue?" Irwin griped.

"Follow me." Luna stood. She took two steps forward, then raised her hand as if in an afterthought. She turned, no longer smiling to face the group. "Take a good look around." Luna paused, waiting for everyone to assemble. "We are standing on only a small portion of the land Cornelia purchased, sight unseen. I want you to know she did this for no other reason but because I needed to escape from an abusive relationship. At the time, she felt I had to go someplace far away from my ex to a place where I could get a fresh start without having to look over my shoulder all the time." Luna stopped as if giving the group time to let her words sink in. "Jax's father was a lawyer. A good one. In all likelihood, he still is. You can only imagine what I had been up against."

Irwin caught Harper side-eye Christopher as she reflexively twisted her engagement ring. Then, just as quickly, she looked away.

"Not only did my ex-husband have the knowledge and money to fight the case, but he knew all the judges on a first name basis. Most of the police officers, and the other attorneys to boot. I didn't stand a chance of fighting him on his own turf. That's when Cornelia, who I had met and liked as a student, approached me. Cornelia ran the school's theater department along with her friend—" Luna paused as if stretching her mind to remember. "a woman named Gilly Satter—"

"Satterfield," finished Irwin.

The group turned toward Irwin. Irwin, his hands folded across his chest, sat stoically still, his expression unreadable.

"Why, yes," nodded Luna, pulling herself to the edge of the rock to face Irwin. "Did you know Gilly?"

"I did," answered Irwin, his voice fractured with emotion.

Unlike most people who would have clumsily continued to pry, Luna did not. Instead, she simply inhaled deeply, covered her heart with her open palm, and lowered her head to Irwin in a single, solemn bow.

Touched by Luna's dignity and compassion, Irwin closed his eyes, losing all awareness of the other eyes fixated on them. When he reopened them, Luna had already shifted her body to shield him, granting him a further moment of privacy, while she continued to address the rest of the group again.

In that moment, Irwin inexplicably understood Cornelia's connection to this woman and her child, grateful to now be a part of it.

"I had been an assistant art teacher at the time, working on the sets for the annual theater production," explained Luna. "Up to that point, Cornelia and I were friendly, but that was about it. Then one day, I showed up to rehearsal with a swollen cheek and bruises up and down my arms. That's when she started pulling me to the side to talk to me, listening to my story. I began to trust Cornelia, grateful for her friendship. It took some convincing, but eventually, she persuaded me to leave—to start over and rebuild my life somewhere safer. For both our sakes." Luna winked at her adoring son.

As Luna spoke, Irwin recalled Stan, Gilly's ex-husband. An emotionally brutal weasel of a man and shameless philanderer. Gilly had confided in Irwin that it had also taken her a while to learn to trust Cornelia as well. Not because of anything Cornelia had done, but because she had lost confidence in her judgment. It had taken a lot of convincing, but once Gilly made up her mind to leave Stan, it had been Cornelia steadfast in her corner through thick and thin, supporting her through the pangs of a messy divorce. Stan had been a real bastard and a bully, but like Luna, and every other victim of domestic violence, Gilly, too, deserved more in life than a malignant abuser.

The sound of Luna's voice cut through Irwin's thoughts, dragging him back to the present.

"As you can imagine, with me being a part-time, poorly paid art teacher and my ex, an extremely well-paid attorney, I didn't have many choices at my disposal. At the time, Jax had been no more than a toddler, and with a baby and limited funds, deciding where to go seemed a colossal and daunting decision to make. However, Cornelia, never one to easily give up, kept reminding me I had skills to fall back on—namely my art and teaching. Unfortunately, art and teaching aren't necessarily skills one can immediately generate a livable income with when one is on the run. Cornelia intuitively understood that."

"Of course, she did," smiled Olivia, squeezing Darren's hand.

"Soon enough, my home life got more dangerous but leaving still didn't feel like much of an option. I knew I had to get us out but didn't know how." For the first time since telling her story, Luna's eyes glistened, tearing up at the memory. Luna moistened her dry lips and spoke in a soft tone. "Cornelia did something I could never have predicted."

Here we go, thought Irwin, sneaking glances at the faces frozen onto Luna's.

"She called the house one day with some concocted, hair-brained story about needing me at the set. Some big emergency. Told me I had to come right over." Luna shook her head. "I remember not having anyone to watch Jax. My bigtime attorney husband at the time didn't believe he should have to 'babysit' his own child on his one day off, but Cornelia insisted I bring him. Said it wouldn't be a problem. Just to rush. And so, I did. But when I pulled up to the school parking lot, it was empty, and the doors were locked. I thought I must have misunderstood her, but a few seconds later, Cornelia came barreling around the corner—"

"Speeding and driving like a lunatic, I presume," announced Irwin.

Luna laughed. "Exactly. She pulled up to my car. Tires screeching, turned off the engine, opened and slammed her door, then opened mine and plopped herself on my front seat."

"'Here you go, babycakes.' That's what Cornelia liked to call me. To this day, I still don't know why," Luna grinned. "Anyway, she then handed me an envelope filled with a lot of cash, two one-way plane tickets, and a deed in her name to this land and house."

"'Take this and hide it somewhere safe,' she told me. 'You're set to leave two days from today. That should give you enough time to sneak pack whatever you can't live without. Do you still have that bugout bag I told you to pack?'"

I told her I did.

"'Good. You know the drill, then.'"

"But Cornelia,' I told her. "I can't take this. Then she said, 'I'm not asking you. I'm telling you to.'"

"But it's too much," I tried to tell her.

"'I hope it's enough.' Then she said, 'Please let me do this,' and then Cornelia squeezed my hand and whispered sternly, "'Listen to me. Your husband isn't going to stop. One of these days, he's going to go too far and hurt Jax or kill you.'"

"I knew Cornelia was right. She told me to take whatever paperwork I needed and be careful. Super careful. She didn't want my husband to find out we were gone until it was too late."

"What kind of paperwork?" asked Harper.

"The deed to this land, a few other papers, mostly directions to get here and instructions. And two bogus birth certificates with a real bankbook under those new names. I asked her how she accomplished it but told me not to ask any questions. I also asked her how I could ever repay her."

"What did she say?" asked Olivia.

"Cornelia looked at me, her expression stern, and said, 'By never coming back.' Then she leaned in, hugged me, and kissed Jax." Luna's voice quivered. "She promised to keep in touch, and kept that promise ten times over, but it was the last time Jax or I ever physically saw Cornelia again." Luna turned to Irwin. "When you called to tell me she had died, it felt like my world shattered. Like the only mother I had in the world had been taken from me. When you mentioned the letter, I hoped Cornelia would finally explain why she did what she did for me—for us."

"I'm sure she has," said Irwin, meaning it. He reached around into his back pocket.

"Thank you," Luna nodded, gripping the letter. "And to all of you for bringing this small piece of Cornelia back home to us."

"Hell, we've got a whole lot more of her if you want," mumbled Darren pointing to Harper's backpack, earning him a swift pinch to the inside of his upper arm.

Luna's head whipped around to Darren. "What did you mean by that?"

"Idiot!" Olivia seethed, cutting her eyes at her husband.

"What? —Cornelia would have laughed," grumbled Darren, nursing his newest wound.

Harper lifted her backpack and tugged the urn partially out. "My dad means this."

Luna gasped and cupped her mouth. "Is that—"

Harper nodded.

"May I?" asked Luna, her hands spread open, pleadingly.

"Of course." Harper yanked the urn the rest of the way out and handed the jar to Luna. Luna, in turn, hugged the container, weeping and smiling at the same time.

"Oh, Cornelia, you came to us at last," she said, tears of joy streaming down her sun-kissed cheeks.

Irwin, prone to being discernibly rude, could only stare at Harper, confused.

Harper, in turn, winced, meeting Irwin's perplexed glare with an equal, albeit baffled probing stare of her own.

"*Uhm, um*, Miss Luna," interrupted Irwin, glancing around for rescue. "You're holding Cornelia's," his eyes narrowed, searching for the right way to put this. "Well, her ashes. You know, her remains."

Luna's upper body braced with an unnatural stillness.

Irwin shuffled his foot under her glare, drawing a circle in the dirt with the heel of his shoe. "What's left *after* cremation."

Mortified, no one dared move a muscle.

"I'm fully aware of that," Luna spoke directly to Irwin, her breathing slow and even. "But none of that matters to me. Cornelia's soul is here and with us now. I can feel her, and for today, that is enough."

And for today, that is enough.

Irwin's face softened under the sudden realization that perhaps he, too, no longer needed to hold on so tightly to Gilly as if she were still here. Not necessarily to forget her, because he would never do that, but because the time had finally come for him to move forward. To make peace with what was while making space for what could be.

Behind Luna, Darren signaled the cuckoo sign, but this time his audience did not laugh. In fact, it earned him another rebuke from an embarrassed Olivia.

"*Ugh!*" he grimaced behind clenched teeth. "I hate it when you do that," he snarled.

"Then shut up for once," Olivia snapped under her breath.

"Play nice, children," muttered Irwin.

Luna turned to Harper. "Where do you intend on bringing Cornelia's ashes? I'm only asking because she is more than welcome to remain here with us."

"Excuse me—" said Irwin, but Harper cut him off.

"Not possible, I'm afraid." Harper shook her head sadly. "Cornelia's already requested we scatter her remains in San Diego."

"San Diego?" Now Luna looked confused.

"Specifically, the Pacific Ocean," Harper explained.

"Oh. I see. Where specifically in San Diego?"

Harper half-shrugged. "La Jolla?"

"*Ah*. That makes perfect sense then," nodded Luna, apparently pacified by Harper's answer.

"Why do you say that?" asked Olivia, never one to leave well enough alone.

"Because of The La Jolla Playhouse." Luna paused, glancing at the circle of blank faces. "Sorry. I should explain. La Jolla has been considered an artist's colony since the late eighteen hundreds. It started as a bunch of small cottages and a place for creative types to live and interact with one another. Then, The La Jolla Playhouse was established, and it ran until about 1959 when it became inactive. However, in 1983, The University of California allowed its campus to house the revived project, which now has three theaters."

The blank stares continued.

Luna exhaled. "Sorry again. Cornelia—if I'm not mistaken, had been a close friend of one of the founding members. I apologize, but I'm terrible with names, but her being a writer, she'd taken an active interest in helping to restore the playhouse."

"*Ahhh...*" chorused the group.

"So, if I understand you correctly," said Irwin, "you're saying Cornelia selected La Jolla as her final resting place because of a particular attachment to the area's history?"

Luna shrugged. "It's a good enough reason as any."

Irwin studied Luna. There was something she wasn't saying, and he wanted to know why. "There's a woman named Elle Reed who also lives there. We're headed to meet her next." Irwin watched Luna's face closely and swore he saw a knowing glint flash in her eyes, but he couldn't be sure. "Would you happen to know this Elle person?"

Irwin saw Luna clamp down on her bottom lip. "Who I

know and don't is, I'm afraid, something I cannot confirm or deny."

"What?" Irwin's head spun toward Harper. "What is she saying? I'm not understanding. Translate."

"'Cannot confirm or deny.' It's a politer way of Luna saying she can't and won't tell you," explained Harper.

"That part I got, but why?"

"For Elle's privacy —*and safety*." Harper leaned in to enunciate the word 'safety' for emphasis.

"Safety?" Irwin's brow furrowed. "We're giving her a letter, not a beating."

Harper groaned. "That's not what I meant."

"Thanks, Harper, but why don't you let me try," Luna offered, kindly.

"Feel free," Harper snorted. "He's all yours."

"Irwin," said Luna softly. "We're a colony of artists, writers, and creatives from all different backgrounds and circumstances. But, as I explained earlier, we also share a few things in common: namely, we each came to Falcon's Nest looking to start a new life, and for many, to escape abuse. Since establishing this place, hundreds of people have stayed with us. One could almost say this place is magical. After a few months, and with the freedom to move about without fear, people start to breathe again. They heal and create, and eventually, when the time feels right, they make plans to leave. However, because we deal with survivors of abuse and assault, we must do everything possible to protect their privacy. And to do this, the identities, even of those who came and left, are never confirmed or denied, to anyone. Call it our policy."

"I see." Irwin nodded, a grave, weighted expression stretched across his face as his thoughts wandered back to Martin Newman. "Then tell me this, can you at least confirm or deny whether or not Cornelia, who is no longer with us and therefore is in no need of further protection, had she ever been a victim of abuse or sexual assault?"

Luna dug her hands deep into her jean's pockets, drew in a large breath as if trying to gauge her response. "Sorry, but I can tell you is this—for as long as I knew Cornelia, she had been a staunch advocate against domestic violence and sexual assault. Granted, she originally purchased this land because she wanted me and Jax to have a safe place to live. However, after a time, we decided together to extend the impact of our—safe haven, let's call it. We both wanted to open an underground safe home for other women and children desperately in need of escape. We wanted to make Falcon's Nest that place—providing others the same opportunity to rebuild their lives without fear. Each year, when funds permitted, we add another house. We currently have twelve homes, not counting mine and Jax's, or the one over there used as a common kitchen, and the one in the front, used as an office and for counseling. Sixteen in all."

"This is pretty impressive," said Harper. "But since you are an underground safe house, how do victims of abuse find out about its existence?"

"By word of mouth," answered Luna. "We work with a select group of specialized individuals I trust."

"Then I have to tell you, we're genuinely honored you have allowed us to come visit," said Olivia.

"Frankly, I almost didn't, to be honest," said Luna. "But if Cornelia sent you, then I had to believe in her trust in you." Luna added, "Cornelia's never let me down." She turned back to Irwin. "We had plans to extend to twenty-four houses, but now with Cornelia gone, I'm not sure what's going to happen. You see, the fact is, I don't own the land or the house I live in. Cornelia did. I'm not sure I can afford to buy it from her estate or the person she left it to."

At that moment, a few of the current residents began to

filter out of their homes, heading off in different directions and looking anxious to get their afternoon started.

Irwin nodded. "Then perhaps it's best we go and let you read your letter in peace."

"Yes. You're probably right." Luna struck the envelope against her thigh and sighed. "No time like the present."

"*Ah*, Luna? Before we go," said Christopher softly. "I need one moment of your time, please."

"Okay..." Luna half-nodded, eying Christopher warily.

"I'm an attorney. Not Cornelia's, except in this particular matter. If you wouldn't mind, could we speak? Alone?"

"*Ah*, sure. That's fine." Luna's facial expression went from soft to visibly anxious. "We can talk in my office if you want."

Harper turned, staring at Christopher, dumbstruck.

"I'll only be a few minutes," he whispered in her ear and winked.

While Luna and Christopher strode off in the direction of the tiny house makeshift office with the brightly painted sign in rainbow colors, Irwin moseyed to Harper's side.

"Did you know about this?" Harper asked him, arms crossed, tapping her foot.

"I cannot confirm or deny," he replied, holding his hands out in front of him as if weighing them in the air.

"Well? Planning for lift-off, Superman, or are you going to tell me?"

"Sorry. My lips are sealed." Irwin clasped his hands behind his back and rocked on his heels, grinning like a Cheshire cat. "However, fortunately for you, I won't need to tell you a thing," he said, tapping a finger against his ear. "Just listen."

And then, the loudest, the most celebrated, the most magnificent yelp of sheer unmitigated happiness one could have ever hoped for sliced through the open, desert air.

Chin quivering, eyes brimming, Harper turned her rosy

face towards Luna's office, then just as quickly buried her wet cheek against Irwin's shoulder to weep happy tears.

"Not all attorneys are the same," he said softly into her hair.

Harper sobbed an inaudible, muffled, *"I know."* Then she lifted her tear-stained face to take a better look into Irwin's eyes. "She did it again, didn't she?"

Irwin, no longer capable of disguising the admiration he held for his long-lost friend, hugged Harper and nodded. "She did indeed."

"I PROMISE." Luna hugged Harper tight. "And here, take this." She handed Harper a small wrapped package, no larger than the size of her palm, and a slip of paper. "It's just a little something to remember us by until we next meet." Luna pecked Harper on the forehead. "Take care of yourself and your family."

"I will."

"And don't forget what I said." Luna clasped Harper's hands, one thumb rolling Harper's engagement ring. "Cornelia's left me more acres than I know what to do with. Certainly, more than enough for you to build a homestead of your own on one day. All you have to do is say the word and it's yours."

"Thank you." Harper's eyes glistened. "For everything." She squeezed Luna's hands. "You know, I can't explain it, but from the second we met, I felt like I knew you all my life. Like, there's this understood connection between us. It's hard to describe."

"You don't have to. I felt it, too. But the Universe is funny that way. She seems to enjoy relinking strong-willed souls together again."

"Harper!" called Irwin, waiting by the staked in the ground welcome sign. "We have a long drive ahead of us, more stops to make, and people to insult. Let's get a move on."

"I don't know what it is about that guy," Luna laughed. "but I honestly really like him."

Harper glanced over her shoulder toward Irwin, heartened to see his arms wrapped protectively around the urn.

"Yeah. He does tend to grow on you." Harper smiled. "Bye, Jax!" she waved, breaking out into a slow jog, Luna's gift and paper held tightly in her grasp.

CHAPTER 19

LAS CRUCES TO LA JOLLA, San Diego, approximately a ten plus hour drive, but by the time the group got on the road, they decided five and half hours later to call it a day. Harper located a decent enough hotel room online with better than good ratings and a few exciting eateries close enough to make everybody's belly happy. And for once, Irwin didn't complain, protest, nitpick, nor criticize.

By ten the next morning, the group found themselves back in the crammed car on the last portion of the journey before flying home. With just about five hours left, they anticipated arriving in San Diego no later than three in the afternoon.

"In and out," announced Irwin. "No long discussions, no life-explanatory consultations, no high tea. We hand Ms. Elle

Reed her letter, bid her a good day, and tomorrow, we spread Cornelia's ashes."

"What? No potty breaks?" goaded Harper. "I'm calling my union rep."

"I'm hungry," said Darren.

"Me, too," said Olivia. "And stiff. I wonder if the hotel will have a pool. I could use a relaxing swim. Work out some of these kinks." She reached up to massage the back of her neck.

"You don't need a pool for that," winked Darren, nibbling his wife's blushing cheek. "I am perfectly capable of helping work out anything you'd like."

Harper groaned and pretended to gag at her parent's latest most disturbing PDA, moving as far away from them as a compact, cramped car would allow.

"They've got to have a pool." Olivia sat forward. "Harper? Do me a favor and check to make sure the hotel has a pool."

"It has a pool, Mother."

"But check to be sure."

"I'm positive. It has a pool."

"Excuse me," Irwin interrupted, clapping his hands, "but did anybody hear a word of what I just said?"

"We heard you, we heard you." Harper pressed her face against the cold glass. "Verbatim, you said you are looking forward to meeting Elle Reed, there was no rush because we have all evening, and—you're hoping she agrees to come out to dinner with us. That way, you added, we can learn more about Cornelia since we drove across an entire freakin' country to do exactly that."

Irwin's shoulders slumped.

"We should be there in about twenty minutes," announced Christopher. "How about we check into the hotel first, dump our baggage, get refreshed, and then head over? What time did you tell her we would be there?"

"I told her sometime before six," confirmed Irwin.

"I'll get the directions from the hotel. What's her shop called?" asked Harper.

Irwin checked his notes. "It's called 'The Bird Bath,' and it's an apothecary."

Harper flinched. "Say that again—"

"It's an apothecary," repeated Irwin.

"No, not that, the name," Harper insisted.

"The Bird Bath."

Harper stopped her online search and whipped out Luna's wrapped package and note.

"Why?" asked Irwin. "What possibly could be the problem now?"

"Hold on a sec. I just need to check something." Harper read the note silently to herself.

Dearest Harper,

    Always remember, this journey started all with a simple birdbath.

    You'll understand everything soon enough.

    Until our souls meet again,

    Luna.

HARPER EXHALED.

Irwin twisted around in his seat, watching Harper unwrap the small package. A beautiful clay birdbath with two love birds perched on the rim. She lifted it for Irwin to see.

"Just like the one Cornelia had," he said.

"Exactly like the one."

"The hotel should be right down this road," said Christopher. "Hey," he pointed. "Isn't that the apothecary you were just talking about?"

Amid a long line of other equally charming businesses stood Elle Reed's shop. Unlike a typical dark wood apothecary with dusty tinctures in antiquated glass bottles lining every available shelf, Reed's shop appeared more modern and airier. The storefront, made entirely out of glass, displayed nothing to indicate what type of shop one would be entering except for the shop's name in bold old typeset, offset by a two-love bird logo design.

"*Huh,*" said Harper. "That's not at all what I expected," she muttered long after they passed the store.

"I suspect our Ms. Reed will have an interesting story to tell," said Irwin, in apparent agreement.

Harper rewrapped and returned her small package to her backpack. "And here you had me believing that all you wanted to do was chuck Cornelia's letter at her and run."

Irwin shook his head. "Not anymore, I don't."

ELLE FINISHED RINGING up the last of her customers.

"Have a nice day," she said, handing the pleasant couple their carefully wrapped package and change. "Enjoy the rest of your vacation. La Jolla's a great place to relax, take in the scenery and unwind."

Elle enjoyed talking with her customers, asking them about their weekend plans or interests. She especially appreciated when they asked her about a particular art piece she carried, allowing her the opportunity to share with them how their purchase had helped to support women in need. Most conversations were of the light and breezy variety—polite, quick exchanges. However, every so often, Elle would come across a fellow lonely soul, or perhaps a woman in dire need of help. Those conversations, while challenging, were at the same time, a welcome and necessary reminder as to the growing demand for the service she provided.

"We will," replied the woman. "And thanks again for all the insider tips. I'm looking forward to taking that stroll along the Historic Coast Walk you spoke about—if I can pull this darn man of mine away from the Murals of La Jolla long enough."

"Hey," replied her husband, playfully kissing his wife's cheek. "Can I help it if I appreciate beauty? After all, I married you, didn't I?"

"Oh, stop it, you," laughed the blushing woman, pretending to be outraged.

Elle smiled, admiring their love.

They waved Elle a pleasant goodbye, and off they went into the midday sun, hand-in-hand.

Elle longed for the day when she too had someone special. Someone to share her life and dreams with. Someone to confide in, but more importantly—someone she could trust. So far, she hadn't been so fortunate, coming to the jaded conclusion those sorts of men didn't genuinely exist except inside the pages of a romance book.

That's not to say the men she had met weren't, well, *nice enough*, but nice enough no longer felt *good enough*. Elle wanted more. Much more, and she wasn't willing to settle for less. Certainly not like her first marriage, when she, desperate to be loved, had put the entirety of Ryan's inexhaustible needs and endless wants ahead of her own—usually at considerable personal risk.

Ryan.

Elle's shoulders quaked at the mere contemplation of his name, ashamed how her memories of him still invoked fear deep within, despite his being thousands of miles away.

Feeling a bit edgy, and with nothing left to do but wait,

Elle paced the store looking for anything not in its proper place. She tidied the front display, *tut-tutting* in mock frustration at items barely askew.

Why dredge Ryan up now?

Elle had worked hard not to give that monster rent-free space in her head, realizing how she connected to her past would set the tone for every other relationship moving forward. It may have taken years of deep introspection to rebuild independence and regain her self-worth, but eventually, the intrusive thoughts had become less frequent. Less terrifying, but never any less lonely.

Elle checked the time. They'd be here soon, —*and with a letter from Cornelia, no less.*

Irwin, Cornelia's friend, had phoned from the hotel saying they were checking in. They wanted to first freshen up and would be by her place within the next hour.

That was thirty minutes ago.

It had been a surprisingly hectic morning and busier midafternoon, but now, as the long day spilled into the evening and people began looking for places to have a nice meal, everything quieted down. For Elle, that was a plus since, in all likelihood, she'd need to close up shop early.

Cornelia had piqued Elle's curiosity. Not so much about whatever the letter contained—a letter, which incidentally could have just as easily been dropped in the mail, but as to why Cornelia had thought it so necessary that Elle meet her friends, especially Irwin Abernathy.

Good Old, Irwin Abernathy—

"This should prove interesting," she muttered under her breath.

Elle had heard countless stories about Irwin over the years, and in far too many ways, she felt as if she already knew more than enough about him.

So why then all the subterfuge surrounding this forced visit?

And then it hit her.

Matchmaking—

"Cornelia!" grumbled Elle, stomping her way into the backroom, angry she hadn't realized this before.

Despite all the different ways Elle had explained how she wasn't the least bit emotionally available to meet someone right now, Cornelia wouldn't take no for an answer. The fact that Cornelia was dead seemed to have done little to sway her determination to force them together.

"Yes, okay, okay," Elle had muttered into the phone to Cornelia during one of their last lucid phone conversations. "I'm not saying he doesn't sound like a lovely man." ... "No, I'm not closed off to finding happiness." ... "Yes, but Cornelia, you're not listening to me. As I have already explained, I'm just not in the right head space to commit right now, and from what you've told me about Irwin, neither is he."

"Oh, phooey." Cornelia had replied, undefeated. "The both of you belong together. Trust me. I know these things."

"Oh, please. Stop this madness, already. I have a good life in San Diego. The shop is doing great, and I can more than comfortably support myself. And, for your information, I have made some wonderful friends here as well."

"But no love life," Cornelia countered.

"I hate to inform you, Ms. Parish, but not everyone needs to be madly in love to be happy," Elle had snapped, losing her cool.

"Sure," Cornelia shot right back. "Keep telling yourself that."

"Oh? Then what about you?" The cutting accusation had slipped out before Elle could stop it. "I'm sorry, Cornelia. That was uncalled for."

"Don't be sorry. You just proved my point."

ELLE LOVED what she did for a living, and the people her line of work allowed her to help. Most of all, she found the people she met the most fascinating, and the quirkier—the better. However, after years of listening to Cornelia's colorful stories about Irwin, she had begun to think 'quirkier' might not be all it was cracked up to be.

CHAPTER 20

EVERYTHING ABOUT ELLE REED'S place screamed magazine-perfect. High-beamed ceilings, freshly painted white walls, and glossy buffed to a high sheen floor accented with genuine Persian rugs. Glass and mirrors amplified the airy, light space. Still, it was the lavish profusion of artistically placed artisan crafts of all types and varieties which lured the curious in, conveying the impression of stepping into an art gallery, as opposed to Irwin's opinion of an apothecary.

In the corner stood three tall tree-like plants with gigantic leaves. Wooden tables strategically placed held various ceramic pots, beaded vases, and large charger plates. By the entrance, Elle had a cluster of half-burnt candles of all different heights, nestled together on a small metal stand.

Irwin sniffed. They had been recently lit, and their white

linen fragrance continued to hang heavy in the air. He sniffed again and grinned, not totally hating it.

In the corner, a single, standalone metal rack jam-packed with long, luxurious scarves of every imaginable vibrant color ever produced. Soaps in glass vessels, oils in tiny glass amber bottles, and other aromatic extravagances were pleasingly scattered throughout the shop with little handcrafted signs encouraging patrons to touch and smell. But what caught Harper's eye first was the stunning painting hanging behind the register of a beautiful young woman standing next to a birdbath, her hands folded together as if in prayer. Resting on her palms, were two tiny love birds.

Irwin, who had been standing a mere few inches behind Harper, gulped, evidently as taken with the painting as she. The two were still gawking at it when a pleasant-sounding voice from the back of the shop called out, 'I'll be right with you.' Seconds later, a striking woman, possibly in her mid-sixties with the prettiest eyes and chin-length wavy gray-steel hair, pushed through white louvered batwing doors to greet them. As she approached the group, she extended her hand first out to Irwin.

"Hello. I'm Elle Reed, and you must be Irwin Abernathy," she said, her lovely voice composed and steady.

"Ms. Reed. Nice to meet you," replied Irwin, looking dumbstruck.

Harper couldn't help but notice the way the crevices around his eyes and lips lifted upward as soon as his gaze met Elle's. Almost like human fireworks.

"Thank you for letting us intrude on your day," he told her, bouncing lightly in place.

"Not at all," Elle returned Irwin's smile. "The pleasure is all mine."

Well, I'll be—Irwin's flirting! mused Harper, quick to mask her happiness as she watched the tips of poor Irwin's ears turn red.

Elle introduced herself to the others, greeting each of them by name with the same welcoming warmth and level of cordiality.

"I have been looking forward to meeting you all. Cornelia has told me so much about you."

As soon as the words left Elle's lips, Harper glimpsed Irwin, half expecting him to start his scowling routine, but nope. Not even a peck of a frown showed up. Instead, he stood with his arms flanked by his side with the stupidest grin on his face.

"I've got a comfortable sitting room in the back if you'd like to relax," Elle offered to the group, "or if you'd rather, I can lock up, and we can head down the street to grab a bite. I know this super quaint eatery a short walking distance from here—five minutes tops. They make the most delicious deli sandwiches, and their pickles are *the* best on the entire planet, outside of Brooklyn, of course. Say yes. My treat."

Irwin shook his head. "No, we couldn't impose on you like that—"

"Oh, but you must," replied Elle. She kept her gorgeous gray eyes with the long fan-like lashes locked onto Irwin, while she gently embraced his upper arm and began walking him toward the door.

Harper braced herself for the inevitable meltdown, but to her complete and utter dismay, it never came. The old faker never even flinched.

"Okay, now I've seen everything," Harper murmured under her breath.

"Give me a sec while I lock up the back and grab my bag. I'll be right with you." Elle floated to the back of the shop, never aware of Irwin tongue-wagging behind her.

"Close your mouth," Harper quietly barked.

Irwin scowled. "Excuse me?"

"Your mouth," she whispered. "You're drooling." Harper plucked a tissue from a box on a nearby table. "Not a good a look for a first date."

"Don't be ridiculous," Irwin scoffed, all while dabbing his lips with the proffered tissue. "Better?"

"Yes, much. And it's nothing to be ashamed of," cooed Olivia, flanking Irwin from his other side. "Elle's stunning, and she sure likes you."

"Stop it. The both of you," Irwin fumed. "—Just knock it off."

"The gentleman doth protest too much, methinks," teased Harper, leaving Irwin where he stood, freeing her to take a quick look around the store, unable to stop herself from touching or smelling everything within her reach. It only took a single glance back to confirm Irwin mind-melding her to 'reel it in.'

Moving further toward the back, Harper noticed a small collection of small crafted items, and precisely what she had hoped to find.

"*Pssst*, Irwin. Come here." She motioned him over. "Take a look at this."

"No," Irwin snorted, glancing around for a rescue. "I'm not falling for your nonsense this time," he hissed back, defiantly twisting his head in the far opposite direction.

"No, seriously." insisted Harper, waving him over. "I'm not messing with you. I swear on the next five purchases of Bones' Shrimp Lo Mein—you need to take a look at this."

Irwin still didn't budge.

"Come on. Okay—I swear on Cornelia's ashes, I'm not joking." Harper batted her eyes. "*Please.*"

Irwin, although reluctant to give in, slowly drifted over to the table, none too happy. "What is it?"

"Look." Harper crossed her arms, triumphantly over her chest. "I told you so."

Irwin glanced down at a collection of handmade bird-baths, identical in almost every way to Cornelia's, and indistinguishable from Luna's gift to Harper.

"Well, I'll be. They're all in this together," he muttered softly. "Cornelia, Luna, and Elle Reed."

"Seems that way." Harper leaned in closer to whisper in his ear. "But the better question is, together in what?"

"I'm ready," Elle announced, emerging from the back room wearing a light salmon-colored jacket, and carrying an expensive leather carryall tote slung casually over her shoulder.

Harper spun around, her expression as innocent as the day is long. "Elle? Before we go, can I ask you about these adorable birdbaths?"

If Harper's question rattled Elle in any way, no one would have ever detected.

"I'll do you one better," she answered. "Let's head over to the restaurant, and once I introduce an embarrassing amount of perfectly seasoned pickles into my digestive tract, I'll tell you all about them and anything else you want to know."

"Now that sounds great" said Irwin, turning into human mush right before Harper's eyes. "Doesn't that sound just great, Harper?"

"Great." Harper nodded, rubbing her palms together. "Pickles it is." She glanced back at Irwin, expecting another snarl, but instead found his mouth wide open again and gaping.

"Let's go, big guy." Harper gently guided Irwin toward the front door, wondering how in the world this geriatric, love-smitten, silly old man would ever survive the next few hours in Elle's presence without sinking into a pool of drool.

As promised, the café looked and smelled incredible. The food, delicious. Although busy, the maître d' immediately led them to a large, circular booth that could comfortably accommodate six. As soon as they were seated, their waitress, who said her name was Bridget, brought over a hefty ornate silver bowl filled to the top with pickles.

"Try one," Elle said to Irwin. "They make them here. They're to die for."

Irwin jabbed the top one with his fork, and then went into a slight panic when he realized he had no plate to lay it down on.

"Go on. Don't stand on ceremony, just bite right into it." Elle did the same with hers. "We don't encourage convention here in La Jolla."

Irwin did as she instructed. "*Hmmm*, they are delicious."

"I told you. Best in the country," said Elle.

"Except for Brooklyn," interjected Harper.

Elle laughed and lowered her voice. "Hush, don't let Earl over there hear you say that. He'll have a conniption."

"Earl?" Irwin asked.

Elle chin nodded toward a squat bald man standing by the register, merrily yakking it up with a few of his customers. "He and wife, Josephine, own the place. Josie's a doll, but I've witnessed Earl turn cantankerous over much less."

"Got it." Harper laughed, liking this woman more and more by the second. "Duly noted."

Irwin reached into his back pocket and slid Cornelia's letter across the table over to Elle. "Before I forget."

"*Ah*, yes," Elle's entire playful demeanor turned inside itself. "I had known for a while about Cornelia's dementia but began suspecting she had it long before her diagnosis when she would phone and keep repeating the same things—

asking the same questions. Much like my mom did when she had gone through it."

"So, you and Cornelia were close?" asked Olivia.

"I'd like to think so." Elle smiled. "I met Cornelia at a pivotal time in my life. In many ways, I credit her for giving me back my reasons to live at a time I didn't believe I wanted to." Elle slipped the letter into her tote. "Thank you, Irwin. I'll read this later."

"How long has your shop been open?" asked Darren, nursing a vanilla milkshake.

"The Bird Bath opened nine years ago." Elle looked at Harper. "You asked earlier about the ceramic birdbaths. Luna originally designed them." Elle paused when she caught Harper's surprise. "She phoned me and told me you were on your way."

Harper nodded and smiled.

"Once I opened the shop, we decided to have the women who stay at Luna's help make them in bulk for me to sell, along with a few other items they send. That way, we could apply the profits from the sales to help keep Falcon's Nest afloat."

"You keep nothing?" asked Olivia.

"Not on those items. Not a dime. Falcon's Nest supported me when I most needed them and helped me get back on my feet. It's also why I named the store, The Bird's Nest." Elle didn't elaborate any further. "It's my small way of paying it forward."

Harper now not only liked this woman, but loved her, and judging by Irwin's lilted lettuce, lovesick idiot expression, he did too.

"I noticed you carry an array of high quality globally handmade pieces in your shop, and not just the ordinary merchandise one would find in an apothecary," said Christopher.

"He's a lawyer," added Darren, as if this descriptor qualified Christopher's inquiry.

"*Ahhh*," Elle smiled. "You are very astute, Christopher. Since the inception of the store, I have remained committed to working within the socio-political ethos of my artists, many who have faced real-life challenges. At the same time, I am also keenly aware I need to market these statement pieces to appeal to a larger audience. The apothecary allows me to do both."

"And the birdbath? What does that signify?" asked Harper.

"We chose the birdbath as our symbol of hope and freedom. For us, it represents the beginning of our collective journey as women to demand a safe space to exist without the fear of violence. It had originally been the brainchild of Cornelia and Luna, with me jumping on board down the line to solidify the business end of it."

"A full circle," murmured Irwin.

Elle nodded at Irwin and laid her hand softly on his wrist. "Luna told me it had been the first craft she kept making over and over again when she no longer saw beauty but danger. The birdbath brought her back to a more peaceful place. When I first arrived at Falcon's Nest, I was a shell of a woman—angry, bitter, and so scared. Afraid of everything. I didn't know where to go or what to do."

"And Cornelia?" asked Olivia. "What part, if any, did she play in all of this if you don't mind me asking."

"Not at all, and I'm glad you did." Elle pushed back her half-eaten sandwich and steepled her fingers. "Cornelia had been my hotline worker."

"Your what?" gulped Irwin.

"Her hotline worker," explained Harper. "The person who answers the phones when—" but Irwin cut her off.

"I am fully aware of what a hotline worker does, thank you. I meant—I had no idea Cornelia did this work."

"You weren't supposed to," said Elle. "Hotline workers tend to conceal what they do for their safety. There's a lot of dangerous abusers out there who would think nothing of taking out their anger on the person they think is responsible for helping their victim escape. My ex was no exception."

"Again. I'm flabbergasted," repeated Irwin. "I had no idea,"

"For the record, Irwin, Cornelia hated hiding all this from you. She told me many times how much she didn't like keeping secrets from you. But the women she helped, well, to put it bluntly, their lives depended on her absolute discretion and full commitment to their confidentiality."

"That, I understand." Irwin nodded, looking surprisingly more at peace with himself than he had for a long time.

"But why the birdbaths?" asked Darren. "Besides the meaning and all..."

"All Luna," explained Elle. "When I arrived at Falcon's Nest, I barely ate or slept. Always afraid my ex would find me and drag me back home. Luna convinced me to take my anger and fear—out on the clay. And believe it or not, it worked. For all its simplicity, it worked. In art, I found healing. Not necessary in the making of it, because honestly, I have no artistic ability to speak of, but from being surrounded by it. And that's when I got the idea to open up the apothecary. I wanted to provide a way for women escaping abuse to procure an income through their art while still maintaining their independence and safety. Quite a mouthful, *huh?*"

"So, all the art you sell is survivor art?" asked Christopher.

"Precisely."

"From women all around the world?" asked Olivia, her voice overcome with emotion.

Elle nodded.

Harper glanced around the table at the faces of her family. Not a single dry eye in the group.

Gosh, haven't we become a bunch of crybabies.

Not only had Irwin fallen head over heels with Ms. Elle Reed, but so had the entire table.

Precisely the way Cornelia knew they would.

ONCE FINISHED, the group convened on the sidewalk.

"It's a beautiful evening. Would anyone care to take a stroll by the water?" asked Elle, standing especially close to Irwin.

"I'd love to, but I have some work emails I need to catch up on," said Christopher.

"I'll keep you company," Harper smiled, and the two kissed.

"A stroll by the water sounds great," said Darren, rubbing his full stomach. "It'll give me a chance to work off that milk-shake, which by the way," he whistled. "Good stuff."

Olivia snatched her husband's hand. "Not so fast, buddy. My back is killing me, and somebody I know and barely tolerate promised me a swim and massage."

Darren smiled and shrugged. "When she's right, she's right. Sorry, but I guess we're bowing out, too." Darren wrapped his arm around his wife's waist, not looking the slightest bit disappointed.

Elle turned to face Irwin. "Well sir, I guess that leaves just you and me. Are you up for a bit of a stroll?"

Irwin's eyes never left Elle's. He lifted an elbow for Elle to hold. "I would be delighted," he said softly. To the rest of the group—using his usual staid tone, "We need to convene in the lobby by ten. Agreed."

Everyone agreed, their faces playfully serious.

"Yes cap-i-tan," teased Harper. Ten it is or walk the plank we go."

Irwin, with Elle on his arm and already strolling away, didn't bother to retort.

"*Yikes.*" Harper bit her bottom lip. "He's got it bad, doesn't he?"

"Looks that way," said Darren, pleased. "And good for him. It's about time."

"I certainly approve," said Olivia. "I think Elle is perfect for him."

"Me, too," said Harper.

"I concur," said Christopher. "It's kind of nice to see him finally happy."

"So, let's agree, here and now, we won't do or say anything to screw this up for him," warned Olivia, sternly. "Agreed?"

They all nodded, smiling.

"No. Wipe those stupid grins off your faces. I mean it," threatened Olivia. "Irwin has just as much right to find happiness and love as we do."

"Then you're thinking this might be the real thing, Liv?" asked Darren in all sincerity.

"I am. I really, really am."

CHAPTER 21

IRWIN LAID on his bed alone, unable to fall sleep. His mind replaying the incredible evening he'd spent with the lovely Ms. Elle Reed.

Besides the fact her beauty made his knees quiver, it had scared Irwin down to his core how easy Elle had been to talk to, to listen to as she shared stories about her life, her friendship with Cornelia and Luna. And how she wound up deciding to put down roots in San Diego, to become the proud owner of such a highly successful apothecary.

More terrifying had been the ease by which Irwin found himself telling Elle about his past. Specifically, about losing Gilly. How he had spent the past eight years visiting her grave, only to pour out his heart to piece of stone.

Somehow, he made Elle laugh, telling her stories about his grandmother. He even spoke briefly about his friend Joe and their time spent in the military. Eventually, Irwin told Elle about his friendship with Cornelia, and how excited she had become when Harper came into their lives—and how much he feared losing Harper when she and Christopher tie the knot, and, in all likelihood, moved away.

"It's obvious how much Harper adores you," said Elle.

"Is it?"

"Oh, yes. Without a doubt."

"Don't tell Harper I said this, but I'm going to miss her. Don't get me wrong, I think she and Christopher will do well together, but her absence is going to tear me apart."

Elle looped her arm in Irwin's. "Silly man. What makes you think she doesn't already know that?"

As the pair walked and talked long into the star-lit night, the rough ocean water below smashed its waves against the bluff, kicking up a discord of foamy spray with each surge. Under the stars, Irwin and Elle shared their dreams, leaving no stone, no matter how uncomfortable, unturned. They spoke of their *what-ifs and could-have-beens* — the kind Life taunts one with as time ticks mercilessly away.

Irwin told Elle all about the concerns he had for the bookshop and how he hoped one day, long after he left for the next unseen realm, it would become a community fixture. A place for lost souls to find residence and acceptance.

"It's not the fanciest bookshop," he told her, "but it feels like home."

Irwin even shared stories about Bones, recounting his cat's annoying antics, which served to make Elle double over with laughter—a sound so chock-full of light and joy that it made Irwin's heart ache in the realization it had already begun to miss her.

Elle told Irwin all about herself, except for the darker details concerning her ex. And Irwin, more than content to let her set the pace of her truths, wanted Elle to have the time and space to reveal them as she saw fit. More than anything, however, Irwin wanted Elle to feel safe around him—and not judged. He wanted her to know she could trust him and that he would do anything to protect her from harm if she let him. Inexplicably, and after only a few hours spent together, Irwin desperately wanted to be the shoulder Elle would want to lean on—*forever.*

"It's time." Harper had dressed for the occasion, wearing a long paisley wraparound skirt, a short sleeve blouse with puffy short sleeves, and the usual work boots.

"You look nice," Irwin told her, not bothering to balk when she threaded her arm into his, tugging him toward the rest of the group waiting along the gravel shelled pathway closer to the cliff.

Irwin checked his watch for the fifth time. "Already?"

"Yep. Everyone's waiting for us." Harper pointed and waved to where Olivia, Darren, Christopher, and Elle stood.

"Okay then." Irwin lifted the urn off the front seat. "Are you okay with me carrying this?"

Harper nodded. "Of course." Harper took a few steps forward, only to stop when she realized Irwin hadn't budged an inch.

"Irwin?" A slight warm breeze billowed beneath her skirt as long strands of wild wavy hair whipped across her face. "Are you coming?"

"Yes." But Irwin still didn't move. He seemed lost—frozen in the same spot as if rooted.

"We really gotta go. Everyone's waiting."

"I know." Irwin held the urn snug across his chest.

Harper sighed and walked back. "Out of everything we've been through, all the crazy ups and downs we've had to deal with, why is this last part of our promise so uncomfortable for you?"

Irwin tilted his head, feigning confusion. "I don't think it's uncomfortable." He wiggled his foot. "It's these shoes. They're biting my toes. I knew I should have worn the other pair."

"Don't try it. I've seen you wear those ugly things over a million times without complaint." She gazed into Irwin's eyes. "Are you worried about something else?"

"Why? My toes popping off isn't enough?"

"You're doing it again."

"What?"

"Word dancing."

"No. What I'm doing is called deflecting."

"Sounds more like stalling." Harper gripped his arm and tugged. "Come on. Let's just do this." She started to walk but almost tripped when Irwin still didn't move. "What now?"

"Nothing. I'm coming."

"No, Irwin. You clearly are not." Harper exhaled. "Look, it's not like we can put this off any longer. It's now or never."

"I'm not trying to put anything off. I'm attempting to..." Irwin stopped talking. He bowed his head and muttered. "I don't know what I'm trying to do."

Harper slowly shook her head. "So, we're back to uncomfortable."

"No, worse." Irwin slouched, looking defeated. "We're back to, 'it's time.'"

IT TOOK A BIT OF COAXING, but Harper finally got Irwin to join those already waiting. Olivia, like her daughter, looked lovely in her pretty pale-yellow sundress, a straw hat, and sandals, while Darren, next to her, chose a crisp white short-sleeve shirt tucked into a new pair of belted khakis. Christopher had on his usual blue jeans, paired with a light blue polo and a pair of sneakers.

And then Irwin's eyes fell on Elle. Beautiful, elegant Elle. She had also worn a sundress, but hers was a pastel blue like the San Diego sky. Her magnificent gray wisdom locks were tucked into a loose, wind-blown bun.

Irwin, knowing how much Cornelia would have hated stuffy funeral protocol, felt deeply indebted to everyone for not wearing anything remotely somber for this crazy woman's send-off.

The morning sun shone over the huddled group, while warming ocean air enticed its waves to dance under clear bright skies. At least for the moment, no other tourists or onlookers were nearby enough to disturb them. Only the occasional lone kayaker paddling close to the shoreline, or a pair of backpackers in the distance making their way along the cliffs could be seen. A sense of calm and stillness surrounded them.

"May I?" Harper opened her arms, waiting for Irwin to hand her the urn. She stepped forward into the circle, indicating the time to begin had arrived.

"We are gathered here together to bid our final goodbyes to our dear departed friend, Cornelia Parish. Before we spread her ashes into the Pacific Ocean as she requested, I'd like to first pass the urn around, so that anyone wishing to say something, can."

All heads silently nodded.

Harper glanced at the urn. "I guess I should begin." She drew in a long, slow breath. "Cornelia, I can feel your adventurous spirit amongst us, watching and listening. There is so much more I want to tell you, and in the coming days, I will, but for now, let me just say—" Harper sniffled. "how much I will deeply miss you, our long talks, your hilarious stories, and our zany escapades. But most of all, your steadfast friendship. You have treated me like a granddaughter. Your love and belief in me never once wavered. I can't believe you are gone." Harper's voice caught. "I will miss you every day for the rest of my life and think of you often." Harper, eyes cast down, handed off the urn to Christopher. Then she pulled Luna's small birdbath from her pocket. "You are an amazing woman who lived her life in the selfless service of others. From something as simple as this ceramic birdbath, you rescued countless lives, never once expecting praise. You are smart, brilliant, funny as hell, and my crime partner for life and hopefully in the next. I love you, Cornelia, and I always will."

Harper turned to Christopher, indicating he could begin.

Clutching the urn, Christopher began. "Everything Harper said times a million, Cornelia. You have been such an incredible friend, and at times, the next best thing to a mother when mine was taken from me. You invited me into your world, your family, your circle of friends, and your life, and for that I will be forever grateful." Christopher cleared his throat. "Oh, and by the way, I just wanted you to know, I didn't hesitate this time." Balancing the urn with one arm, Christopher reached for Harper's ringed hand and gently lifted it to the heavens. "She said yes, Cornelia." He kissed the top of Harper's finger and handed the urn to Darren.

"Hey, old gal. It's me, Darren. If you're listening, which I'd bet the farm you are—you being the nosiest woman I've ever met and all." Darren kicked up some sand with the tip of his shoe. "We had some great times together, and a ton of laughs. And don't think I don't know how you always had my back." Darren's squinted his eyes and blinked. Olivia, her own two eyes glassy with tears, handed him a tissue. "You already know how much I'm gonna miss you." He dabbed his eyes. "Anyways, I'm not gonna stand here and get all sentimental, but I want you to let those folks where you're at now know that if they mess with you, well, they're gonna have me to deal with eventually, and it won't be pretty. That's for sure."

Irwin rolled his eyes toward the sky but remained quiet.

"Take care of yourself, old gal. I love you." Darren handed the urn off to Olivia.

Olivia smiled. "Oh, Cornelia. You will be so missed—and not just by us, but by your extended family and friends, and from every soul you've touched. Thank you for sharing your life with me, and for always making me feel like I mattered." Olivia paused. "That's what you did, you know? —you made every person who knew you feel important and appreciated. To you, we all counted, no matter what baggage we had or flaws we still carted around. Your belief in me helped heal me. I'm not the same person you met years ago—a woman frightened of her own shadow. Gosh, in so many ways, you believed in me even before I believed in myself. I promise, dear friend, to keep moving and growing like you expect me to. I owe so much of who I am today to you. Thank you, and I will always love you."

Olivia handed the urn to Elle.

Elle exhaled. "Wow. What can I add to what has already been said?" Elle hugged the urn. "You were and will always be my rock, Cornelia. You saved my life and countless others. How does one begin to repay that?" She tilted her head back and spoke to the sky. "We can't. Your shoes are too deep, too big, too exceptional to fill. But I promise to continue paying it forward, finishing what you started." Elle smiled. "And speaking of which, Luna and Jax asked me to send you their love and rays of light and happiness. Luna said you should try to behave, but Jax said that he doubted you could."

Everyone around the circle laughed. Elle handed off the urn to Irwin.

Irwin stood holding the urn once more—his head bowed as if in prayer. When he finally lifted his face, streaked tearstains blotted his cheeks. He lifted the container eyelevel, and said, "We need to talk."

Harper's mouth dropped open. "Irwin?"

"I'm sorry, but I can't do this. I need a few minutes alone with Cornelia before we, you know." Irwin looked miserably out of place amongst the clear blue sky, the bright sunshine, and the crashing waves. "I'll be back."

"Take your time, Irwin," said Olivia, setting herself down on a boulder nearby. She patted the space next to her for Harper to join her.

Harper shrugged. "Okay."

Elle, understanding Irwin's need to be alone, walked back to her car to wait. She leaned on the hood, periodically dabbing her eyes with a tissue.

Irwin, the urn in his hands, walked closer to the cliff's edge. From where he stood, he could make out the large boulders walled by foamy water below, protruding prominently in place—their once sharp corners worn down by centuries of ocean surf.

He felt suddenly small again.

Inconsequential.

"Cornelia," he said, placing the urn down on the turf and shells below his feet. Irwin paused to breathe. If anything taught him how to conduct a successful monologue, it had been his many years spent conversating with Gilly at her grave.

"I read your letter—this last one. Three times, in fact." A more potent, cool breeze blew past. "Word for word. I have it mostly committed to memory at this point." He paused. "I waited until this morning to read it." Goosebumps traveled up his arm. "And that's because I've been furious with you and needed to clear my head. But now, well, most of that anger is behind me." Another, equally stiff cooler breeze blew past.

"I've been in a state of irritation virtually this entire trip, mainly because of you." Irwin crooked his chin. "At the same time, I have also been blown away—impressed to learn of all the lives you have touched. Proud even, although I can't help but feel slightly disheartened and confused as to why you never shared even a kernel's worth about the people in your life who were evidently important to you. Nothing. And as a result, I began to question the validity of our friendship."

Below, a massive, foam-tipped wave crashed and splintered against the jagged side of the rocks, sending an expansive spurt of spray high and wide, but not nearly close enough to douse Irwin.

"In your letter, you explained your reasons for all the confidentiality. And, to be perfectly honest, I now understand most of them. The secrecy, your incessant need to overprotect me, and your obsession with trying to control everything, and apparently, everyone. All well and good. That is who you were, and I can learn to accept that."

A short distance away, a flock of noisy seagulls glided and coasted, their wings set back as they dove into the ocean.

"That said, a big part of me still wishes you would have shown more faith in me and our friendship. Like what Olivia said, I'm not the same broken person you met all those years ago. I've grown, Cornelia. I've healed. And in large part to you. I could have listened to whatever you would have told me, and I know I would have found a way to understand, had you given me a chance to prove it."

More water pounded against the cut cliffs, doing its part to erode further and reshape the rocky shoreline.

"About Martin—your shockingly very undead husband and the man you tricked me into believing had died during the war." Irwin felt a tightness in his throat but continued. "In your letter, you said that you didn't recognize the man you had married after he returned from his tour. You wrote about Martin's PTSD and how his being exposed to combat and being in a warzone had traumatized him into behaving in ways you would have never expected. How one day, out of nowhere, he started shouting at you, shaking you, grabbing your wrist and twisting it—almost to the point of breaking it. How he even tried at one point to strangle you, which left you understandably afraid and angry." Irwin paused, choosing his words carefully. "You also wrote how at first you covered for him, hoping to keep your marriage together, but that soon enough, it became clear Martin needed a whole lot more help than you could give him. You said you felt guilty about leaving him in his hour of need, but frankly. Cornelia, I'm grateful you did. Martin could have killed you." Irwin's brows drew together, and he sighed. "In truth, in many ways, the husband you knew and loved did die in the war."

Irwin rubbed at his chest as if trying to force the tight-ness away.

"Nevertheless, I did as you asked and delivered the letter and wedding band to him. He accepted both without explana-tion, not that he owed me one, but more than that, I can't tell you.

'In your letter, you said you didn't tell me anything about your husband out of guilt and shame. That somehow, me knowing he still existed would have changed my impression of the woman you were—that somehow us talking about him would have kept the pain and disappointment alive, and would have added to the remorse I already carried from losing my best friend during the same war. Then you went on to say how sometimes it's better to keep parts of our past lives confined, socked away and hidden for the sake of others. Well, to that I say, rubbish, Cornelia!" he snapped. "All of it. Bull-dinky. Sure, I won't lie, I regret losing my friend, and at times, especially when I least expect it, the anger from that dark period of my life reappears suddenly as if Joe had just stepped on that landmine minutes before." Irwin's voice cracked. He curled his fist into a ball and pounded his chest. "But that's my pain to feel, Cornelia. Mine —not yours. You don't always get to decide how I deal with it." A steady stream of frustrated, hurt tears slid down Irwin's cheeks, but he didn't care. "I," he slowed his breathing. "I just needed you to know that."

Heart racing, Irwin inhaled, then exhaled, struggling to regulate his breathing before continuing.

"Moving on," he said in a lowered, calmer voice. "Which brings us to Mildred. I get that something horrible must have happened to her, and since then, she's had a hard time learning to trust. From what I picked up, she's pretty much a loner. Which I, as you know, have no issue with, but it's apparent she's afraid. And before you send the locusts down on me, I already know what to do. Let's leave it at that.

Luna and Jax. Those two are pretty self-explanatory. I understand why you needed to protect their privacy. No worries, their secret will remain safe with me and the others."

Irwin swallowed hard and cleared his throat.

"Now, Elle. Here's where you and I part ways, Cornelia *Yenta* Parish. I thought about this all last night. Yes. Elle's a lovely woman, but you and I both already know I'm not ready to make another commitment. You do recall how well the last one worked out, don't you? Don't forget—I'm Irwin—the guy whose love causes everyone to die."

Irwin stared out to the open sea. "Besides, Elle lives here, and, well, I don't. It could never work anyway."

A cold, crisp breeze blew past Irwin. "My question to you is this—why do you always feel compelled to interfere in my love life? Even, surprisingly enough, when you're dead? And despite what you may think about my aloneness, I don't need you—ghost or not— meddling around in my affairs and playing matchmaker. I'm a grown man, for goodness sake, and perfectly capable of finding someone for myself."

Just then, a single seagull broke rank and file from the flock and soared directly toward Irwin.

Caw-caw, caw-caw.

"Idiot bird!" snapped Irwin as the gull swooped at him, causing Irwin to duck and flinch.

Caw-caw, caw-caw.

Squawking, the highly agitated bird hovered above Irwin's head, circling closer and lower...

"Okay. Okay!" Irwin shouted. "Fine, I admit it—all right? I like her!" Irwin's hands flew to protect the top of his head. "I could imagine falling in love with her! Now call off your stupid bird."

Caw, caw-caw

The renegade gull soared back offshore, away from the bluff to rejoin his drove of raucous gulls.

"That was close." Irwin wiped the sweat off the top of his brow with the back of his hand. "Nevertheless, Ms. Nosey, just so we're clear, I am no longer mad at you. However, please don't assume this admission means I agree with all your meddling and excuses because frankly, I-do-not."

Irwin released a weary sigh as his voice lowered to that of a faint, woeful whisper. "It's just that I'm no longer dejected by them."

The chill in the air increased. Irwin glanced over his shoulder, realizing everyone looked tired and past ready to go. It had been a long morning, and they still had packing and a flight to catch early the next day.

"Looks like I'm going to have to wrap this up, but before I do, I also want to thank you for being my closest and best friend. I'm going to miss you. And by the way, your line in the letter about this whole sham you cooked up—about throwing your ashes out to sea just to get us closer together—

Well, it worked. Just like your know-it-all-butt knew it would."

Irwin removed the heart-shaped white gold locket from his pocket. The same one Christopher had gotten equipped with a GPS device, years back. It had come in handy on more than one occasion when Cornelia's symptoms had begun to manifest.

Irwin recoiled his arm and tossed the chain as hard as he could over the cliff. "That's so I'll always know where you are," he muttered, his craggily, ruddy cheeks wind burnt and flushed. Irwin yanked a hanky from his pants pocket and blew his nose.

"I've never been the praying type. You know this. Still, I can't help but wish I could be sure you were here listening to everything I said." Irwin opened his palms and lifted his face to the heavens. "So, for what it's worth, here is my unabridged version of holy supplication.

"Cornelia Parish—if you're in heaven listening, please send down a sign that you've heard me, and that you're okay and at peace where you are. It doesn't have to be anything fancy. No parting of the sea, spare me the locusts and floods. Any sign will do," Irwin pleaded. "Anything at all."

Splat —a full sloppy wet load of seagull poop landed right on Irwin's face.

Not exactly the sign from heaven Irwin had asked for.

"*UGH*" he yelped in distress, unable to see through the dark, gummy gook.

"That's NOT funny, Cornelia," Irwin yelled, stammering, thrashing his arms wildly in the air. "I specifically said a sign!" he sputtered and spat. "How the hell is bird crap landing on my face a sign?"

Bent from the waist, Irwin coughed and spewed, his bony fingers wiping feverishly at the smeared bird gunk caked like wet plaster all over his eyelids, cheeks, and mouth.

"*Ack*—"

Spit, spew.

Irwin, close to retching, tugged his belted shirttails out of his slacks to wipe his face.

"Hey," pointed Darren. "What's up with Irwin? What the hell is he doing?"

Everyone stopped to look.

Although Irwin's every bombastic move centered on his being able to see and breathe again, to everyone else's horror standing from afar, it appeared as if he were preparing to take the final Pacific plunge.

"Oh my God, he's gonna jump," shrieked Harper, breaking out into a run. "Don't you dare, Irwin," she screamed, her legs pumping as hard and as fast as she could make them. With the agility of a gazelle, Harper bounded over rocks and soared through dry, overgrown brush. "Please—don't do this to me," she cried, nearly tripping over an exposed root. "I love you."

The rest of the stunned group watched the scene unfold, the shock cementing them in place, unable to fully comprehend what was happening.

Unable to see, Irwin spun in wild circles, his hands and face obscured by globs of greenish-brown seagull poop. Head twitching and body rocking side-to-side. He moved awkwardly about, half-blinded in the direction from where he thought he had heard a carnival of shouting coming from.

"What?" he shouted back, off-balance and wobbling a wee bit too close to the cliff's edge. "*Harrr*—?" Irwin stammered out just as Harper lunging her body forward, tackling Irwin face-first to the ground and onto a patch of high-weeded thick grass.

"*Nooooo!*" Harper screamed, grabbing for his calves, pulling him away from the threshold of certain death.

Irwin lifted his head, "—*per*," he managed to sputter, his lips hidden by grass and sand.

"I can't lose you, too," Harper sobbed into his filthy torn pant leg, her long yet surprisingly strong arms locked tightly around Irwin's exposed scuffed calf. "I won't let you—I won't let you."

"*Argh...*" Although slightly muffled by the earth, Irwin deployed several obscene grunts, groans, and curses.

"Please, Irwin, don't do this," Harper begged, her leg locked around his in a clamped vice grip. "I can't live without you, too."

Irwin lifted his neck and spat out what he hoped was a pebble and not a tooth.

"What-in-the-hell-are-you-talking-about?" he tried to say, although what came out sounded more like a garbled growl. "And why—why, why, why—on God's name did you just do that to me?"

Harper, her glassy eyes opened big and wide, stared at the back of Irwin's head. "Because I thought you were going to jump."

Irwin's head slumped to the ground. With most of the fight inside him gone, he rolled onto his back, gripping his stomach. Although his face still had matted bird excrement and grass all over it, he clenched his teeth, and took two cleansing pants. Then, out of nowhere, he began to *laugh*?

Not a giggle, a chuckle, or even anything close to a chortle, but a full-blown, no holds barred, down in the gut belly laugh—the likes of which Harper had never heard come out of Irwin before.

Her mouth dropped open, causing Irwin, already rolling in fits of laughter, to hoot even louder. Gripping his stomach, he swayed back and forth on the ground, kicking his feet, hysterical. "Great horny toads," he bellowed, unable to stop laughing.

"What the heck is *wrong* with you?" Harper blinked,

though no longer crying. "I don't find any of this funny—*at all*."

Irwin clasped his bony knees and pulled them toward his chest while continuing to roll around on the ground in stitches.

Harper, who had already released his calf, snorted. "You're mental. You know that?"

Nevertheless, maybe because Irwin's unconstrained joy was acting like a contagion or maybe the fact that he couldn't stop laughing like a lunatic, but Harper's once weeping face morphed into the biggest, goofiest smile, and soon enough, she too joined in, albeit probably not precisely knowing why.

Finally, despite a few false starts and stops, their laughter began to wane. The two friends locked eyes as years of pent-up grief and misplaced bitterness seemed to coalesce, crowning into an unspoken but clear understanding of how they could no longer allow the anguish and sorrow they had been carrying to control the rest of their lives.

"My stomach hurts," tittered Harper, hiccuping.
"Mine, too," Irwin muttered faintly, once he caught his breath. "This funeral, or wake-memorial—or whatever you want to call this disastrous trip—by the end, has turned out to be everything Cornelia wanted, and exactly what she planned for all along."

Harper clasped and squeezed Irwin's hand. "Because she knew."

Irwin grinned, exposing a tiny piece of grass wedged against his tooth. "She did, indeed."

By this time, everyone had shaken off the shock and had caught up.

"Oh look, the cavalry's here," mocked Harper. *Hiccup.* "Nice of you to join us."

Darren bent at the waist, out of breath and panting. "I'm getting old."

"You certainly are," gasped Olivia, doing her best to breathe.

Christopher, not at all winded, shot Harper a sheepish shrug and chin nod, indicating on the sly that her parents were the cause for his delay.

Darren stopped puffing. "Hold on a minute." Darren craned his neck to stare down at Irwin, still sprawled on the ground with his long thin arms flailed wide to his side, staring at the cloudless blue sky in a bug-eyed wonderment. "Is he *smiling?*"

Irwin flicked Darren a thumbs-up. "Yes. I am smiling," confirmed Irwin.

He looked so peaceful that nobody had the heart to mention the bird droppings still coating his face.

"Oh, Irwin— look at you." Olivia crouched down and extended a hand to help yank him up, but Irwin gently waved it away.

"I can't believe I have to qualify this," Irwin finally manages to say, albeit through intakes of choppy laughing breaths. "But for the record, I was not, and let me repeat myself—not trying to kill myself!"

"Yeah, I know that now." Harper's hair was now sheathed in broken leaves, twigs, and other odds and bits. She lifted herself onto one elbow and propped her dirt-covered chin onto open palms, shooting Irwin a highly exasperated glare. "You scared me half to death, you know?" Then she playfully poked him in the chest. "All of us."

"Evidently." Irwin stretched an arm up to Darren. "Okay. I'm ready. Give me a hand, would you?"

Once upright, Irwin felt a peculiar sensation taking over his senses, specifically his acute sense of smell. "*Ugh.*" He started coughing and gagging.

Spew, cough, gag.

"Somebody," *gag, spit,* "Quick! Give me something to wipe this crap off my face!" he yelled at no one in particular.

"Hold on, Irwin—I think I've got something." Olivia stuck her entire arm into her handbag, combing in search of a pack of handy wipes. "Got it," she yelled, but as soon as she tugged the package, something hot pink and missile-shaped flew out instead, striking the ground once before springing over the nearby cliff with almost a magical lift to its dramatic escape.

"*Ahhh!* —Isn't that just great!" bellowed Olivia, flinging the unearthed pack of wipes at Irwin's head. "So much for that option."

Everyone inched closer to the cliff's edge, craning their collective necks to watch Olivia's battery-operated 'little friend' hit a rock and smash to smithereens. Soon enough, a succession of strong waves crashed against the bluff's side, taking what little remained of the hot-pink contraption out to sea.

Olivia's shoulder's slumped. "I'm going to miss her," she moaned wistfully, any past mortification long gone.

Darren wrapped an arm firmly around his wife's waist. "Not to worry, Liv," he said, feigning a severe glower. "I'm sure Cornelia will find a way to keep your little friend company."

Olivia rolled her eyes while everyone else turned to glare at Darren.

"What?" Darren crimped his shoulders and grinned. "Too soon?"

CHAPTER 22

THE SMALL BOAT Irwin chartered to comply with the permit that allows for the spreading of ashes at sea cut its engine approximately three miles from the La Jolla shore where the waters were typically over 600 feet deep and at least three nautical miles from land. The captain, a stately gentleman, gave a slight, friendly wave to Harper, letting her know they could begin.

The group huddled together at the stern in a tight circle, hands clasped. Harper held the urn up toward the sky and recited the short verse she had written for this final farewell.

'Mighty sea,
    To you, a sacred soul we gift.

Protect her consecrated ashes and safeguard her from harm.

Keep this gentle soul close until the winds lift her to the heavens,

and carry her to her final resting place.'

"AMEN," murmured the group.

"Cornelia would have wanted you to do this next part." Harper handed the urn to Irwin.

Irwin moved closer to the boat's starboard and waited until the air stilled enough before lifting the top.

"I will always and forever love you," he whispered as he poured his friend's life essence atop the welcoming water. "— you meddlesome, interfering, know-it-all, brilliant, kind friend."

AFTER SCATTERING CORNELIA'S ASHES, all except for Elle, who had to get back to open the shop, the group convened in the hotel lobby to talk before heading upstairs to change and finish packing.

"It took a bit of finagling, but I finally got us on a flight home," announced Christopher, handing each person a copy of their boarding pass. "When I say early, I mean at the butt-crack of dawn early. That means no delays, no procrastination, and no excuses. We need to be dressed, packed, and ready to jump into the cab by four if we want to get to the airport on time."

"Where are we going to find a cab at four in the morning?" asked Irwin.

Harper wiggled her phone. "Welcome again, my techno-ridiculous friend to the new world, sir, where you, too, with the press of a few keys, can call for an Uber."

"I can't believe this is our last night." Olivia stared down at her pass, sounding oddly nostalgic. "I mean, I know we've had a few bumps here and there, but I've enjoyed meeting all the different people on this trip." Olivia grinned. "I suspect this was all part of Cornelia's grand master plan."

"I wouldn't doubt it for a hot flash," teased Darren, folding his pass in half. "Hey, Irwin—bet you're anxious to get back to the bookshop?"

"Are you kidding? Irwin's been ready to leave before we even left," laughed Harper. "Right, Irwin?"

Irwin pressed his lips like a wizened old man. "Not exactly," he replied, much to everyone's shock.

On the one hand, Irwin had always prided himself on living a life grounded upon caution, not presumption—and certainly never, ever, *ever* with any type of unsolicited meddling, despite the company he kept. To now lead this particular charge and intentionally intervene in somebody's life without being asked—*whether needed or not*—upended every gray cell left alive in his old, irascible body. And yet, as hard as he might want to try, Irwin couldn't shake the feeling that by him not doing so meant letting not only Cornelia down, but himself.

Chronic loss had taught Irwin that the time to act was in the present. Not tomorrow, not yesterday, but now, especially at this stage in his life. He adamantly refused to add even one more regret to his already much too high pile. Whatever reservations he had harbored were now overshadowed nine to one by a sense of accountability—in particular, his dignity, plastered on the mug he had to face every morning.

"Change of plans for me," he announced. "I have one more stop to make before heading home. I've already spoken to both Roger and Regan, who, by the way, have assured me in no uncertain terms that my shop is still standing, and my cat is still an idiot."

Everyone waited in disbelief for Irwin to elaborate—and for a welcomed change, he did just that. Irwin told them everything, making sure not to leave a single detail out.

"Well, I'll be," muttered Darren. "Did you guys know about this?"

Olivia and Christopher shook their heads an emphatic no, while Harper remained too conspicuously quiet.

"I should have known," groaned Olivia. "Bonnie and Clyde are back at it again."

"I'd prefer the parallel of Hercule Poirot and Captain Arthur J. M. Hastings," implored Irwin.

"Who?" asked Darren.

"Hercule Poirot." Harper tore up her boarding pass. "The famous Belgium detective created by Agatha Christie? Come on, Dad, we carry all of her books."

"Agatha Christie, I know about," Darren said in a huff. "but never heard of Captain Hastings?"

"He was Poirot's trusty side-kick, his companion-chronicler and all-around best friend."

"Yes, Harper. Thank you," interrupted Irwin. "All very illuminating, but if you would all excuse me, I'd like to go to my room. I am in dire need of a long, disinfecting hot shower and a clean set of clothes." Irwin started to leave, but Olivia blocked his way.

"Not so fast."

"I'm sorry, Olivia, but is there a problem?" Irwin noticed a renegade bird feather sticking out from under one of his shirt buttons and plucked it off. "I abhor seagulls," he said.

"Is he kidding?" Olivia waited for everyone else's reaction, but they stood looking as stunned as her. "Okay, I'll be the first to bite." Olivia faced Irwin. "Maybe, Irwin, I'm a little taken aback. From the onset of this trip, you've made it emphatically clear our only mission this entire time was to deliver the letters and dump Cornelia's ashes in the sea. Correct?"

"Correct," agreed Irwin. He started to walk, but Olivia grabbed his arm.

"No. Not yet. Still talking."

Irwin stayed put.

"You've had us rushing around, holding our bladders until we're ready to burst, and reminding us continuously about the need to rush back to the shop." Olivia released Irwin's arm to fold hers over her waist. "And now, out of the blue, and at the spur of the moment on the very evening before we're supposed to *all* fly home, you casually inform us of a drastic change of plans?"

"Yeah," nodded Darren, crossing his arms over his chest like his wife. "What about that?"

"I see." Irwin grinned. "The problem lies in the fact that you, my compendium of unenlightened friends, will soon come to realize how certain matters in life take precedence over others."

"Don't misunderstand us." Harper grinned. "It's not that we necessarily disagree with you or your motives, which are astoundingly altruistic, but face it, Irwin—it's strange as hell hearing it come out of your mouth."

"Everything about this trip's been strange if you ask me," whined Olivia. "Listen, I can't speak for the rest of you, but I strongly suggest we fly this extra last leg. No offense, Irwin, but I've had my fill of open highway, greasy cold road food, hotels from the seventh level of hell, cramped seating, dismal AC, snakes, and now, seagull poop." Olivia sniffed the air near Irwin and scrunched up her nose, making a big deal of breathing through her mouth. "You so need a shower."

"We?" asked Irwin while sniffing warily at his soiled sleeve, only to gag.

"Of course, we!" Olivia looked downright offended. "Don't be ridiculous." She glanced around for support. "I'm right—*aren't* I?"

Funny how the power behind a single stern glower from Olivia could make Harper and Darren dare not utter anything but a mumbled affirmative.

"Fine," bemoaned Christopher, watching from the side, "—just fine." He walked around and collected the rest of the boarding passes. "I should have assumed it wouldn't be this easy." Christopher motioned for Harper to hand him the remains of her tattered pass. "This is going to take a while, but I'll start making new reservations."

Harper was all too happy to hand Christopher her torn scraps. She pecked him on the cheek, then draped an arm lovingly around her fiancé's waist, pulling him close to whisper in his ear, "I wouldn't have it any other way."

AFTER SHOWERING and dousing himself with enough body soap and shampoo to clean a militia, Irwin dressed and packed. He had already excused himself from having an early dinner with the group. There were a few pressing matters he needed to address with Ms. Reed before leaving.

"I hope you don't mind, Irwin, but after this morning, and the day I had at the shop—I'd rather just grab something quick to eat and relax by the water," Elle told him when he came to pick her up. "I need to calm my nerves and reset my peopling meter, which frankly, is way past overdrive."

While Irwin had originally planned to impress Elle with fine dining and wine, he didn't mind the change. In fact, he appreciated how, like him, Elle also had an internal peopling meter, although he safely assumed her capacity to people, compared to his, was double in size.

They headed down the bustling main street together until they came upon a quaint bistro where they ordered two large fried chicken sandwiches, chips, and two cold bottles of water to go. Grabbing their food, they crossed the street and found a bench situated near enough to the water to get the full tranquil effect, but still far enough away from the locals out for a quiet evening stroll.

"You're leaving tomorrow?" asked Elle, unwrapping her sandwich with the deliberate delicacy of someone opening a cherished present.

Irwin nodded, doing his best to disregard the oncoming sudden surge of loneliness. As peaceful as being near the water should have made him feel, Irwin felt the opposite— jumpy. Not surprising considering he'd been running on empty these past few weeks, with barely any sleep to think of the night before. He'd spent a good portion of the previous night tossing and turning, wracking his brain to come up with some right way to tell Elle how he felt about her, even after this ridiculously short span of time knowing her. And, in doing so, not scare her off for good.

"Take another chance on love, Irwin," Cornelia the interloper had written to him. "Don't try to make sense out of what your feeling because Life doesn't work that way, my fine neurotic friend. It's not a neat, check-off the box kind of existence. Way too messy for all that. For now, as difficult as it may feel for you, go with the flow. Allow your churlish, unexercised heart the opportunity to lead for once instead of that obstinate, inflexible head of yours. And although you will hate to admit I'm right, because, well, I usually am, but isn't Elle just perfect for you?"

There were times Irwin thought he could still hear Cornelia's voice in his head enunciating the words in that *know-it-all* way of hers. And yet, despite his hating that she had been right—*again*—he also wished he had the wherewithal to do what she had advised without feeling as if failure lurked around every corner, ready to trip him up.

Irwin wished he and Cornelia could be back in Pennsylvania, sitting at his kitchen table. Just the two of them like they had done most evenings. Cornelia would park herself in a chair, nursing her tea while packing away a nice amount of butter cookies. Between bites, she'd give him the rundown on the people who had come by the shop. Small snippets of conversations she'd overheard—translation: *eavesdropped*. Sometimes, she'd wind up lecturing Irwin on whatever recent overreaction he had to something or someone that day.

"You really should take it down a notch," she'd chastise him, plopping another cookie on his plate.

And Irwin would pretend to be annoyed, but he never really was.

I should have told her that. I should have shown her how much what she shared with me all these years meant.

And now, Elle.

With the trip nearly over and the whole urn debacle behind him, Irwin understood the time to act was now. Not later. Not tomorrow. Not in a letter or phone call or God forbid—a text! No. What he had to say couldn't be told through the wizardry of technology. Only a face-to-face would suffice. Being with Elle tonight and telling her exactly how he felt about her meant doing something so contrary to his personality, it made his teeth ache.

Irwin stared at Elle. Beautiful, kind Elle, waiting on *his* answer.

That had to mean something good, right?

Irwin plowed on. "Yes. Tomorrow morning, bright and early," he said. "Christopher's already put us all on notice."

Elle's mouth smiled, but her eyes did not.

"We initially were scheduled to go straight home, but it turns out there's an unexpected stop we need to make first."

Elle nodded as if weighing her words. "Another letter recipient?"

Irwin thought about explaining but decided to err on the side of discretion. "Exactly," he answered, not entirely comfortable with this half-truth. At the same time, Mildred's right to privacy demanded a slight bit of fudging.

Elle lowered her stare to her lap. "Then what?"

Irwin, sporting his 'no big deal' smile, cleared his throat. "Then it's back to Pennsylvania to rescue Regan from Bones or Bones from Regan. I haven't quite figured out which one yet. Then salvage whatever's left of my bookshop from Roger."

"I see."

Irwin, a bit jittery, paused to undo the top button of his shirt, then took a big swallow of water before continuing. "Elle?" he said, uncharacteristically reaching out to hold her hand.

"Yes, Irwin?" Elle glanced up with gentle, hopeful eyes.

Irwin had to fight the urge to do something idiotic, like kiss her, so instead, he stuttered.

"I...I, *err*, wanted to, *umm*, ask you something." His skin flushed. Irwin nervously crossed and re-crossed his feet at the ankles, forgetting all about his half-unwrapped sandwich balanced precariously on his knees.

"Ask away."

The nerves in Irwin's eyes began playing muscle-tic-ping-pong with his eyelids, making him look about ready to pass out.

"Are you okay?" Elle quickly placed her sandwich and bottle of water to her other side. "Try breathing slowly," she said, rubbing his shoulder.

Irwin's skin broke out into a cold sweat. "I think I'm having an anxiety attack."

"Focus on your breathing," Elle instructed soothingly.

"Whatever you're feeling right now feels scary, but it's not life or death."

Irwin snorted. "Let you tell it."

"You can get through this, Irwin," Elle said, calmly. Supportively.

Irwin tried pacing his breaths.

"That's better. Keep doing exactly that."

Irwin slowly inhaled, then gradually exhaled.

"What you're feeling will pass. Just keep breathing steady."

Irwin stretched his back and exhaled.

"Excellent." Elle waited. "Are you feeling any better?"

Irwin nodded, eyes locked onto Elle's.

"Good. Now, tell me what you need now."

"You."

"What?" Elle's breath hitched. "I'm sorry, what did you say?"

"I said, I need you. In my life," repeated Irwin, boldly going where no Irwin had ever gone before. "I know we've just met, and what I'm about to propose doesn't make the least bit of sense. I also am aware I live incredibly far across the country, and it will be hard to maintain any kind of relationship, and even if I do, it'll probably end in disaster anyway because everyone I love either dies or—"

Elle cupped Irwin's face and kissed him passionately on the lips. Not once. Not twice, but for a long, long time.

"I need you, too," she murmured, her nose pressed against his. "In my life."

Irwin eyes widened like a deer in headlights. "Say it again."

"I need you, too, in my life."

"One more time."

Elle laughed, face bright. "I. Need. You. Too."

"—in your life," he prompted. "Don't forget that part. It's the best part."

Elle pressed her forehead against Irwin's. "In my life."

Practically delirious, Irwin wrapped his arms around Elle's back, but when he did, his sandwich fell onto the ground and rolled, much to the delight of a nearby belligerent seagull.

Elle laughed. "Your friend's back."

"Cornelia's paid him to torture me." Irwin grinned. "Well, go ahead," he shouted at the gull. "Take it. You know you want to, you fetid feathered mongrel of the bird world."

"You do know your way around words, sir." Elle kissed Irwin again.

Perhaps sensing his food in danger of being filched by another feathered friend, the bird tensed, twisting his head side to side. Then hastily, he ripped the wrapper away, stabbing the sandwich between its beak before flying off.

"I sincerely, and without exaggeration, dislike that bird," grumbled Irwin. "However, I do admire his tenacity." Irwin drew Elle in close. "I don't want to lose you. I don't know how to pull this off, and in all likelihood, I'm going to screw it up, but I want to figure out a way to make whatever this is between us work."

Elle's eyes filled with tears.

"Oh no, I've already messed things up. I didn't mean to make you cry."

"These aren't sad tears." Elle used her palm to rub her cheeks.

"Happy tears?"

Elle grinned. "I'm not entirely sure if I should tell you this, but Cornelia—"

I should have known.

"Go on," Irwin groaned. "Just say it."

"Well, she's told me for ages about what a good man you are."

"*Mmhm...*"

"And a kind man."

So far, so good.

"Keep going."

"A bit of a grouch at times, but also a man of unquestionable integrity—honest through and through."

Irwin rubbed his forehead, waiting for the 'but.'

"She also said you would never intentionally hurt me."

Irwin's head snapped to attention. "Never," he murmured.

Elle tilted her head and poked Irwin softly in the arm. "Cornelia also said you and I were a perfect match. In my letter, she wrote how head over heels she was that we finally got the chance to meet. Although, and this is a quote, 'It's a damn shame I had to wait until after I died for you two to do it.'"

Irwin laughed. "That's Cornelia."

"She blamed you for that."

"I have no doubt."

Elle snuggled closer to Irwin, resting her head on his shoulder. "Did Cornelia happen to mention me in your letter?"

Irwin had read Cornelia's letter over so many times in the past twenty-four hours that he had most of it committed to memory. "She did."

"And?" toyed Elle. "Aren't you going to tell me what she said?"

"She said," 'Irwin," Irwin changed his voice to imitate Cornelia's. "Elle is a kind, gentle soul. Scared to death to be in love and be loved, but despite her understandable trepidation, she's the perfect woman for you. Don't go screwing it up.'"

"That's mighty fine advice she gave you." Elle chuckled. "Do you plan on taking it?"

Irwin's expression grew thoughtful. "That's the plan,

ma'am," he murmured, leaning in to kiss Elle with every ounce of passion resurrected within his craggy, old body. But as their lips parted, a gentle warm ocean breeze blew past. Irwin cocked his head, willing to swear on a stack of dictionaries he just heard Cornelia's voice whisper past.

"*It's about time, you old fool.*"

Irwin smiled, not in the least bothered with how Cornelia had been right all along. Again.

CHAPTER 23

THEY LANDED at Columbus International Airport the next day, where they picked up their next rental, ready and waiting to take on their short drive to Mercy Hospital.

Typically, only two visitors max were permitted at one time, but the head nurse, after having been subjected to the Irwin-Christopher tag team, reluctantly acquiesced.

"Just for a little while," he warned, his brows knitted together in that practiced, 'I'm a seasoned nurse, don't screw with me' glower. "She needs her rest. Room twelve, to the right."

The group of five made their way down the quiet corridor. Along the way, they passed by tiered carts filled with empty food trays, patient monitors, an empty stretcher, and other random medical equipment.

"I hate hospitals," murmured Harper. "They give me the creeps."

"Tell me about it," muttered Irwin.

"What if she's not happy to see us," warned Olivia in a hushed whisper. "I feel like we're invading her privacy."

"It's a bit late for that, Liv," said Darren.

"I know, but we should all agree to go if she's the least bit upset."

"Why would she be mad?" asked Darren. "I think you're overthinking this."

"*Argh*, just appease me, Darren," snapped Olivia, her cheeks flushed and turning redder. "Sugar muffins—here comes another one of those hot flashes. —And in a hospital, no less."

Darren, now a pro at avoiding perimenopausal divergence, took a full step behind Olivia for safe cover while mumbling, "I appease thee, I appease thee."

"Are we ready?" said Irwin as he turned the knob to enter Mildred's room. He found her alone and resting—the curtains partially were drawn, allowing the day's sun to penetrate the room. Besides the sound of a few beeping monitors, she looked peaceful.

Either the sound of the door opening or the footsteps jarred Mildred awake.

"Irwin?"

Mildred rubbed her eyes, blinking as if not sure whether she was hallucinating or not.

"Hello, Mildred," said Irwin softly. "We didn't mean to disturb you."

"It really is you." She blew out her cheeks. "Thank goodness. I thought I was losing my mind." She paused. "What are you doing here?" She glanced around. "—And Harper, too?" Mildred blinked as if clearing her vision. "I-I don't understand—"

Harper leaned in to gently peck Mildred on the cheek. "Hey, Millie. How ya feeling?"

Mildred tried lifting her neck, but it was too much too soon.

"Here, let me help you." Harper fluffed and adjusted the pillows behind Mildred's neck.

"Hi, there," murmured Olivia, moving closer to help Harper get Mildred settled in and comfortable.

"Olivia!" Mildred's eyes watered. "Don't worry. We have no intention of staying long. Nurse Ratched already warned us you need your rest but he said we could come back later in shifts—if you're up to it."

"And Darren. Oh my! And Christopher." Mildred struggled to sit up. "You're all here, but how? I mean, how did you know where to find me?" Mildred frowned. "Cornelia told you, didn't she?"

Irwin shook his head. "She didn't have to. She left her interloper in-training here to take charge of things."

Harper opened the screen on her phone and showed Mildred the photo she'd taken of her preop form.

"Oh, right," Mildred chuckled. "—on the refrigerator. I'd completely forgotten all about that."

"Hope you're not mad at us," said Harper.

"Mad!" exclaimed Mildred. "Don't be silly. How could I be mad? If anything, I'm touched you're all here. But what about the trip? Did you already sprinkle Cornelia's ashes? Oh no. I hope you didn't cut your trip short on my account." Mildred's voice trailed off.

"We took care of everything and no worries. It all went as expected," said Irwin, doing a lousy job of disguising the irony flooding his voice.

"Oh." Mildred grinned.

Irwin thought she looked pretty when she smiled.

"I see. Well, you'll have to fill me in on all the gory details at another time, then."

"That's a promise," agreed Irwin.

Mildred slapped the bed. "Come closer, all of you. I want to see you." She cleared her throat and pointed to her cup. "If you wouldn't mind, Irwin? I'm parched."

"Not at all." Irwin positioned Mildred's cup carefully on the nightstand. He measured and poured equal parts ice chips and water, then snapped on the top with a bit of difficulty.

Mildred, biting back a smile, observed Irwin jab the top with a plastic straw—careful to bend it at nothing less than a perfect forty-five-degree angle before handing it off.

"Thank you," she said, taking small, guarded sips, and wincing in-between.

"Are you in pain?" asked Harper, ready to call for the nurse.

"I'm okay. Just so surprised by this visit. Happy-surprised. I never in my wildest imagination expected to wake up and find you here of all places."

Harper adjusted Mildred's blanket, careful to tuck it under her bandaged arm. "That's because for better or worse, you're one of us now."

Mildred, who had for so long spent most of her adult life alone, couldn't help but tear.

"Now, now," soothed Olivia. "We can't have any of that." She dabbed Mildred's eye with the corner of a tissue. "What would Cornelia say?"

Mildred grunted, "Cornelia? Why, she'd say, "Mill, stop all this ridiculous boohooing and get on with it.""

"I see she liked to interfere in your life as well as in mine," said Irwin, only half-joking.

Mildred looked long and hard at Irwin. "She never stopped talking about you. Did you know that? Irwin this, or

Irwin that. I have to admit, your friendship, at times, left me feeling jealous."

"Jealous?" Irwin snorted. "Page the nurse. Hurry! This woman is delirious."

Mildred chuckled.

"Hell, had I only known, I would have gladly shipped Cornelia to you and let her obfuscate your life instead of upending mine."

Mildred laughed again. "She could be a little over assertive sometimes."

"A little?" Irwin's head recoiled, and his eyes grew wide. "The woman drove me nuts." He reached into his shirt pocket and tugged out an old black and white photo showing two pretty young women, each holding the other by the waist and smiling for the camera. "She wanted you to have this," he said, handing it over.

"Oh, my, would you look at this." Mildred held the captured memory taken of her and Cornelia many decades ago. Two friends, plodding through life during a time when the country around them felt as if it would implode any second. Mildred couldn't stop staring at the faded image and smiled. "This is wonderful. Thank you for bringing this to me, Irwin." Mildred tucked the photograph under her blanket. "All of you."

Harper stroked Mildred's hand gently while Olivia, on the other side of the bed, used her fingers to move wispy strands of hair away from Mildred's eyes.

Irwin, not known to handle his sentimentality well, briskly cleared his throat.

"I'd like to make a toast if I may?" He joined Darren and Christopher at the foot of Mildred's hospital bed and lifted his Styrofoam cup filled with apple juice high in the air, tilting it ever so slightly.

Everyone quieted.

"We've been sent on quite the adventure these past few weeks, courtesy of our long-lost friend, Cornelia Parish. A journey, which for me, started the day she and I first met and has continued until the day we laid her ashes to rest. We've shared many laughs, some tears, a few arguments, and more mishaps and calamities than I care to admit."

"—Like the snake," said Darren winking at Millie.

"Like the snake," agreed Irwin. "Long story Mildred but remind me to fill you in when laughing no longer hurts."

"He's not exaggerating about that one," winked Harper.

"However," said Irwin, "through it all, there has been one constant—our friendship, which has grown stronger and more committed over the years. Most of all, less—"

"—afraid," murmured Harper, pressing her diamond ringed finger to her lips.

"Less afraid," Irwin repeated warmly. "Mildred, to quote our dear mutual friend who needs no further introduction, 'You're stuck with us now.'"

"Hear, hear," everyone murmured.

"If I may," continued Irwin, "I'd like to share a quote from Brené Brown who said, 'We run from grief because loss scares us, yet our hearts reach toward grief because the broken parts want to mend.'

"Well, we've done our fair share of running, haven't we? But in the end, we came full circle, reaching toward our grief, collecting our broken pieces, and opening our frayed, tattered hearts in the desire to heal from our profound loss.

"And so, my friends, my family, without further ado, I make this final toast. To our unlikely friends, to our devoted friends, to our newly acquired unexpected friends, but most importantly, to our eternally cherished, never forgotten, and always admired forever friends. Cheers."

"Cheers," they all shouted.

And although slightly unconventional, even for this

haggard, road exhausted, disparate looking bunch, they raised their hands together in salutation, clanking whatever cup, car keys, Styrofoam cup or half-eaten candy bar they held high in solemn, yet jubilant celebration.

"To Cornelia," said Irwin.

"To Cornelia," echoed the assembled hearts.

"May she rest in peace," toasted Irwin, "—and not drive everyone else in heaven insane."

THEY EACH TOOK turns visiting Mildred in shifts, and the days spent together flew by. Still, there were several plans to make, arrangements to solidify, and even a few residual tears left to shed. But through it all, the Abernathy & Crane crew, which now included Mildred, promised to remain forever committed to one another—making all their shared future minutes together, whether good, not-so-good, painfully awkward or occasionally disastrous—count.

THE END

Indubitably.

DOMESTIC VIOLENCE

Many characters depicted in this story, including our beloved Cornelia Parish, faced some form of domestic violence during their lifetime.

"Domestic violence does not discriminate. Anyone of any race, age, sexual orientation, religion or gender can be a victim – or perpetrator – of domestic violence. It can happen to people who are married, living together or who are dating. It affects people of all socioeconomic backgrounds and education levels.

Domestic violence includes behaviors that physically harm, arouse fear, prevent a partner from doing what they wish or force them to behave in ways they do not want. It includes the use of physical and sexual violence, threats and intimidation, emotional abuse and economic deprivation. Many of these different forms of domestic violence/abuse can be occurring at any one time within the same intimate relationship." —National Domestic Violence Hotline

This danger propelled my characters to eventually escape, but even after leaving, they remained constantly under threat. Alone and frightened, and desperate to be believed, they set out to discover unique ways to reinvent and rebuild their lives, and to find safe spaces to live. Most of all, to heal.

The fictional hide-out created for this story is not so fictional. There are people and places doing this kind of heavy lifting all across our country, providing the necessary help and survival tools to those facing violence within the home and relationships. But survivors of abuse cannot do it without our help and support. To Donate: https://www. thehotline.org/donate/

> "The Hotline provides confidential, one-on-one support to each caller/chatter/texter, offering crisis intervention, options for next steps, and direct connection to sources for immediate safety. Our comprehensive database holds more than 5,000 agencies and resources in communities all across the country. Bilingual advocates are on hand to speak with callers, and our Language Line offers translations in 170 different languages." —National Domestic Violence Hotline

If you or anyone you know needs help, please do not hesitate to reach out to The National Domestic Violence Hotline whose mission is to "answer the call to support and shift power back to those affected by relationship abuse."

1-800-799-7233 / 1-800-787-3224 (TTY) /
https://www.thehotline.org/help/

BE THE CHANGE

ACKNOWLEDGMENTS

I wrote *Unexpected Friends* during a global pandemic, COVID-19. A strange, bizarre time filled with overwhelming uncertainty and devastating loss. A time when human beings, social creatures that we are, were forced by dire circumstance to mask-up, quarantine for months at a time, and above all, stay away from one another—not only for our safety but to save the lives of those we love and care about. And while loneliness [not COVID-related] is a premise frequently revisited throughout this book, and despite the pandemic, I was anything *but alone*.

I want to especially thank the following individuals for sharing not only their time and energy but also their encouragement and reassurance throughout this truly daunting creative process—especially when my struggling torn-to-shred-heart has felt immensely heavy and sad.

In no particular order—the publishing team: Shaggy Dog Productions LLC. Thank you for your unwavering belief in this project. My editor, J.C. Wing, whose enthusiasm and tenderness for these characters match or surpass my own.

Interior Design by *Wind Lark Publishing*—who takes the core of these books and makes them look as cute as can be. Also, a huge thank you, once again, to *Deranged Doctor Designs*—who never cease to make each book cover in The *Abernathy & Crane Series* unique (and so darn cute!)

And what would writing a novel be like without my Lady Writers? I don't even want to contemplate such blasphemy! Belinda Nevill Gordon, Kelly Jensen, Susan Moore Jordan, Catherine Schratt, Evelyn Infante and Mary Ann Moore— you ladies rock. Plain and simple. You are not only my fellow writers, my cheerleaders, but also my friends. I am blessed.

To my early reader who poured over this book over so many times during its haphazard construction that I honestly think she has large sections of it memorized—Harriet Van Houten. Thank you with all my heart.

I must also thank my grandchildren—whose silly antics, wild capers, and ridiculous escapades kept me laughing, *hiding*, hopeful, and immeasurably grateful through what can only be described as a heartbreaking and painful pandemic. I remain in total admiration, grateful for your goofiness, silliness, and unmatched ability to face uncertainty and doubt with tenacious kindness and resolve. Most of all, I adore and cherish your incredible inner strength and loving little souls, which frankly puts most adults to shame.

Finally, to all my incredibly compassionate, bighearted, and hilariously off-the-wall grown children and my wonderful, longsuffering husband: *Gosh*, guys—how can I ever thank you for all the material you unwittingly provide for these books? —for the stuff, you do that you don't even know I'm using! I mean, honestly, if it weren't for your collective unhinged lunacy, your relentless ability to make me laugh and cringe, or the never-ending action-packed drama you dump on my doorstep—these books would totally snooze and drag. Trust me on this. So, big thanks again for being in my life and most definitely on my pages!

PS: I am *crazy-in-love* with you all. *Can't you tell?*

ABOUT THE AUTHOR

When not busy plotting a stabbing, a garroting, or a murder —all on paper, of course—Sahar is busy writing about her crew of highly-entertaining, quirky, unpredictable book characters. Some characters have been lovely, big-hearted, gentle souls, merely temporarily lost and in desperate search of life's answers. Others have leaned more to the eccentric side. Highly unconventional. Difficult personalities accustomed to writing their own rules and determined to live their 'best life' to the fullest. A few...*okay, probably more than a few*, have been downright devious. Duplicitous, dangerous types—undeniably not the kind of personalities one would want to cross paths with in a dark alley or locked in some seedy hotel room.

Suspense writer Sahar Abdulaziz is the author of nine novels—including *Expendable, Tight Rope, Unlikely Friends, The Gatekeeper's Notebook*, and her latest release, *Devoted Friends*. Most of her work is in realistic fiction: psychological thrillers, suspense, and satire. She writes about characters who find themselves facing complicated life challenges. However, despite whatever life-trajectory her invisible idiosyncratic friends face, Sahar is determined to tell their stories. She's eager to put pen to paper to share their compelling accounts, no matter how hilarious or convoluted their adventures become.

Rep'd by Djarabi Kitabs Publishing, Limitless Publishing, and Shaggy Dog LLC.

Facebook:
https://www.facebook.com/AuthorSaharAbdulaziz
Twitter:
https://twitter.com/Sahar_Author
Website:
https://www.saharraziz.com
Instagram:
https://www.instagram.com/saharraziz/

www.ingramcontent.com/pod-product-compliance
Lightning Source LLC
Chambersburg PA
CBHW030811260626
47169CB00001B/281